Praise for *A Dangerous Woman*

"Original and beautifully written . . . Somehow, the author has managed to inhabit Martha so completely and bring her to life on the page so vividly that we lose our own sense of how 'different' she is. I'd call this a heartbreaking novel, except there's a certain triumph in it, so I'll just say that it's a wonderful novel, and that it will absolutely transport you."

—*Cosmopolitan*

"Brilliantly acute . . . Remarkable . . . Morris's magnanimous ability to portray her characters with so much tenderness and cruelty may be her novel's finest strength."

—*The Boston Sunday Globe*

"Martha Horgan is at once the most irritating and engaging character to inhabit a novel in a long time. . . . Morris has shown us that those who live outside the magic circle of friendship and family have a rich inner life like the rest of us, only much sadder and unforgettable."   —*Time*

"Morris has created a remarkable portrait of a disturbed woman who is a fully sexual creature."   —*The Washington Post*

"Morris has given us a small town American tragedy that Dreiser would have recognized and found very real. She brings to American fiction a realism that has been absent far too much and for far too long."   —*Newark Star Ledger*

PENGUIN BOOKS

A DANGEROUS WOMAN

Mary McGarry Morris is married and the mother of five children. She lives in Massachusetts. She is the author of three novels: *Vanished*, which was nominated for the National Book Award and the PEN/Faulkner Award; *A Dangerous Woman*, which was made into a major motion picture; and *Songs in Ordinary Time*.

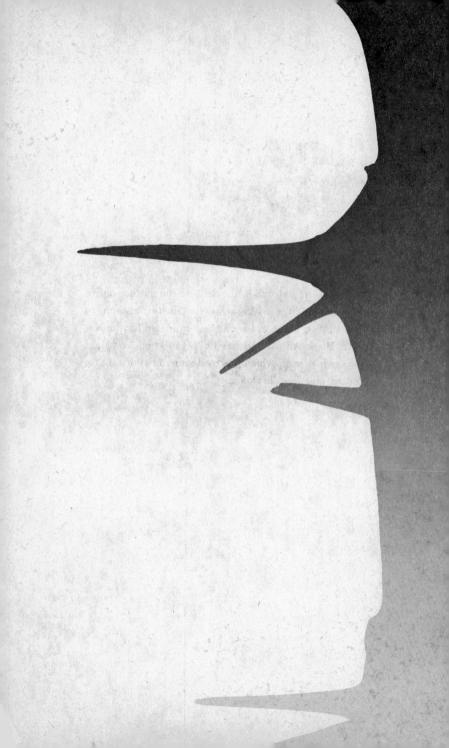

A DANGEROUS WOMAN

MARY McGARRY MORRIS

PENGUIN BOOKS

PENGUIN BOOKS
Published by the Penguin Group
Penguin Putnam Inc., 375 Hudson Street,
New York, New York 10014, U.S.A.
Penguin Books Ltd, 27 Wrights Lane, London W8 5TZ, England
Penguin Books Australia Ltd, Ringwood, Victoria, Australia
Penguin Books Canada Ltd, 10 Alcorn Avenue,
Toronto, Ontario, Canada M4V 3B2
Penguin Books (N.Z.) Ltd, 182–190 Wairau Road,
Auckland 10, New Zealand

Penguin Books Ltd, Registered Offices:
Harmondsworth, Middlesex, England

First published in the United States of America by Viking Penguin,
a division of Penguin Books USA Inc., 1991
Published in Penguin Books 1992

7 9 10 8 6

PUBLISHER'S NOTE
This is a work of fiction. Names, characters, places, and incidents either are the
product of the author's imagination or are used fictitiously, and any resemblance
to actual persons, living or dead, events, or locales is entirely coincidental.

THE LIBRARY OF CONGRESS HAS CATALOGUED THE HARDCOVER AS FOLLOWS:
Morris, Mary McGarry.
A dangerous woman / by Mary McGarry Morris.
p.   cm.
ISBN 0-670-83699-0 (hc.)
ISBN 0 14 02.7211 9 (pbk.)
I. Title.
PS 3563.0874454D36   1991
813'.52—dc20   90–50405

Printed in the United States of America
Set in Perpetua
Designed by Michael Ian Kaye

For Agnes, who wanted a love story

A DANGEROUS WOMAN

ONE

———◻———

The murder is seldom discussed without someone recalling that warm autumn night years before when Martha Horgan was only seventeen and Bob Hobart, a classmate, offered her a ride home from the library. Pretending she hadn't heard him, she brought her book closer to her face. The girls at the end of the long table giggled. Everyone knew what Hobart was up to. The library was so packed with students that many sat cross-legged against the walls, and yet the chairs flanking Martha Horgan were empty. It was always that way; she walked alone, sat alone, but it was hard to feel too bad about it, because she could be such an unpleasant girl. Bob Hobart slid into one of the empty chairs and asked again if he could give her a ride. Muttering angrily, Martha jumped up and stalked out of the reading room. The girls collapsed in laughter over their books. Martha's temper was legendary.

She was a tall skinny girl whose wide crooked mouth seemed perpetually askew, a ragged boundary between laughter and tears. Behind her thick, smudged glasses her eyes, with their slow-moving myopia, cast a watchful intensity that was unnerving. Her aunt constantly scolded her for this, but she couldn't help it. She watched people hoping to discover what it was that made her so different from them. Sometimes it seemed she might be just a step off, a moment behind, and so, if she ran faster, laughed harder, smiled brighter, she would catch up. She would get there.

"It's Donny," Bob Hobart whispered, at her heels when they were past the checkout desk. "He wants to see you. He told me."

"Really?" she asked, grinning. She was madly in love with Donny LaRue. Every day she wrote him anonymous notes which she wedged through the grille on his locker door when no one was around. She always called his house after his mother left for work. She never said anything when Donny answered, but just listened to his voice. For the past few days, though, his little brother had started answering. The brat would blast the stereo and hold the phone against the speaker.

Once she was in the car, Hobart barely spoke to her. The minute he turned onto the rutted logging road, she cringed against the door. She told him she had forgotten that she was supposed to go straight home. He assured her it would only take a minute. He just had to drop something off at this party some guys were having; in fact, it was a birthday party for Donny.

They bumped along the unlit narrow road for about ten minutes until he pulled in behind three cars as old and battered as his.

MARY McGARRY MORRIS

2

"I'll wait here. I don't want to go," she said, panicking. None of this made sense. Or did it? Maybe that's what was wrong with her, always being too suspicious and afraid to take chances.

"It won't take long, honest. Besides, you don't want to sit out here all alone in the middle of nowhere." He smiled. "Come on!"

She followed him through the woods to a clearing known as the Meadow, where twelve boys sat around a small campfire, drinking beer and passing around two joints.

The boys' eager greetings made her feel better. They usually either avoided her or made fun of her, and now they actually seemed happy to see her—all, that is, but Donny, who stood at the edge of the clearing gesturing angrily while he spoke to Bob. The flames cast jagged shadows on the boys' faces as they called up to her. Tom Gately offered her his beer, which she refused, but he stuck it in her hand, then rushed back to the fire as if he were afraid of her. They kept coaxing her to drink it, even though she insisted she hated the taste.

"What DO you like the taste of?" one boy called.

"I don't know." She felt nervous and giddy now, with Donny watching. "A lot of things."

"Like what?"

"I don't know." She shrugged uneasily. She couldn't think of anything she liked other than Donny. He wore a dark-green shirt she had never seen before. She knew all of his clothes. She knew what he did every minute of the day. She knew what everyone in his family did. Lately she thought about Donny so much that there wasn't a lot of room left for other thoughts.

"Do you like candy?"

"Yes. But not caramel. I don't like caramel." She glanced at Donny. He was still standing, but his face was shadowed. Bob Hobart sat down in the circle.

"Martha doesn't like caramel."

"Jeez, I don't either."

"How 'bout ice cream?"

"Some flavors I like." She nodded, flattered by their rapt attention.

Maybe they had changed. Or maybe it was her. Maybe she had changed over the summer.

"Yah, me too. Some I like, some I don't. How 'bout you, Ed? What's your favorite flavor?"

"Cherry. Long as the cherries are big fat juicy ones," Ed said and everyone laughed so hard she tried to laugh too. She didn't know why they were cracking up over cherry-chunk ice cream. She stopped laughing, because she could tell by their expressions that it was probably something lewd.

"How about come? You like the taste of that?" Craig Lister asked, getting up from the fire.

"No." She hated Craig Lister. He had tripped her on the stairs the first day of school, and then tried to act like it was an accident when a teacher grabbed him. But he had done it on purpose. After a lifetime of bumps and shoves, she could always tell.

"You ever tried it?" His smile was cold and thin.

"No."

"Then how do you know you don't like the taste?"

"I just know, that's all," she said, her chin out. Thought he was so smart. She hated boys like him, rude, strutting, cocky boys, hated them.

"I don't know, Martha, I hear it's pretty good. You want to try some?"

The fire crackled and spit.

"No." She turned quickly and stared at Bob. "You said a minute. A minute's up and I have to go home now."

"Come on, Martha, try it. You'll like it," Kevin Moss called.

"Yah, Martha, come on!"

She saw Donny laugh now, so she smiled.

"See, she already did! She did Hobart. On the way here," someone called.

"Hey, Hobart!" Craig Lister said, shaking his finger down at Bob. "Not nice, Hobie, sampling Donny's surprise."

Hobart's head sagged with helpless laughter onto his drawn-up knees.

"Okay," Craig Lister said. "Let's see what you got here, Martha. See if it's anything we can use." He had just undone the top two buttons of her shirt.

Shocked, she stepped back and slapped his hand. He reached toward her again, and this time she hit his hand hard. Laughing, he kept coming at her as she backed away. Suddenly he leaped with a whoop and yanked open her shirt. Instead of a bra, she wore one of her father's old undershirts that was so flimsy, Lister ripped it in two with just a pull; the way you'd tear up old rags, she thought, such a strange thought, with everyone staring up at her; threadbare, useless old cloth for the rags her father buffed her aunt's car with.

"Holy shit," Lister said, seeing her long full breasts. "Take a look. . . ."

She held her shirt closed and ran toward the woods. But suddenly he was behind her, his arms pinning hers as he butted her back to the campfire with his body.

"Now, let me see," he said, looking over her shoulder down at the hysterical faces ringing the fire. "We got a lot of your favorites here tonight. Okay, Justin, Jim, Tom. You go first. Show Donny how."

One by one they stood before her and stared at her chest. Eyes closed, she hung her head so that her hair obscured her face.

"Come on! Come on!" Lister said, disgusted that no one would touch her. "Martha loves this," he grunted, jiggling her body against his. "She loves you guys. She's been after you guys ever since first grade. You know that. Come on! You're gonna make Martha feel bad."

"Oh no," she gasped, as the first cold hand clamped over her breast, squeezing one, then both. "Please don't," she begged. She was choking.

"Good tits."

"Excellent."

She was gagging.

"Come on, Hobie!"

"Pass."

"Come on, you creep, they don't bite, you know."

"I said no."

"You're holding up the line, pit face," Lister growled.

"Please don't," she gasped.

"Are you nuts?" called a voice she recognized as Donny's. "This shits."

"Fuck off, dickhead. She likes it! That's what she came for. Ask Hobart. She told him."

"Let her go, you fuckin' creep. You're making me sick."

Someone was unzipping her pants, and now they yanked them down to her ankles. A stick was being dragged across her chest, poking her breasts, jiggling them, now flipping them up and down. Behind her Lister laughed into her hair and rubbed his pelvis against her. A can whooshed open and a spray of ice-cold beer hit her chest and ran down her belly. She screamed, struggling to get away. Her arms were being pulled from their sockets. Another can whooshed open and sprayed her face. The beer smeared her glasses and stung her eyes.

"Let her go!"

"You creep, you fuckin' sadist, Lister, let her the fuck go!"

She tripped and fell forward as someone yanked Craig Lister away from her. Sobbing, she scrambled to her feet and pulled up her pants. Her slick beery fingers fumbled at her shirt buttons. The boys were running into the woods. She heard their cars start, then peel off into the darkness. She ran most of the way back down the road. It was close to midnight by the time she got home.

"I knew this was going to happen," her aunt Frances screamed as she staggered through the door.

"They oughta be arrested," her father said, averting his embarrassed gaze.

"What did she expect, going into the woods with them," her aunt said when she had heard the story. "I told her! I've warned her! Always staring at people, haunting them. I knew this would happen!"

"It's not her fault," her father said, and she did not know if he meant what the boys had done or the strangeness that was her life.

Over Frances's objections, Floyd Horgan called his friend Sheriff Sonny Stoner, who rounded up the boys and their parents in the aldermen's dark conference room at Town Hall. There was no denying the incident had taken place. Some of the boys wept, recalling the details. Poor Martha Horgan . . . Oh, they were so ashamed.

A few parents vowed that, come hell or high water, they would stand by their sons' sworn accounts of how sexed up Martha Horgan got after she drank that first beer. She had started it, and the boys had only done what any normal boys would have.

"Now, let's not go off the deep end here," the sheriff cautioned. "Let's not see any more harm done."

Yes, most agreed, the sheriff was right. Enough harm had already been done to one of the more fragile members of the community.

"One of the more disturbed!" Mrs. LaRue piped up, dumping onto the table a bag of the notes Martha Horgan had written to her son just since the start of school. "Over two hundred," she announced, crumpling the bag and throwing it onto the pile of tightly folded notes. "Letting a girl like that roam all over the place—seems to me that aunt of hers is just asking for trouble, or else maybe she just don't give a damn. Well, I know one thing'll shake up Mrs. Horace Beecham, and that's the lawsuit I'm gonna file against her if one single thing happens to my son—if she dares file any kind of charges against him. Sonny, you're so damn worried about protecting Martha Horgan, have you given any thought to protecting my son from her? All our sons. Think about it!"

There was dark grumbling. It was a shame about Martha Horgan. On that they could all agree. Oh, she was bright enough and certainly pretty enough to pass for normal, but everyone knew she was about as odd as they come, poor thing, muttering to herself and chasing little kids if they so much as looked at her, which they were bound to do, of course, kids being kids.

Nutty as a fruitcake, always had been, always would be, and so, really, wouldn't it be better just to drop the whole thing and not ruin the lives of a fine bunch of young men who would be graduating high school in a few months—not to mention the shame the poor thing would be subjected to in testimony of that sort? Sonny explained all this to Steve Bell, who was Aunt Frances's longtime attorney and lover, and he spelled it all out to Martha's father, who, while he said it didn't seem right to drop it, agreed it also didn't seem right to pursue it.

And so the matter was dropped. The only problem was everyone's sense that, in some inexplicable way that defied all reason and logic, Martha had somehow asked for it, that she had brought it on herself with her attractive figure and her peculiar ways. The young men went off to school and the service, then careers and families of their own. And there grew with time the rancorous certainty that she had probably instigated the whole pitiful thing, not only that, but (and some said they knew this for certifiable fact) that she had actually had relations of one sort or another that night with every single one of those fine boys. The joke in town was how no man dared be alone on the same side of the street with her for fear she'd chase after him. Even now, some fifteen years later, a teenager was sure to get a rise out of his buddies by suddenly darting across the street with Martha Horgan's approach.

She never returned to high school after that night. And if there were people who felt she should have, they never said so, relieved as everyone was that things had worked out so well. Dressed in baggy shapeless clothes, usually her father's old work shirts and pants, Martha kept to herself. The most that ever happened was the loneliness that grew in her heart. She had no friends, no life beyond the upkeep of the garage apartment she shared with her father. Even the parties across the way, in her aunt's elegant home, had little to do with her. Frances's friends were uneasy around her. She made people nervous because they made her nervous, and on the rare occasion when she met someone she liked, her attention was so rapt as to be frightening. There were some days when she felt as if there were a net around her, a spell that had been cast on her at birth, a spell that only love could undo.

When she was thirty-one, her father died. During the wake, she couldn't cry or speak to people. It was on the morning of the funeral service, just as the casket was about to be closed, that she finally broke down, sobbing and retching, causing a nasty scene in front of the dry-eyed chatty mourners, who were all Frances's friends. Everyone looked away with the same thought: Poor, poor Frances. Wesley Mount, the funeral director, rushed to comfort Martha, but unaccountably, after a lifetime in the business, not a word of solace came to him. Nothing. And so he put his arms around her and held her until she was calm enough to breathe normally.

Later that same day, Frances cornered Martha in the kitchen. Frances was distraught and panicky; without her brother, it was all on her shoulders now, the house, the grounds, everything, even Martha. She started off by saying that the scene in the funeral home had been humiliating.

"What are you talking about?" Martha demanded.

"You know exactly what I'm talking about, leaping into Wesley Mount's arms like that and then standing there . . ." Frances shuddered. "Just standing there with your eyes closed, making that weird sound, that moaning."

"I wasn't moaning!"

"Didn't you know what everyone was thinking? Didn't you care?" Martha glared at her.

"I mean, you just confirmed every rumor they've ever heard about that night in the woods."

"Don't talk about that," Martha warned, starting to get up.

"I will talk about it and you will listen!" her aunt insisted, blocking her way. "From now on, you will consider every single consequence of your actions before you say or do anything! Do you understand? Do you? Do you?" she was screaming as Martha pushed past her in a rage.

That very day, Martha moved into town. She got a job at Kolditis Cleaners and a room in Claire Mayo's boardinghouse. And for eight wonderful months she was on her own. She had her first real friend, and everything seemed possible.

T W O

———□———

Right now Martha Horgan was the only worker behind the counter. She was glad there weren't any customers in the Cleaners. Mercy and Barbara, the women who ran the pressers, were both on break. In the little cubicle at the end of the counter, Birdy Dusser, the manager, was trying to explain the shortage that John Kolditis, the owner, had discovered in the cash drawer this morning. John's harsh voice carried over the flimsy partition.

"What? What is it? You think maybe mice? No, no, I know. Some-body's breaking in here a coupla nights a week and all he ever takes is fifteen or twenty bucks a crack. The rest he leaves. Makes sense, huh?"

Birdy replied in a low voice.

Martha wished there was some way to help Birdy right now, even though she had brought this all on herself. Ever since Birdy had started going out with Getso, one of the laundry-truck drivers, she couldn't seem to do anything right. On the slips she would check "heavy starch" for bed sheets or "rainproofing" for men's shirts, and for three weeks straight she had mixed up everyone's work schedule. She had marked last Friday as a day off for Martha, Mercy, and Barbara, leaving no one to run the machines or service the counter. Thank goodness Martha had gotten bored in her room and had come downtown to visit. Usually that irritated Birdy, seeing Martha show up here on her day off, but that morning people had been lined up out the door. Now Martha tried to double-check everything Birdy did.

"Would you stop?" Birdy had snapped at her this morning when she found her examining a slip she had written up only moments before. "Why are you doing this?"

Soon after, she overheard Mercy telling Birdy how Martha had even looked in the coffee maker after Birdy started it.

"It's so weird!" Birdy said.

"She loves this friggin' place so much, she's probably after your job."

"And she can have it," Birdy said in disgust.

Martha felt sick to her stomach. She would never, ever do a thing to hurt Birdy, who was her very dearest friend in the world. When no one else had even let her fill out a job application, Birdy had hired her on the spot.

"Then who?" John boomed, and Martha shuddered. She picked up a rag and began to wipe the dull glass countertop, scrubbing the same gouge over and over. "Don't yell at her like that," she muttered. "You better not yell. I mean it. I mean it. I mean it."

The bells rang on the opening door, and she looked up to see a man in shirtsleeves rush at her with his yellow slip. "I'm in a hurry," he said, then went to the glass door, where he stood looking out onto the busy street.

She searched through the racks where the cleaned clothes hung in clear plastic bags. Today's date was on the slip. "Won't be hard to find," she said, pushing the hangers aside. "Should be right here . . . right . . . right here. But it's not," she whispered. "Not there. Not there," she said nervously, hurrying over to the cubicle. Birdy would know. Now she recognized John's handwriting on the slip. He was always making mistakes. He never knew where anything went, but he always accused everyone else of inefficiency. Well, she'd show him that he made mistakes too. He might be the boss, but he was just as human as the rest of them. She threw open the door to the cluttered little office, and it banged back, shaking the partition walls.

"Martha!" Birdy said, shocked to see her rush at John.

"Here," she said, holding the slip in his face. "Out of sequence. I looked, but I can't find it." For Birdy's benefit, she rolled her eyes at his incompetence.

"Shit!" John hissed. "I forgot." He reached behind the door and pulled out a navy-blue blazer with brass buttons. "I promised him by noon. And I forgot. Here," he said, flinging the jacket at Birdy. "They're coffee stains. Go do a pre-spot, then bag it."

"He'll know," Birdy hissed back.

Martha nodded. Of course he'd know.

"He's not gonna know. Jesus Christ, don't just sit there. That's Gately, the fucking president of the fucking bank I'm tryna get on the board of. Go! Go!" He waved and Birdy scurried into the back room.

Martha stood, staring. John flipped his hand, gesturing her out of his way. When she didn't move, he squeezed past the desk to get out of the office.

"Andy!" he called, shaking the man's hand. "It'll be right out. I didn't like the way it looked, so I'm making the girl do it again. She's hand-pressing it. Might be a little damp, but it's better that way, hand-pressed. Here she is. Here you go. Here." John held up the jacket and Mr. Gately slipped into it.

"I appreciate this, John. Next Chamber breakfast I'll wear a bib," Gately chuckled.

"Ah!" John said disgustedly. "It's the same everywhere. Lousy service, the hallmark of the modern marketplace. You can't get good help anymore. I can't. Nobody can. It's all going down the tubes."

The door jangled open onto a slack-jawed young man shuffling in with a sheaf of laundry slips clutched in his fist. This was Hock, one of the residents of Harmony House, a home for retarded adults. "Pickup day," Hock announced, dropping the slips onto the counter. Down in the street, a car idled, waiting. The counselor was letting Hock run this errand himself.

"I appreciate this, John. How much do I owe you?" Gately asked, taking out his wallet.

"Pickup day!" Hock said again. "My turn for pickup day!"

"The girl's got the slip," John told Gately with a nod at Birdy. He turned his back to Hock.

Birdy looked skeptically from the slip to John. "Five dollars?" she said hesitantly.

Everyone ignored Hock. He picked up his slips and waved them at Birdy, who usually waited on him. She was the only one with enough patience. "Pickup day, my turn!" he called, his voice rising anxiously. He touched both sides of his face and then his chest, as if to make sure he was there and not invisible.

Martha was stunned: the full charge for a jacket that hadn't even been dry-cleaned. Talk about honesty. Talk about stealing from someone.

Gately paid John, thanking him again as he opened the door.

"Excuse me, sir!" Martha called, rushing at him before he got outside. "Excuse me, sir, but this isn't right. He's lying to you. This jacket has not been dry-cleaned, and I don't think it's right. Not at all. It's not one bit right!"

They stared at her, all but Hock, who paced back and forth in front of the counter, peering at his slips.

"You're paying for work that wasn't even done!" Martha said, growing breathless. "That's not right."

A DANGEROUS WOMAN

"Martha," Birdy warned. "You're losing it." She glanced at Hock, who made a whimpering sound.

Losing it? Losing it? Well, she was sorry, but she had been hired to do a good job and give good service, and if the boss wasn't going to be honest—the people who run businesses, the people who run this country—then who would be?

"Look, the jacket's clean," John said, first to her, then to Gately. "Not a spot on it." He turned anxiously to Birdy. "Right? The jacket's clean. Tell him. Tell him!"

"The jacket's clean," Birdy said, eyes downcast.

"I'm sure it is," Mr. Gately said. "Great job. No problem." He started to open the door again, and Martha grabbed at him.

"No!" she cried. "You should leave it here. . . ."

"That's all right!" Gately insisted.

". . . and make him really clean it!"

"Please!" Gately said, trying to pull away.

"Martha!" Birdy gasped.

She looked down, shocked at the blue wool pocket that dangled from her hand.

Hock waved the slips at Martha and laughed heartily.

"Jesus Christ, I'm sorry, Andy. But you see what I'm dealing with here? See? See what happens!" He turned on Birdy. "What is this? I'm tryna run a fucking business here and I don't have time for these screwballs. Do you hear me?"

Birdy nodded.

He turned to Gately. " 'Please, John,' " he said in a high voice, mimicking Birdy. " 'Give her a chance, poor thing. As a favor. A favor for me.' So look what I end up with. Martha Horgan!"

"I know," Gately said quietly.

"Oh Christ, I forgot," John said with a stricken look. "That night, your boy."

It was starting. First the choking. Martha held her breath and thumped her chest. The ceiling was sinking, the floor rising, and she felt herself getting bigger and bigger.

MARY McGARRY MORRIS

Hock stared at her. He had stopped laughing. Now he looked afraid. The door opened, and a young woman with straight blonde hair entered. Hock hurried to stand by her. "Is everything all right?" the young woman asked, putting a hand on his shoulder.

"Are you kidding?" John said, throwing up his hands. "Things couldn't be better here in the sheltered workshop."

THREE

———□———

While she waited for the curling iron to get hot, Martha leaned close to the mirror, practicing what she would say tonight when the party ended. "Well," she began, then took a deep breath. She took off her glasses, thumped her chest twice, and cleared her throat. "Well, thank you for inviting me. I've had a good time . . . a fine time . . . I've had a very fine and enjoyable time." Oh, that was awful. She squared her shoulders and smiled. "This has been so much fun!" she said in the clench-jawed manner of Frances's friends no matter how dull the evening had been. "I've really had a wonderful time! The food was delicious. The conversation was lively. . . ." She cleared her throat. "Oh God," she moaned, burying her face in her hands. She was just too nervous. What if her hands shook like this at the party and she spilled coffee on Birdy's sister's furniture? The only reason Birdy had even invited her was because of John's blow-up yesterday. Birdy had begged him not to fire her. She said Martha needed to socialize more. She was too rigid, too uptight. She didn't know how to act around people.

She held her breath, trying to remember the ten easy steps to becoming an engaging conversationalist that Birdy had cut out of *Cosmopolitan* for her. "Wear bright friendly colors. Be calm. Smile. If your instinct is to laugh, then by all means laugh! Make and maintain eye contact." She couldn't remember the rest. In any event, she had one of her own—she wouldn't lose her temper, no matter what anyone said or did. She would be in total control. "Only you can help you," she said in a firm voice, pointing at the mirror. "Only you can help you. Only you can help you!" she muttered, her voice trailing off as she looked up.

Turning in a panicky little circle, she sniffed at the sharp chemical smell . . . hot plastic. . . . The curling iron—the dot on its tip had turned black. She held the directions close and read, PLACE END STRAND OF HAIR ON WAND AND ROLL TOWARD HEAD. HOLD FOR 20 SECONDS. "One . . . two . . . three . . . four . . ." she began to count. It burned her temple, so she twisted it away from her head. She had never used one of these before.

Birdy's sister was having another PlastiqueWare party. Mercy and Barbara had gone to all of them, but this was the first time Martha had been invited. She had found the invitation this morning in her box at work. The first thing she did was sniff the small blue envelope, with her name scrolled in Birdy's elaborate handwriting. It smelled of Birdy, fresh and sweet. She had been so jittery that she waited until her break before she opened it, in the back room, with her hand cupped hard to her mouth so no one would hear her squeal.

"Nineteen . . . twenty." There. She tried to see in the mirror.

Something was wrong. She couldn't unroll the wand from her long hair. The more she turned the curling iron, the tighter it tangled. Her fingertips were burned and there was a red mark on her temple. She smelled singed hair. "Oh no!" She angled her head to the dim, blurry mirror. The curling iron had no "On/Off" button. Frantically, she began to break strands of hair from its tight rows of hot little teeth.

"Help!" she cried, barely able to touch the curling iron, which she was only twisting tighter against her seared scalp. "Help!" she cried again. But no one would hear her all the way up here on the third floor. Straining toward the door as far as the cord would allow, she began to yell, but the boarders, like her landlady, Claire Mayo, were all old women. The only one who might hear her would be Mrs. Hess, whose room was directly below this one. "Help! Help!" she cried, stamping her feet.

"You stop that!" Mrs. Hess shouted from the bottom of the stairs. "You just stop that!" She slammed her door.

"Mrs. Hess, please help me. My head's on fire!" she hollered, and then she thought to pull out the plug. Of course. "Stupid fool," she muttered, looking for scissors in the sewing kit Birdy had given her the first time John threatened to fire her from the Cleaners. Birdy had suggested she take up mending, something she could do at home alone, where people wouldn't bother her. Birdy meant well, but just the thought of not being with her every day made Martha feel queasy. The best part of the job was Birdy.

She was snipping her hair from the hot curling iron when the door flew open. Claire Mayo stood there, breathless and glassy-eyed from the long attic climb. "What's burning?" panted the old woman, her hand at her heaving breast. "Where's the fire?" From the hallway, Mrs. Hess peered into the room.

"Leave me alone!" Martha roared, slamming the door and turning the dead bolt now with the shock of what she had done. She looked down in horror at the handful of chopped hair. She put on her glasses and leaned close to the mirror to examine the jagged bald spot on her temple.

MARY McGARRY MORRIS

"That's it!" Claire Mayo called from the hallway. "I told you last time I'm sick of your temper!"

"Leave me alone!" Martha begged. Now what would she do? This was probably the most important night of her whole life, and her hair looked as if a rodent had gnawed on it. "Leave me alone, just leave me alone!" she panted as she tore through her drawers looking for her new red scarf. Next she scrambled through the few things folded on the closet shelf, and then she remembered. Birdy had admired the scarf and so she had given it to her. After that she bought two more scarves and gave them to her, until Birdy insisted she stop.

"I told you before. I warned you!" The old woman kept it up.

Martha kicked aside the clothes that were all over the floor, and then she picked up the pink cloche Loiselle Evans had knit for her last winter. She put it on, then, seeing how ridiculous she looked, tore it off and threw it across the room, moaning.

"I won't put up with any craziness!" Claire Mayo banged on the door.

"Just leave me alone!" she moaned, her face in her hands. "Please! Please, leave me alone!"

"Up here, screaming the house is on fire like some kind of insane person . . . One of these days . . ." The two old women muttered their way down the dark, creaking staircase. ". . . in there talking to herself all hours of the night . . ."

———□———

She had circled the block twice before she could bring herself to climb these four brick steps, and now she did not even ring the bell, but tapped lightly on the door frame, holding her breath, chewing her lip. She kept touching the top of her ear, where she had parted her hair to cover the bald spot.

Maybe she had the wrong night. Maybe no one had come. But the street was lined with cars. She shifted from foot to foot, then stepped down. She stepped back up, then down again. The door opened.

"Oh!" said a woman with small startled eyes. "Martha Horgan!" The woman tried to smile—as if that could make up for anything, Martha thought. Rude people, everywhere she went, such rude, rude people. Always knew her name, but never said theirs. "Birdy invited me," she said, lifting the plait of recombed hair that sagged over one eye.

If she had known the party had already started, she wouldn't have come in. But it was too late now. One of Birdy's sisters set a straight-backed kitchen chair in front of the television for her. She sat next to the PlastiqueWare salesman, who stood, the two of them facing this audience of smiling women. They all stared at her. She crossed her arms. No. Clasped her hands, sweaty, slimy fingers. Crossed her feet. No. Crossed her legs. Her face was hot, burning red hot face red hot ears all that heart blood pumping, pounding in her ears. Take a deep breath, don't choke. Can't see anything in this glare. Can't swallow calm down. If she opened her mouth birds would fly out. The salesman was tall and skinny with long bony fingers and thick black eyebrows that fused over his nose. The women laughed and she blinked. They were laughing at him, not her. Okay, calm down, calm down.

On his long narrow folding table were displayed nests of clear plastic containers for food storage, plastic mixing bowls, bread boxes, and clear rectangular boxes with ridged covers for stacking, "also perfect for sweaters and whatever lacy unmentionables you ladies . . ." From his jacket pocket, he fished out a knotted string of panties, stockings, camisoles, which he dropped into one of the boxes, the silky mound growing higher. The women laughed even harder now as he began to pull more knotted strings from his sleeves and the back of his jacket. A fat woman in white pants doubled over laughing. Martha pressed her knees together and clenched her teeth in a miserable smile. All the women wore either pants or skirts. She was the only one this dressed up. She had on a silky turquoise dress with big red pinwheels, which she had bought in Cushing's on her way home from work. Her feet were rubbed raw from these new black heels. In the mirror over the sofa, her lopsided reflection grinned back at her. The women were all looking at her hair. What in God's name was she doing here? Why had she come? Oh, Birdy! She forced her eyes on Birdy, dear, sweet Birdy,

MARY MCGARRY MORRIS

20

who was in the kitchen, sliding a foil-covered platter from the refrigerator. There. Birdy was coming into the living room now. She winked and all at once the air grew smoother, easier to breathe.

The PlastiqueWare demonstrator was pouring a pitcher of water into a juice container. When it was full, he twisted the cap tightly, shook it, then, holding it high overhead, dropped it onto the hardwood floor. Her hand flew to her mouth as it bounced up and down, and then rolled by her feet.

"It bounces. Just like my checks at the end of the month," he said, wiggling his eyebrows and flicking an imaginary cigar. "But it will not break!"

It took her a minute to catch on. Oh, like Groucho Marx. That was good. Now, that was funny. She clapped her hands and laughed. She kept laughing until she realized everyone else had stopped.

Birdy's pregnant sister, Carol, watched from a chair in the kitchen doorway. Shifting the heft of her belly, she glanced down at the floor as the sudden high whine of an electric saw buzzed through the brief silence. Birdy's brother-in-law, who had been on a yearlong strike from the wire plant, made extra money building redwood bird-feeders in his basement workshop. Everyone who knew Birdy owned a feeder. Telling Birdy they were for the ladies at the boardinghouse, Martha had bought six of them. But they were for her, every single one. Recently, at work, when she asked to buy more, Mercy and Getso burst out laughing and Birdy's face drained a bloodless white. "You've got to stop this," she said in a low voice so the others wouldn't hear. "Do you understand? It's really starting to get to me."

At first Martha's feelings were hurt, until she realized it was because Getso was there. He made Birdy nervous when he came upstairs into the Cleaners. Getso had recently totaled one of the laundry trucks, and Birdy was always trying to cover up for him to John.

Birdy had made a point of reminding the women at work that Carol got ten percent of everything sold here tonight. The most expensive item was this forty-five-piece matched set, the DeluxeWare, its clear plastic bowls sprigged with flowers of the same bright blue as the lids.

There were juice jars, nested freezer-and-refrigerator containers, an eight-piece canister set, napkin and paper-towel holders, graduated mixing bowls with handles and lips for pouring, a ring of six blue measuring spoons, a measuring cup, salt and pepper shakers, two flowerpots, a bathroom wastebasket, and a tissue-box cover.

Martha's heart swelled with each new item added to the display. How lovely they were, how perfect. A set like that meant order and peace and her own kitchen, her own life with Billy Chelsea, the widower who lived with his two young daughters in the white cottage down the road from her Aunt Frances's house. Her eyes glazed and her face flushed with the familiar daydream of his strong rough hand cupping the back of her head, his hot mouth crushing hers.

". . . the last DeluxeWare set left, but ordering only takes ten days parcel post," he was saying.

It was hers. Of course it was.

"I'll take it," came Mercy Reardon's girlish voice. Mercy attended these parties all the time. She already had a husband, three children, one side of a duplex, and her own car. She had curly bleached hair that she swore was naturally blonde, and she told people that Birdy was her best friend, which was a lie, and now she was up at the table opening her checkbook to take this away from Martha when she already possessed everything a woman could ever want.

"It's mine. I already said." She jabbed Mercy's arm.

"What?" Mercy glanced down at her.

"What?" echoed the startled demonstrator.

A hum pervaded the room full of chattering women. As if drawn by it, Birdy came out of the kitchen with a dish of brownie squares in flattened silver-foil cups. Her sister followed with a tray of rattling cups and saucers that she slid onto the table in the dining alcove of the stuffy, green-walled room. For a fraction of a second, from the cellar, the saw buzzed, then held like a throb in the hard blue swell of a vein.

"I'm buying this set. I told you I was!"

"I didn't hear you." The demonstrator's smile quivered.

"Don't be ridiculous, Martha. You don't even need this stuff." Mercy glanced back at the demonstrator. "She lives in a room! In a boarding-house!" She wrote out her check, chiding in a low voice, "Martha, Birdy doesn't expect you to buy the most expensive thing here!" She scribbled her name, then held out the check. Martha snatched it away from her. "Martha!" Mercy cried, reaching for it. "Martha!"

She was tearing it into such tiny pieces the blue-and-white confetti fluttered onto her lap and shoes. Birdy and her sister loomed over her. The room had grown very still. The DeluxeWare set was hers. She had spoken first and everyone knew it. The women stared at her.

"That's ridiculous!" Mercy sputtered.

"Drop it," Birdy warned Mercy, her eyes holding Martha's.

"Maybe I could get another one even quicker. Maybe by Wednesday," the demonstrator said.

She wrung her hands and stared at the floor. That was her set, but all Birdy cared about right now was that Martha not cause any trouble. Oh, she had to get out of here before anything else happened. She lurched past them. With a cry of astonishment, Birdy's sister staggered heavily out of her way.

"Martha!" Birdy called after her.

She had made it to the door, and when it opened she plunged not into the starlit night, but into the suffocating closeness of this tiny bathroom that reeked of dried rose petals. She sat on the cool toilet lid, sneezing and sobbing.

At first they tapped lightly, calling to her in the gentle, coaxing tones they probably used on their children. Then they knocked and demanded she open the door. Finally they returned to their visiting and ordering. They ignored her. She winced with each peal of laughter and, every few minutes, shivered with the swell of the saw downstairs. She arched her feet against the sweaty toilet bowl now as the bright tide of their voices seeped in under the door. They were leaving.

"Tell Thorny I said hi," a woman said, her breathy happiness like a slap in Martha's face.

"Tell Thorny I said hi," echoed Martha's singsong whisper.

"Oh, he was a riot!"

A DANGEROUS WOMAN

"Oh, he was a riot."

"Good night!"

"Good night."

"Thank you, Carol."

"Thank you, Carol."

"Goodbye!"

"Goodbye."

"I've got a ride."

"I've got a ride. Oh, aren't you lucky, you've got a ride. You've got a friend. You've got someone who likes you, someone who cares about you." She sobbed.

There was a knock on the door. "Martha?" Birdy called. "Everyone's gone now."

She unlocked the door and rushed past Birdy.

———□———

With the shade drawn and the curtains closed in the stifling attic room, she sat in bed watching the staticky little black-and-white television that had become hers after Gert from the first floor rear died.

The stairs creaked. This morning Claire Mayo had called in sick for her at the Cleaners and now this was her third trip to the third floor to see if Martha was feeling any better.

"I thought I'd make stew," the old woman said, pausing hopefully, and now Martha realized the real purpose of each arduous climb was to see if she felt well enough to cook dinner. Claire sighed. "Or maybe I'll just heat up some hash."

"My head hurts," she called back dully, leaning against the heat-filled eave over her bed. Sometimes in the winter the same wall furred with frost.

"You should eat," the old woman called, with a rising note of panic on the word "eat." Martha had been doing just about all of the cooking in the house. For the most part she enjoyed it, but lately she was bewildered by the way Claire's increasing dependence on her was accelerating into a volatile possessiveness. She never knew when the old woman would fly into a tirade.

MARY MCGARRY MORRIS

"I'll get crackers or something later," she said.

"Hiding out never solved anything, you know," Claire said.

"I'm sick. I'm not hiding out." She glared at the door.

"Your boss wants to know if you're coming in tomorrow."

"Birdy?" she asked, throwing back the sheet.

"No, that rude John."

She closed her eyes. Tomorrow was Saturday, the Cleaners' busiest day. As much as she missed Birdy, she still couldn't face her. Not yet. How could she have done that to her best friend, who had hired her, who made her laugh, who last week had chased the two boys who had hounded her all the way from the bank to the Cleaners, mimicking her headlong stride and the long swing of her arms, chanting "Marthorgan! Marthorgan!" until they had gotten her so riled up she kept skidding to a stop every few feet to scoop up stones, which she pegged back, sending the boys into giddy dives behind trees and parked cars. Birdy charged out of the Cleaners, calling them by name as she threatened to call their parents, their principals, and even the police if she had to. "You ought to be ashamed of yourselves," she had called down the street as they fled. "Picking on Martha Horgan like that." Birdy had come inside, trembling, and for the rest of the day hardly spoke to anyone, including Martha.

She buried her face in her hands. Picking on Martha Horgan like that. Thirty-two years old. A grown woman pegging stones at boys. She was the one ashamed.

"I can't go in tomorrow. Will you tell him I'm still sick?"

"I can't do everything around here, you know." Claire said. "Cooking and checking on people and making phone calls for everyone all the time."

"I'll make the stew," Martha sighed, swinging her legs over the side of the bed as Claire headed downstairs to call the Cleaners for her.

By Sunday she felt much better. It was one of those late-May twilights in a world so suddenly, tenderly green that every time someone walked through the park Martha thought she could see each blade of grass spring back into place. The sweetness of lilacs and lilies of the valley drifted from yard to yard, with a fine yellow dust that coated every roof, porch, and windowsill, and all the passing cars. Tracing her finger through it on the porch railing, she could tell this was no common dust, not at all the particles of atrophy and blight, but proof of all this living, this aliveness she felt charging the night.

Dinner was long over. She sat with the five elderly women on the wide veranda in rocking chairs, watching the park across the street fill up with people. The weekly band concert would be starting soon. Ann McNulty and Suzanne Griggs were knitting. They sat on Martha's left, and on her right were Mrs. Hess, Loiselle Evans, and Claire Mayo. Across Main Street, at the center of the park, in the round stone bandstand, the musicians tuned their instruments in a grating skirmish of screeches and riffs, and now, in rude interjection that made the white-faced women blink and blink, the rat-tat-a-tat-tat-tat of the drum. A car horn tooted as a young man in white pants darted across the street.

A few stars glimmered in the thin night sky. Knots of people hurried by the porch, hugging blankets and carrying babies. Some Martha recognized from the Cleaners, but they pretended not to see her. She kept watching for Birdy. Wouldn't that be something, to go over there and have someone to sit with on a blanket? The very thought of it raised a dry lump in her throat.

"Oh, look—there's the Massinneault boy. Yoohoo! Arthur! Arthur Massinneault!" called Miss Griggs.

"Hello, Miss Griggs," the blonde young man called as he came by with three other young men. Miss Griggs had been secretary for the Recreation Department for forty-five years. "Hello, Miss Griggs. Hello, Miss Griggs. Hello, Miss Griggs . . ." The voices passed in echo. She smiled sweetly, her soft voice abridging each person's history: "Helena's stepson . . . the boy that set the Tarsey fire . . . the Minzner girl, she eats lard . . . little Billy Sullivan, his mother and sister both born without a single eyelash between them . . ."

"Marthorgan!" came a cracked voice.

Her toes clenched. Her nails dug into her palms. Her eyes widened.

MARY McGARRY MORRIS

Claire Mayo stationed herself at the top step, arms folded as she scanned the shadows for the adolescent taunter. After a minute, she eased watchfully back into her rocking chair, and for a brief but painful time, no one spoke or moved.

"Oh! Now, doesn't Wesley Mount look good?" Loiselle Evans observed too eagerly of the tall man coming slowly down the street. Mount's funeral home was just a block away. Mount wore his customary dark suit and crisp white shirt. His snug vest glittered with a thick gold watch-chain. Because of his long face and wide shoulders, Wesley Mount seemed an enormous presence, but he was actually so thin that as he came briskly along his suit could be heard flapping on his bony frame.

"Sickly little boy," Suzanne Griggs said. "Afraid of his own shadow."

"Well, who wouldn't be," Mrs. Hess allowed through a clenched smile as he neared the porch, "your whole life involved with death."

"Never fit right," Suzanne Griggs continued, after each stitch giving two quick twirls of yellow yarn around her long red needle. "Kids all thought he was weird."

"Bet they're laughing up their sleeve now," said Ann McNulty with her customary bitterness. After twenty-nine years of marriage, her husband, Willis, had left her for a handsome young cabaña boy they'd both taken such a shine to their one time in Clearwater, Florida, inviting him up here to ski and stay with them any chance he got.

"Good evening, ladies," Wesley Mount said, his large white face tilted over the railing, his voice the same whispered mellifluence that could soothe the most distraught mourner. The ladies leaned forward in a flutter of greetings. Wesley had seen them through enough friends' and relatives' funerals that they sensed a kinship with him. Martha peered toward the bandstand as if she were looking for someone.

On Saturday mornings in the Cleaners, customers lined up to be waited on. Birdy said that for twenty years Wesley Mount had been bringing in his laundry on Saturdays and the only reason he had switched over to Mondays was so he could be sure of having Martha service him, and Birdy meant that just as lewdly as anyone cared to take it. Every time she said it, Mercy and Barbara laughed themselves weak. That bothered Martha, because she had told Birdy about his embrace in the funeral home, but she knew Birdy would never tell anyone. Birdy said all Martha had to do was look at Wesley and his ears and the back of his neck would turn beet-red.

"You're out and about early tonight," Claire Mayo said with a glance at her watch.

"I am," said Mount. "But, you know, it's the strangest thing—for three days there has not been one single death in Rutland County."

"Lord have mercy. . . . Imagine that. . . . That must be some kind of record . . ." the women murmured.

The band had just begun to play "The Camptown Races," their first song of the concert season. Martha stared at the park, wishing he'd leave.

"Well," Wesley Mount said, then gave a little cough and cleared his throat politely behind his hand. She was conscious of his uneasiness now as he spoke to her, and the ladies' curious bemusement.

"Are you feeling better," and it seemed the longest pause before he uttered her name, "Martha?" said with such gentle trepidation that the old women looked on with weak tender smiles, their faces just sad enough to confuse her. Oh, she didn't want to hear any talk from them after he left.

"I'm fine, thank you," she snapped, squinting toward the Chinese lanterns strung in intersecting lines of color across the park. Why had she come out here? She hated it when people talked to her in front of other people, singling her out like this. At least in the Cleaners she knew what to say. But out in the world like this . . . the air thinned and her heart lurched as the bandstand lifted up through the treetops like a great stone blimp, hovering against the stars while the band exploded into a gusto of galloping beats to end the song . . . she had to be very, very careful. So many things could happen. Sometimes she had to hold her breath just to stop it all from turning too fast. But in these last few months away from home, she was getting better and better at living out here, in the world, with everyone else. There. It always settled into place if she sat very, very still and did not breathe.

MARY MCGARRY MORRIS

Did not blink. The moment returned itself, falling as a scarf falls, soft settling folds. . . .

"They said you were sick," Wesley Mount said.

She was motionless in the rocking chair, her reply just the slightest nod. The drape of patched hair sagged over her eye.

"She had the flu," Loiselle Evans said dreamily. A soft-haired, soft-eyed woman, Loiselle lived for love, any kind of love. Dogs. Cats. Man. Soap operas. God. Even the tale of Willis McNulty's fling with the nut-brown cabaña boy stirred her.

"It's been going around," Wesley Mount said.

"Yes, it has," Loiselle averred in a tremble that seemed to lift the Chinese lanterns in a ripple of colored light through the tall dark trees.

"Leaves you feeling real punk," Wesley Mount sighed.

"Well, she's on the mend now. In fact," Loiselle said with a coquettish wag of her finger, "Martha made us all just the tastiest meatloaf today. Crispy onions on top, and just the fluffiest mash potatoes you ever saw. She's quite the young cook!"

Wesley glanced shyly at Martha, then as instantly reeled in his attention to the beaming ladies. He wished them all a good night and continued on his splay-footed way.

"Martha," Loiselle whispered in a tone of pure wonder, "I think Wesley Mount has got his eye on you."

"Hmph," she said, her eyes hot with blushing. "The Grim Reaper. That's what John calls him. He comes in on Mondays now and picks up on Fridays." That made no sense, but who could think with a heart beating this loudly?

"Well, he's quite a gentleman," Loiselle sighed. "And let me tell you, there aren't many of those left." Loiselle patted her hand. "Nossir." Her hairy little chin quivered.

"It makes you wonder," Mrs. Hess said, as he disappeared in the distant shadows, "successful young man like that never getting married."

"He diddles the stiffs," Martha said.

"What?"

"Martha!"

"What she say?"

"What's a diddle?"

"Loiselle!"

Miserably, she closed her eyes. Birdy could get away with saying things like that, but she couldn't. Across the way, in the park, young couples sat on blankets in the dark grass, shoulders touching, heads bent close. How did they get there, she wondered, the old yearning like a beak at her ribs. How did they manage to know what clothes to wear, what conversations to have, which friends to choose, lovers to take? What invisible rudders steered them through waters as unnavigable for her by daylight as by night?

Did she have a blankness where others possessed that code of information necessary to guide them through dinner conversation and the proper way to comb their hair or simply say hello to a stranger without having to thump their chest and cough and clear their throat—until she would be not only choking, but starting to veer so much off course that the sudden realization that she'd never belong, that there'd never be a place for her, could either enrage or paralyze her.

No. She had to keep reminding herself how much better she had gotten with so many little things.

The ladies' knitting needles froze.

"Look at that," Claire Mayo muttered as a tiny woman in baggy gray pants and a man's wrinkled plaid shirt teetered drunkenly on the opposite curb before stepping heedlessly into the double lane of traffic. She was Anita Bell, Steve Bell's alcoholic wife. Steve Bell and Martha's aunt Frances had been lovers since Martha's childhood. Steve continued to live here in town with Anita while halfway up Beecham's Mountain Frances maintained her status as widow of Horace Beecham, at one time the wealthiest man in southern Vermont.

Suddenly two southbound cars squealed to a stop, just inches away from the startled woman. With her hand shielding her eyes from the headlights' glare, she turned in a jerky little circle. The traffic had clogged all the way up Main Street, past the corner lights and gas stations. Horns honked. The band continued to play.

MARY MCGARRY MORRIS

Anita Bell held up her middle finger and roared, "Bastards, you no good son-of-a-bitching bastards!" She pointed to the northbound traffic that still crept past. "Stop! I said stop!" she commanded. And it did.

She crossed, lurched onto the curb, where she reeled for a few feet, then caught herself on the old granite hitching post at the end of Mayo's weedy, frost-heaved brick walk. Glancing up, her eyes snared Martha's, and she pointed at her. "Don't you look at me like that, you crazy slut. I know what you did with those boys. I know," she called, her husky voice careening down the street, startling dogs and scraping houses and gouging the bark off trees. Martha cringed as twigs and chips and little stones flew back at her.

"Just don't say anything," Claire Mayo hissed, her hand steadying the arm of the rocker. "Let her go."

"Poor Steve Bell," Loiselle Evans said.

"The way he's stuck by her all these years," Mrs. Hess said.

Ann McNulty, her mouth puckered and thin, said, "Yes, and if one pot's cold, he's always got the other to cook in."

FOUR

————o————

Monday morning, she was the first one at work. She had come early to get fig squares and sugar doughnuts before the bakery sold out. Birdy loved fig squares. It was twenty minutes past opening, and Martha was still waiting on the front steps when Birdy finally arrived, with Getso driving her car. Birdy had been giving him a ride ever since his car had broken down last month.

She wondered how Birdy could stand him. He had been a boxer as a very young man, and his nose was crooked, and there was a thick scar over one eyebrow so crudely stitched the right eye had been pulled up higher than the left. His mouth was red and full—lewd, she thought. His ex-wives used to come by the Cleaners with their children for their support money until a fight broke out one payday between the two women. John said Getso was through if either woman so much as stepped a foot on his property again.

A vague nausea like motion sickness always overtook her when Getso came near. It was as if he exuded poisons that she alone could sense. She would only speak to him when she had to, and then with her head down, eyes averted, breath held.

After getting out of the car, Birdy tucked in her blouse and tugged her skirt band straight. Late as she was, she waited by the car while Getso locked it.

Martha's throat tightened at their approach. She coughed. She needed to be alone with Birdy so she could apologize for the way she had acted at the party.

Birdy's eyes were red and puffy, obviously from crying. Avoiding Martha's stare, Birdy looked at her watch and then at Getso. "I told you we were late," she said, hurrying past Martha to unlock the dusty glass door.

"No, she's early," Getso called after her. He braced one scuffed boot against the step Martha sat on and, with both hands on his waist, leaned in, stretching his left leg behind him. "It's Monday, and Martha can't wait to see her man," he grunted, switching feet, now stretching back the other leg with a series of grunts. He laughed, then looked up at her, squinting in the early sun. "You know, I know Mr. Mount pretty well. I'll bet if I said something he might, you know, ask you out or something. Would you go? Well, would you?" he persisted when she didn't answer.

"No!" she said, wishing she had gone right in with Birdy.

"You ever had a date before?" He angled his face near hers.

She grabbed the pastry bag and jumped up, but he was blocking her way.

"Hey! Now, don't go flipping out on me or anything. I didn't mean nothing personal or like, you know, what happened that time, them guys, you know. Like I was just saying to Birdy, you know, in this life we're all poor bastards."

She tried to get by him, but he held the door. She couldn't believe that, just moments after causing Birdy's tears, he would make a pass at her best friend.

"Just remember. No matter what happens, we're all in this together." His red lips trembled. "I know. I got feelings. . . ."

Horrified, she pushed past him into the stale heat of the Cleaners.

"You're late. I've been waiting for a half hour," she said, and followed Birdy through her routine of turning on the lights and fans, and unlocking the register and storage rooms. "Here. I got these for you," she said, shaking the bag after her from task to task. "I got there early and I got you the figs before they sold out. You know how fast the figs sell out." And now it poured out of her. "I'm sorry for what happened. Really, Birdy. I really am. You've been so good to me and so patient, and every time I mess up, you always act like nothing happened—but this time . . ."

Without a word, Birdy turned from the safe and set the cash drawer on the counter. Suddenly Martha threw her arms around her soft shoulders. "Oh, Birdy, I'm so sorry. I'm so ashamed. You've been so good to me. You treat me better than anybody ever . . ."

"Martha!" Birdy gasped, struggling back. "Stop that. Don't do that." She looked toward the doorway, where Getso leaned.

"Hey, whatever comes natural you know," he said with a smirk.

Birdy grabbed a cellophaned pad of new laundry slips and threw it. He ducked, laughing. She stalked into the back room and called for Martha to follow. "Sit down," she ordered, continuing to point even after Martha sat at the wobbly break table. "First of all, I'm not mad at you. Personally, as far as I'm concerned, the other night's gone, past tense. It's history," Birdy said.

She attempted a smile, but Birdy's weariness was too sobering.

"But . . ." Birdy shook her finger. She seemed troubled. "I've got to tell you . . . just so you'll know where it's coming from . . ." She closed her eyes and sighed. "I hate having it just sprung on you. . . ." She sighed again and patted Martha's shoulder. The loading-dock buzzer rang insistently. "Look, when John comes in, let me talk to . . ." She looked toward the stairway. "Damn, damn, damn," Birdy muttered and she ran downstairs.

Martha could tell from the kidding voices and the rush of truck exhaust up the stairs that the rest of the drivers had arrived and were getting their delivery slips from Birdy. She got up quickly to put the bag out front, in Birdy's basket under the counter. Left back here on the table, the fig squares would be gone before Birdy got a one. The drivers were the worst. They ate everything in sight and never brought pastry in themselves. Birdy said they counted on the women for that.

Seeing Getso at the counter, Martha froze in the doorway. Leaning over the cash drawer, he slipped out two bills, then folded them with a flip of his fingers down the front of his tight jeans.

She raced back to the table and sat down with the bag on her lap just as he came into the back room. "She still down there?" he called irritably on his way past. His boots hammered down the wooden stairs.

She jumped up and put the bag into Birdy's basket. In her own basket she found a pint-sized PlastiqueWare container. Birdy must have bought it for her. Smiling, she snapped the blue lid on and off. Also in the basket was a small white envelope with her name printed on the front. Her heart raced as she held the envelope up to the fluorescent light. It must be an invitation to another party. Of course; this would be Birdy's way of setting things straight without a lot of embarrassing talk. Grinning, she pressed the envelope to her chest and shook her head. Birdy had to be the kindest, most considerate person she had ever known. Hearing Birdy's voice now in the back room, she slipped the envelope back into her basket. She would open it later. Right now she had to tell Birdy about Getso.

She winced, hearing Mercy and Barbara in the back room. Their laughter caught in the sudden trawl of Birdy's low, anxious voice.

"Oh God," Barbara groaned. "Why couldn't it happen on my day . . ."

"Shh," Birdy said.

A DANGEROUS WOMAN

The strap of bells rang on the opening door as Wesley Mount entered with two grocery bags stuffed with laundry. "Oh, good morning." He smiled, relieved to see her back. Birdy had come out of the back room, followed by Mercy and Barb. They didn't want to miss this, she could tell.

"Wasn't that quite a concert last night?" he asked, and she heard Barbara stifle a little squeal.

Birdy wet her thumb and began to count the money in the cash drawer.

"I heard it all the way home and in the house too. I don't usually. But last night I heard it as clearly as if . . . as if I'd been on Claire Mayo's front porch," he said pulling his balled-up shirts from the bag.

She shook out each shirt. The white one had a red smear on its front.

He paused, his hand in the bag. "You know what I think it was," he said, cocking his large head. "I think it was one of those perfect, perfect nights when every single aspect of the universe, every star in the constellations . . ."

From the corner of her eye she saw Birdy's head jerk up. She had discovered the shortage.

"Blood or lipstick?" she interrupted in her practiced drone, raising only her eyelids to look at him, the way she'd learned from Birdy.

Birdy stared at her, then wet her thumb and began to re-count the bills.

"Well . . . well, blood," he stammered, and she dropped the shirt. "But it's my blood," he assured her. "I cut myself."

"Oh God," Mercy groaned, and Barb giggled. They had just begun pressing shirts. Their machines hissed and flapped as each woman raced to finish first.

BLOOD, she printed on the slip. "Heavy starch, folded?" she asked, marking an "X" in the box before he answered.

"Yes!" he said, flattered that this time she had remembered.

Birdy slid the cash drawer into the register. The door bells jangled and John entered, looking so pale and sweaty Martha thought he must be sick. She tagged and bundled Wesley Mount's shirts while the two men exchanged greetings. Wesley stood close to John, and each time

MARY MCGARRY MORRIS

John, who was a head shorter, stepped back, Wesley moved closer. Birdy said this came from years of Wesley's listening to the whispered secrets of the bereaved. Wesley was telling John about a disagreement he was having with some of the Chamber members. It was, he explained, his property, for which he had paid good money—top dollar, in fact—and no one was going to put that kind of pressure on him. And besides, Grolier, who owned the nursing home next to Wesley's property, was way off the mark. Seeing the hearse parked in the lot wasn't going to depress Grolier's nursing-home patients. In fact, just the opposite would be true.

"It'll give them a good feeling. I know how they are. They tell me. John, they look forward to dying," Wesley Mount whispered.

Rubbing his neck, John smirked at Birdy. For the rest of the week they would all be imitating Mount and shooting her looks, as if she cared, as if it bothered her in the least. She wheeled out one of the huge canvas carts for his shirts. They must think she was stupid, that all the secret little smiles and quick remarks went right over her head. She looked up sharply, but the two men were talking about the potholes on Main Street.

It had taken her a long time to get used to John's vulgarities and sarcasm whenever she made a mistake. All he had to do was look at her the wrong way and she was certain to drop things, mislabel bundles, count back the wrong change, bump into people, lose her temper, and end up in one of those miserable choking spasms that people who knew her would ignore but that had more than a few times sent strangers running to thump her back while they inquired in panicky voices if she was all right. All right? How could anyone be all right whose existence was fueled by this terrible, self-consuming energy, this frenzy of fear and anger, a crippling power, driving her . . . driving her . . . She had never been all right. Never. No—always the butt of everyone's jokes perfect strangers children were the worst nipping at her heels like savage dogs all the way along the streets calling her name so that it had become a NAME, a bad word, MARTHORGAN a taunt synonymous with bogeymen and bums and crazed old women in unpainted, crooked houses.

She jammed the cart against the wall, and it rolled, so she jammed it again, then again, until it finally stayed. When she turned, they were staring at her.

"My bags," Wesley Mount said softly.

She had thrown away his bags, his stupid bags. "Imagine saving paper bags like an old lady, and won't they all have a good laugh over that too when he leaves," she muttered as she fished them out of the barrel. She handed him the bags, and no one said anything.

"Well. Well, I'm off," Mount said uneasily. He folded the bags into tight squares and put one into each jacket pocket. "Have a good day," he said at the door.

"You too," she said, her voice sludged with thickness. One by one she swung the weekend's laundry bundles into a cart. The bells gave the briefest little jingle as Wesley Mount closed the door softly behind him. Under John's scrutiny, she worked faster and faster. The minute the cart was full, she ran it out to the huge machines, then returned so quickly she was panting. She loaded the second cart.

"Well?" John said. He kept tapping a pencil against his palm.

Birdy stepped back against the curtained doorway.

"So what's the story?" he asked. Watching her, he unwrapped a powdery stick of gum and chewed it to folds on his front teeth.

"I was sick Saturday," she said, her head down.

"Yah, well." He waved impatiently. "I mean the notice. The notice!" He gestured at the counter.

What notice? She lifted the metal slip-box and pushed aside the plastic-coated price sheets, but she didn't see any notice. "You want Birdy?" She looked back. The curtain wafted in and out of the empty doorway. She thumped her chest and swallowed hard. Had some procedure changed without anyone telling her? Behind her the steam plates rose and fell with a hiss as the two women kept pressing shirts.

He shrugged and held out his ringed hands with a look of bewilderment. "The notice! What do you think I mean? The notice—didn't you read the notice? In your basket. The notice!" He raced around the counter and from her basket snatched the envelope with her name on it. "Here." He thrust it at her. "It's a layoff notice. I gotta let you go.

Nothing personal." He rubbed his hands together, then blew into them as if they were cold in this swelling wet heat. "It just gets slow now."

"No," she moaned, unable to break her gaze. The envelope trembled in her hand. "No!"

He rolled his eyes. "Shit," he muttered. "I should've gone with the Grim Reaper there," he said, gesturing back at the door.

The flat lids of the machines flew up and down with each shirt's continuous readjustment, collar up, front, back, sleeve, cuffs, then collar again under the plate of steam, while the women looked on dully.

"I'm not the one you should fire!" she blurted. "I'm a good worker. It's Getso you should fire."

"Not firing, now, Martha—but laying off. There's a difference," John said.

"I saw him take money right out of the cash drawer. I did! Right before you got here! I was going to tell Birdy. She should know! Birdy! Birdy!" Breathlessly, she yanked open the curtain and was startled to find Birdy right there, staring back at her. "You counted it! How much is gone? How much did he take? I saw him!"

Birdy's blank look puzzled her. Didn't she care? Martha ran to the register and, with the pen she kept nearby—oh, she couldn't bear the cold, hard touch of metal, the way it made her skin crawl—she stabbed the cash key to open the drawer. "Count it! Count it! You'll see!" she demanded, slapping the counter.

John wouldn't look at her. "Talk to her. Do something," he said to Birdy.

"Count it! Go ahead! Count it!"

"Calm down! You just settle down!" Birdy ordered.

"I saw Getso take it right from there," she said pointing. "Right out of the drawer. Count it! You'll see! I saw him take it." This wasn't the way she wanted to tell Birdy. But at least it was all out in the open now, she thought, trying to smile as Birdy hugged her.

"Just drop it. John's trying to make it easy for you. Okay?" Birdy said at her ear. "At least this way you get benefits."

She broke free of Birdy's hold. "Don't you even care? That's why money's missing all the time. It's Getso! I saw him take two bills and go like this down the front of his pants." She grabbed John's arm and shook it.

John looked at Birdy. He bit his lip, then nodded. "Call him up here."

"He's right out there," she said, lifting back the curtain.

Getso stepped out, squinting. With his back to her, he spoke to John in a low voice. Her head throbbed. He wasn't going to get away with this. She rocked back and forth, trying to calm down. He wasn't going to take advantage of Birdy anymore. Birdy would never have to come to work again with tears in her eyes.

"Tell her," John said. "Tell her to her face."

Getso turned. He shuffled his feet. "I saw you take them two tens out of the cash drawer."

At first she nodded. She could barely hear him. It wasn't sinking in. "No!" She looked at Birdy. "No!"

Birdy's eyes were closed.

"He saw you last week too," John said. "Thursday you took fifteen. Friday you're out, nothing's short. Saturday, same thing. Today you're back. Bingo! Twenty short!" He held out his hands. "But that's not even why . . ."

"No!" she cried, lunging at Getso, trying to shove her hand down his pants. "That's where . . ."

"What the . . . Jesus Christ," Getso hollered, grabbing her wrist.

In a quick scuffle, Birdy and John had pulled her away. "Stop it! Do you hear me? Just stop it!" Birdy was trembling.

They could say what they want say what they want her name over and over repeating her name Martha Martha Martha please say what they want as she stuffed her pocketbook with the contents of her basket, the red ceramic mug with the white "M" Birdy had given her on her birthday, a *Good Housekeeping* magazine, a small bag of birdseed, a box of shortbread cookies imported from Scotland, and her plastic container.

"Hey! Martha!" John said as she charged grimly around the counter, head down, shoulders slack as it all fizzled away.

MARY MCGARRY MORRIS

40

"Where you going? It's a two-week notice!" He put his hand on her arm.

"I have to go," she said, jerking back so quickly that her purse flew open and her mug fell and shattered on the floor.

She stepped into the hot dusty sunlight, then paused, certain Birdy would say something. Anything.

"This means she's quitting! This means no benefits! You're all witnesses," John raged in the sigh of the closing door. "Goddamn screwball, gives me the creeps!"

"Did you see where she tried to grab him?" Mercy squealed.

"I told you she had the hots for Gets," Barb said.

Getso was laughing.

———□———

Panting, she darted through the park, zigzagging on and off the path to avoid people. She ran across the street and into the boardinghouse, relieved to find the sunny front parlor empty. The Aid Bus had brought the ladies to the senior center. Where was Claire? She would have to tell Claire. No, she couldn't tell Claire, couldn't tell anyone. She'd just pack her things and go.

She ran upstairs. She threw open her closet door and yanked her clothes off the hangers. She emptied the drawers, jamming everything into two shopping bags and the bird feeders into an overnight bag. Bending over her tiny sink, she splashed cold water on her face, then patted down her heat-frizzed hair. Her face dripping wet, she put on her glasses, picked up her bags, and took a deep breath. The hair on her arms bristled and a cold itchy sweat prickled her scalp as she stepped into the dark hallway. On the top step she paused, then hurried back into the room. She smoothed the wrinkled bedspread and picked up the wire hangers from the floor. She wiped the sink dry with wadded tissues, then ran them over the bureau top and headboard. When the tissues crumbled, she used her shirttail to dust the windowsill. She moved the lamp over the brown tea ring on the white plastic porch table she had used as a nightstand. "I've been a good boarder," she said under her breath as she backed out of the room. "A very good boarder. I've been a good boarder, a very good . . ."

Downstairs, in the kitchen, she pressed the telephone to her ear.

"I can't come now," her aunt Frances said. "Besides, I thought two . . ."

"Two's too late!"

"I didn't mean . . ."

"Now! I need a ride now!" She stamped her foot. "Right now!"

"Martha! Calm down! Tell me what happened. John let you go? Didn't he give you notice? Didn't he give you two weeks?"

"I quit."

"Quit, why'd you quit?"

"Because I did."

"Oh God."

"Are you coming?" she asked.

Sighing, Claire Mayo came through the back door, her dingy apron sagging with dirty rhubarb stalks.

"Martha, I'm in the middle of something. You can't expect me to just . . ."

"Forget it. I'll just take the bus." She hung up quickly. "That's what I'll do."

"Trouble?" Claire asked. She dumped the rhubarb into the long soapstone sink.

Martha shook her head. She still hadn't moved from the phone.

Claire ran cold water over the rhubarb. She glanced at Martha. "What's in the bags?"

"I'm going home," Martha said.

The old woman's head whipped back. She turned off the water and stood by Martha, wiping her hands with her apron.

"I got fired!" Martha blurted, her face twisted in disbelief. "And I'm his best counter person. I give good service! I look right at people right in their eyes," she said, tapping the lens in her glasses. "And I never even blink. Not once. The whole time they tell me what they want—Starched! Folded! Hangers! Pre-spot! Waterproof!—I keep look-ing right at them." She buried her face in her hands and sobbed.

———□———

She sat on the rough concrete bench at the corner of the park. She had been waiting for the bus for well over an hour. It embarrassed her to have the same people pass by and see her still here. Every few minutes, across the road, the curtain parted slightly in the parlor window. She had missed the first bus because Claire Mayo had blocked the doorway, trying to talk her into staying. When she heard the bus coming, she got so upset she pushed the old woman out of her way.

She dug into her bag now for her magazine and hunched forward, pretending to read. A young woman in tight shorts came through the park pushing a double baby stroller; the redheaded twins, a boy and a girl, banged their feet on the metal footrest. Alarmed by the noise, Martha held her finger to a line, stabbing it into the page.

A car blared its horn. "Hey, Martha! Martha! Wanna go for a ride?" boys' voices called in a blur of arms whizzing past. She got up and hurried across the street to the pharmacy, where she hid her bags in the dusty lilac bushes by the steps. Once inside, she felt better. The bags marked her. People saw them and they knew she had been fired, knew she had no friends, never had, never would. She stood by the window, turning the card racks. From here she would be able to see the bus coming.

A pale-pink card embossed with a white rose caught her eye. I'M SORRY, read the gold script. The card was blank inside. She took it to the cashier, a fat girl with earrings of yellow feathers. She set down the paperback she had been reading and turned over the card. "Dollar forty-eight," she said as she rang it up. Martha picked up the card and opened it. What would she write? She had already apologized for the other night. If anything, Birdy owed her an apology.

"Ma'am? Excuse me. Miss Horgan? You still want the card?"

Her head shot up. "No!" She slapped it down on the counter and hurried outside. All she could think of was Getso's brazen face while he lied. And Birdy's blank expression. Did Birdy really believe she would steal from her best friend? That she had been stealing all along? Maybe it wasn't too late. Maybe she could still set things straight. She went to the phone booth at the bottom of the steps.

"Cleaners!" Mercy Reardon answered on the first ring.

Martha hung up. Birdy must be on break. She waited a few minutes before she called again.

"Cleaners!" Again, Mercy's voice.

Just as she hung up, she heard Birdy laugh. She had one coin left.

"Cleaners!" Mercy answered irritably.

"May I speak with Birdy, please?"

"She's not here."

"I know she's there. This is very important. It's an emergency, tell her."

"She . . . she stepped out."

"But I heard her. I know she's there."

"She went to the bank."

"It's only noon. She doesn't go till one-thirty."

"Martha, today she went early. Okay?"

She didn't say anything.

"Martha?"

"Will you tell her I called? If she wants, she can call me back—at my aunt's. Well, tell her to wait a while. I'm not there yet."

"Where you calling from?"

"A phone booth."

"Where? Which one?"

"The one by Marco's. The drugstore."

"Oh!" Mercy sounded relieved. There was a hollow silence as if she'd briefly covered the receiver. "Hey, look, I'll tell her you called. And, listen, you take it easy now, Mart. Keep your chin up, kid. Okay, now?"

She dragged her bags out of the bushes and started walking north on Main Street, past the big old homes that had been converted into antique shops and real-estate agencies. When she heard the bus, she would flag it down.

Maybe Birdy had gone to the bank early. She must have. Otherwise she would have come to the phone.

Uneasily, she remembered that wire-hanger salesman Birdy had dodged all last winter, hiding in the ladies' room when he delivered, not taking his calls. It had been a riot, the way she had enlisted them in the conspiracy. The thing Martha liked best about Birdy was the way she incorporated people into her life, the good and the bad, her happiness and her troubles. But with Getso it had obviously gotten out of hand. And for some reason, Martha was the only one to see it.

A red pickup truck slowed, then pulled to the curb, and Billy Chelsea leaned across the seat. "You heading home, Martha?"

She stared, flattered, not knowing what to say. She hadn't seen him in months.

"Come on, I'll give you a ride." He waved.

Just then the bus roared past.

"I gotta go see Frances for a minute anyway," he said as she climbed in.

"Hear you been working in town!" he said, and she nodded, licking her lips, her eyes struck by the sun through the windshield and the hot dust of the dashboard. She cleared her throat. "Yes, I have," she finally managed.

He glanced back at her a few more times, then seemed to realize the lead would have to be his.

"I been doing some stuff for Frances," he said as he drove. "Different things. Plumbing. Some wiring. That deck is next. The steps gotta be replaced, and some of the boards. That's gonna be the biggest job. She wants it done before Steve Bell's big birthday party. It's tough now too. My little girls' sitter quit. Most people don't mind, though, if I bring them along. They're pretty good. They read comics and color and stuff like that in the truck."

She caught his glance in the mirror. "How old are they?" she asked slowly, so she wouldn't stammer. She listened carefully, hoping for some clue what to say next.

"Five and four." He laughed. "You gonna be up the house tomorrow morning?"

She nodded.

"Then you'll meet 'em. I figured I'd mention it to Frances while I was dropping some stuff off," he said, gesturing at the lumber in the back of the truck. "Think she'll mind?" He looked at her.

Unsure of his meaning, she shrugged.

"Well, it's that or nothing, I guess," he called over the engine and the rush of air through the windows and the rattling lumber. "For a while anyway. Lately it's sort of a package deal with me. Till I get a full-time sitter anyway." He glanced at her bags. "You still working at the Cleaners?"

With the sting of tears in her eyes, she took a deep breath. "It's very hot today, isn't it?" she said.

"What?" He leaned toward her. "What?"

When she repeated it, he called back, "Sure is. I guess summer's finally here after all."

She held on to the door as the truck sprang up and down over the narrow mountain-road.

"But, then, we don't have much choice in the matter, do we?" Bouncing on the seat, he smiled over at her. "Just take what we get."

"I guess." She winced. That was dumb.

He lived a couple of miles down the road from Beecham's in a small white farmhouse. She used to see his wife walking or picking berries, with the baby sacked on her back and the older girl lagging alongside. She had been a handsome young woman, with bunned hair and a hardy smile. And then one day she died in an accident, on her way to the dentist. After that, the vision that soothed Martha to sleep at night was of herself and Billy Chelsea, wading hand in hand through a brilliant field of black-eyed Susans and Indian paintbrushes. But whenever she actually saw him on the road or in town, she always looked the other way before he could.

His sideburns were just starting to gray, and his eyes and mouth were deeply lined. His belly sagged over his jeans. "Here we go," he said, turning into the driveway. Of the three cars parked there, the only one she recognized was Steve Bell's low black Jaguar.

He pulled in front of the huge brick house, then jumped out and opened her door. "Let me give you a hand. Here," he said, taking her bags.

"No! That's all right," she said, snatching them back. After all, he was here on business, and she didn't want to waste his time. "First things first," she muttered as she hurried toward the house. "Take care of business and the business'll take care of you." The door slammed, and she realized she hadn't even thanked him.

She was surprised to find the cool dim tedium of Frances's house so soothing. Last fall she had vowed to never step foot in here again. Peering through the sheer bathroom curtain, she could see four people sitting on the patio. Behind them the swimming pool shimmered. With his hand shading his eyes, Billy Chelsea stood talking to Frances, who sat in the pale-blue shade of the table umbrella, her long legs crossed, a thin white sandal dangling from her foot. Across from her sat two women with their backs to the house. Also facing the women was Steve Bell, in white bathing trunks and a bright-pink shirt. He seemed to be looking right at the window.

She hurried out of the bathroom. To get up to the garage apartment where she and her father had always lived, she would have to walk past them, and right now she didn't want to talk to anyone, especially Frances's gushy friends.

"Martha," a woman called softly from the end of the hallway. A tall slender figure came toward her. "I've been hearing such good things about you," she said, lightly touching Martha's arm.

Martha smiled. She liked Julia Prine, who was the only one of Frances's friends who ever hung in long enough for Martha to get past her self-conscious miseries.

"Home for a visit? You've been on your own for quite a while now," Julia said, walking with her. "I think that's wonderful."

"Well, not . . . n-n-now," she stammered, flustered to see Frances come into the kitchen. Their last time together in this room had been the day of her father's funeral. In her rage, Martha had dumped all of the drawers onto the floor. She remembered clattering through silverware and ladles and knives as she had stormed out.

Frances turned from the sink, where she was filling glasses with ice cubes. Her face was already deeply tanned, her wide, full mouth coated a startling pink. People were always amazed to find out she was fifteen years older than Martha.

"She's through with that place, thank God," Frances said to the tiny, bright-eyed brunette who sat down at the table and lit a cigarette. They called her Betty. Martha had never met her before.

"They're a weird bunch in there," Frances said, as she swept toward Martha in a jangle of bracelets and gold chains and lifted her cheek to be kissed.

"Especially that John Kolditis." Betty shuddered. "One look at him and I swear to God I almost quit. I mean, really! How did he EVER get in?"

"Maizie," Frances explained, naming John's wife. "Old, old money," she said with an airy wave. They were all members of the Atkinson Country Club.

Arms folded, Martha waited awkwardly to leave. She felt bruised inside.

"God. It's scary, isn't it?" Betty grimaced.

"Betty Mestowsky, you are such a snot!" Julia Prine said, laughing.

"It's the nouveau riche in me," Betty sighed. "I can't help it. New money, new furniture. It makes someone like me very insecure and very nasty."

Julia laughed, and Frances smiled uneasily.

"I mean, the only antiques I own are the ones I've bought," Betty whispered. "Not like Frahnces here. Tell me, Mahtha, are you old money or new, dear?"

"Mustard!" Frances said. She wet her fingertip and dug furiously at a spot on Martha's sleeve. "How do you do that? How do you get mustard on your shoulder? Explain that to me. I'll bet you were the Cleaners' best customer." Frances glanced over at the women. "What about the Ramshead, then?" She checked her watch. "I'll make reservations for nine." Suddenly she turned back, her mouth open. "Your hair! My God—it's been chopped. . . ." She reached toward Martha's head.

"Don't." She stared at her aunt. "Don't touch me again."

———□———

The garage apartment was hot and airlessly stale. Except for the dust, it felt as if she had never been gone. She moved from room to room now, pleased to find her father's clothes still in his closet and dresser. The narrow bathroom closet was filled with his shaving gear and his medicine bottles. She had never realized how cramped each room was, and she had lived here all her life.

When Martha was a year and a half old, her mother died. Unable to be Horace Beecham's caretaker and also raise a toddler, Floyd Horgan sent for his pretty teenage sister, Frances. For the next few years, the three of them shared these small dark rooms, until Horace Beecham fell in love with Frances and, flaunting all propriety, moved her into his big brick home. They were married when she was twenty-one and he was sixty-one. Five years later, Horace died, leaving Frances a wealthy young widow. To the end of his days, unveering in his rigid veneration of duty, Floyd Horgan insisted on staying here in the caretaker's apartment. It was the taciturn man's hard-earned station, and to have sought more would have been a violation of Horace Beecham's trust. This sense of uneasy tenancy had continued to dog brother and sister all the years since Beecham's death. They were the dirt-poor Horgans, who through some sleight of Fate's hand had been transported from the dark hard Flatts to this spectacular mountainside. They didn't have to tell Martha how her peculiar ways tolled their past. She had always felt it.

She went into her bedroom. Most of her clothes were Frances's hand-me-downs, which she seldom wore. Her favorite things were big and baggy and sexless. Dressing quickly now, she changed into an old shirt of her father's and a pair of his work pants she had cut at the knees.

She kept looking up at the clock. At six-thirty, she dialed Birdy's home number. She counted twenty rings before she hung up. Next she called the Cleaners, even though she knew they'd be closed by now. No one answered.

In the bathroom, she rinsed out the gritty tub, splashing water after a delicate yellow spider until it had swirled down the drain. She laid out two towels and a face cloth for her nightly bath, then set her slippers facing the door. Such rituals were the fretwork of her life. As a child she had discovered that it took 284 steps to get from the start of the driveway to the school-bus stop. The counting of those steps became as vital a part of her school days as packing her lunch, alternating between bologna sandwiches and plain peanut butter. There were always two or three favorite outfits, usually shapeless and dark, and a favorite pair of shoes worn to a soft, floppy comfort, and for a while there had been the scarf, a soft gray-plaid wool of her father's, which she pulled up over her nose. She grew so attached to the scarf, it began to seem that without it she couldn't breathe the sharp winter air. Because she was so afraid of losing the scarf, she had to know where it was every moment. She began to wear it tied around her waist. Soon her classmates were trying to pull it away, which sent her into such a frenzy that her teachers insisted she leave the scarf at home. Instead, she wore it under her shirt. The gym teacher called Frances, who sat Martha down and made her watch while she cut the scarf into little pieces. "It's a scarf," she kept saying. "That's all it is, an old scarf. Just an old scarf you don't need anymore." Of course Frances had been right, it wasn't the scarf but the ritual of the scarf: not things so much as the safety their sameness allowed her.

There were her books on the left of her desk, piled by subject, according to her schedule, and the two pencils and two pens aligned on the right corner with her milk money, first nickels, pennies, then dimes, always stacked the same way under her anxious scrutiny. Boys soon learned that a quick scramble of her desktop symmetry would provoke a spasm of teary gasping and choking, as she tried to rearrange it all before the bell rang for the Pledge of Allegiance, which had its own ritual, a quick three thumps of her heart, and a deep breath with her eyes closed, the only way she could get through it without a stammer, or so it would seem in the scheme of dreaded moments finally made tolerable, endurable. Soon the entire class would be thumping three times, breathing deeply; and yet another teacher would pull her aside, cautioning, "Now, Martha dear. The only reason I mention this . . ." There had been foot tapping and throat clearing, lip chewing, nail biting, snorting, blinking, and choking, the choking having become, even to this day, the worst. All her tics and rituals were only parts of other things, engine-revving incantations against fear and failure. Without them she would get so dizzy she could feel the earth spinning around and around, and she could see this familiar speck, hair and legs flying, holding on for dear life.

She looked up, startled by the sound of the buzzer. She ran to the intercom above the square wooden table in the kitchen and pushed the button to listen.

"I'd like to talk to you before I go out," Frances said.

"What about?"

"I'll tell you when you come over."

"In front of your friends?"

"They're gone. Steve's the only one here, and he's upstairs dressing."

"I'm in the middle of something," Martha said, repeating what she had been told when she had asked for a ride home.

"Well, when you're finished, then. I'll wait."

———□———

Frances waited for Martha in the living room. In all her years here, this was the one room Frances had redecorated. And she had only done it this past winter—with both Martha and Floyd gone, she suddenly realized. Again now, as it often did, the room's airiness struck her as jarring and out of place compared with the rest of the house. She got up and paced back and forth. It wasn't the room. It was the quiet. The aloneness. She missed Floyd, and yet this terrible insecurity she suffered with every change was her brother's fault. For forty years he had been the caretaker here. After Horace's death, Floyd had chafed with every one of her orders. If she had listened to him, she would still be driving the same twenty-year-old Thunderbird. He had kept that car running perfectly without ever once having it repaired in a garage. God, when she thought of how much he had done all those years—the house, the furnace, the garage, his own apartment, the pool and the lawns, and the constant pruning of all the shrubs and trees—it really was amazing. Without him the place was falling apart. Everything. It frightened her . . . everything sinking into ruin.

She sat down. The water dripped from the kitchen faucet with a steady plink plink plink. She looked up, comforted by the creak of Steve's footsteps overhead in the bedroom. Thank God for Steve, who was every bit as positive and cheerful as he had been when they first met, in this very room. She had been sixteen and Pearl had just died, leaving Martha with Floyd. Steve had been a new young lawyer joining his father's practice, the firm that handled Horace's work. He used to watch her whenever he came here on business, and she in turn couldn't take her eyes off him. She had been so unhappy up here with two older men and a fussy toddler that Steve's visits had been all she had to look forward to.

She smiled, pleased to hear him whistling. Anita's DT's had been so bad this morning that it had taken Steve and both of his daughters just to get her dressed and to the hospital. Thank God, they had admitted her. At least he'd get one night of peace.

Where was Martha? She got up and began to blow the dust off tabletops and shelves and picture frames. She wanted to talk to her before Steve came down. She had become accustomed to the peace around here with Martha gone. Of course, every time the phone rang she would cringe, certain it was John from the Cleaners complaining that Martha was annoying his workers or that she had offended another customer.

"I feel bad for her," he had said on the phone the other night, "but now I gotta draw the line."

Dreading the answer, she had asked what had happened.

"Last week she attacked a customer, and now the latest is she got the wrong kinda bowl or the wrong kinda something at this party, and she flipped! Screaming at everybody! She locked herself in the bathroom for two hours. For two hours! People are scared of her. Look, Fran, I been good. You know I been good."

"You have been, John, and I appreciate it. I'll talk to her. But please don't fire her. She'll go to pieces."

"All right, Fran, I'm gonna give it to you straight. She's dipping from the till. I mean, give me a break! Flip-outs are one thing, but she's stealing me blind."

"She wouldn't do that. I know she wouldn't." If anything, Martha was too honest.

"I didn't believe it either. But then, the two days she doesn't come in, everything tallies. To the penny!"

Unable to dissuade him, she had asked if he would keep her on just for two more weeks. At least that would let her down slowly and give her time to find something else and help her save face.

"No!"

"Please, John. I'll pay you the two weeks."

"What about the five bucks here, the ten there? It adds up!"

"I'll take care of that." She was already subsidizing the raise he had refused to give her in January, when everyone else got raises. Of course, Martha didn't know that.

"All right. Two weeks. God, I must be nuts."

Not nuts. Greedy, Frances thought. But, then, leave it to Martha. Instead of staying on with a two-week notice while she looked for another job, she had quit on the spot. Poor Martha, every incident was high drama, every confrontation a disaster, every slight a blow. Such an exhausting life, without subtleties, propelled by fear and anxiety. Frances sighed; well, she was home, and in a way it was a relief. At least she would know where Martha was now and what she was doing. Those first few nights last fall after she had stormed out of here, Frances had lain in bed, staring up at the dark ceiling, wondering if she had gone off with some total stranger, if she lay dead in a ditch somewhere.

Heavy footsteps trudged down the hallway, and this soft room, with its pink-tinted walls and pale upholstery, its brass and glass and pastel porcelain, grew coldly stark. Her eyes darted from corner to corner, and instinctively her hands flew out as if to reshape this formlessness back to its dull oak floors and woodwork, its heavy mahogany tables, and all the dank-smelling upholstery, dark-green and old-rose velvet, that had been Horace's.

Martha came to a dead stop in the doorway, glancing around the room, obviously startled by the change. Like a child, Frances thought, with her unkempt hair and her mouth cresting with every surge or quiver of emotion. It was a face of alarm, its flesh too pliant, too easily shaped for concealment, or secrets. Of course she hadn't stolen John's money.

Frances could tell she was on the brink of tears. But, typically, she appeared to be smiling. Her foot tapped, impatiently, as if she were in a hurry, on her way somewhere, as if SHE had more important things to do.

Frances's teeth clenched.

"What?" Martha repeated, rubbing her arm. "What do you want?"

All patience vanished. Obdurate and dull . . . "What do you want?" Like a knife blunt at the bone. "What do you want?"

"Well? Do you like the way I've done the room?"

"It's all right. I liked the old room better, though."

Frances smiled. "I knew you'd say that."

"Then why'd you ask me?" Martha snapped.

"All I meant, Martha, was that I know you don't like change," Frances sighed. "That's all I meant."

"I don't mind change. Don't start putting words in my mouth!"

"Oh God," Frances sighed, closing her eyes.

"I'm sorry I'm bothering you. You're the one who called me over here. Is that all you wanted to know? If I like the room? Yes! I do, I like the room!"

"Martha!"

"It's beautiful! Everything you do is beautiful!"

"Martha, stop it!"

MARY McGARRY MORRIS

"Don't talk to me like that," Martha warned.

"All right. Okay. The reason I called you over here is to ask you if you're here for good now," she said, as gently and yet deliberately as she could. "Because, if you are we have to get a few things straight."

"I said, don't talk to me like that."

"All right. What I'm trying to say here is, you must watch your temper. And you must make every effort to be friendly to people. I don't want any of that peeking out windows or listening behind doors and lurking. . . ."

"I don't do that!"

"Good. That's good." Frances took a deep breath. "Now, there are two very important things I want you to keep in mind." She lowered her voice. "There's Steve's surprise party in July, and I'd like to be able to count on your help with it. And . . . and the apartment. You can live in it this summer, Martha. But come winter, you'll have to move in here with me. It just doesn't make sense to heat two places. Money's too . . ."

"Don't worry," Martha interrupted. "I won't be here."

"Where will you be?"

"I'll have my job back," Martha said, her glasses slipping, her gaze just that fraction shifted so that there was no way of knowing what she was looking at.

"All set?" Steve asked with a hesitant tap on the door frame. He was straightening the knot on his plaid tie. Thin, wet strands of hair had been combed from above one ear across the pate of his sunburned head. She was pleased to see him wearing the new blazer and linen pants she had bought him. But she was surprised at how shapeless his loafers were getting, and they weren't even that old. She would call Wickley's tomorrow and have a new pair sent to his office.

"Nice to be back, isn't it?" Steve said to Martha with a quick smile. He handed Frances her purse, eager as always to smooth out any discord. "Always good to come home," he crooned, easing her out the door.

From the hallway, Martha muttered, "This isn't my home." Quietly adding, "And it's not yours either."

A DANGEROUS WOMAN

Steve chuckled softly. "She doesn't miss a beat. I'll say that for her," he said as they stepped into the dark heat.

She waited while he opened the car door for her. She slid onto the plush seat, then glanced up, surprised to see him looking down at her through the open door. "I think being on her own's made a real difference," he said hopefully, and when she didn't respond, he closed the door.

As she stared out at the huge brick house, she was consumed by the strange thought that this was no one's home. Not really.

———□———

At eleven-thirty Martha tried Birdy's number one more time before going to bed. Birdy answered on the first ring, her voice so hoarse Martha apologized for waking her up.

"Actually, I just got in," Birdy yawned.

"Oh." Martha bristled at the thought of Birdy out partying while she had been dialing her number every fifteen minutes all night long.

"So! How're you doing?"

"Okay."

"You all settled at home now?"

"I guess so."

"The reason I know you're home is, you left your raincoat. If that's why you're calling, it's up at the boardinghouse. Claire Mayo's got it."

Martha grinned. "That was awfully nice of you, Birdy. You're so thoughtful. You're probably the most thoughtful person I know, and I mean that. I really do." She couldn't stay mad at Birdy.

"You're gonna have to thank Mercy for that one. She dropped it off on her way to bingo. . . . You still there? Mart?"

"Yes. I'm here." She covered the mouthpiece and tried to clear her throat.

"Mart? What's up? You still there?"

"It's about Getso. I know you don't want to believe me, but I saw him take two bills out of the cash drawer and stuff them down the front of his pants. It wasn't me. I swear to God it wasn't. Please believe me, please, Birdy. In my whole life I never had anyone be as good to me as you. I never had anyone to talk to. I never even talked to anyone the way I talk to you. You . . . you made me feel so, so real, Birdy! Like I was there! Like you could touch me and I'd be there. Oh, I don't know how to explain it. Do you know what I mean?" She paused, wincing. "Birdy? Birdy, I love you so much!"

"Yah, well, listen, umh—this isn't such a good time for me. I've got, uh, company here, if you know what I mean?" Her breathy laugh told Martha she meant him.

"Can I call you back?"

"Sure," Birdy said.

"When? Tonight?"

"Umh. No, that's not such a good idea."

The thought of him sitting there, listening, turned her stomach. But maybe Birdy wanted a private conversation so she could hear the truth about him. "Tomorrow?" she asked.

"Sure," Birdy said.

"Okay! I'll call right before you leave for work. I'll call at six-thirty. You don't leave until six-forty-five, right? That way, if I call at six-thirty, we've got fifteen minutes."

"Sure."

"And I won't make you late. I promise. I'll time my . . ." She was talking to the dial tone.

———□———

She had set her alarm for six, but from five on she lay in bed wide awake. At six-thirty sharp, she called, but Birdy's line was busy. She kept dialing, her eye on the clock. Whoever it was, Birdy wouldn't let them talk too long, not when she was expecting Martha's call. At seven o'clock, when the line was still busy, it came to her like a slap in the face. Someone had taken Birdy's phone off the hook.

FIVE

Ever since Billy Chelsea's arrival at eight, the bright warm morning had been filled with the squeal of wrenched-out nails followed by the landing whack of tossed boards.

Arms folded, Frances watched from the driveway, her agitation growing with the pile of boards. "Oh my God!" she called out. "You said just a few boards, Billy. You never said the whole deck!"

In the kitchen, Martha checked her watch. By now all Birdy's setup tasks at the Cleaners would be completed and she'd be right by the phone. Martha held her breath and dialed.

"Cleaners!" It was Mercy.

Martha hung up. A few minutes later, when she called again, Mercy answered.

Martha pinched her nose. "I have to speak with Birdy Dusser, please."

"Oh." Mercy paused. "She won't be in today."

"Is she sick?" Martha asked, alarmed, forgetting to hold her nose.

"I'm not allowed to give out personal information about employees," Mercy said.

She hung up and quickly dialed Birdy's home number, but it was busy. She waited a few more minutes. Still busy. But at least now she understood. The phone was off the hook because Birdy was sick and trying to sleep.

She returned to the window and, through the sheer curtains, saw Billy Chelsea toss aside his crowbar. Now, in the planks nearer the house, the decay was so pervasive he yanked out the boards by hand.

His T-shirt hanging from the railing, he labored bare-backed and sweaty. Parked nearby was his truck, where his daughters played dolls in the back. Every now and then, wiping sweat from his eyes, he went over to check on them. The younger girl whined after him now as he walked back to the deck. "I'm thirsty, Daddy."

"There's soda in the cooler," he called, bending to the deck again.

"I don't want soda," she called back, her arms slung over the tailgate. "I want milk."

"Annie," he ordered the older, reddish-haired child. "Get CeeCee a soda."

"She don't want soda," Annie hollered back.

Billy turned and walked back with the crowbar, which he laid in the truck bed as pretext for talking to the little girls. They both leaned toward him, their hot pouting faces threatening tears.

"Now, you just better mind," he said, his face at the younger girl's.

"I wanna get out," CeeCee cried. "It's too hot!"

"I wanna get out," Martha mimicked under her breath. "Brat. Little brat," she whispered.

Billy Chelsea climbed into the truck and started it. Frances hurried out of the house, staring as he moved the truck into the shade of the beech tree. He jumped down and swung open the back gate and quickly spread a blanket in the truck bed for the girls to sit on. "They were getting too hot," he explained sheepishly.

Sticking out of her shirt pocket was the spiral notepad in which she recorded his hours. "This is unbelievable!" she said, surveying the mess.

"Carpenter ants did most of it," Billy said with a grunt, making sure he worked as he spoke. "Musta been a huge nest to do all this damage." He jiggled another board, then pulled it out, its ends exploding in a puff of fine reddish powder as it hit the pile.

"What do you mean, must've been?" Frances asked.

"Well, they're gone now," Billy said.

"Gone? Gone where?" Her voice rose.

"They just go." He looked back at her. "They just, like, move on."

"Move on!" Frances cried, bearing down on him. The children watched wide-eyed. "Where? Are they someplace else now? In the walls? In the floors?" She gestured back at the house. "Where?"

"No," Chelsea assured her. "The walls're brick. They go in dead trees. In fence posts."

Martha rinsed off the last breakfast dish and set it in the plastic drainer. She let the water run as she sponged the sink clean. The vibrant whack whack whack of Chelsea's hammer shot through the house. She was picturing herself working the counter with Birdy, just the two of them on a busy Saturday, and gradually, in her focused way, she would get everyone waited on. Then she and Birdy would have a nice long visit over coffee and fig squares, and she would explain what Getso had done, and then Birdy would finally see him for the scum he was, compared to Martha, who would never take advantage of a friend oh Birdy must know that. "She must," Martha gasped, rubbing her eyes with the dish towel.

"Here she is! Here's Martha! Martha, turn the water off! Look who's here!" called Frances with such strained gaiety that Martha spun around with a grin, expecting to see Birdy.

Frances gripped Annie and CeeCee Chelsea's hands. "I told the girls they could play in here. That you'd keep an eye on them." Smiling wearily, she phrased everything like an emphatic question. "Maybe get them some lunch? Billy was going to bring them home to eat, but this'll be better." She leaned close and through clenched teeth said, "Keep them away from him! For every five minutes of work, it's ten with them!" She drew back from the girls. "I have some errands to run. Okay?" As she left, she flashed a bright smile.

"Okay," Annie Chelsea said with an uneasy glance at Martha.

"Okay, okay, okay," she panted, looking everywhere but at them. She felt hot. She touched her cheek. She was no good at this. You had to be good at small talk to be good with children. She never knew where to start. They stared up at her. She wiped her hands on the sides of her baggy pants and folded the dish towel into a small careful square; first she set it behind the faucet, then, changing her mind with a mutter, shook it out and bent over the sink to rub it dry, every inch of it dry, dry, dry. She couldn't face them until every single drop was gone. There. She refolded the towel into the same tight square and, turning, took a deep breath and, with three hollow thumps of her collarbone, said, "Do you like ham? I got some cheese here too." Fenced by the open refrigerator door, she stared in at the bright sweating pitcher of orange juice.

"I like ham," the older girl said behind her. "And so does CeeCee."

"You like cheese?" Martha asked without turning.

"We like everything," the older girl said. "My father said we got no business being fussy. He said beggars can't be choosers."

"I'm not a beggar!" CeeCee protested.

"I didn't say you were!" Annie snapped back.

Her arms loaded with bread, cheese, ham, and the mustard jar, she kneed the refrigerator door closed. The two little girls followed her to the glass table and watched her make the sandwiches.

They looked at each other. Whatever CeeCee whispered made the older girl frown. Maybe they didn't like mustard. Was that it? Well, if they didn't, too bad. It was their tough luck. The sandwiches were all made, and she wasn't throwing them out to make more. Brats. Spoiled brats.

"Can we sit down?" Annie asked.

"Oh yah!" she said, thumping her chest and nodding too earnestly, relieved that it had nothing to do with mustard. They couldn't keep their eyes off her. Such rude girls staring like that, didn't anyone ever teach them manners? Probably not, she thought with a sudden sense that they might be as unmoored on this earth as she was. "Sure! You sit down! You both can. Right there in the chair. Sure! Go ahead!"

Halfway through the silence of eating, CeeCee, looking at her sister, said, "I'm thirsty."

"She's thirsty," Annie said.

"Oh yah, sure!" Martha jumped up and offered them milk, juice, water. They both wanted milk. "Here. Here's your milk," she said, placing a glass in front of each girl. "I like milk. It's good for you. I like milk a lot. Makes your bones strong. Makes your teeth strong too." She blinked, alarmingly adrift in the realization that there was nothing more to say about milk—about anything, for that matter. If she told all she knew about milk, that it came from cows, was white, creamy, pasteurized, homogenized, they wouldn't care. So what was the sense? Why not just set the bottle on the table and let that be that? She wasn't going to talk just to fill up dead air. Why should she? She fiddled with the brass napkin-holder, conscious of their uneasy glances as they chewed. Setting her feet squarely together on the floor, she removed the blue cloth napkins and refolded them, placed them so precisely in the gleaming brass swan that their edges were perfectly aligned, like sails, like bright-blue wings. There, there, she thought, letting it out, taking another breath with three quick taps on her chest. Now what? In all the world there were so many things to talk about, but what were they? And if she could think of even a single one, would they even care, these hard-eyed children, who made her squirm, made her hate herself, them, all things?

"Do you have a husband?" CeeCee asked, letting fall the last of her uneaten crusts, curled like a rind.

MARY MCGARRY MORRIS

"No," she answered, barely able to expel the word.

"How come?" CeeCee asked.

" 'Cause she's not married," Annie said too quickly, obviously anticipating some gaffe from her sister.

"How come?" CeeCee asked, looking at Martha.

" 'Cause she's not!" Annie said. She grabbed her sister's wrist and squeezed it. "Now, shut up!"

"I didn't say anything!" CeeCee's voice quavered.

"No, but you were gonna," Annie said, her freckles pale with tension.

"You got cable?" CeeCee asked, jerking her hand away and rubbing it.

"No. Do you?" Martha got up and rinsed off their dishes while CeeCee listed her favorite television shows. Annie had excused herself to go to the bathroom.

"My daddy said the kids were mean to you in school," CeeCee said in a sudden veer off course. "What'd they do?" she rushed on. "They hit you? They throw things at you? They ever spit at you?"

"They . . ."

"CeeCee!" Annie gasped from the doorway.

"They were just mean," Martha said at the sink. She was folding the towel.

"I don't want to go to school!" CeeCee said. "If they be mean to me, I'm going home and I'm never going back!"

"They won't be mean to you," Martha said, turning to find CeeCee's eyes bulging with tears. Poor thing. Poor little thing. "You're so pretty and so nice."

CeeCee sniffed. "Is that why they were mean . . ."

Annie pounced too late.

". . . you're pretty, but my daddy says you're not nice."

Martha stared as the two girls wrestled with each other. Outside, the hammer blows struck the hard flat sheen of noon in an agitation of heat and blinding light. She had a headache. Both girls were crying. Annie had slapped her sister and then been bitten on the upper arm with such ferocity that the deep black imprint of sharp little teeth seemed permanently embedded in her soft flesh. Their rage spent, the

A DANGEROUS WOMAN

girls sagged against one another. They asked to go into the living room.

She followed them from window to window, shelf to shelf, table to table.

"Look," CeeCee said, pointing to the tiered collection of cut-glass dogs that had been Mr. Beecham's.

"Don't touch," Martha warned, and CeeCee drew back her hand. Through the window she glimpsed Billy Chelsea, still shirtless, with a saw at his side, heading doggedly toward the garage. Anger flared through her. Why had he discussed her with his children? What right did he have to perpetuate her miseries? None. He had no right. None at all! No one did! They should leave her alone, she thought in a welter of throbbing temples and the girls' nettlesome voices. Just the way she left them alone. They had no right. That was the trouble. People should leave other people alone. . . .

First came the crash on the marble tabletop, and then, turning, she saw the shattered porcelain pieces fly up in countless, irrecoverable pale slivers. Mr. Beecham's porcelain cabbage rose had been destroyed. They had broken it, these nasty sweaty children. . . .

"You shouldn't have done that," she screamed. "I told you not to touch! I did! You know I did! And what am I supposed to tell her? Do you know what she'll say? Do you have any idea what she's going to say?" She had been shaking the older girl's arm and now she flung it away. "You shouldn't have done that! You shouldn't have," she gasped to the weeping girl, breathless herself now and wet-eyed. She hadn't realized the younger girl had run outside until this moment.

Billy Chelsea ran into the room and swept up Annie. Sobbing, she buried her face in his neck.

"She broke the cabbage rose!" Martha said, her voice piercingly sharp. She was out of control, but now there was no stopping, no way back. There was only this spew of monstrous rage, stupid and repetitive and unstoppable, volcanic and so all-consuming that in school they would goad her to it, then stand back to watch with wonder and giddy fear.

"That was Mr. Beecham's rose! And look what she did! Look what she did!" she panted, holding out a palmful of the pink-and-white-and-green pieces.

MARY MCGARRY MORRIS

64

"I don't care what happened or what she broke, goddamn it!" he roared. "You had no right to lay a hand on her! No right! Do you hear me?"

Head hung, she nodded. There was so little air to breathe. She was ashamed. Her brain reeled with apology, but he had already stormed outside, carrying both girls. She buried her face in her hands. "Stupid, Martha, so damn stupid, can't do anything right," she groaned.

He had just thrown the last tool into his truck when Frances drove into the driveway. She jumped out of her car and followed him around the side of the truck.

"Nobody touches my kids," he hollered from the driver's seat. "I don't care what the hell's wrong."

Frances's pleading voice rose and fell.

"But she did and I'm not putting up with it."

Again Frances's voice.

"I told you. I said this was the only way I could do it. That I had to bring them with me."

Frances's voice.

"Yah, but you don't like it and it shows and my kids can feel it. Plus I told you before I even started I had no idea how much rot I'd find, and now, every board, you act like I'm tryna pull something on you. I don't need this, Mrs. Beecham! I don't need this job! I don't need this shit!" The truck door slammed. "I don't need anything from anybody!"

"Your first day home! That was good," Frances said, her lips white and drawn. "That was very good. Now what do I do? Because you have absolutely no self-control, I am left with that mess out there." She shook her head. "And, you know, he asked me about hiring you to babysit this summer and now that's gone too. This is so typical."

"Leave me alone."

"I wish I could!"

"Don't talk to me like that."

"Martha, the way you act . . . you . . . you . . . Why did you hit that little girl? My God! I mean, I could be sued."

"I didn't hit her! I shook her arm." Head throbbing, she sat with her hand over her eyes.

A DANGEROUS WOMAN

"You shouldn't have touched her. You shouldn't have screamed. You shouldn't have acted like that."

"She broke the cabbage rose!" Martha stared so fiercely that her head trembled.

"So? She broke the cabbage rose! I would have dealt with it. I . . ."

"You would have screamed at me! You would have blamed it on me. Like you blame everything on me. Like everything I do is wrong! Well, I'm going to tell you something—I DO act right. I do! When I'm not around you I do!"

"Yes, you certainly do act right, don't you? Locking yourself in a bathroom for two hours and then stealing from your boss. Oh yes, that's very normal behavior, Martha. Just like your . . . your obsessions with people, that's just the way everyone acts."

"That's not true."

"It's true. It's ridiculous. It's bizarre. It's disgusting. Depressing. Disappointing. What else? Did I leave anything out?" Frances screamed.

———□———

In the next few days, Frances had met with five different carpenters, whose estimates were all so similar she was convinced of their collusion, their treachery, their jealousy, their dislike—no, their hatred, yes, hatred that Frances Horgan had come this far, had risen above what anyone had ever expected or predicted of her.

"Don't be ridiculous," Steve Bell said. He kicked aside a splintered board.

"It was written all over their faces," Frances said. "They were gloating."

"Frannie." He looked over his glasses at her. "You don't mean to tell me that five separate carpenters—and two of them don't even live around here—that all five got together and conspired to set a ridiculously high price . . ." He leaned toward her. "Because they don't like you?"

"I just can't stand this mess anymore! It's driving me crazy. The whole house is falling apart!" She paced back and forth under the beech tree.

"Well, you know what my next words are."

"Please," she warned. She was sick of hearing it, from him, from everyone.

"But with Floyd gone it doesn't make a bit of sense to hold on to this big ark anymore. It's just too much of a drain. Sell this place. Do something with your money. Have some fun, Frannie!"

Her head shot up. "I am perfectly content with my life."

He looked at her. "Really? Because lately I . . ." He shook his head and swallowed hard. "I worry about you, Frannie. I do."

"Then help me find someone!" she said quickly, to avoid the banter that had seesawed them through the years: him wanting to leave his family, her not wanting his daughters to hate her, him insisting he couldn't abandon Anita in a crisis, her pointing out that Anita's existence was rooted in crisis. Patience, each would counsel the other. Patience. Their time together would come soon enough.

"All right, look, I've got this client. A builder. I'll send him up."

Six

—□—

Steve's contractor arrived early on a morning dark with the threat of rain. Martha was in Frances's kitchen, chipping open the hot shell of a soft-boiled egg. She had to eat over here, because there wasn't any food in the apartment, but that didn't matter, because all she really needed, all she cared about right now, was talking to Birdy. Every time she called the Cleaners, Mercy or Barbara answered, so she would hang up. Last night she had dialed

Birdy's home number every fifteen minutes, only to hear the jarring throb of the busy signal. Finally, at one in the morning, the phone actually rang, and she let out a squeal. But then a recording clicked on to say Birdy's number was now unlisted. Stunned, she continued to dial, praying with each ring that there had been a mistake. She had tried again first thing this morning, only to be tormented by the recording's crisp voice. Getso was behind this; to protect himself from the truth, he had to keep Birdy away from her.

The contractor nudged the side of the steps with his boot, then grimaced as the bottom step collapsed. Spotting her at the window, he gestured for her to open the door.

"Three days' work for a three-man crew plus materials," he told her through the screen. He slid his pencil back and forth over his ear, calculating. "Twenty-eight hundred. It's a monster deck, and the steps're gone." He took a few steps back and, shading his eyes, looked up. "Roof's curling, and them gutters don't look so hot. Steve said to look around."

"I'll get my . . ."

"How the hell do you figure twenty-eight hundred?" Frances called out, tying her robe and combing her fingers through her hair as she opened the door. "I've had five estimates, and not one of them was that high!"

"Then you better grab one fast, ma'am. I'm only here as a favor to Steve. I don't go around begging for work. I got a hell of a lot more than I want. Believe me!" he said with a curt nod before climbing into his truck.

Frances came inside and flopped down in the chair. "What am I going to do?" she sighed.

"Claire Mayo gets people out of the want ads," Martha said, realizing those were the first words she had spoken in days.

Frances looked at her. "Maybe I could find somebody. Somebody to keep things up. Maybe somebody older. Not too old—but settled." She took a pad of paper from the telephone stand. " 'Wanted,' " she said, starting to write, " 'caretaker for large house and grounds' . . . No."

A DANGEROUS WOMAN

She scratched out a word and above it wrote, " 'Handyman.' Sounds cheaper. I'll put 'housing a possibility.' " She glanced up. "But he certainly couldn't live in the house." Her gaze narrowed on Martha. "He'd be in the apartment. Do you understand?"

She swallowed the last string of cold runny egg. As a child she had yearned to live in this beautiful house and not in the drab oily-smelling garage apartment that was stifling by summer and drafty and damp every winter. It had always seemed selfish of Frances not to have shared her home with them. Now she realized it didn't matter in the least, because as soon as she talked to Birdy she would be back in her job, in her old room. She would be back in her own life. Birdy always told her to give people more space, not to smother them so. She would. She would wait a few more days and give Birdy time to think things through, time to miss her. Smiling, she washed the egg cup and set it in the drainer while Frances called her ad in to the paper.

As she crossed the yard to the garage, lightning flashed, and she hunched forward and ran up the outside wooden stairs. Thunder crashed like an underground explosion that made the steps tremble. She closed the door just as the downpour began.

The usually dreary brown slipcovers and flat, stale rug deepened into a cocoon of shadows and hollows, with a comforting sense of her father's somber presence.

She filled the tub with warm water and bubble bath. She put the kitchen radio on the toilet tank and turned it to her favorite country-music station. She set a candle on the closed toilet lid and lit it. She took off her glasses and now, as she pulled her nightgown over her head, she glanced in the mirror, stirred by the sight of her wide, nippled breasts. Stepping into the tub, she slid through the bubbles' cool dry fizz into the hot water. From the radio there came the wail of a jilted man.

. . . she's cut the strings from my heart
. . . and tied me all up in a knot of misery . . .

MARY MCGARRY MORRIS

A guitar and harmonica tore into each other like bickering lovers. Goosebumps rose on the back of her neck. The candle's long yellow flame thinned to a taper of soot. Waves of rain poured down the dark windowpane. She lay with her knees apart, her hands cupping her hard, slippery breasts. Smiling, she closed her eyes, waiting for the heat to seep inside, but it was Getso's blade-boned face she kept seeing. No! Not him, not that pig, that thief. No, it was Billy Chelsea she always pictured. Billy Chelsea's tanned face squinting at her through the door screen, apologizing in a shy, faltering voice. "I lost my head," he'd say. "No, no," she'd say; she was the one who should apologize. She'd insist he come in, and he would, head down in that uneasy shuffle. Well, he'd say, turning to explain, turning so suddenly they'd bump into each other, her hard breasts jammed into his muscular chest, his hands catching her shoulders, as if to push apart, but then pulling her in to him, his eyes closing as his soft wet mouth met hers. . . .

Head back, her neck pressed against the hard cold rim of the tub, her lips parted in a little moan, her hips rocking in a crest of rhythmic splashes, when the ceiling light flared on. The radio died in a glare of silence. She gasped with the shock of Frances's looming shadow.

"Oh my God!" Frances said, staring down at her. Most of the bubbles had dissolved. "Oh for Godssakes!" she said, turning away in disgust.

"You get out," Martha roared, ineffectually swinging a wet arm, then bringing it back to cover herself. "You get out, you bitch, you bitch, you dirty bitch!"

"Telephone!" Frances screamed back at her. "I've been buzzing you, but . . ."

"Get out!" Martha bellowed into the wet mask of her shriveled palms. "Get out! Get out! Get out!"

"It's Wesley Mount! He wants to talk to you," Frances said with utter contempt.

———□———

Wesley Mount called back later that day. He had just found out that she had left the Cleaners and he wanted to see how she was doing.

A DANGEROUS WOMAN

71

"I'm doing fine," she said, her face reddening. This was the second time his concern had caused trouble with Frances.

"Well, I'm glad to hear that," he said in that strained formal voice she remembered from the funeral home. There was a pause. He cleared his throat. "So . . . so, does this mean you'll no longer be living in town?"

"Yes." Why did he pester her? Couldn't he tell how miserable he made her feel?

"Well, then, I'd like to come see you sometime, if you're at all . . . at all amenable to such a . . . a pro . . . a possibility. If you don't mind. If you'd like me to, that is."

"I can't."

"Can't?" He laughed nervously into the silence. "Well, I didn't mean right now. Or even today. Maybe . . ."

Her throat constricted. "I have to go. Bye," she said, and hung up. She looked down at the phone. "Will you leave me alone!"

———□———

For the past few days, she had managed to avoid Frances, who was busy with the yearly compilation of all her bills, receipts, and statements for her accountants. The handyman ad had run in last night's paper, and so far this morning Frances had received two phone calls. The first man hadn't shown up for his eleven o'clock appointment, and now the second was due at one.

At one-twenty an old dusty pickup truck, in a smoky rattle of metal and combustion, churned up the road and into the driveway. A skinny blonde man with small pinkish eyes got out and came to the door. He reeked of kerosene and sweat. When he said he had an appointment with Mrs. Beecham, Martha told him to wait in the driveway. She dawdled a few moments in the kitchen, counting on the truck's noise to summon Frances. They had not spoken since the other morning.

"For the ad," she said, pointing. Frances went outside to speak with him, and Martha watched from the window. In the truck sat a moon-faced young woman, her hair skinned back in a thin dull ponytail. Beside her, standing on the seat, sucking his thumb, was a pot-bellied little boy in a tight undershirt and sagging diapers. The woman watched alertly as Frances and the young man moved quickly from one end of the deck to the other. Frances was shouting to be heard over the engine. The young man turned with a frantic signal for the woman to shut off the ignition. The woman gestured reluctantly and he signaled again, his rigid jaw set until she reached over and turned the key. The engine rattled, then died with a whine. The woman shook her head as she pulled down one side of her shirt and lifted the other, shifting the infant she had been nursing.

The young man knelt by the collapsed steps and turned over a board. He flipped it back onto the heap.

"Some're still good. Most of your cost'd be lumber. We need a place—so, I mean, you could pay me what's fair. You know," he said with a dismal gesture toward the truck, "enough for food and diapers."

"I'm sorry," Frances said, shaking her head. "But I can't have a whole family."

"They're just babies," he said with a vapid smile. "Just two little babies."

"You don't understand," she said, turning resolutely toward the house.

"YOU don't understand!" he cried, lurching after her, his unlaced work boots riding up and down his skinny legs. He reminded Martha of a boy. "I'm desperate. We don't have no place to stay."

"I'm sorry. But this isn't what I want!"

"Okay! Okay! I wasn't gonna say it 'less I had to, but I'm Binky Herebonde." Grinning, he offered his hand, which she ignored. "I'm Adolph's son and Lyle's grandson-in-law," he said with a smart nod.

"I know who you are," she said, stepping along the planks Steve Bell had propped to bridge the black muck.

"You and Velma's grandpa are first cousins. You used to live with him and Velma's grandma," he said, moving beside her through the mud, his proud smile fading as she hurried along the board.

"That has nothing to do with this," she said, climbing nimbly into the kitchen. She closed the screen door and, with a quick fumble, latched the hook into its eye. "This is business, young man. Purely business."

"But we're related. I wouldn't never do a bad job for family, Miz Beecham, and you can ask around. I'm a hell of a hard worker," he said, his face taut at the screen, and added, "And Velma too. She don't look it, but she's stronger'n I am." He tried to laugh, but his voice splintered and seemed to snag on everything.

"I'm sorry," Frances said, stepping back, her own face revealing nothing.

An hour later, the truck was still in the driveway. With the woman steering, the young man had pushed it off to the side. Now the hood was raised in the boiling sun as he bent over the engine. He kept reaching into his back pocket for his screwdriver, then his wrench.

Dozing in the shade, the woman sat against the beech tree's scar-ruptured trunk. Between her legs, as if newly expelled onto the open diaper, lay the sleeping infant. Next to her, with his head on her thin white thigh, was the older child, his knees to his chin, his mouth pumping some milkless hunger from thumbs Martha knew must be filthy and gritty. Just before he fell asleep, he had been sifting dirt from fist to fist.

Earlier, staring grimly ahead, Frances had driven off on some invented errand. "One hour," she had hissed to Martha. "And if they're still out there, call the police."

Martha watched through the window, fascinated that they were her relatives living only a few miles away and she had never met them. There were still sleepless nights when she felt so empty and alone since her father's death that every sound reverberated inside her. She blinked now with the urgent clankclankclank of the young man's wrench on his engine. How was it, she wondered, stirred by the woman's hand capping her young son's skull, that some people, this woman, this man, had found love and she never had? What charm did they possess, what knowledge? As a girl, she had thought that the missing element was simply someone who would love her, someone time would provide. But now it seemed more and more evident that there were people in this world who were the Unloved, and she was one of them. That it might be just that simple, that immutable, was, in a strange way, almost a relief.

"Ma'am?" he called, scowling behind the screen. " 'Scuse me, ma'am, but my wife'd like to use the . . . the ladies' room, if you don't mind."

His wife stood behind him with the baby and the toddler in her arms, her face squinched in pain. This close, she appeared to be only fifteen or sixteen years old. "I'll only be a minute," she said with a little groan as she padded after Martha on flattened rubber sandals. "Thanks," she gasped, hurrying into the bathroom with both babies. "I got the runs real bad today," she grunted on the other side of the door.

After a few minutes, Herebonde squinted through the door screen. "All fixed! She still in there?" he asked, wiping his hands on a greasy rag. The toilet flushed, sending a clangor through the water pipes. "Them damn runs again," he said, shaking his head. "She's been so sick. Makes her real weak."

Martha nodded. She had heard of the Herebondes when she had lived in town, drinkers and fighters and dirt poor. It was hard enough to imagine her father related to any of them, much less Frances.

"Maybe I oughta go check on her," he said with a gesture of his rag. "If you don't mind. You know, get the babies."

She led him to the bathroom, then stood back.

"Velma?" He tapped on the door. "You okay in there?" he called so tenderly that Martha glanced away.

There was a faint moan.

"Want me to take 'em?" he asked, listening, eyes closed, at the jamb.

The door opened onto a stripe of bare knees and the woman's shorts ringing her ankles. Embarrassed, Martha went up the hall.

"She's in a bad way," he called after Martha, as he carried the babies. "We're both in a bad way." He followed her into the kitchen. "You think there's any chance she might change her mind?" He regarded her with those raw, almost lashless eyes. "I do real good work. Real good." As if for solace, he drew his chin over his boy's head.

She cleared her throat and rubbed her arm. "She said, if you weren't gone in an hour, I'm supposed to call the police."

He glanced up at the brass clock over the stove. "Did you call 'em?"

She shook her head.

"Are you Martha?" he asked.

"Yes."

"I heard about you." He looked at her. "But you're a nice person, I can tell." He worked out a hand from behind the clinging child and she shook it.

Again the toilet flushed. The infant began to cry.

"Shit," he muttered, setting the child down so he could prop the infant to his shoulder, then jiggled him up and down as he spoke over its catlike cry. "They said she was a real bitch. They said, don't bother, you know, but, Christ, I'm desperate. Velma's grandma said, if she fell down dead in front of her, she'd just step right on over her, she's that way."

A car had pulled into the driveway. The toilet was flushing again.

"Oh Jesus," he muttered, scooping up the child. "I'll get Vel."

The man climbing out of the old blue Ford was tall and unshaven. With all his stretching and yawning, he appeared to be working out the kinks of a long trip. Or a long night. He wore a lettered T-shirt inside out, and his pants rolled up over bare ankles. Laces dangled from his scuffed brown shoes, as if he had just stepped into them.

"Hi," he said at the door with the tip of an imaginary cap. "The name's Mack. You Mrs. Beecham?"

"She's not here," Martha said. Behind her, both babies wailed as the Herebondes hurried into the kitchen.

"When'll she be back?" the man called.

"Soon," she told him, and with another tip of his hand he left, saying he would catch her later.

"Here," Binky Herebonde said, handing her a grocery register slip. "On the back," he said of the clumsy lettering. "My name and my brother's number, case she changes her mind."

"Thanks," whispered the scrap of a woman, a girl, her eyes deep in her head, her thin shoulders curled against cramps. "Wait a while," she cautioned, gesturing back. "Smells kinda gross in there."

———□———

"What city, please?"

"Atkinson," Martha said. "You see, I have a new number. It's unlisted, and I'm trying to call the new number at home, my home, but I can't remember what it is. I know the old number. That's 723-7682. But if you could give me my new number, I'll write it down this time, and that way I won't forget it again." She tried to laugh, but her throat was so dry she coughed. "Excuse me," she gasped.

"I'm sorry, but I'm not allowed to give out an unlisted number to anyone."

"But I have to call! What am I supposed to do? How do I get the number?"

"Come into the main office with proper identification and a supervisor will be glad to assist you."

"What's proper identification?"

"A driver's license will do."

"But I don't drive." Her eye fell on Frances's stationery on the table. "What about a letter saying who I am?"

"I'm sorry. It has to be some primary means of identification, like a birth certificate or a license."

"But I don't have those with me right now, and I'm in a terrible situation here! You don't understand! This is very, very important! I mean, this could affect someone's whole life! In fact, it does! A terrible, terrible thing has happened, and I have to get it straightened out!" She was banging her fist on the table.

"Just a moment, please, and I'll put you through to a supervisor!"

"Hello, this is Jane Martin, may I help you."

Again Martha explained her dilemma, stressing the fact that this was an emergency.

"Give me your name and the number you're calling from, and I will advise the unlisted party of the emergency nature of this call."

She couldn't very well say she was Birdy Dusser. "Martha Horgan," she said giving the rest of the information in a small hopeful voice. She waited.

The operator came back on. "Yes, Miss Horgan. The unlisted party has been apprised of your situation."

"So will you put me through?"

"I'm sorry. I'm not able to do that."

"Well, is Birdy going to call me, then?"

"As I said, someone at the unlisted number has been apprised of your situation."

"Someone? Who?" It had been Getso. She just knew it. "Who did you tell?"

"I'm sorry, but I . . ."

Suddenly the door opened, and she hung up the phone. Frances rushed in, throwing aside her purse, bags, a large folder. "I've been trying to call for an hour and the line's been busy. Did Steve call?"

She opened the freezer and began to crack the ice trays over a bowl. She filled the trays with water. "We're supposed to go out to dinner with the Pierces for Julia's birthday and I don't know what time to tell everyone to come." She put the trays back into the freezer. "Steve must know if I wait much longer I'll never get reservations. Damn! He's been out of the office all day. Something's wrong. I can feel it. It's been one thing after another ever since his daughters came back. God! The two of them, emotional shipwrecks, always turning up in their father's life." Both of Steve's daughters had recently gone through divorces.

Frances went down the hallway, then came running back. "What's wrong with the toilet? It sounds funny. And what're these?" She pointed at the soiled diapers jammed into the trash. "You let them in here, didn't you?" she asked, glowering.

"Here," Martha said, holding out Herebonde's strip of paper. "If you change your mind, he said."

Frances balled the paper and flung it onto the table.

"Oh. There was this other man that came," she said as Frances turned to go. "He said his name was Mack and that he'd catch you later."

"Oh God, that ad," Frances groaned. "I'll have every fool in town up here."

It was early evening, and everyone was in Frances's living room, where for the past hour and a half they had been waiting for Steve. He was on the phone now, urging Frances to go on without him. Anita was "in a bad way." He and Jan, his older daughter, were trying to get her admitted to Peaceview, an exclusive sanitarium in upstate New York.

"Why can't it wait till morning?" Frances asked. She was in the study. "I'm sure SHE'S in no rush."

"Actually, she's the one," Steve said in a low muffled voice, no doubt with his hand cupped to the phone. "She's begging us to help her. She thinks she's dying."

"Steve! She always says that!" God, he was gullible; after all these years, still falling for the same lines.

"No. I can tell. This is different." It was unbelievable, she thought, but he almost sounded excited.

"What's different is she's got Jan there to feed her lines to." She paused, but he didn't say anything. "Look, Steve, why don't you do yourself and Jan a favor and just . . . just let her be. You know as well as I do what's going to happen. The two of you are going to spend the whole night—what?—calling this one and that one, and then you're going to drive all the way out there, and she'll change her mind. You know she will. She always does."

He didn't say anything. Poor Steve, all knotted up in his daughters' selfishness; sometimes he just needed some hard plain talk to get himself back on track. "It's Jan, Steve. She just feels guilty, I think, because she's been away all this time. Anita's no fool. She'll play this to the hilt. And poor Jan—I mean, as if she doesn't have enough problems. Look, Steve, have Jan stay there with her. That way, you can make a decision in the morn . . . Steve? Steve, are you there?"

The background rumbled with the aftershock of Anita's croupy voice, her words falling like bricks into rubble. ". . . help this son of a . . . I had some . . . he talkin' to?"

"Yes, Jan," he said away from the phone. "Yes, Jan. Yes."

Jan was telling him about blood. Her mother was passing blood. Frances's stomach turned. The woman had destroyed herself. And, as always, who picked up the pieces? Steve.

"Tell them I think there's some real bad kidney damage. . . ."

"It's not the hospital, Jan," Steve interrupted his daughter.

"Is it Dr. Warren? Did you get him?"

"Jan, I'll be right with you," he said.

"Oh," Jan said coldly. "It didn't occur to me you'd call HER in the middle of this."

"I said I'll be right there," he repeated.

"Steve!" Frances shouted. She looked toward the warm glow of the living room, where everyone sat, then caught herself. "Call me in the morning," she said before she hung up. Bitch. Little bitch. God, after all these years. After all she'd done, not just for him, but for all of them.

From here she could see Martha in the kitchen. With a fork, she mashed bouillon cubes into a mug of boiled water, then began to whip them furiously. Pausing, she peered into the mug, and her glasses fogged with steam. She set down the mug and bit by bit crumbled a cracker into it with an intensity that hunched her entire body round the cup.

Frances gripped the arms of the chair. It took all of her willpower not to run in there and grab the mug and dump it into the sink. It was unnerving, the way Martha could become the task itself, focusing until there was only that compulsive stirring, a blur beyond anything human. How does she do that, she wondered. To so totally obliterate one's self, it gave her the chills.

Just then she saw Heidi Pierce pause in the kitchen doorway on her way to the bathroom. "Well, look at you," she called in to Martha. "Just as busy as a bee around here, aren't you?"

Head bent, mouth pinched, Martha fused her concentration on the clinking fork.

Heidi shrugged and continued down the hallway.

"Just as busy as a bee," Martha mimicked Heidi's childish voice. "Just as busy, busy, busy as a stupid little bee!"

Is it me? Is it me? Frances thought with a surge of terror. The thick wiry hair. The same broad shoulders. The heavy white breasts bobbing in the bathwater. "Stop that!" she cried, charging out from the study. "You'll chip the mug," she added weakly. Not a sound came from the living room.

They were finishing their drinks now that she had told them Steve wouldn't be coming. Heidi and Bill Pierce perched in the pale-yellow chairs opposite the down sofa where Julia Prine sat with a dour-faced young woman named Tyler Spaulding, whom Frances had just met tonight. Tyler Spaulding's head was a crown of skinny blonde braids, and the bodice of her shapeless brown dress had been worked in colorful Indian beads. Julia was a people collector—the more offbeat, the better.

"This is the worst one yet," Frances explained, conscious of everyone's rapt attention. Anita Bell was always a gripping subject. "She checked herself out of the hospital yesterday and Steve just found her."

"I didn't want to say anything," Heidi confided, picking her cuticles excitedly. "But a few months ago I heard she was out at the lake." She leaned forward, her hand at her sternum, as if to contain some horror. "You know, in one of those cabins the kids rent. With some, well, some bum, and I guess it was pretty dis . . ."

"I'm sorry, but I don't believe that for a minute," interrupted Julia, her lofty tone obviously meant to impress her young friend.

Frances wondered what cause would be championed tonight, which endangered species. She envied Julia's intellect and natural goodness. Good bloodlines, she thought. All the bitterness and fear had been bred right out of her.

"I'm only telling you what someone told me, Julia." Heidi sniffed. "Someone who should know!"

"Steve's a saint," Bill Pierce said, so quickly it was obvious he had been his wife's source. Bill was Steve's law partner, the poor boy who had managed to become the bulwark of the Bell family's firm. "I tell you—what that man goes through," he sighed with a long sad look at Frances.

"Where did they find her?" Julia asked.

"In the Moonbeam Motel," Frances said. "Out cold. And alone," she added with an icy glance at Heidi, bristling with her peculiar proprie-torship if not of Anita Bell, then of the woman who was Steve's wife. Any discussion of Anita Bell had to be carefully orchestrated through Frances. In a strange convolution of jealousy and pride, she had become the keeper of Anita's reputation, present as well as past. She was fond of relating Anita's lineage and even knew the name of an ancestor who had been among the first elected officials in Plymouth Colony: Jeb Sitwell—one son, three daughters, two cows, and a wife, his inventory began. "In that order," she would always add, sensitive to the irony that she knew more about Anita Bell's ancestors than she knew about her own, or wanted to.

"How long has this been going on?" Tyler Spaulding asked of Anita Bell's condition, and Frances's mouth fell open. The nerve. Imagine, asking a question like that of someone you had just met. But look, they were answering her.

Ever since they were married, Heidi thought, but Bill disagreed. No. No, he thought sometime after: maybe even after the children. Yes. Heidi nodded, frowning, troubled by her recollection of Anita as a devoted young wife and mother.

"You know what you often find in these situations," Tyler Spaulding said. "You find out the perfect spouse is not so perfect after all."

They glanced anxiously at Frances, their voices crossing in a nervous defense of Steve.

"I don't think I've ever heard that man raise his voice," Heidi said. "Bill, have you?"

"God no. Not Steve." Bill looked to Frances for approval.

"Steve's a . . . Well, he's just a dear," Julia said. "But maybe that's it. Maybe he's just been too dear."

Frances couldn't believe this. Who had authorized this analysis? They were talking as if she weren't even here, as if Anita Bell were just some common drunk. She gathered up the empty glasses.

"Well, he's done her no favors, from the sound of it," Tyler Spaulding said. "It's like a disease. I mean, it infects the whole family. They're all perpetuators."

MARY MCGARRY MORRIS

Perpetuators. Frances paused in the doorway, glasses dangling from her fingertips.

"There has to be a sick member," the young woman continued. "Everyone has their role to play, the caretaker, the patient, the attendants. It's amazing how comfortable everyone gets in their roles, and how entrenched—no matter how miserable they are. Families are probably the sickest, most brutalizing unit in our society."

"That's fascinating!" Heidi sighed, twisting the pearl-and-emerald cocktail ring on her pudgy finger; Heidi, who had no children, no family beyond Bill, Frances thought smugly. "You know, I always wondered what kept them together."

"He's obviously part of the illness. They feed off each other. She needs a caretaker and he needs a patient, a ward to justify his . . ."

"That's sick!" Frances exploded. Still holding the glasses, she stood in front of the startled young woman. "That's the biggest and sickest load of shit I've ever heard."

"But you'd be amazed how common it is," Tyler observed, so coolly Frances had all she could do to keep from dumping the melting ice cubes in her lap.

"When you think of it, it makes sense," Heidi said in her baby voice. She looked at Frances as if this really deserved credence.

"But not Steve," Bill said with a motion to take the glasses from Frances. She stalked into the kitchen then, with Julia at her heels, laughing quietly.

"Where do you find these people?" Frances asked, so tense her mouth felt numb.

"I don't know. I think they find me, thank God," Julia mused, looking toward the living room, where Tyler Spaulding's voice rose in some fierce condemnation of love.

"My God! Listen to her, an answer to everything. Isn't it wonderful that life is so goddamn simple for some people."

"She's the new director of Harmony House."

"She's obnoxious!"

Julia paused, looking at her. "Frances, honestly now, don't you get tired of it?" she asked, lowering her voice. "Bill's old car and his Golden Oldies and—God—Heidi! After a while you don't even hear the words. You need a break. Come on, Fran, you know what I mean. It's always the same thing. We meet here. Bill puts the top down; he turns on his tapes, we hold our glasses over the side so they don't spill, and then, when Roy Orbison comes on, Steve and Bill sing 'Pretty Woman.' We not only eat in the same three or four restaurants. But we say all the same things. We even order the same food."

If she weren't so stunned, she might have been amused that Julia's captious dismissal was of the very estate she had spent her lifetime tending—respectability, harmony, constancy. There had been enough bizarre and violent nights growing up in her cousin's cramped house to see her to the end of her days. A woman like Julia had no idea how tenuous it all was, how fragile; and, once toppled, how deep the wreckage, and how insidiously pervasive.

Her hand trembled as she splashed gin into the plastic tumblers. She added tonic water, then squeezed a plastic lime over each one, counting one, two, three drops. Her hair slipped across her face and her heart pounded and her breath whistled in her ears like wind through a chasm.

In spite of Steve's not being here; in spite of this house's falling so vindictively apart, springing leaks and shedding roof tiles, dropping its drainspouts and rupturing its plumbing lines as if it could not sustain itself without Horace, without Floyd, and knew her for the intruder she was; in spite of Martha—she would have a good time tonight. She could do that, could raise the sluice gates so hard and fast that nothing hurt. She looked up and smiled.

Relieved, Julia patted her arm. "The truth is, I really wanted Tyler to meet Martha. I think she can help her."

"Help her? What in God's name are you talking about?"

"She was doing so well in town," Julia said. "And now up here she's totally isolated again."

"Isolated? I'd hardly call being home isolated!"

"Frannie, there she was busy, going places. . . ."

MARY MCGARRY MORRIS

"And being taunted," interrupted Frances, "and laughed at and completely obsessed with those . . . those people she worked with! At least here I know she's safe."

Julia stared at her. "She's no more safe here than she is in town! At least there she's got some purpose, a life of her own," she said, her voice rising.

Frances put her arms around Julia. "Happy Birthday, dear," she whispered, "and, for once, mind your own goddamn business!"

———o———

Martha was glad they were finally leaving. She wanted to call Jane Martin, the telephone supervisor, and see if she could find out if she had talked to Birdy. At the end of the hallway, Frances and Julia and Heidi Pierce lingered in the wide foyer by the open door. The headlights from Bill Pierce's old Cadillac bounced off the women's faces as the shark fins of the long white car turned in the circle. A song blared outside: Elvis Presley singing "Jailhouse Rock." Laughing, the three women sang together as Frances swiveled back and forth in an exaggerated version of the Twist.

Just then the bathroom door opened a crack and Julia's friend Tyler Spaulding peeked out and waved her over, the very person Martha had been avoiding. She remembered her coming into the Cleaners right after she had torn the pocket off Mr. Gately's jacket.

"Excuse me, but I'm so embarrassed," she said, gesturing behind her. "It won't flush." She grimaced. "I hate to just leave it."

"Oh. It was the Herebondes," Martha muttered, her eyes avoiding this young woman's keen blue stare.

"Hair? I don't know. . . . I . . ."

"The Herebondes," she said, rubbing her arm up and down, up and down, staring past Tyler Spaulding at the bathroom window. "The Herebondes!"

"Hair buns," said the young woman, recoiling. "Hair buns?" Her pale cheeks colored.

"It was all her flushing. Her, the Herebonde girl. She kept on flushing it," Martha explained, mired in the futility of it all. "You don't know her. So I'll fix it. I'll fix it. But you have to get out!"

"I'm sorry." Tyler Spaulding fled down the hallway.

Martha lifted the cover off the tank and set it on the floor. The metal hook connecting the arm to the ballcock had broken off. One more thing Frances would blame her for.

She opened the medicine cabinet and broke off a strand of dental floss, which she threaded through the holes in the metal arm, then into the ring at the top of the slimy ballcock.

"Ty forgot her bag."

Martha looked up to see Julia Prine slip a canvas purse off the doorknob. She stepped closer and peered into the toilet tank.

"What a good idea! Aren't you clever! I'll have to remember that!"

Martha pressed the lever, and smiled when the water flushed through the bowl.

"It works!" Julia laughed.

"I just thought of it!" she said, grinning.

"You're a very clever woman, Martha!" Julia looked at her. "A lot more clever than you give yourself credit for!" she said with an embarrassing intensity. "Listen! How about dinner some night? Just the two of us," Julia said, her cheeks flushed, her eyes bright. "We'll have a great time. I'll call you," she said, and left before Martha could refuse. She had only gone out to dinner twice in her life, both times with Frances.

The minute the door closed, she dialed "0" and asked to speak with Jane Martin. The operator said Jane Martin was not on duty; would she like another supervisor? She hung up without answering and dialed Birdy's number repeatedly, hanging up each time she heard, "I am sorry . . . I am sorry . . . I am sorry . . ."

"No, you're not!" she screamed back. "No, you're not!"

SEVEN

Sunday had been a long hot yellow day. Now, as the sun went down, the cicadas' crackling intensified, and in the distance a bright haze clung to the mountaintops. The mud where the deck had been was cracked and gray, and its fine powdery dust had sifted through the open windows onto all the sills and tabletops.

Frances's drive to Albany today with Steve had had to be canceled when he could not get Anita into Peaceview. The only other alternative was the state hospital, which his daughters wouldn't even consider, so Steve had spent the day trying to hire three shifts of private nurses.

"Well, let me know," Frances had said into the phone, her eyes closed. "I know. . . . Of course, I understand. . . . Where? Oh yes. I've heard of that. . . . When? But, Steve, that's your birthday! She'll be better by then!"

After she hung up, she came into the kitchen, where she banged pans and slammed the cupboard doors as she made herself a cup of coffee. She turned and glared at Martha, who was eating a sandwich at the table.

"They want him to take her someplace out west. The same time as his birthday!" She shook her head. "This isn't fair. It really isn't." She went to the door and looked down at the cavity of dry mud and groaned. "What does it matter, with this mess, anyway?"

Martha continued to chew as she read the Sunday paper. Turning the page, she saw an ad for the Cleaners. This week's special was six shirts cleaned for the price of five. That was always a popular coupon special. They would be so busy they would keep forgetting to ask for the coupons. She never forgot. Never once. As she folded the paper, she felt like crying.

A car labored up the driveway, its loud engine racing. Frances shaded her eyes and peered through the sink window. A door creaked open, closed, and then the board to the door rattled.

"You Mrs. Beecham? My name's Colin Mackey and I'm here about this ad."

Martha looked up.

"Come in," Frances was saying as she opened the door.

He was the same man who had come when the Herebondes had been here. This time he was clean-shaven and his pants were wrinkled but rolled down. He wore the same scarred shoes, still without socks but now tied. His hair looked as ragged as before. His hands trembled and he wet his cracked lips constantly.

"I figured you'd be an old lady," he said, his eyes fixed on Frances, his smile a wince.

MARY MCGARRY MORRIS

"I will be if this place gets much worse," she said, glancing away from his urgent stare. "Do you do carpentry work?"

"That and some electrical and some plumbing. I'm very handy." His smile widened. "And very desperate for work."

Frances stiffened. "Do you have any references?"

"You serious?" he said with a nervous laugh, then added quickly that of course he had references but they were all out of state. He had spent most of the last two years in Oregon and Washington. Frances asked what kind of work he had done there.

"Whatever I could get." He laughed. "Odd jobs, even dishwashing. My longest was two months with a fence company, digging postholes. I dig a mean hole, ma'am."

Even from here, Martha could smell the liquor.

Frances stepped back. "Why don't I call you, Mr. Mackey? Leave your number and I'll let you know," she said, starting to open the door.

"I don't have a phone," he said, not moving. "I'm staying with these people, but they . . ."

"Well, you call me, then," she said.

"When? When should I call?"

"Wednesday."

"What's today?" He looked over at Martha with a tight wave at his waist. "Today Saturday?"

"Sunday," Martha answered, so faintly he asked again.

"Today is Sunday," Frances told him, her cold tone and gaze underscoring his confusion.

He shrugged. "So what's going to change from now to Wednesday? You're not going to like me any better. Your deck's not going to get built, unless you get someone else." He squinted at her. "You got someone else?" he asked in a thin voice.

"I have a few people in mind," she said, nodding. She opened the door and held it for him. "You can call back if you'd like." She extended her hand, Martha knew, only to draw him to the door. "It was nice meeting you, Mr. Mackey."

"I'm a respectable person, Mrs. Beecham. I'm very well educated and

I'll do a good job for you," he said, gripping her hand and looking directly into her eyes. "I'm extremely overqualified."

"Then you call," she said icily, removing her hand. "And I'll let you know."

He tried to smile. "Yah, I'll bet you will."

Frances locked the door behind him. "Bastard!" she muttered as his old car turned in the driveway. "Half smashed and he's got the nerve to ask for work."

The next morning, Frances was up at six. The dining-room table was covered with financial reports, bills, and bank statements. Today was the annual meeting with her accountants and lawyers.

"Turn off those lights!" Frances called into the kitchen.

Martha switched off the one light that had been on.

"They better not say one word," Frances said. "I have been so careful. So frugal . . ."

Martha had never understood why, after all these years, Frances continued to be so nervous, so apologetic about her own money. It was the same with the house, as if it weren't genuinely hers, as if she feared someone might take it away from her if by some misstep she proved herself careless, or unworthy. It was the same insecurity Martha had seen in her father, that strange sense of tenancy, of always having to appease an invisible master, a dead man, Horace Beecham.

Frances charged into the kitchen with an accordion-pleated folder under her arm. "I don't believe it," she said glancing up at the clock. "He's twenty minutes late." Steve had called at eight to assure her he would be there on time. Frances picked up the telephone now and punched in three numbers, then changed her mind and hung up.

Bent over her cereal bowl, Martha tensed under Frances's scrutiny.

"Don't leave the milk out in this heat," she said, taking the carton from the table.

"I'm still using it," Martha said.

Frances put it in the refrigerator. "It'll spoil. But, then, what would you care? You didn't buy it."

Martha stood up and dug into her pants pocket and pulled out a handful of change, counting to a dollar fifty. "Here," she said.

"Oh for Godssakes," Frances sighed as Martha held out the change. "That's not the point," she said, turning away.

"Take it," Martha insisted, stepping in front of her. "I'm buying the milk." The last thing she wanted was Frances's charity. She wanted her job and her room back, and Birdy.

"Please!" Frances said, leaning over the sink to look out the window. "Will you just please stop it!"

A horn sounded as Steve's low black car squealed into the driveway. Frances ran outside, and Martha stacked the coins on the windowsill. In the distance she could hear the high-pitched irritating laughter of the Chelsea girls. Head down, she charged out of the house over to the apartment. She had just eaten her last food in that house. She would buy her own groceries. And she would see Birdy.

———□———

Heart pounding, she was so nervous she didn't hear the knocking right away. She was dressing. "Wait," she called. "I'll be right there." She put her bathrobe back on and opened the door.

"Mrs. Beecham in?" the man named Mack asked through the screen. His eyes were puffy and even in the shadows he squinted, his breath reeking of the same stale foulness. When she said Frances would be gone all day, he sighed and shook his head.

"She said Wednesday, right? She said to call Wednesday."

"Yes, but it's Monday."

"It is?" He winced when she nodded. "When'd you say she's coming back?"

"Tonight. But she said for you to call Wednesday." She closed the door, then listened. It was a moment before she heard his footsteps down the creaking stairs. That was stupid, telling a perfect stranger she was all alone here. "Good," she muttered, dressing quickly. "That was really, really good." She hurried to the door, then ran back and called the Cleaners again. When Mercy answered, she hung up and dialed Birdy's number, listening to the end of the recording. Nothing had changed. The only way to contact Birdy would be to go to the Cleaners, and she couldn't bring herself to do that. But if she got her groceries at the little Superette near the Cleaners, she knew she might run into Birdy, who bought their coffee and break supplies there every Monday afternoon.

As she came around the side of the house, she was startled to see Colin Mackey dragging a board from the lumber pile. He set it against the cinder block and, with one foot bracing it, began to saw off the rotted end.

Rubbing her arms, she watched in fearful silence. "What're you doing?" she finally forced herself to call out.

"I'm sawing this two-by-four." He paused, looking up at her. "No sense wasting the whole day."

"You're not hired! She didn't hire you!" She thumped her chest angrily.

"No, not yet. But if she does, I'll be way ahead of the game." He started the saw going back and forth. "Besides, I haven't got anything better to do."

"No, you can't! I have to go someplace, and I can't leave with you here."

He stopped sawing and straightened up. The sun lay across the yard in a dizzying white square, and the pool water had bleached to a pale blue. "I'll just do a little, I promise. Just to show her. Like a sample, you know, of my work, and then I'll leave. I promise."

An hour later, he was still out there, sawing and hammering under the hot sun. She waited in the house. She kept peeking out the kitchen window. She had never seen anyone work so fast. Instead of walking between the lumber pile and the section he was framing, he ran. His hammer was a glinting stream of motion, and now, as he glanced up anxiously at the house, it occurred to her that he would work until she told him to stop. The only way she would catch Birdy at the Superette now would be if she ran most of the way.

"I have to go now," she said, coming outside. She locked the door, then waited as he drove in two more nails. "I said, I have to go now!"

MARY McGARRY MORRIS

His head jerked up and he teetered dizzily, his face such a ghastly gray that she was afraid he was going to pass out.

She took a few steps onto the driveway, turned, and watched him gather his tools and put them in his trunk. He pulled out a dingy yellow towel and patted his face and neck dry, before tossing it back. She walked a few more feet, and stopped. He opened the car door, then stood with his hands on his hips, watching her with a puzzled expression.

"Where's your car?" he called.

"I don't have one. I'm walking."

"Where you going?"

"Into town."

"Well, so am I!" He jumped into the car, got it to start with a fumy wheeze, then pulled alongside her. "Get in and I'll give you a ride."

Empty beer and soda cans rolled between her feet. The back seat was a mound of stale clothing he had tried to cover with a sheepskin-lined jacket and an army blanket. The back window ledge was strewn with faded magazines, a leather boot, and a typewriter with a curled sheet of yellowed paper in it. At least by car she might still make it in time to catch Birdy.

"So what do you do?" he asked as he drove. "You work?"

"I used to. At the Cleaners."

"What do you do now?"

She folded her hands in her lap. "Nothing."

He laughed. "Hey, that's what I do! Same thing. What do you know. Small world." He held out his hand to shake hers, but she peered fixedly out the side window.

They drove a mile or so in silence. She glanced at him. From this angle, he looked a great deal older. His face was deeply creased and the hair at his temples was gray and the skin under his eyes sagged in dark pouches.

He caught her studying him. "You married?"

"No!" she said, so emphatically that he laughed.

"My sentiments exactly." He turned onto the main road.

As they neared town, she stared down at her tightly gripped hands.

Maybe she should just march right into the Cleaners and talk to Birdy. Of course she should. Just march in there and tell her the truth. But what if John was there? Or Getso? She closed her eyes. What would she do then? What would she say? She'd say, Birdy, please come in the bathroom. You have to hear the truth. "You have to!"

"What? I have to what?" Mack asked. He glanced at her as he drove. They were on Main Street, approaching the park, where a swarm of little girls rode bikes with training wheels up and down the paths. Someone sat in one of the rocking chairs on the front porch of Mayo's boardinghouse. But she couldn't tell which old woman it was.

He signaled for a right turn. Not here, she thought in a panic. Oh, she didn't want to see any of the ladies. Not yet. Not until she had her job back.

"I don't know where you want me to stop."

"Downtown!" she cried.

"Yes, ma'am!" he said with a laugh, brakes squealing as he swerved around the corner.

She slouched low on the seat as they passed the gas station and the pharmacy and the armory. She didn't want to see anyone she knew. She closed her eyes. This was a mistake. She wasn't ready for this. It was all Frances's fault, nagging her about the milk, riling her until she wasn't thinking straight. She punched her open palm. Frances should have left her alone, but she never did, never would.

"Any particular place?" he asked.

"The supermarket." She glanced up, not sure where they were. All she could see was the bright-blue sky over the dashboard. Conscious of his stare, she sat up and did not move, taking her breath in shallow draughts. "Right here's fine," she said, swallowing the wrong way. She hit her chest.

"You okay?"

She nodded and wiped her eyes. Her nose was running.

He pulled up to the curb and she opened the door and got out. Most of the stores here on State Street were small, a florist, an auto-supply shop, a party-goods store.

"I don't see any supermarkets." He looked over the wheel. When she told him the Superette was just around the corner, he leaned across the seat and insisted she get back in so he could take her there. Pretending not to hear him, she closed the door and started up the street, tensing with the approach of his loud engine. When it was alongside, the old car slowed a moment, then accelerated up the street and out of sight.

The air-conditioned Superette smelled of ground coffee and pungent cheese. Red peppers and webbed salamis dangled over the meat case at the back of the store. It was still the same white-haired woman as before, sitting on a stool behind the counter, watching soap operas on a miniature television. Martha moved slowly up the three short aisles, filling one red plastic arm basket with fruit, lettuce, cucumbers, crackers, a jar of cheese spread. She set that basket on the counter and got another from the stack by the door. These next items had to be selected with care. Nothing too heavy to be carried, and nothing that would melt or spoil before she got home. Four cans of soup, a package of shortbread cookies, a jar of peanut butter, and a bag of peanuts. She glanced up at the clock. Two-thirty. Birdy would never come in this late in the day for coffee supplies or cigarettes. She was probably working on the books now, head bent over the stacks of slips, her feathery dark hair catching the light, her plump upper arms moist with sweat.

She carried her basket to the register. She had just made up her mind to go from here to the Cleaners. She didn't care who was there, Getso, John. She had to talk to Birdy.

"Fourteen seventy-eight," the old woman said, starting to pack everything. "Haven't seen you in a while," the woman said. She shook out a second bag and put the soup cans in it.

"I just want one bag," Martha said, her head down. She held her breath as she counted her coins. She always gave the exact change. It upset her to break a bill when she didn't have to. It didn't seem right.

"One bag'll break."

"I just want one bag," she insisted.

"Then I'll double-bag," the woman said, removing the cans from the bag with stained fingertips.

"No! I said I only want one bag!"

A DANGEROUS WOMAN

The old woman stared at her as she piled the rest of the groceries into the first bag. She realized now what the woman had meant by a double bag, but it was too late. The woman watched coldly as she backed out the door with the bulging bag in her arms.

The heat of the parking lot met her in a sheet of glare. Lifting one arm as best she could, with her shoulder she nudged her sweaty glasses back onto the bridge of her nose. Straight ahead, there was a gray van with its familiar red-and-white lettering. It was one of the Cleaners' smaller vehicles, parked with its rear doors open. She stopped. Pulling alongside the van was the big laundry truck, with Getso at the wheel, a cigarette dangling from his mouth. Hoping he hadn't seen her, she turned frantically in the opposite direction. Her glasses slid down her nose and the bag shifted in her arms. She was headed toward a row of hedges that blocked this side of the parking lot. She kept going, judging them low enough to step over, to get her out of Getso's sight.

"Hey! Hey, wait up!" a man's voice called. She did not know it was Mack.

As she turned, a cold sweat rose on the back of her neck. Getso came around the back of his truck. He threw his cigarette on the ground and, with his thumbs hooked in his pockets, stared at her.

"Wait!"

In a blind turn she stepped over the knee-high dusty hedges that were budded with Popsicle wrappers and faded cigarette packs and Styrofoam cups. Suddenly she pitched forward, the heavy bag spewing its cans and jars onto the opposite sidewalk. She fell down on one knee, wedged between the shrubs, watching her lettuce roll to the end of the sidewalk, then stop at the curb.

Getso bent over her, one hand digging into her armpit, his other pulling at her shoulder. "C'mon," he grunted.

"Leave me alone!" she cried, trying to push him away, but he only leaned closer, tugging with a stream of hoarse curses.

"Jesus Christ . . . c'mon . . . get the hell . . ." he muttered as she batted him away.

"Get your hands off me. Don't touch me! Leave me alone!"

MARY McGARRY MORRIS

"C'mon, damn it. Just get up." Again he bent down, reaching toward her.

She slapped his face, and his head jerked back. "Don't you touch me!" she screamed, pointing at him. She kept trying to stand up, but her foot was snagged in the sharp branches.

He looked down at her, rubbing his cheek. "You screw . . ."

"Don't lay another hand on her!" It was Mack. Stepping past Getso, he grabbed her wrists and pulled her up. He set her bag on the asphalt and squatted down to retrieve her spilled groceries.

"What the . . . Hey!" Getso sputtered. "I was just tryna help her, that's all!"

"She sure as hell didn't think so," Mack said, getting up. He stepped over the hedge and, palming the lettuce, dropped it into the bag. Martha lifted the bag, careful to hold its bulging tear against her chest.

"What? You think I was attacking her or something? C'mon're you fuckin' nuts?" Getso shouted with an indignant jerk of his hand at Mack, who was picking up soup cans.

Mack glanced back at him. "Just get the hell outta here," he said.

"Yah, and next time I'll step right over the fuckin' screwball!"

Mack stood up and walked toward Getso, shaking his head. "You didn't really say that. I mean, you couldn't've said that, right? I must've heard wrong." He twisted his finger in his ear. "Tell me I heard wrong."

With a disgusted swipe of his arm, Getso started to walk away.

"Hey, Lancelot, go fuck yourself," Getso hollered as he jumped into the truck. "And do her, do the fuckin' screwball too," he called, grinning over the open door.

At this, Mack lunged forward, but Getso had already slammed the door shut and thrown the truck into reverse. As the truck squealed by, Mack's hand jerked back and the can of tomato soup shot into the windshield, turning it into a glittering web of shattered glass.

"Who was he?" Mack asked as they drove up Merchants Row.

She stared out the side window. In a flat voice she told him about seeing Getso steal from the register and how he had accused her.

"Greasy slimeball," Mack said.

"You shouldn't have broken the window," she said, chewing the inside of her lip until it was shredded.

"Yah, and maybe I shouldn't have been born either," he sighed. He stopped for the red light, and while he waited he banged the wheel with the heels of his hands. He looked at her. "But there are some forces of nature that can not be denied." He laughed, and she looked away; her stare dulled the passing houses and trees until there was nothing to see. No colors. No sharp edges. No contrast.

She went straight up to the little apartment and stayed there. She knew exactly how it would go: Getso would blame her. To keep from being fired he would have to; this new truck replaced the one he had totaled. John would call Frances. And, of course, Birdy would become even more inaccessible.

Now he was out there sawing and hammering and Frances would say that was also her fault. It wasn't fair the way such simple things, fig squares for Birdy, or a man showing up on the wrong day for a job, or buying a few groceries, could run so amok for her and never for anyone else. She stood in the window with the sun on her face, stood absolutely still, and closed her eyes. She could almost feel it, that huge blank echoing space where nothing, not even the beat of a heart, could regulate all the turmoil that found its way inside. She pulled down the shades and closed the curtains. With the pillow over her head, she dreamed that she huddled on a child's small wooden chair in the middle of a dark empty room of a house that was being constructed around her.

———□———

The black-shaded brass lamps on Mr. Prowse's desk and conference table diffused the light at eye level, so that it was difficult to look away from the accounting printouts and all the other documents without constantly refocusing one's vision to the layered dimness of the elegant office. Blinking, now Frances could make out the intricate ring pattern in this red-and-blue Oriental carpet she had first seen twenty-seven years ago, when Horace had first brought her here to meet his accountant

MARY MCGARRY MORRIS

and old friend, Thomas Prowse. Little had changed. Mr. Prowse, who had seemed like an old man then, still looked much the same, except that he grew smaller each year. The pads in his gray suit jacket sagged over his shoulders, and his collar curled away from his stemlike neck. At least his white hair was still as thick and unruly as ever.

Mr. Prowse sat so small behind his massive burled-ash desk that she was sure they probably had to swivel his chair higher and higher each year. She wondered if his feet even touched the floor anymore. He was reminiscing about a long-ago land swap between himself and Horace. Each man thought he had finally bested the other, only to discover both parcels were worthless. "He wouldn't admit it," Prowse recalled gleefully, his upper plate shifting with a clack. He pushed it into place with his tongue, giving his speech a lisping thickness that was starting to turn her stomach. "To the point where he even drove pilings into the muck and put up this tin warehouse. It started to sink that very first spring," he lisped, the wet corners of his mouth gleaming.

His gums must be shrinking, she thought. Even his eyes looked smaller in their sockets as he described the property he had received in the swap. If Horace were still alive, he'd be like that, she thought, recoiling; her husband, a shriveling, drooling old man telling pointless stories.

Beside her, Steve's polished black shoe jerked up and down impatiently. He looked at his watch and raised his eyebrows. Irritated, she looked away. God, when she thought of all the interminably dull legal conversations she had endured for his sake over the years . . .

Her business had been over for at least a half hour. While Mr. Prowse dozed on and off, the tax increase had been explained by one of the firm's junior accountants, a somber young man who had excused himself right after his presentation. He obviously had not wanted to get caught in the old man's stream of consciousness, which was meandering further and further now from any logical connection to Horace.

Steve cleared his throat. He slid his leather portfolio from the desk onto his knees, grunting her name.

What was the harm, she thought, avoiding his stare. She drew in her breath and smiled at Mr. Prowse, lost in a rapt description of the best chicken pie he had ever eaten. An old stonecutter's wife in Barre had baked it for him. It was during the Depression, and the stonecutter could not pay his bill. "He offered to carve me a tombstone, whatever I wanted on it. And the old stonecutter did beautiful work. But what does a hungry young man want with his own tombstone?"

"Frannie!" Steve nudged her.

"And just coming out of the oven was the biggest, juiciest chicken pie I'd ever seen or smelled." Mr. Prowse clasped his thin, spotted hands and laughed.

This was all part of the ritual, benediction in this ceremony of acceptance that had begun, to everyone's shock and disgust (especially Mr. Prowse's), when Horace had taken a girl as his bride. Every year she dreaded sitting through this examination of the books, because it always seemed like an annual review of HER. But now that Horace's venerable friend and business adviser had once again judged her worthy of the Beecham name and money, she could relax and look forward to an ice-cold martini at the Sugar House in Burlington, where she and Steve would be meeting their old friends Bob and Enid Fowler.

A gash of light cut into the office as the door opened. The secretary, a trim gray-haired woman with an English accent, leaned over Mr. Prowse's shoulder and whispered, "See the red light flashing on the console, sir?"

"Oh my, yes," Mr. Prowse said, squinting at the console of buttons before him.

"There's been a call from Attorney Bell's office. Um, an emergency, it seems," she said, pointedly addressing only Mr. Prowse.

They hurried down the granite steps into the parking lot. The morning nurse had found Anita unconscious in the shower. An ambulance had taken her to Atkinson Hospital. Steve fumbled his keys from his pocket. "Damn it!" he groaned when they flew from his hands. He knelt down and groped under the car for them.

She didn't see the need for all this panic. He had already talked to his office. He knew what the situation was at home. Even the dark circle of sweat staining the back of his jacket annoyed her.

MARY MCGARRY MORRIS

His hand shook as he unlocked her door.

"Well, that's a relief, now that she's finally in a hospital," she said. "At least we can take our time getting back." What he obviously needed now was to hear a calm and clear-thinking voice. She smiled. "You can relax."

He looked at her, startled.

"Now that she's in good hands," she added, patting his arm. She realized how insensitive that had almost sounded. Her tongue prickled with the thought of that martini, All of a sudden she was starving. Poor Steve, she would let him drink as much as he wanted tonight, and then she would drive home. "As soon as we get to the Sugar House, you could have Bob call the hospital and get an update for you." Bob Fowler was an internist. She frowned. "Do you know who admitted her? I hope it's someone we know and not that fool Kessel she saw last . . ."

"We're not going to the Sugar House," he said, opening his door.

"But we always go there." For a moment she thought he had somewhere else in mind.

"Frannie, Anita tried to kill herself," he said, looking at her over the roof of the car.

So what else is new, she thought. "How?" she forced herself to ask.

"I don't even know," he sighed. "Apparently Jan wasn't making much sense when she called." He closed his eyes and tapped his keys on the roof. His voice broke. "She said for them to tell 'the son of a bitch' to get back as fast as he could."

"My God, after all you've put up with! After all you've done for them and for her, to treat you like this! You don't want to hear it, but they're manipulating you, Steve. They're using you."

He slid down into the car and sat staring over the wheel. "I never should have come up here today. I could tell when I got up this morning, she was in a deep depression." He looked over at her. "It was even worse than a depression. It was this terrible sadness, this overwhelming and deadening sadness. And I couldn't stand the sight of it or the feel of it. She came down the stairs and it was like this cloud, this darkness that moved with her. . . ." He put his face in his hands, and for a moment the only sound in the car was a strangled wheeze. "She was doing so well yesterday. It was like the old Anita. I almost called you last night and then again this morning to say I couldn't go, that I knew you'd be fine alone. And then she came down those stairs and her eyes were just filled with so much pain"—he winced, his voice hoarsening to a whisper—"that I couldn't stand it. I kissed the top of her head and I got out of there as fast as I could." Tears rolled down his flushed cheeks.

"Do yourself a favor, Steve, and don't say another goddamn word to me."

They were nearing her turn onto Cuttle Road, both of them stiff and dry-mouthed now after the last hour's reproachful silence. Shivering, Frances stared at the winding road ahead, her fiercely crossed arms mottled with goosebumps from the car's frigid air conditioning. She had already closed the vents on her side, but his were still open and blasting away. She'd be damned if she'd give him the satisfaction of saying one word about how cold she was, which was exactly what he was waiting for, and then he'd be off and running. He'd go from this temperamental thermostat, to how pale and easily tired she had been lately, and, by the way, speaking of low blood, had she heard about Mimi Lukas's father, Marion—the one who'd made a fortune importing acrylic baby-furniture. Well, acrylic furniture was perfect for cramped spaces, because of the dreamy ambience it gave a nursery, with the baby seeming to float in a kind of amniotic state; that is, if couples were actually even reproducing anymore; tell me, when was the last time someone you actually knew had a baby. Steve was a master at free-associating people from anger to conciliation, deftly sweeping them in and out of moods, anger, threats, probing questions; anything to avoid confrontation. She could picture him over the years doing it to Anita as well. He prided himself on settling most of his clients' cases in the comfort of his office and not in the courtroom.

He hunched over the wheel, his grim expression and constant sighing all for her benefit. He knew as well as she did that as soon as he got home he would find out that she had been right after all, that Anita was fine and Jan's hysterical phone call had been another false alarm, calculated to spoil Frances's day with her father.

When he turned, the knot in her stomach tightened. He would be dropping her off, letting her out of his car, alone. Alone. She was almost forty-eight years old. Forty-nine then fifty. And after that, what? What would become of her?

He pulled onto the gravel circle and she got out while he was still down-shifting. He raced back down the road. Turning, she was conscious of the first flowers blooming along the walks, limp with the late-afternoon sun. Her eyes froze on the dirty old car, deep in the shadows of the beech tree. She looked back at the house, startled to see this newly built section of posts and joists where the deck had been. At the sound of splashing, she spun around. A man in dark shorts was swimming the length of the pool, back and forth, his face submerged, his curved arms meeting the water with weary slaps.

Halfway across, his face lifted and he saw her. He swam to the side and hoisted himself by his elbows onto the white coping near her. She remembered him from the other day, but she had forgotten his name.

"I came by to see if you'd made up your mind," he said, rubbing water from his eyes. "But you were already gone and . . ."

"Where's my niece?" she demanded, looking around with alarm. She stepped back. "Where's Martha?"

"Up there. In her apartment," he said, gesturing at the garage. "She said it wasn't Wednesday, but it didn't seem to make any sense to wait around and not do anything and let two more days go by without anyone doing anything, so I figured I'd just . . ."

She was on her way to the garage. She heard him climb out of the pool, the dripping water fizzing onto the hot concrete. She couldn't swallow, she felt her shoulders tense, expecting him to come charging after her, his hands to tighten around her neck the way they had strangled Martha, and now the door at the top of the stairs opened and there was Martha. She was all right.

They began to shout, their voices writhing in a high-pitched tangle. "What in God's name . . ."

"I told him to go . . ."

". . . were you thinking of, letting a perfect . . ."

"But he wouldn't listen and so . . ."

". . . stranger spend the day here . . ."

". . . what could I do, I didn't know what to do, I couldn't make . . ."

"You should've called the police, that's what . . ."

". . . him go. I tried, but he wouldn't."

"I'm sorry," Colin Mackey said. He stepped next to her. "It's my fault. I just figured . . ."

"You don't just figure, Mr. Mackey," she said. "Not here. Not on my property!" She walked toward the house.

"Mack," he said, catching up with her. "Call me Mack," he said, his tone so sleek her eye went instinctively toward the ripple in the grass.

"There's no need to call you anything. You don't understand. I want you out of here. And don't come back!" She hesitated by the board to the kitchen door.

For a moment he stood speechless, his hands clenched at the sides of his dripping shorts, his knuckles white. "I'll be honest. I figured I'd do what I could and maybe you'd be desperate enough for a good carpenter to hire me."

"Desperation is not the way I do business."

His head drew back. "Of course not. I'm sorry. It was presumptuous of me." He started for his car. "I'll get my crowbar and rip this out of here."

"No!" she called, and he spun around with a grateful smile.

"You don't have to. You can leave it. It's all right. You can go," she said, her voice high and thin as she kept waving him toward his car. "Just go." When he had driven out of sight, she took her first deep breath.

"I told him to go," Martha said from behind, startling her. "I tried to make him leave." Her hair stuck out in bushy clumps, and there were grease spots down the front of her shirt. It was sickening. She was such a mess, such a slob, careless about her appearance, about her own safety, her life.

MARY MCGARRY MORRIS

Martha followed her inside, her voice buzzing after Frances with the dull persistence of a gnat. She filled the kettle with water and set it on the stove for tea.

". . . So I got the groceries at the Superette and I was going to see Birdy. But then, when I came out, Getso was there."

Frances stood by the door, staring dismally out at the section Colin Mackey had framed. Steve's birthday party was only a month away. Since Friday there had not been a single call about her ad, and now it had run out. Maybe she should hire him. What would be the harm? Let him do the deck, and then she would look for a permanent handyman later.

". . . and so he helped me pick up all the cans and stuff, but then . . ."

Frances wheeled around. "Martha! Please."

She was all wound up, her eyes glowing behind her smudged glasses. God, it was like listening again to all her teenage ramblings about who had snubbed her and who had knocked the books out of her arms or thrown her clothes into the shower in the boys' locker room. It would pour out of her, and then for days afterward she would hole up in the apartment, refusing to leave or talk to anyone.

"I have so much on my mind. You have no idea," Frances said, pressing both temples with her fingertips.

"I just want to be sure you know it wasn't my fault," Martha said, striking her breast. Her mouth quivered.

"I already said that. I told you that." She turned off the stove and poured the sputtering water over the camomile tea. With the mug close to her face, she inhaled the fragrant mist.

"But you're not listening. You don't understand. I mean the windshield he broke. The one on the laundry truck."

———□———

John called from the Cleaners early the next morning. Sheriff Stoner had arrested Colin Mackey for smashing the windshield of John's brand-new delivery truck.

She could tell Martha was on the extension in the apartment. They had both picked up at the same time.

John claimed that whatever Martha had said to this Mackey character had triggered the whole incident.

"It wasn't me," Martha broke in. "It was what Getso said Mr. Mackey should do to himself and then to me. And I think you know what I mean."

"Who's that?" John demanded. "Is that her?"

"Yes, it's me!" Martha snapped.

"For Godssakes," Frances groaned, and closed her eyes with a sudden image of herself and Martha as two old women in long dark coats, dragging their possessions around in shopping bags.

"Listen, you, you better stop calling here! It's driving everyone nuts."

"I don't call there."

"Ten, fifteen, twenty times a day she calls. The phone rings and nobody's there. She listens and she hangs up."

"It's not me," Martha said in a weak voice.

"Jesus Christ, of course it's you!" John hooted.

"John? John, listen! I saw Getso steal that money from the cash drawer." Her voice coiled small and tight in its dark corner. "You shouldn't have fired me. I was your best worker. I was such a good worker I never even missed a coupon on the specials. Never. Not one. And I never stole anything from you. I would never do that. Never. I mean that."

"Frannie! Help me out here. I can't take much more of this shit," John implored. "You gotta keep her outta my life! Please!"

"Martha, hang up. I said hang up! Now!" Frances demanded.

The phone clicked.

"This is getting totally outta hand, Frannie. Birdy Dusser had to get her number changed. My girls are all scared. They think she's gonna go after them next."

"That's ridiculous and you know it," Frances exploded. She had had enough. For Martha's sake, she had put up and paid out, but no more, damn it. "I have to go," she said before he could reply. She hung up, then quickly dialed Steve's office number. From now on she would have him deal with John. Gretchen, his secretary, said he was on another call; would she like to hold, or be called back?

"Neither," she said. "And no message."

"Anita's regained consciousness, Mrs. Beecham," Gretchen whispered. "He's been up there all night, poor man. I don't think I've ever seen him look so bad."

"How did she do it?" Frances asked.

"Valiums," Gretchen whispered. "Poor things, they're all in a state of shock, the two girls and Mr. Bell."

Drifting in and out of sleep, Frances lay by the pool on her stomach, her limp arms hanging over the chaise longue. Suddenly her eyes opened wide and her head shot up. Nobody was going to screw up her life. Not Anita Bell. Not John Kolditis. Not Martha. Not even Steve. She hadn't been to the club in over a week and already it was starting to show. She pinched a roll of tanned flesh at her waist. She had put on weight. Her deck wasn't built. On the kitchen table were two boxes of printed invitations that still had to be addressed and mailed. She jumped up and wrapped herself in her towel, knotting it as she went inside. She would call Patty and Hank Brewster for tennis, and then maybe early dinner at the club. Cradling the phone to her ear, she opened her telephone file to "B": Barnes, Brewster.

There was ringing on the line.

"Cleaners! Can I help you!" a woman shouted over a din of voices, and music, and hissing sounds.

Martha hung up.

"Guess who?" the woman on the other end shouted, and then a man barked in a long, chilling howl.

She ran over to the apartment and banged on the door, which Martha opened at once. Martha stared at a point over Frances's left shoulder, only looking at her when Frances said John had asked the telephone company to put a tracing device on his line. Frances leaned closer. "One more call and they'll arrest you."

"But I have to talk to Birdy!" Martha blurted.

"Forget about Birdy. Damn it, Martha. You've got to stop this!"

"She's my friend, and I can't have her thinking I'd steal money and get her in trouble. And he must still be doing it. I just know he is. That's why he won't let me near her. We were such close friends, he knows she'll believe me. Don't you see? I have to talk to her! I have to!"

"Stop it! Stop it right now! You should see your face, how twisted it gets when you even say his name. Don't you see what's happening, what you did? Because you HAD to see Birdy, you got into a car with a man you didn't even know, a stranger! Martha, it's just like that night all over again."

"Don't!"

"But it's the same. . . ."

"No!" Martha covered her ears. "I can't hear you, so you might as well stop it. Just stop it."

"All right, I'll stop," she said, and Martha looked up. "But you've got to forget about Birdy Dusser and the Cleaners and get on to new business." She sighed. "We both do, okay? We'll start in the morning. First thing, bright and early!" She reached for her arm, but Martha drew back stiffly.

E I G H T

———□———

The air was ripe with the smell of sweet cut grass and fresh cedar chips. Colin Mackey was building her deck, and young Johnny Henderson was doing the yard work. Frances checked her watch. She always knew to the penny what she owed, and the minute Henderson gathered his tools he got paid.

He had trimmed all the shrubs and mowed the lawns, and at the corners of the pool, in the ornate clay pots festooned with bunches of grapes and the cruel little faces of gargoylian children, he had planted bushy pink and white geraniums and slender vines of dark ivy that with each breeze swept back and forth over the white apron. When he finished weeding the flower beds, he piled his clippers and rakes and shovels in the wheelbarrow and pushed it to the side of the garage, where he uncoiled the garden hose and rinsed off every single tool. As soon as he put the first tool into his truck, she hurried outside with his check. He looked at it, then glanced at her. Both this time and last, he had worked almost fifteen minutes over the hour. Hoping to distract him, she described how she wanted pink and white impatiens planted in front of the deck when it was finished.

"Awful lotta sun for impatiens," he said, squinting that way.

She could already picture them against the white lattice. "They only have to look good for three weeks. Until Steve's party," she laughed, then immediately regretted it. He was such a humorless young man. She was always explaining herself while he would look at her with this same blank expression.

The power saw came on with a deafening whine. They waited while Mack cut a long post into three sections.

"Who's your carpenter?"

"His name's Colin Mackey."

He shook his head, the name meaningless to him. "He got a helper?"

When she told him no, he smirked. "At the rate he's going," he said behind his hand, "that deck's going to take him the whole summer."

"He said two weeks," she said uneasily. Mackey had spent most of the day driving back and forth to town for supplies.

"No way!"

Mack's mallet pounded the newly cut post into the ground. The new windshield for the laundry truck had cost $375. Though he had tried to talk her out of it, Steve had arranged it so that, if Mack came up with the money, John wouldn't press charges. The deck would cost her the price of the lumber, the new windshield, and, for Mack, an additional three hundred dollars, which she had just this minute decided he would not get until the job was done. He was the desperate one; let him meet her terms. In any event, it was her best bargain in a long time—since Floyd.

"He's here first thing in the morning and he doesn't leave till dark," she said, annoyed with herself for explaining anything to this twerp. The curtain in the apartment window moved, and she was further irritated to think that Martha had been up there all morning, both hiding from Henderson and watching him.

"Well, you get in a bind, remember, me and my dad do decks. And we wouldn't be setting the posts directly in the ground like he's doing neither."

"You wouldn't?" She bit her lip. Damn. Didn't the ass even know what he was doing?

"No, ma'am. We use footings."

"Footings?"

"Yes, ma'am." Smiling, he extended her check. "Seems about five dollars short, I think."

After he drove off with the additional five dollars, she stood with her arms folded, watching Mackey work. He had twisted a white rag around his brow to keep sweat out of his eyes. His bare back had burned to an angry red.

"Why aren't you using footings?" she called shrilly the minute he stopped hammering.

"Because you don't need them," he answered over his shoulder, as he set a board into place. "Just more work, time, and money." He checked the board with the level, then shifted it a hair bit higher before nailing it into place. "These posts are all pressure-treated. Guaranteed not to rot for forty years."

Massaging his waist, he went to the new lumber that he had spent the morning stacking. Stapled to the end of one length was a small rust-stained tag, which he yanked off and told her to read. It was a forty-year guarantee. When she put it into her pocket, he laughed. "You going to save that?"

"Of course."

"You think you'll still be here in forty years?"

"That's hardly the point."

"I mean in this house." He was still smiling.

She glanced at her watch. "I really shouldn't be wasting your time like this. You've only got another week and a half."

"Yessum, that's right, that's right, that's right," he muttered, running back to the deck.

It wasn't until she was in the house that she realized he had been making fun of her.

Less than an hour later, she heard him calling her from the kitchen. She hurried out of the study, where she had been addressing invitations.

"Mrs. Beecham! Excuse me, Mrs. Beecham!"

He held up his hands. "I'm sorry, but I need work gloves."

She cringed at the sight of his palms, raw with cuts and blisters—not hands that had done a lot of hard labor. "I told you, everything's in the garage, in my brother's workshop."

He winced. "I was just looking in there, and Martha . . ." He winced again. "She came down and threw me out."

"Oh God. All right," she sighed, going outside.

She climbed through the heat of the sun-beaten stairs and knocked on the door. There were dark sweaty circles under Martha's eyes, and she wore baggy corduroy pants and a flannel shirt. Behind her, the apartment was dark and musty-smelling. All the shades were down, with the curtains drawn. A pair of Floyd's work boots stood on a folded paper bag by the door. That was Floyd's shirt Martha had on, and his pants.

When she explained that Mack had to use the workshop, Martha insisted those were her father's tools and her father's gloves down there, and no one would use them.

At that, Frances marched into her brother's bedroom and threw open the closet door. She took his few limp shirts and pants and laid them on the bed. From the bottom of the closet, she took his one pair of dress shoes and another pair of stiff work boots and tossed them onto the bed.

Conscious of Martha staring at her from the doorway, she emptied his bureau drawers onto the bed. "I want this all cleared out," she said, struggling to sound calm. This had always been the trouble, her outbursts igniting Martha's. Pointing, she came toward her. "Including the clothes you have on. You are a thirty-two-year-old woman, and from now on that's how you're going to dress and that's how you're going to act. Do you hear me?"

Martha glared at her.

"Shades up! Curtains open!" she ordered from window to window, yanking back curtains and snapping up shades. "We have a lot to do and there's no time for breakdowns, Martha. Life marches relentlessly on."

She didn't have her father to hide behind anymore. From now on it was just the two of them; instead of saying it, though, she forced a smile. Maybe this was exactly what Martha needed. A good harsh dose of reality. Finally.

Later that night, she and Steve sat in the study. It was their first drink together in over a week. He hadn't called first, but had dropped by, explaining that he had wanted to see how the deck was progressing and, more important, he whispered, nuzzling her ear, how she was doing.

He needed a haircut. His new yellow tie was stained, and his suit pants were wrinkled and bagged at the knees. When he put his arm around her, she flinched with shock at his sour body odor.

He spent every night at the hospital. Anita had gained five pounds, and today Jan had brought her new makeup. His younger daughter, Patsy, a teacher in Hanover, New Hampshire, was subletting her apartment for the summer and had already moved back home. Everything was ready for Anita's release in the morning. "Jan's taking the day off, and Patsy and I will be picking her up. Both girls are so nervous, you'd think . . ."

"Shh," she said with her finger to his lip. She unknotted his tie and undid his collar button.

"Where's Martha?" he asked as she reached up to turn off the lamp.

"In the apartment." She unbuckled his belt and unzipped his fly.

"We better go upstairs," he said, starting to get up. She tugged him back.

"She won't be over. She's mad at me. She's not speaking to me." She was stripping him down to his underwear.

"Oh God, Frannie. I need you so much. Oh my God," he kept sighing as she stood over him, pulling her shirt over her head.

She knelt beside the couch and laid her face on his chest.

"I'd rather be upstairs," he apologized. "I keep thinking somebody's coming."

"Nobody's coming," she assured him, bending over him.

"Please, Frannie!" he insisted against her breast.

She followed him upstairs, amused and aroused by his panic. Theirs had always seemed more a domestic relationship than an adulterous one. In fact, it occurred to her now, as she folded down the spread and pulled back the sheet, that she had probably felt more like a mistress as Horace's young wife than she had ever felt with Steve.

She sighed as he pulled her close and lay trembling against her. He kissed her, and her eyes opened with the sudden vivid memory of Horace pulling her into his lap and kissing her for the first time. She had been eighteen and he had been fifty-eight. She closed her eyes, remembering the touch of his hand as still the most stirring experience of her life.

"Oh my God!" Steve moaned, and she opened her eyes. "You're so good to me, Frannie," he whispered drowsily, his face buried in her long hair.

She fell asleep with her arms and legs locked around him. Later she woke up grinning at the sight of his narrow backside darting through the doorway. Moments later he returned with his clothes balled in his arms.

"Don't go!" she said as he started to dress. "It's only nine-thirty."

"I'm late. I forgot Patsy said she'd hold dinner." He pulled up his pants. He was out of breath.

"Steve!"

He sat on the chaise longue and shook out his sock. "She thinks I'm at a meeting."

MARY MCGARRY MORRIS

"Then call her." She grabbed the telephone and carried it to him. "Tell her you've left the meeting and you're at my house now."

He closed his eyes. "I can't."

"Then tell her you got held up." She stepped closer and pulled his scratchy face against her belly. "Tell her to go to bed and you'll see her in the morning."

"I can't."

"What do you mean, you can't? Steve!" She tilted his face up to look at her. They were grown women with lives of their own. They knew their mother and father had no kind of a marriage. They had known about her for years, and now all of a sudden they thought they could come back home and change everyone's lives and all the rules.

"Because," he said, "I promised them."

"Promised them what?" she demanded.

"That I'd help. That I'd do everything I possibly could. That I'd be there," he said, tying his shoes while she watched, the phone still in her hand.

NINE

———□———

        Martha stirred her cereal. She had remembered that today was Birdy's monthly hairdressing appointment, and her plan was to meet her when she came out of Lucille's House of Coiffures. She checked her watch again; just five more hours to go.

    Frances leaned in the doorway, sipping coffee while she watched Mack work. He had been out there since sunrise. Frances wore a pleated pink-and-white tennis skirt. Again she reminded Martha that she would be at the club all day.

"Remember, now, I want you to get all of your father's things packed and out of the apartment today. It'll make your . . ."

"I'm going into town," she interrupted, knowing better than to mention Birdy's name.

Frances looked at her. "Under the circumstances, I'd think that's the last place you should go."

The milk-bloated corn flakes made a wet, mealy sound against the spoon. "I need groceries," she said. That was true. With most of her own food gone, here she was, caught again in the tentacles of her aunt's charity.

"Will you stop that stirring!" Frances closed her eyes and sighed. "Make a list and I'll get what you need," she said, turning back to the screen.

"No! I want to do my own shopping!"

Frances spun around. "Look, I told you yesterday . . ." She paused for a long deep breath. "For your own sake, Martha, don't go into town. I'll get whatever you need. Let things settle down. Please! You've got a lot to do here. All your father's things. Today's a perfect day to get them all out of the apartment."

"No." Martha had been shaking her head. "I want to get my own groceries. I'll get the apartment cleared out, but I'm going to get my own groceries. I didn't do anything wrong and I can do what I want and go where I want and people aren't going to stop me and they're not going to keep blaming things on me that I didn't do. It's not fair! It's not fair! It's not fair! I never stole any money! I never smashed any windshield." She was hitting the glass table.

"Martha! Stop it!"

"But everyone thinks I did. They all think I'm a thief, and it's not fair. I worked so hard there."

"I know you did," Frances said wearily. She stepped closer to the door and peered outside.

"It was very hard for me. I tried very, very hard to be a good

A Dangerous Woman

employee and give good service and to be a good person and a good . . . friend," she said as the screen door opened, then banged shut after Frances.

The board rattled under Frances's running feet. "No, no, no!" she cried. "It's out too far!"

"Six inches," Mack said. "In just this one place. Six inches, that's all."

"No! It has to be exactly the way it was! Exactly!"

Angrily he began to tear out the section he had been working on since early this morning.

"Bitch," he muttered as Frances drove off.

Martha hurried over to the apartment, and he called to her, but she ignored him and kept going. The other day, when she had stopped him from going through her father's trunk at the back of the garage, all he had to do was say he had permission. Instead, he had run to Frances. He was a weakling, another coward, like Getso. "Nothing but trouble looking for a scapegoat," she muttered with the sun on her back as she ran up the stairs. She opened the door with a swoop of joy at the thought of seeing Birdy and getting the whole mess straightened out. As soon as she got her father's things packed and in the attic, she was going into town.

Frances wanted her to throw everything out. But all she been able to discard was her father's medicine; the rest she deposited neatly in a corner of the attic near Mr. Beecham's ancient sporting equipment and cameras. Her father would have liked that, she thought with a twinge of childish jealousy for the white-haired old man who had commanded her father's respect and attention and had received most of his love.

She hadn't been up here in years. The high ceilings of rough boards and the long windows on every side filled the attic with light. She had forgotten the peace of this deep, hot dust, which felt, as she gazed around at the stacked pictures and domed trunks and bodiless hanging suits, like such a desiccation of time that she had the strange sensation of being an image herself, someone's fleeting thought intruding on all these memories.

"There you are!" Mack said from the doorway, and she turned with a startled cry. "I've been all through the house looking for you," he said. "You know when Frances will be back?"

"Probably not until supper," she said, tensing back. He didn't belong up here. He made her nervous, walking around like this and touching things.

"I can't find the small toolbox," Mack said. He was poking through a stack of framed pictures. "You didn't see it, did you?"

"No."

"I thought maybe you came out and saw it and you put it somewhere. You know, to get it out of the way or something."

"I wouldn't do that." She turned to watch where he went now. "Why would I do that?"

He shrugged. "Just figured I'd ask."

He squatted in front of a yellowed portrait of a young man posing by a table of books, his dark suit trimly tailored to his long thin body, his pale-blonde gaze aloof to the point of boredom. "That's Mr. Beecham," she said when he asked.

Tilting it, he blew soot off the glass and held the picture close to his face. "Ooo, the same scum look your aunt gave me this morning. They say, after enough years together, people start to look alike."

He was right. She could see that same cutting disdain in Horace Beecham's rigid smile.

"But she didn't even know him then. And, besides, they were only married five years," she said, so anxious for him to put the picture down that she could not take her eyes from it.

"Five years!" He looked up at her. "Then how long has she been a widow?"

"Twenty-one years. I was eleven when Mr. Beecham died." Why had she told him that? It was none of his business, and, for that matter, he shouldn't even be up here. She began to push the last box into the corner.

"I'll do that," he said, coming quickly to lift it. His arms were slick with sweat, and his T-shirt stuck to his back in wet puckers. He looked around. "Any more?"

"No. That's all. I'm all done. I'm done!" she said, too emphatically.

"This all your father's stuff?" he asked, nudging the largest box away from the smaller ones.

"I had those straight," she warned, the sight of the crooked boxes as unnerving as blaring sirens. Her breath came tighter and tighter.

He set a carton on the smaller one in front, the entire pattern now totally misaligned.

"Leave that alone!" she ordered. "Don't you touch those boxes!"

His hands flinched back as if scorched and he spun around. "I thought maybe you put his tools up here."

As she hurried past him, he stepped so quickly aside she heard a thud and then a painful curse as he banged into something.

"There aren't any tools up here. It's all his clothes and things," she muttered, heaving the boxes back into place. "Why would I bring tools up here? All his tools are in the garage. You've got all his tools. . . ."

"These his too?" he asked, touching the clubs in the sooty golf bag that sagged against the whitewashed chimney.

"Those are Mr. Beecham's!" she warned, adding that just about everything here was Mr. Beecham's.

She followed him as he roamed between the cedar chests and old trunks and wooden crates of books and ship models and tarnished silver platters and golf trophies and a rack of overcoats and tails and now a dusty top hat, which he put on. She bit her lip. He was trying to antagonize her, to goad her.

"Look at this!" he called. He had found the mounted animal heads that used to hang in Mr. Beecham's dark study downstairs. "That's a lion, and a water buffalo, and a . . . Christ, a gazelle. Why the hell would anyone shoot a gazelle?" He stared at the creature's blank lustrous eyes. "What could have been the point?" he asked. "A gazelle! All they do is run. They're so graceful and small," he said.

"I guess it's like a deer," she said defensively. "People shoot deer and stuff them like that." Her skin crawled. He shouldn't be touching things that weren't his. Especially Mr. Beecham's things. She never touched Mr. Beecham's things. If he broke anything, she would be blamed. "Please don't!" she said, seeing him stroke the spiraling horns.

MARY McGARRY MORRIS

He spun around. "Don't what?"

"You don't belong up here!" she said. "You're going to break something!"

"Break something!" He laughed. "Me, who would harm neither man nor beast, break something?" He looked at her, shocked. "What do you think I am?"

A prickle of fear grazed the back of her neck as she remembered the soup can smashing the windshield. She looked toward the distant door.

"Tell me! Do you think I'm good? Or do you think I'm bad?" he asked, his bright eyes cutting to hers with an intensity of sore heat, a sudden rawness like stripped skin.

She shrugged, and he asked again, in a menacing rumble.

"I think you're good," she said, her whisper weightless as the shafts of lightdust at all the windows. Her glasses slid heavily down her nose. She pushed them back and held them in place with her finger.

"And I think you're good," he said solemnly. "But are you pure of heart? Are you?" he asked, taking a step, then another toward her. "Are you pure of heart, Martha?"

She darted past him, through the door, and down the stairs, her heart pounding as he ran after her.

"Martha!" he called. "Wait! Don't run!"

He was crazy. A crazy man was chasing her. At the end of the second-floor corridor, she slipped inside the white alcove that opened into this cavernous old linen closet with its paper-lined shelves of unused sheets and pillow cases and table linen, all covered with dusty plastic, and its deep wall bins for blankets, the small brass latches black with disuse. As a child she had hidden in these bins, sepulchered for hours on end, only to find, when she would finally reappear, that no one had missed her.

Downstairs, doors opened and closed as he searched for her.

"I was only kidding!" he called near the bottom of the stairs. "Martha! I was just fooling around! Jesus Christ," he muttered, and then the screen door banged shut.

The saw screamed on and she hurried downstairs and out the back door, running toward the garage stairs.

"Martha!" he called, and she turned with a gasp as he came toward her, shirtless, his face and arms in the sun coated with grime. He held up his hand. "I was kidding around. I was just saying weird, off-the-wall things. I do that. It's just a weird thing I do. It scared you and I'm sorry. Really . . . Martha?"

She rubbed her arm, nodding, staring at the worn spot on the toe of her canvas shoe.

"Okay?" He touched her forearm and she flinched. "Okay?" he asked again.

She nodded. "Okay," she said, backing up the steps. Just leave her alone. Let her go. She had less than an hour now to get into town and meet Birdy coming out of the beauty parlor.

———□———

The square white house with its mauve shutters and gray front door stood close to the sidewalk, behind a fence of unpainted lattice sections that had buckled and sagged back in places, as if caught in a permanent breeze. Each time Martha passed the house she slowed way down, staring at the lavender venetian blinds on the little cellar windows. She had never been inside, but she knew from Birdy that the beauty parlor was down there in Lucille Faro's basement. There were two sinks, two chairs, and three hair dryers, with most of the floor space taken up by a huge playpen for Lucille's twins. Lucille's husband had joined two playpens together by welding the sides and weaving the mesh and rebuilding the bottom. The twins' names were Ivy and Rose, and though she had never seen them, she knew Ivy was blonde and Rose was the redhead.

Birdy knew everything about everyone in town and was so candid about her own life that, listening to her, Martha would get this bloated feeling and her eyes would smart with the pure dazzle of so much talk.

She paused in the cool shade of a maple tree. It was getting late; Birdy was due back at the Cleaners in five minutes. Maybe she wasn't even down there. Maybe she was sick or had switched her day. Martha might be out here pacing back and forth all afternoon and unless she went to the Cleaners she wouldn't know where Birdy was and she couldn't go there couldn't go there couldn't go there. Not to the Cleaners. Not there where they called her thief. Not yet. Be calm, now. Just open the rickety gate and ring the bell. All she could do was ask. That's all. "Just ask. That's all you can do," she muttered.

"Oh!" said the skinny young woman in a pink nylon uniform when she opened the door. "Can I help you?" she asked through the screen.

"Is Birdy Dusser in there? I have to see her. It's very important."

"Well, gee, I . . ." the woman stammered, in a flutter of frosted pink eyelids. "I'll go see."

She seemed to be gone a long time. Maybe she had stopped to perform some crucial next step on a perm and she had forgotten all about her out here on this narrow wooden step. Or maybe Birdy was hiding in there, hoping she would get tired of waiting and go away. Martha turned and came off the steps.

The door opened. She followed the young woman down steep cellar stairs that were carpeted in a thick purple shag. She sniffed at the smell of sweet chemicals and mildew. She sniffed eagerly at the damp redolence of hair chemicals and mildew and now at the churning washer and dryer and the musty piles of soiled towels. It smelled of secrets. It smelled of women, an intimacy of women so deep in this fertile darkness that she gasped, as starved for air as if she had burrowed straight through to the core of the earth.

Birdy was getting up from one of the dryers. The short yellow cape on her shoulders reflected the light, so that for a moment, in the darkly paneled basement, her glowing face was all that Martha saw. Her dark hair was tubed on pink-and-white foam rollers. An older woman in green shorts sat under the adjacent dryer, which she switched off the minute she saw Martha. Lucille Faro stood with her back to the huge playpen. The twins faced each other in a litter of bright plastic toys that squeaked and honked under their fat legs now as they scrambled upright, their round bellies pressing against the mesh.

"Martha!" Birdy said, hugging her, and Martha's eyes closed as she sighed Birdy's name in a soft deflation of longing.

"You look great!" Birdy said, stepping away.

Her hands opening and closing at her sides, Martha had all she could do not to pull her back.

"Doesn't she look great?" Birdy asked the women, but their stony stares and angled heads never wavered. "Must be all that mountain air," she said, pulling out her curlers and dropping them into a pink sand-pail monogrammed LUCY in a swirl of silver glitter. "You even look like you put on a pound or two in all the right places." She winked. "As you can see, mine're still piling up in all the wrong places. But I'm thinking of joining that exercise place on Cottage Street, the one that just opened." She climbed up into the chair. "Comb me out, Luce?" she asked through the mirror.

"You still want me to make that call for you?" Lucille Faro asked, staring.

Birdy's eyes widened and she shook her head. "No, I think it'll be okay. Anyway," she said, her eyes back on Martha's in the mirror now, as Lucille styled her hair with a long-handled brush. Martha smiled, watching Lucille's rough red hands shape Birdy's sausaged curls into a soft cap of shiny waves. "It's this whole new concept where they strap you onto these machines that push and pull and pump and do all the work for you. My sister signed up. Beverly. You remember Beverly?" Birdy bent her head and closed her eyes while Lucille sprayed her hair from a gold can. "She's on third shift at the General and she says it's great. She lays there and sleeps while the machines do all her exercising."

Martha nodded vigorously, interjecting "yup"s and "uh huh"s whenever she could. Still talking, Birdy slid out of the chair and paid Lucille.

They came along the sidewalk with Martha so deep in the thrall of Birdy's bubbly monologue that she tripped for the third time. Birdy's arm shot out, but she caught herself. "Watch your step," Birdy warned now, as they crossed Merchants Row. They were nearing the Cleaners. "I have to talk to you," Martha said, grabbing Birdy's arm. "It's very important."

Birdy's eyes flickered in the direction of the Cleaners, then back at Martha. They sat on the bench at the downtown bus stop. Martha raised her voice over the rumble of passing traffic.

". . . And I went in to put the fig squares in your basket and I saw him. He was taking money right out of the cash drawer and he did this," she said, sliding her hand down the front of her pants. Encouraged by Birdy's weary smile, she went on. "It's not fair that I get fired when he's the one that's stealing. But worse than that, Birdy, as far as I'm concerned, is that it's probably still going on. I know he's still stealing money every single day and you're probably putting your own back in so he won't get in trouble. He's using you, that's what he's doing! He doesn't care about you like I do!" Her heart swelled in the silence; Birdy finally believed her. "Birdy, you're my best friend," she whispered. Seeing Birdy this sad just tore her apart. Poor thing, she probably thought Getso was her last chance. "You're the nicest person I've ever known. I could always talk to you. You were always so kind and you made me laugh and I've missed you so much. . . ." Her voice broke.

"And I've missed you too. Aw, poor kid," Birdy sighed, patting her hand. "You know, Wesley keeps asking if anyone's heard from you. Mart, I'm not your only friend. You've . . ."

"Yes, you are!" Martha cried, seizing her arm with both hands. "You are! You're the only one!"

"Martha, let go of me."

The look on Birdy's face frightened her. "I'm sorry. Oh, Birdy, I'm so sorry. Did I hurt you?" She tried to stroke Birdy's arm where it was red, but Birdy pulled away. "I never want to hurt you. You know that."

"Sure, honey," Birdy said, standing up.

"All I want is for us to still be friends," she said. She held out her hands, and then, to still their trembling, clasped them to her chest. "That's all I want!"

"I know."

"I mean, we don't have to do anything together or anything." She laughed nervously. "I just want you to like me, that's all I want."

"I like you. Of course I like you."

A DANGEROUS WOMAN

"Then will you tell John I didn't steal his money; that I'd like my job back?"

"Well, I'll certainly mention it," Birdy said, her voice like her smile, suddenly too bright. She had seen Birdy do this to others. She was being placated. Being humored.

Breath held, Martha sat very still, certain something was going to fall and break. Any sudden movement or noise might trigger the catastrophe that loomed.

She watched Birdy swatting the wrinkles out of her pink skirt. Wrinkles. She was worried about wrinkles.

"You don't believe me, do you? You think I did steal that money," she whispered.

"Of course I don't!"

"Then who do you think stole it?"

"It was probably just one of those crazy mixups. Like the wrong night-count or something."

Martha grabbed her wrist. "No! Don't you understand? It was Getso! I saw him! I watched him! What do I have to do to make you believe me? Go to the police?"

"The police! Oh my God!"

"See, that's what he's afraid of. That's why he won't let us talk on the phone! That's . . ."

"Martha! Keep your voice down!"

"That's why he tried to attack me at the Superette the other day!"

"Martha, you fell. He saw you fall. He tried to help you up. Charlie, in the van, saw the whole thing."

"Then Charlie's lying too. He attacked me! That's what he tried to do!" she shouted. "And I have a witness! He'll tell you! You wait! You wait right here. I'll call him and he'll . . ."

"Listen to me! You listen to me!" Birdy panted, her face raging at Martha's. "I didn't want to say this, but there haven't been any more shortages since the day you left. Do you understand?"

"No! No, I don't! I don't understand!" she cried, thumping her chest, and then it came to her. "He's waiting! Don't you see, Birdy! That's how evil he is. He's waiting, that's what he's . . ."

MARY McGARRY MORRIS

"Martha, I'm going now. Please. Please, stop." Birdy stepped off the curb.

"How can you believe him and not me? You're my best friend. I wouldn't lie to you! Birdy! You're my best friend! Come back here! Birdy!" She started to chase her, but Birdy had already crossed the street. The light changed, and now the cars surged forward, trapping Martha on the island in the middle of the traffic.

TEN

———□———

The sun was starting to set. Frances
sprawled in a lounge chair by the pool. After twenty-seven holes with
Heidi Pierce and Ann Clyde and Ruthie Baxter, her body was as drained
as her nerves were frayed. All they had talked about was Anita Bell's
suicide attempt and the ugly scene that had taken place between Steve
and his daughters in the hospital waiting room.

When they had finished playing, Frances had come straight home.

After her shower she had come out here and plunged into the water and she still felt grimy.

Mack stood over her, talking. As anxious as she had been to get away from everyone at the club, the thought of being alone filled her with dread. She nodded, only half listening; the man would talk to a wall as long as it didn't move. Her face flushed angrily. Steve's daughters had called her a whore in the hospital waiting room. A whore. And, according to Ruthie, Steve had wept.

Now Mack was laughing. When he couldn't find the toolbox, he said, his first thought had been Martha. "I thought, you know, because they were her father's tools, maybe she didn't like me using them. Especially after the incident with the gloves," he said, shrugging with a sideward glance up at the garage. His voice dropped. "She really got upset."

God, what now? What had she said? What had she done? Would he quit too? Then what would she do? No! she thought, raising her head slowly. She couldn't be alone right now—not with this mess, not with Martha teetering on the brink of hysteria. Frances could tell. She could always tell. . . .

"And then later I found it," he said, slipping into the chair. "I'd built a whole section over it! I tried to explain when she got back from town, but by then I think I'd already freaked her out. She was in a really bad way." He leaned forward. "This is none of my business, but . . ."

"You're right," she said, her eyes meeting his. "It's none of your business."

"You don't even know what I was going to ask!" His incredulous voice made her smile. His boyishness surprised her.

"Whatever it was," she said, tensing herself, "it couldn't possibly be any of your business!"

He slapped his knee. "You're right. You're absolutely right." He glanced toward the shade-drawn windows over the garage. "But I can't help wondering what I'm dealing with here."

"My deck. That's all you have to deal with."

"And I'm working real hard at that." He smiled. "But someone like Martha, she . . . I don't know. . . . I look at her and I see all that . . .

that . . ." He turned back now. "I don't know what I see. I guess that's what's so fascinating. She's so vulnerable and so . . . so . . . so overwhelming." He sighed.

"I didn't realize I'd hired a psychiatrist." Her eyes watered as she took a long sparkling swallow of her drink. Vulnerable, overwhelming. Try draining, she thought; try depressing, try lifelong burden. The sun burned a raw red hole in the sky.

"I'm a writer," he said with a rueful laugh. "You hired a writer."

"Really!" It was all she could do to keep a straight face. Calling himself a writer, this seedy, middle-aged brawler whose beer paunch and battered face belonged in a roadhouse with some frizzy-haired tramp hanging on his arm. She shivered. God, he was everything she had ever detested in a man. But right now, for a little while, she'd let the empty hour be taken up with his easy talk and his quick laughter. Eventually the gin could make anyone good company, she knew, amused now by the careless spread of his long tanned legs and his hand grazing hers as he took her glass. Yes, it was the ice-cold gin. She yawned, watching him refill her glass. Without being asked, he poured himself a drink. What surprised her more than his nerve was her own amusement as he sat back down.

He needed a shave and his ragged hair curled over his ears and down the back of his neck. Men like this were nothing. Life slipped through their fingers. They took and gave little back, and their every word was calculated according to some base measure of self-promotion. She knew just how quickly that squinting smile could arch in a brutal sneer.

But what did it matter? For now she felt like talking, needed to talk, needed someone to sit there, someone in that chair, someone tall enough to block her view of the town below. She was telling him about her birthday party for Steve. The guest list was already too long, but every day at least two or three more names would occur to her or a friend would call and remind her of someone else she HAD to invite.

He said she was lucky to have enough friends to muster for a party. His friends were all over the place, the whole country. Even his kids were all spread out now, he said, two in California, one in England.

"My wife's still in Boston," he said, and added, "my ex-wife."

"You're divorced?"

"Legally," he said, and she laughed. "But not emotionally," he added.

"What does that mean?" she asked, knowing exactly how he wanted it taken.

"I still see her." He gestured with his hands. "We get together."

Eyebrows raised, she made the same gesture. "You mean you . . ."

"Yah, we," he said, laughing and returning the gesture. "But maybe only once a year."

She sat up and crossed her legs. In the slant of the setting sun, she was conscious of their shadows deepening on the white concrete, and the press of the night at their backs. He was telling her about the book he had written nineteen years ago.

"What was the name of it?" she asked, smiling, perfectly willing to play the game.

"*Last Man In*," he said, and paused hopefully.

She enjoyed telling him she had never heard of it.

"It's about three soldiers in Vietnam and what their lives are like once they get back to the States." As he described his characters and the plot, his voice softened so that she had to lean forward to hear him.

"It was, I guess, what you'd call a critical success. It sure wasn't a financial one. But at the time, that meant so little to me. The money, I mean. Hell, I was young, and I had so many ideas for books; I remember telling my wife one night I was afraid, if I wrote them all, people would consider me a hack. I couldn't get to sleep, worrying about it. I was really afraid of that—of becoming a hack. Me, a hack!" He shook his head.

"How many did you write?" she asked, yawning.

"After the first one?" He laughed. "Not a one. Not a single one."

"But you must have tried."

"No. Not really. I thought I was, but all I was really doing was talking about writing."

He poured himself another drink, this one just about straight gin. She stared at his glass as he sat back down, so he'd know she knew his type—oh, did she ever. Without a word, she set her glass on the patio and swung her legs off the chaise longue to go inside.

"Oh, I'm sorry!" he said, jumping up and refilling her glass. "I should have asked you." He handed it to her. "I'm not used to being companionable. . . . And I haven't talked about this in so long, I'm getting carried away." He hoisted his glass. "To the dearth of Colin Mackey."

She looked up, but did not return the toast. People who revealed too much of themselves inevitably wanted something back. She smiled at the sudden image of a little boy with his underpants circling his ankles as he waited for her to pull hers down too. Her irritation grew as he paced barefoot, drink in hand, back and forth on his shadowy stage, delivering his maudlin soliloquy.

". . . and then nothing. There I was, the boy wonder, all alone with my dust-covered desk, my pregnant wife, and two little kids who didn't give a damn who I thought I was. They insisted I was their 'daddy' and she insisted I was her husband, and there was no way they were going to get away with that shit. So I left."

His abrupt silence sparked a commotion of crickets and squawking birds. She raised her head and sniffed hungrily at the smell of charred-meat smoke from some stranger's barbecue. Mosquitoes had begun to swarm from the darkening tree line. Soon it would be night.

She turned, surprised to hear this clearly the hum of cars from the distant highway. From the garage apartment came the scrape of a balky window being raised, and she knew Martha was watching them. The pool filter clicked off with a gurgling rush. What am I doing out here, she wondered, and yet could not bring herself to go inside. He had gotten them another drink. Between sips, she spoke carefully, conscious of her thickening tongue.

She was describing the misery Anita Bell forced on everyone. Mack hunched forward. Raising a hand, he interrupted to ask why Steve had stayed with such a wife so long and, more bewilderingly, why Frances had stayed in such a dead-end relationship all these years.

Dead-end relationship! She suddenly felt so feverish that her skin bristled and her eyes felt hot. "It just happened. Time passed and then it just seemed too late."

MARY MCGARRY MORRIS

"Too late!" he cried, leaning closer to touch her arm. "It's never too late for happiness! How can you say that? My God. That's giving up! That's like dying."

She stood up and, with a flick of her wrist, dumped her drink, the ice cubes streaking light into the dark lawn. Fireflies glimmered over the pool. Below, in town, house lights were coming on amid the bright gridwork of streetlamps.

"You have to do something!" he said as she cleared the empty gin bottle and the ice bucket from the table. "You owe it to yourself! You owe it to Steve!" he cried, so close behind that she felt heat on her neck. "You have to do something! You have to!"

She paused at the door. "You're drunk," she said. His head snapped back and she gripped the knob. She didn't trust people or things that might rage out of control. Even fires in the fireplaces frightened her. For years none had been lit here.

"Just a little, though. Just enough to feel very, very good," he said, grinning with a childish wave of his fingers. "I've enjoyed talking with you."

"You better go now," she said, her head reeling.

He peered at her so closely that his whiskers scratched the screen. "I need a favor. You mind if I sleep out here in my car? Just for tonight. I don't snore," he said solemnly.

"Yes, I do mind," she said. She closed the inside door, wincing with the breech of the sliding bolt. She clung dizzily to the banister, and it seemed that she was battling her way to the top of the stairs. She groped along the hallway to her door, then crawled onto the bed, so exhausted that she fell asleep in her damp bathing suit and robe.

Martha watched him walk back to the pool. He yanked his shirt over his head, took off his shorts, and dove into the water in his underwear. In furious choppy strokes, he flung himself through two churning lengths of the pool, then climbed out and bundled his clothes under his arm. His car lumbered out of the driveway. She left the bathroom light on and she got into bed, where she fell into a quick sleep.

———□———

A few hours had passed. Martha's eyes opened wide. At first she thought a branch was hitting the garage roof. She bolted up, the sheet clutched to her chin. Someone was knocking on the door and calling her name.

When she turned on the outside light, Mack waved through the glass.

"Can I use your phone?" he asked over the taut chain when she opened the door.

She stood by the kitchen table while he dialed the same number four times, listening with closed eyes while it rang and rang. He sank into the wooden chair and shook his head.

"I'm getting too old for this shit," he sighed, then chuckled. "Now the hangovers start with the first drink." He looked up, studying her a moment through eyes that were raw slits. "I'll bet you've never even been drunk, have you? Have you?"

"No." She moved back against the door. The knob pressed into her spine.

"Mind turning off that light?" he asked, shading his eyes from the overhead glare. "Please!" he said when she didn't move.

"I want it on!" she said, determined not to be intimidated by him again.

"I can see through your nightgown," he said, peering at her again. "Your underpants are striped and your . . ."

She flicked off the light.

"That's better. That's much better," he said.

Now the only light came from the open bathroom. She reached behind the bedroom door for her bathrobe, which she buttoned to her knees before turning around.

He was dialing the phone again. "Nobody's home," he sighed, hanging up. "Now what do I do? I don't feel so good."

He laughed when she set the aspirin bottle and water in front of him. In the half-darkness, he seemed calmer. She opened a box of saltines and poured him a glass of milk; she remembered doing this in the middle of the night when her father had stomach trouble.

He was talking about his wife. He laughed and put his hand to his mouth. "She's fat," he whispered. "I gotta be careful. She's married to

MARY McGARRY MORRIS

this tough little guy. He's an insurance agent in Boston. I write her these long, horny letters. She's got a secret post-office box I send them to. And once a year I go there and we get a room and old Hal thinks she's with her old roommate—which, of course, she is." He laughed. "It's very romantic," he sighed, and then he frowned. "You think it's very romantic?"

"I don't know."

Dismal and gray, all his worn features slackening, his stare fixed on her. "Actually, it's sad. It's very, very sad. A whole month after, I'm no good. I can't eat. I can't sleep. I drink too much. I talk too much." He tapped his watch. "It's been almost a month. So by tomorrow I should be feeling better." He sighed. "It gets worse every year. Takes longer and longer to get back on track. And you know what the worst of it is? Every year I realize how much I gave up, roaming around all that time, thinking I was some hot-ass genius, thinking all I needed was a . . . a cabin somewhere or a patron or a grant, so I could write decent again. So I could just finish something. And every year she looks fatter and happier, and this time it hit me." He leaned across the table and whispered, "She's so damn glad she's got what she's got. I mean, one look at me and she's GOTTA be grateful to old Hal, right?" He shook his head in amazement. "Jesus Christ, I'M even grateful to old Hal. If it wasn't for him, I don't know what would've become of my kids. You know, he made them go to church every Sunday and holy day of obligation and wash the car every Saturday and change the oil every three thousand miles and go to college. All three of them! They know about things like OPEC and prime rates and the best shoes, and cars I've never even heard of. Sometimes I don't even know what the hell they're talking about. Hey!" He waved both arms. "C'mere and sit down. C'mon!" he said, gesturing until she sat down. "Sit like this," he said, demonstrating, his elbow on the table and his hand visoring his brow. "Are you Catholic?"

"No."

"Well, that's even better, then. You don't know what the hell I'm talking about. Okay, close your eyes," he said, and when she did, he leaned so close his breath grazed her cheek. "Bless me, Martha, for I have sinned," he whispered. "I have lied and cheated and stolen things. I have fornicated and I have been slothful and cruel and, sweet Jesus help me, I have never voted. But for all my sins, I am most sorry for being cruel. . . . No! I take that back. I'm most sorry for being a shithead. Well, actually, I guess it's the same thing. So I am most sorry for being a cruel shithead. Okay, give me absolution. I'm waiting!" He grabbed her hand, and she opened her eyes to see his hand waving. He opened one eye. "I'm forgiving us both. This is gonna take a few minutes, because you got some mighty bad sins in your past." She tried to pull away and he laughed. "I'm only kidding," he said. "I'm kidding." Still holding her hand, he looked at her. "Tell me something, what's your tribe? You're a Tasaday, aren't you?"

He gripped her fingers so fiercely they cracked. His smile was thin and mocking. "You're like some primitive thing that's never been spoiled. Like a creature that's never stepped out of the jungle. Nothing touches you, does it? You might as well live in a glass cocoon."

He held her hand in both of his. His bright watery eyes and the turmoil of his words reminded her of his angry, battling swim earlier, in the pool.

"I would like a drink," he said, getting up quickly. "I'm absolutely— what's the word, what's the word—incubating! Incubating! Things are happening." He struck his breast. "Germinating! I can feel all the hard seedpods swelling and softening. It's been a long time," he said, returning to the table. He bent and put his hands on her face. "For once I'm going to shut up. I'm not going to say another word! I want you to tell me things. Promise me you will. Promise you'll talk to me all night. Promise?" He was squeezing her cheeks. His eyes kept closing.

"About what?" she whispered, afraid to move.

"About everything!" he growled, his face meeting hers, his mouth open and wet, his teeth gnashing at her lips. He got up, and she touched her mouth to see if it was bleeding. She wasn't sure, but she thought she had just been kissed.

He was in the kitchen, searching through the cupboards, until he found her father's Scotch, which he set on the table with two glasses. She refused a drink, but when he insisted, she managed one fiery sip. She wiped her eyes and sniffed.

"Now, next time take two sips," he said, and downed the rest of hers in one gulp. "Then three, then four. Build up. Acquire a taste for it. Before you know it, you and Frannie'll be out there every night, belting 'em down, having a hell of a time."

As he drank, he told her he had been a high-school English teacher before his book came out. He had tried teaching a few times since then, but that had been years ago. "Oh shit!" he groaned, burying his face in his hands, strands of his hair hanging over his stained, nicked fingers.

She kept thinking of his mouth on hers, his harsh smell still in her nostrils. She felt that same danger, that paralyzing sense of inevitability, she would get when she and her father used to climb Loomis's ledge behind the lake. If she looked straight up, the huge tilted, balanced boulders would seem, in the sun's glare, to teeter, to shift, their movement so slight, so fractional, that with a blink it felt as if she were witnessing the misalignment, the plate-wrenching shudder, of the earth itself.

"Mind if I ask you something?" He peered sourly at her. "How old are you?"

"Thirty-two," she said, and the word tasted bad.

"Where'd you go today?"

"To see my friend."

"Who's your friend? Not that fucking Getso, I hope," he said with a bitter chuckle. "Next time I'll break more'n his fucking window, windshield." He flipped his hand. "Whatever." His eyes half closed, he laughed. "So tell me about your friend. What's your friend's name?"

"Birdy." Just saying it made her feel better.

"Birdy! You don't have a friend named Birdy!" He pointed at her. "See, you're laughing. You made it up, right? You figure, This fucking Mackey, I can tell this asshole anything, he's so screwed up." He shook his head. "Birdy! Whoever heard of Birdy!"

"Birdy Dusser! There really is such a person! She's my best friend.

We used to work together. I told you about her and how Getso stole the money. Remember?"

"Oh yah, fucking Getso. It always comes back to fucking Getso." His head bobbed up and then down, and she thought he had fallen asleep in the chair.

"Mr. Mackey?" she said, and his eyes opened.

"Birdy! Whoever heard of Birdy," he muttered, wiping his mouth with the back of his hand.

She was afraid if he didn't keep talking he was going to fall asleep right here in her kitchen. "See?" She showed him the plastic bowl she kept on the table. "Birdy gave me this," she said, snapping the blue lid off, then sealing it back on.

He took it and peered dully at it. "What's this Birdy?" His eyes closed, and the bowl rolled onto the floor.

She picked it up. "Well, they had all sizes, and I almost got the DeluxeWare set, but they said I didn't really need it living alone, well, where I was living. In the boardinghouse, that is." She took a breath. "I really wanted that set. I really did." She kept nodding. She was getting upset. Why was she telling him about the PlastiqueWare and snapping this lid off and on, off and on? Now he was awake and looking up at her with a kind of horror. "She was so nice. Her mother's a crossing guard at a school I used to go by on my way to work. Once she stopped all the cars and made them wait for me to cross and I was so embarrassed," she said, her face flaming even now with the memory, "I thought I was going to faint. I did," she said, rubbing her arm and shrugging. "I was halfway across and all the drivers on both sides were all staring at me and it felt like I couldn't breathe or swallow. It was awful. It felt like I was way high up, with everyone down there watching me, and then finally I made it to the other side and later Birdy came up to me and she said how her mother had called and asked if I was sick. And I said, 'Tell her not to ever do that again.' That I'd cross myself. That she should tell her mother to leave me alone!" She looked at him and he stared back with glazed eyes. "I shouldn't have said that to her," she tried to explain. "I mean, it was my fault." This was awful. What was she talking about what was she talking about what was she talking about. Oh God. She cleared her throat. Sweat trickled down her sides.

Muttering, he put both hands on the table and tried to get up, but he slid back into the chair. Drool shone on a corner of his mouth as he held his head back to focus his bleary eyes. He managed to move the chair back and stand up. "You've been very kind," he said, leaning his long marred fingers along the tabletop, to feel his way. "I'll just sit here a minute," he said, and sighed himself onto the hard brown couch. "And then I'll be gone and will not pass this way again. Ever," he said, his head bobbing. "I promise," he whispered as his eyes closed.

She waited ten minutes, then bent and gently prodded his arm. "Mr. Mackey. Wake up, Mr. Mackey. You have to go. You have to wake up. It's one in the morning, Mr. . . ."

His eyes flared open. "Get your fucking hand off me, bitch," he snarled.

"You get out of here!" she shrieked.

He reached up and snatched off her glasses and tucked them under his arm. "Good night," he sighed, and sank into a deep flaccid-faced sleep.

She closed the door softly behind her. She tiptoed quickly down the stairs and let herself into the house, careful not to turn on a light or make a sound that might rouse Frances. She went straight to the study and curled up on the cool leather sofa.

—◻—

Bang! Bang! Bang! Bang!

The room was blurred with sunshine. Jumping up, she stubbed her toe on the massive claw base of the oak coffee table then limped blindly into the kitchen. He was outside, hammering boards onto the deck. Without her glasses she couldn't see what time it was. She stood directly under the clock, tilting her head and squinting, but its face seemed handless. She pulled a chair from the table over to the wall and climbed up and peered at its face.

"What're you doing?" Frances groaned from the doorway.

Startled, she teetered, bracing herself against the wall. "Just trying to see what time it is. I don't have my glasses." She gestured toward the garage. "I forgot them."

Frances was at the window. "It's seven o'clock." She yawned, leaning over the sink. "And look at him out there. Where's his car? My Lord, he must have walked." She began to make the coffee. "At least he's reliable."

———□———

Her glasses were crooked, the right lens riding higher than the left, giving her a startled, contorted look. She couldn't bend them any more than she already had; the wrenched hinge was barely attached. She had found them in the apartment, wedged behind the sofa cushion.

It was mid-afternoon and she had cleaned all the bathrooms in the house. Before leaving for the club this morning, Frances had asked her to clean the bathrooms and mop the kitchen floor.

She wrung out the mop in the bucket of warm water and ammonia. She had started to draw the mop back and forth when there was a hard rap at the door.

"Martha? Martha, it's me, Mack. Martha, I'd like to talk to you. I want to apologize," he said after a pause. "I feel really lousy about how I acted. . . . Martha?"

He told her through the latched screen that, while he wasn't exactly sure what he'd said last night, he knew he had acted like an ass.

"I'm very sorry. I really am. Will you forgive me for every stupid, insensitive, asinine thing I'm sure I said?" He brought his unshaven face close to the screen. "What happened to your glasses?" He winced. "Oh. I did that, didn't I?"

Because he insisted he could fix them, she let him in. As he hunched over the table, working on the hinge with tweezers and a pen knife, he thanked her for not saying anything to Frances. "She thinks I couldn't wait to get back on the job. What she doesn't know is, that's my penance. It's how I prove I'm not a bum—not yet." He glanced up at her. "Not as long as I can get up the next morning and kill myself working. Here," he said, his hands shaking, as he held out the glasses.

MARY MCGARRY MORRIS

They were tighter, but still crooked.

Standing in front of her, he studied them, dipping his knees to be eye level with her. "They're still off. The right's up too high. But I'm afraid I'll snap the hinge if I tighten it any more."

"That's okay," she said, turning from his anxious scrutiny when she realized she had been staring at his mouth. The mouth that had been on hers.

———□———

A long black limousine pulled into the driveway. The driver wore black pants, a short-sleeved white shirt, and a black tie. He got out and put on his suit jacket. He tightened the knot on his tie with a nervous glance up at the house, then reached onto the seat for something that was long and bright yellow and hung on a coat hanger. As he walked toward the house, she recognized Wesley Mount. Mack stopped hammering and stood up.

"Can I help you?" he called, wiping sweat from his eyes.

"Uh, yes. If you would, please. My name is Wesley Mount, and I'm looking for Martha Horgan."

"You delivering something?"

"Well, in a manner of speaking, yes," Wesley said, raising her raincoat. She ducked back from the window.

"I'll see that she gets it," Mack said, wiping his hands on his pants. He reached for the coat, and Mount drew it back.

"Actually, I'd like to see Martha, if I could. If that wouldn't be any kind of imposition." He gestured apologetically with the raincoat. "Particularly since I see you're right square in the middle of quite a project here. Quite a project!"

Mack tilted his head and chuckled. "Well, I certainly am," he said, managing to sound just like Mount. "But you wait here and I'll see if Martha's around."

"Thank you! I do appreciate it!" Wesley Mount nodded.

Mack returned the nod with equal vigor. "I'm sure you do!" He grinned.

"Martha!" Wesley smiled, his cheeks reddening, when he saw her in the doorway. Mack jumped off the skeletal deck and dumped a can of nails onto a flat paper bag, to sort through them.

"I ran into Loiselle Evans," Wesley said, "and when I asked if she or any of the ladies had heard from you, she informed me they hadn't. She was quite concerned about your raincoat still being there. She reminded me that we've had quite a few storms already, with one predicted tonight, as a matter of fact. So I told her, no problem, I'd run it right on up to you." He held up the raincoat again, and Mack took it and passed it to her.

"Thank you," she said, wetting her finger and rubbing intently at a spot on the sleeve to avoid the look of amusement on Mack's face.

"You're welcome." Wesley nodded. He started to turn, then looked back at her. "Oh! Careless of me," he said, tapping his temple. "I almost forgot. I don't know if you're at all familiar with the Atkinson Choral Society, of which I'm a longtime member, but, in any event, we're having our annual dinner-dance and installation of officers this week. Saturday night, as a matter of fact. And though I quite understand that this invitation is proffered on extremely short notice, I'd be honored if you'd accompany me." He blinked and licked his dry, quivering lips.

Neither one spoke. She hugged the raincoat. Mack looked back and forth between the two of them. "She have to buy her own ticket?" he asked.

"Oh my Lord, no!" Wesley said, flustered, addressing Mack. "All Martha has to do is have a good time."

Mack nodded. "Sounds like a good deal. Free eats. Good time. Good music?"

"Oh yes! There's a few of us doing a brief Handel presentation. Actually," Wesley said, leaning forward and lowering his voice, "it's an absolute surprise. The presentation, that is."

"You're kidding!" Mack said.

"No, I am not!" Wesley said with an eager shiver. "We've been preparing for weeks now."

"I can't," Martha said, and she swallowed hard. "Thank you for my raincoat. I have to go in now." She closed the door and fled into the study, where she turned the television up high. "Leave me alone, leave me alone, leave me alone, leave me alone," she pleaded under her breath.

"Excuse me," Mack said, opening the door. "This isn't any of my business. But who was that?"

She told him, and he seemed to be struggling not to laugh.

"So you do know him? It's not like you never knew him or anything." He shrugged. "So why not go? I mean, the Choral Society, Handel, dinner, it's not like the Hell's Angels or anything. You should go!"

"I don't want to go!" Arms folded, she stared at the television.

"But you'd probably have a good time! A few drinks, a lotta laughs . . . Well, scratch that, maybe with him a lotta drinks and just a few laughs. But either way you'd have a good time."

She glanced at him. "I don't go out on dates!"

"Why?" he said with a laugh.

"I just don't!"

He was quiet for a moment, studying her again. "You mean, you've never gone on a date?"

"Yes!" she lied. "I've gone on dates. I just don't go on them anymore."

"Why? Did you have a bad experience, or some long relationship or something that didn't work out?"

"No. Well, I guess so." She looked right at him. "Yes."

"Who'd you go with?"

"You don't know him, so never mind!" She thumped her chest.

He chuckled. "That's right, so tell me! What difference does it make?"

The girls in high school used to talk like this. And if they caught her listening, they'd ask her, Who do you like, Martha? Come on now, you can tell us.

"None of your business," she said, which was just what she used to tell them.

"C'mon! I spilled my guts to you last night and now you won't even trust me enough to tell me who you went out with?"

"His name's Billy Chelsea." Her face flushed at the mention of last night.

"I met him! That's the guy down the road, with the little girls. Nice guy."

She looked up and could barely see him, her eyes burned so. "That's not true. I hate to lie. I hate liars! I never went out with him."

Mack looked at her sadly. "Well, then, maybe he's not such a nice guy."

ELEVEN

———□———

Tonight she felt very sad. She lay in the tub with her eyes closed. It was almost midnight. The candle on the back of the toilet had burned itself out, and she hugged herself under the still, cold water. She had tried picturing herself with Mack, but it wouldn't work. All she could think of was Birdy. She shouldn't have spoken to Birdy the way she had. The poor thing had enough troubles. Birdy must have known all along that Getso was stealing.

Maybe she wasn't protecting him. Maybe she had been too afraid of him to defend Martha. Maybe she was afraid of what he might do to Martha. That was it. Of course. He was probably still stealing, but Birdy was trying to protect her. Suddenly it was all coming clear. Getso was planning to set Birdy up the same way he had set her up. That was it. Of course. Oh, poor poor Birdy, being lured into that snake's nest.

She was climbing out of the tub when she remembered the names of Birdy's next-door neighbors. George and Lee Penny. "Penny-PennyPenny," she kept saying as she wrapped a towel around herself and ran to the phone book. Their number was right at the top of the page.

"Hello!" a woman answered anxiously on the first ring.

"Hello," Martha said, as calmly as she could manage. She had to keep swallowing. A clock had begun to tick in her head. "I was wondering if you could help me. I'm a friend of Birdy Dusser's and I don't have her new number and I have to talk to her right away. It's an emergency."

"Who is this?"

"I told you! A friend of Birdy's."

There was a pause. "Birdy's friends all know her new number."

"Well, I'm sorry, but I don't, and I'm a really close friend of hers and this is a very, very important phone call. I mean, this is serious! Someone wants to hurt her very much and I've got to tell her before it's too late!"

"Who is this? Tell me your name, and I'll give you the number."

"Martha Horgan."

The phone went dead. When she dialed again, the line was busy. She slumped against the refrigerator, numb with the realization that Getso had even turned Birdy's neighbors against her. That such a cruel, vile man could be so powerful was terrifying.

She looked up. Outside, the stairs creaked. They creaked again, and she darted into the bathroom and put on her nightgown and robe. There were three faint taps on the door. She came out of the bathroom to find Mack, staring dismally through the glass at her. She opened the door the length of the chain.

MARY MCGARRY MORRIS

"Sorry to bother you so late," he whispered, "but the guy I've been staying with, his wife won't let me in."

"You can't stay here!"

"Listen, I wouldn't have bothered you, but I'm in a real bind here. I parked way behind this old factory, and just as I'm falling asleep, a cruiser pulls in and the cop says, if I don't have a place to stay, he's got one for me—jail."

"Then go ask Frances!" She started to close the door, but he stuck his arm in, and she pulled the door back quickly, afraid she had hurt him.

"She already said no the other day. Look, I was really drunk last night. I was way out of line. But I'm stone-cold sober now. I'd just as soon sleep in the car, but I can't end up in jail again. I can't get a room and I haven't even got gas money to get the hell out of here. She won't pay me until the job's done. Martha, I'm like some kind of prisoner here, with this windshield thing. I can't leave. I can't stay. It's like this weird trap I'm caught in." He looked as panicky as he sounded.

She closed the door to release the chain. When she opened it, he had gone down to the bottom step. He looked back, then ran up the stairs, grinning.

She gave him sheets and a pillow for the couch, and a towel and a face cloth. He came out of the bathroom smelling of soap and toothpaste, and she hung up the phone. The Pennys' line was still busy. She stood in front of the cupboards, moving around the few cans and boxes left in there. "Would you like some iced tea or fruit cocktail or anything?"

"No thanks," he said, whipping open the sheet onto the couch. "I'll be asleep in no time. I'm beat," he sighed, lying down. He stretched out his arms and legs.

"There's a little box of raisins here."

"No thanks."

She pushed aside a can of crackers. Her hand jerked back at the touch of dry mouse-droppings on the shelf and she slammed the cupboard door. She opened the refrigerator. "Want some apple juice?" she asked, needing to linger by the phone just a while longer. Maybe the

Pennys' line was busy because Lee Penny was relaying her warning to Birdy right now.

"No thanks."

She closed the refrigerator and dialed the Pennys' number again. Still busy. She said good night and went into the bedroom and closed her door, but every time she closed her eyes she saw Getso's sly face slide over the cash drawer. She got out of bed and tiptoed past Mack, snoring on the couch.

The Pennys' number was still busy. She kept hanging up, then dialing again, faster and faster, because now the busy signals sounded different, fainter, briefer, as if she were actually penetrating some barrier, as if she were working her way into Birdy's consciousness, getting so close now that she was sure she could hear their voices beyond the incessant signal. "Birdy!" she whispered into the phone. "Birdy! Birdy, it's me, Martha!"

"Martha?" answered a man's voice, and she turned, startled to see Mack up on one elbow, watching her through the darkness. "What's wrong?"

She tried to explain it to him.

"You're obsessed with this, aren't you?" he said.

"I'm not obsessed!" she said angrily. "I just want the truth to come out, and I don't want Birdy to get in trouble."

"But she obviously doesn't want to hear it, Martha, and that's something you can't force. The truth's right in front of her, but you can't force her to see it."

"No, you don't understand. I'm the only one who knows what he's up to, and he's got it so I can't see her or call her."

Mack yawned. "Then write her a letter."

————— □ —————

When she woke up the next morning, he was already working on the deck. She sat down at the table in the hot little apartment and began her letter. She told Birdy the whole story, relating every detail: the weather that morning, and how Getso's shirt had been yellow and Birdy

MARY MCGARRY MORRIS

had worn red flats and her heart pendant. Birdy would see what a reliable witness she was.

Later in the afternoon, when she saw Mack putting away his tools, she ran out and asked him if he'd do her a favor.

"Name it!" he said. He was in a great mood. He said he was going to buy himself a big steak and find a place to stay. Before Frances had left for the club this morning, she had given him a hundred dollars. She said she was pleased with his work and she figured he could use it.

Martha held out a pen and a sheet of paper. "Would you write and tell Birdy how you saw Getso try to attack me that day?"

"But is that what I saw?" He winced. "Maybe he was trying to help you up, like he said."

She was shocked. "You don't believe me either!" she said, grabbing for the paper. Maybe they were in on this together; maybe this was even bigger than she thought.

"I'll write it!" He leaned over the workbench, writing, and when he finished, he read, "Last week, I witnessed Martha Horgan struggling with a man named Getso, who in my opinion intended to cause her harm. Most sincerely yours, Colin B. Mackey." He folded the paper, and she put it in the envelope with her own letter and asked him if he would mail it when he got to town.

"You won't forget, now," she called as he got into his car.

"First mailbox I see," he said, waving it out the window as he drove by her.

"Don't lose it!" she called uneasily.

"Don't worry!" he called back.

She was lying on the couch, watching television, when Frances buzzed her on the intercom to say she was home. She asked what time Mack had left today.

"Five, I think."

"His car was in front of Brennan's," Frances said disgustedly of Atkinson's most notorious bar. "I suppose that's the last we'll see of Mr. Mackey."

The post office was near Brennan's. The letter would be delivered tomorrow. Tomorrow the phone would ring and it would be Birdy, sobbing and begging her to come back to work.

"Martha?"

"What?"

"I asked you if he said anything before he left. Something's up with him," Frances said. "It's been bothering me all day."

———□———

It was midnight. All the lights in the house were off. Frances had gone to bed soon after she got home. Martha was in her nightgown, brushing her teeth while she walked around the apartment and turned off the lights. She had just come out of the bathroom when she saw Mack grinning at her through the door glass. He held up a paper bag and jiggled the doorknob.

"I got you something," he whispered, handing her the bag when she opened the door.

"Did you mail it?"

"Mail it?" He frowned.

"My letter."

"Oh. Oh yah, the letter. Don't worry about it. Open the bag!" He smiled, watching her.

It was a large square plastic container.

"Take the top off."

When she did, she found a smaller container, and in that, another one; in all there were six, all nested under blue lids.

"Thank you," she said, stunned that he had remembered.

"You like them?" he asked, flopping onto the couch.

"They're very nice . . . but you can't stay here," she blurted.

"It's a whole set," he said.

"I know. They're very nice." She nodded, still standing. "I like that blue. But you can't . . . ."

"Like your eyes," he interrupted.

"My eyes are brown."

"No! No, they're not."

"Yes, they are! They're brown!" she insisted. She laughed. "I should know."

He dragged himself up. "Poor kid," he said, coming toward her unsteadily. "All this time you thought they were brown." He anchored himself on the back of the chair, and she knew by his dull stare that he had been drinking. "They're blue. . . . Lemme see here," he murmured, lifting her crooked glasses.

Opening her eyes wide, she saw his eyes close. His mouth was soft and wet. He pushed back her hair with both hands and kissed her eyes and her ears and her neck. He led her to the couch, hugging her so tightly that his hairy forearm rubbed her chin. He sank down and pulled her next to him.

"I kept thinking about you all night. You been thinking about me?"

She nodded. She had been thinking about him mailing her letter.

He laughed. "No, you haven't. You've been thinking about Birdy and Getso and calling people, that's all you've been thinking about."

She tensed. He was making fun of her. She tried to get up, but he held her tight.

"Well, instead of thinking about them all the time, I want you to think about . . . about me! How's that sound? From now on, we're gonna practice good mental health, the two of us. You, you think about me instead of Birdy and whatsisname, and me, I think about you instead of my own personal obsession, which is what a flaming shithead I am." He leaned toward her and sighed. "You're mad at me. Don't!" he breathed at her ear. "Don't be mad at me. I like you. And you like me, don't you? And neither one of us knows why." He kept talking like this, muttering, almost arguing, scolding himself and her, as his hands ran up and down her hairy legs and belly and breasts. "You think I'm just some bum, don't you? You don't understand. How the hell could you? I don't even understand. But I'll tell you this, you feel so good . . . you feel so warm and so soft."

He slipped her nightgown from her shoulders to her waist. Her eyes closed at the shameful sight of her nipples shriveling on her heavy breasts, then opened wide as his rough cheek scratched her belly. She moaned and raked her fingers through his hair. She couldn't think. He had crawled into her brain, swelling her skull with his pounding heat.

"Mack," she groaned, bending over him. "Mack!" But his only response was a warning growl. He had fallen asleep with his head in her lap.

———□———

She woke to the persistent song of a bird even though it was dark outside. She stared up at the ceiling fan over her bed and wondered if he was still on the couch. His snoring had awakened her at different times through the night. But now everything was still.

"Shit!" she heard him suddenly mutter, then curse again in weary, muffled tones. Water ran in the sink. The cupboard doors creaked open, then shut with a heedless bang. It was quiet again for a little while. And then her door opened. He came to the side of her bed, and she grinned so foolishly that she covered her mouth with the back of her hand and bit it. He said her name, then jiggled the bed with his knee.

"I feel sick," he whispered, exuding the hot breath of the Scotch he had just helped himself to. He said he had looked in the bathroom and kitchen for something for his stomach but hadn't been able to find anything.

"If you don't mind. I hate to bother you," he muttered after her.

When she returned, he was sitting on the side of the bed, with his eyes closed. She shook the bottle, then poured the glutinous pink liquid into a shot glass.

He gulped it down. "I'm a son of a bitch to be imposing on you like this," he said, fumbling to set the glass on the nightstand. It tipped, and he let it roll near the edge. He buried his face in his hands. "Jesus Christ," he moaned.

"Are you sick?" she asked, stepping closer.

"I'm dying. Christ almighty. I don't know what the hell I'm thinking of." He looked up at her through the fraying darkness.

There was a sudden intensity to the window light, as if it did not come from the rising sun but had been smoldering all along within the night itself. The sun didn't matter, she thought, looking toward the brightening shade, for it seemed right now utterly within her power to fill the stale little room with whatever degree of light she wished.

"I'm too old for this shit," he muttered, kneading his eyes with his knuckles. "What the hell am I doing? Christ, twenty years have just gone like that," he said with a weak snap of his fingers. "The next twenty'll go even faster, and here I am at the end of the line. I got nothing left. My last friend tells me he's sick of my whining." He laughed bitterly. "HE'S sick of it! Oh Christ, Colin Mackey, what a fucking fucking loser you are!"

He took a deep breath and raised his head sheepishly. "It's not easy being a professional asshole. I gotta find a new line of work. This is taking its toll." He reached for her hand. "I'm sorry. I seem to have a real knack for taking advantage of good people." He started to get up.

She sat beside him quickly, her hands folded in her lap. "If you want, you can stay there. You can go to sleep." Her hair fluttered in the quiet stir of the fan. He didn't move or say anything. Biting her lip, she held her eyes tightly closed, her body tensed. Stupid Martha, she thought. He didn't want to sleep here. He wanted to leave, but he didn't know how now that she had said that, now that she had plunked herself down, almost on top of him. She tried to clear her throat.

His arms slipped around her. "Don't cry," he whispered, his voice breaking. He lay back with her, lifted her nightgown, kissed her. He took her hand and slid it between his legs, his laugh quick and harsh as she pulled back, startled by the thick coldness there. He had to help her, parting her legs, and after a moment's fumble, the bed creaked and rattled, its headboard banging crazily back and forth against the wall as if propelled by an engine gone mad with the heat and their gasping and the ceiling fan, an enormous gear, spinning round and round, not only turning the earth, but fusing in place every star and planet. It became all she could hear, her head tossing and turning, until suddenly she cried out in a loud unfamiliar voice, "Oh God. Oh my God! Oh . . . oh . . . please . . . please!"

It was over.

A DANGEROUS WOMAN

"Quiet!" he gasped and clamped his hand over her panting mouth, his face slick with sweat that dripped onto her face. She could see the little gray and black hairs in his nose tremble as he breathed.

"I thought I heard something!" he warned, getting up. He stood by the window.

She covered her mouth with both hands to muffle the one word perched on her tongue, straining and beating its wings.

"If I had a gun right now, I'd blow my fucking brains out," he said, staring down into the shadows.

TWELVE

He had been avoiding her for days. When she came near him, his hammer struck double-time. Unintelligible grunts and curt nods were his replies when she spoke.

"Would you like a sandwich?" she asked, coming into the kitchen and finding him at the refrigerator.

"Frances said to help myself," he said, wincing.

"I made some tuna." She grinned, recalling the salty taste of his dark, dusty shoulders.

"Maybe later," he muttered, and hurried outside.

———□———

The next morning, she went into town with Frances to check on the new stone on her father's grave. They planted red geraniums at the base of the marble marker, then bent their heads as if in prayer. With the sun's heat on her head and the rough fresh scent of the geraniums on her hands and the smothering drone of bees all she could think of was Mack, her lover, with whom she had made love, by whom she was loved; her beloved. When she opened her eyes, she reeled dizzily to see, in the bright-green sweep of mica-flecked tombstones, a beautiful elm tree, its height and symmetry suddenly so startling that for a moment she couldn't breathe. The world had become a perfect place.

Frances was calling for her to come.

"I miss Floyd," Frances said when she caught up to her.

Martha turned her head to rub away a smile. She missed Mack, who by making her body his had made it finally hers, swathed with an unfamiliar grace. She smiled out the blurred side window as Frances drove her to the bus stop. That she was just like everyone else amazed her. All of her, all her parts were real, her limbs and organs finally blessed by love. She watched a young girl ride by on her bike, then stop alongside as the light turned red. In a glance their eyes met, and Martha smiled and did not look away. She had these arms, these legs, and, inside, this violent heart, and she was a woman. A woman who had been loved. The girl lowered her head to the handlebars before she sped past the changing light. Suddenly Martha felt too alive, too bright, as fragile as one of Mr. Beecham's glass pieces.

"Could you straighten up the downstairs when you get back, and make some ice cubes?" Frances asked before Martha got out of the car at the bus stop. Frances was on her way to the club. She had offered to take Martha grocery shopping, but Martha wasn't interested now that eating in the house had become a way to be near Mack. At night she hardly slept, listening for his tap at the door, but he hadn't been back. Yesterday she had worked up her courage to ask him if he had gotten a room in town. "I'm all set," he had muttered.

"There'll be some people by later. Just a few," Frances was saying, and Martha knew by the sigh that Steve Bell wouldn't be among them. The most he and Frances had managed lately were long late-night telephone conversations. His daughters demanded his complete attention to their mother's recovery. "Fools," Frances had scoffed. "They don't know what they're doing." Now Frances's bitterness included these mousy girls, whose hungry affection she had always solicited and possessed over the years, often to Martha's great envy. But she couldn't gloat or feel the least bit smug now at Frances's unhappiness, not when she felt so good, so full of Mack.

He was confused, she told herself, taking a seat in the back of the bus, where she would be alone to think. She would be patient and pleasant, and then he would snap out of this gloom. Self-control, she whispered to herself, wadding the tissue in her lap to bits that clung to her dark skirt. She had even started to dress up more at home. "Self-control," she whispered, nodding emphatically at her reflection in the grime of the metal-banded window. "I won't get mad. I won't yell. And I won't tell any more of those stupid stories about myself! No, I won't!" she vowed, rubbing her arm. "Think before you speak, Martha Horgan! Oh, I will! I will!" She nodded, her smile fading when she saw the two smirking teenage girls peek around their seats at her, at Martha Horgan, Marthorgan, talking to herself, but talking about love, something they knew nothing about.

———□———

He was painting the deck when she got home. The long walk up the hot mountain road had drained her. Her feet were sore and she was sweating. He had attached a paint roller to a broom handle, which he worked back and forth in careful swaths of pale-gray paint.

"It looks nice," she called, coming toward him, shading her eyes.

"You've done a beautiful job." She stood there. "Very nice!" she called louder.

He muttered something, then turned and started to paint a new section.

"Does Frances like it?" she asked, moving below the railing so that she walked beside him as he worked. She looked up and repeated her question in a louder voice.

"I guess so," he said, pausing to reload the roller, working it back and forth in the paint tray.

She watched him paint this corner section, then take the empty tray down the steps to the paint cans that were on a tarpaulin in the shade. She stood behind him while he squatted down and stirred the thick paint with a long screwdriver.

"My father had a special paddle for stirring paint. He made it himself. Want me to get it?" she asked eagerly, bending over him. "I know right where it is."

"I'm all set," he said, pouring paint into his tray. He carried it back to the deck.

"He wouldn't ever use a roller," she said, on his heels. "He always used brushes. But that looks nice," she assured him, afraid she had sounded critical. She peered through the balusters at the wet gleaming boards. Her head hurt. Her mouth was dry.

The sky was that perfect blue that is the cobalt of purest air. The small square windowpanes above them gleamed in the sun, and now there appeared, in the pattern of red and blackish and white-washed bricks, a line she had never noticed before, a jagged fissure from the upper left-hand eave down to the granite lintel over the door. She blinked and it was gone, then blinked and saw it jump again, a lightning bolt of split mortar.

"Why won't you talk to me?" she was demanding in that thick, dull, obdurate voice she would never be free of. "Why are you mad at me? What did I do wrong? I don't understand why you're mad. I don't know what I did. Tell me what I did! Tell me why you're mad!"

MARY MCGARRY MORRIS

He jumped off the deck. "I'm not mad! Stop it! Just stop it!" he said, scrubbing his hands furiously with a rag.

"Why won't you talk to me? If you're not mad, then why won't you talk to me?" Oh God, there it was, that singsonging ugly rhythm, her head tossing back and forth, her chest sucking up and down. "Why? Tell me why!"

"Martha! Stop that!" he said.

"What's wrong with me? Why can't you talk to me?" She jabbed his chest. "What's wrong with me?"

"Nothing's wrong with you." His eyes darted everywhere.

"You can't even look at me."

"What if Frances comes? She'll have me out of here in two seconds!"

"I don't care about Frances! I just care about us!"

His head jolted back. "Martha, I don't want to hurt you!"

"You don't hurt me!" she said, surprised. She smiled. Hurt? How could loving someone as much as she loved him ever hurt?

"I hurt everyone! I've hurt everyone I've ever laid my hands on!" he shouted over her objections.

"No! No, you don't!" she cried.

"Yes, I do! Everyone! I'm like her, like that bitch Frances, cold and selfish and harmful! I feed on weakness! I suck up what I need, and it disgusts me! Do you understand? Do you?" he demanded, his marred face at hers. "I don't want to hurt you. Especially you. I'm sorry for what happened. I took advantage of . . . Martha? Martha, listen to me. I was drunk!"

"But that's all right!"

"No! Martha, please!" He grabbed her arm, squeezing it. "As soon as I'm done here, I'm leaving. There's nothing between us. Do you understand that what happened was so disgusting I feel sick when I think of it?"

She couldn't say anything. She couldn't even look at him. She stared at the house.

He stepped away from her. "Martha, you're too easy to hurt. You've never been exposed. You don't see what I am. I'm nothing. I'm no good. I'm a bum! And you're . . . you're . . ." He held out his hands. "I don't even know what you are."

Frances's small group had swelled into a party. Frances and Betty Hammond had set a course record today, and so Frances had invited everyone back to the house. Now, with the lowering sun, the mosquitoes had just forced everyone off the pool patio and inside.

Moments ago Martha had been summoned to the house. Mr. Weilman wanted to see her; she didn't have to stay long, Frances assured her, just a quick hello. He was insisting she come over. Everyone considered the old man a nuisance, but what could she do, Frances whispered into the phone, he'd been playing pinochle with Betty's husband.

He was also a relative, in the sense that his deceased wife had been Horace Beecham's cousin. Obviously watching for Martha, he waved as she entered the kitchen. He was tall, thin, and white-haired, with a pale sunken face in which his soft voice seemed oddly lodged, because when he spoke his lips barely moved. "Martha, come sit by me," he said, patting the sofa cushion. "How've you been? I haven't seen you in so long."

"I'm fine," she said, her throat still raw from her outburst with Mack. She felt small and pale. She tried to concentrate on what Mr. Weilman was saying. He was reminding her how in the past when he came to Frances's parties he usually ended up over in the garage workshop. "I learned more from watching your father than I ever did from any other one person," he was saying. "The man was a mechanical genius. In a place like Detroit, he could've named his price and they'd have paid. But you couldn't talk him into it. He'd charted his course and that was that. He was Horace's caretaker, and with someone like your father to oversee his existence, the old man didn't need another soul in his life." Mr. Weilman leaned and whispered behind his hand: "Tell you the truth, I always thought the old man married Frances just as a way of forging one more bond with Floyd." He looked up, grimacing, then winked at her. "Now, don't go telling your aunt I said that."

MARY McGARRY MORRIS

160

The last of the old line, Mr. Weilman had always seemed more like family to Martha than the unmet blood relatives who lived only a few miles from here in the Flatts. A widower since she had been a little girl, he had spent much of his time traveling.

"I'm afraid I've lived a very dull life this last year, shuttling in and out of clinics," he said. "It's been an education in itself. I've discovered that, just as the cancer advances of its own invincibly blind accord, so too does the treatment." His eyes lightened, and she nodded, not at all sure what he was talking about.

"Once the forces are set in motion, there's no stopping them. With my orders in hand, I was shipped from doctor to doctor, from coast to coast, clinic to clinic." He laughed softly. "I began to think of myself as this grand battlefield, like Waterloo or Omdurman. I'd lay on those cold metal tables with that huge cannon trained on me and I could feel the armies lining up, the forces preparing for battle. Many's the day . . ."

A chill went through her as Mack entered the room. His baggy chinos were torn at the waistband, and his long-sleeved blue shirt was wrinkled, with a rust stain down the back. Frances rushed over to him. "Here he is," she said, steering him to a swarm of eagerly rising heads just inside the dining room. He shook hands, nodding, repeating names as they were given. He smiled. In the distance, he was a handsome man, his expression as gracious and watchful as any of theirs. Not at all a bum, she thought with a covetous gaze and her insides aching.

"*The Last Man In!*" Frances announced, then had to repeat it over the din of voices.

"A writer!" said Henry Hammond. "You up here for that Breadloaf thing?"

"Now, don't think I forgot," Mr. Weilman was saying, as he withdrew something from his pocket. "Sea coral," he said. "I found it on the beach last winter in Tortola. I never come empty-handed, do I?" He grinned, handing her the smooth black stone, still warm from his pocket.

"Who's that?" he asked, following her gaze. "One of Frances's new friends?"

When she told him, he repeated Mack's name and sniffed. "Never heard of him." He looked around. "Where's Steve? Seems odd not to have old Steve here."

Together they stared at the two tanned women in gold jewelry and bright sundresses who had just arrived.

"Oh my," Mr. Weilman sighed as each woman brushed cheeks with Frances. "I've got to get back in the swing of things, I can see that."

Mack eased out of the crowded dining room, pretending not to see her as he passed.

"Okay, okay, okay, okay," she whispered, taking deep breaths.

The cold bones of Mr. Weilman's hand settled over hers. "There, now," he crooned softly. "There, there, there."

The two couples by the fireplace looked away quickly and resumed their conversations.

———□———

Now they only talked when Frances was there. Martha had found that he would answer her politely, but nervously, in her aunt's presence. When they were alone, he ignored her. He would be leaving any day now. All that had to be done on the deck was the skirt of latticework underneath. More than once she had considered holding a match to the fragrant new lumber, so that he would have to start over. She was sure he was sleeping in his car at night. His back seat was filled with clothes, and again this morning he had sneaked into the little bathroom off the kitchen to shave. He had been halfway down the hall when the wet bottom of his paper bag had burst and his shaving cream, razor, and cologne had fallen out. He had looked up to see if anyone was around just as Martha had ducked back from the doorway. She watched him all the time now, and every night, just before he drove off, she would run outside with another letter for him to mail to Birdy. The letters seemed to embarrass him; it was almost as if he could tell they were about him, which they were, though she never referred to him by name. This new link to Birdy had become her strength. She knew that Birdy must be reading the letters, because none had been returned to her.

MARY McGARRY MORRIS

Every letter ended with the same warning. Watch out for Getso! Don't trust him! And if Birdy needed help of any kind or someone to talk to, Martha assured her she would be waiting, always.

———o———

Martha's ankles wobbled in her high heels, and all the big white buttons on her dress clattered as she tiptoed down the apartment stairs. She wanted to avoid Frances, who was down in the workshop, examining the shutters Mack had taken down today. When Julia had called this morning to tell Martha she'd be picking her up for dinner tonight, Frances had pretended to hang up, but Martha could tell she had stayed on the extension, listening. Martha came off the bottom step and Frances hurried out of the garage just as Julia's little silver car turned into the driveway. She tapped her horn and waved.

Frances waved back then gripped Martha's wrist. "You still haven't told me what this is all about," she said through a rigid smile. Again she waved at Julia.

"I told you, I don't know."

Mack watched from the doorway.

"With Julia there's always a reason. I mean, you've known her for how many years and suddenly she's taking you out to dinner?"

"I don't even want to go!" She had been a nervous wreck about this all day. She had even called Julia an hour ago to tell her she was sick, but Julia hadn't been home.

"And where did this come from?" Frances pointed at her dress.

"In town," Martha said, flinching.

"Why?" Frances shook her head, looking her up and down. "Why?"

"I told you, I don't know why!"

Mack came toward them with more shutters in his arms.

"I mean, this . . . this thing you have on, this dress," Frances said with a shudder.

"You look very nice, Martha," he said, and Frances looked at him.

"I've got reservations at Ramshead," Julia called over the rush of air through the car's open windows. "It's Frances's second home." Julia laughed. "It's like in the movies. She sweeps in and they all know her name, her favorite table, favorite drink, favorite entrée." She drew up her eyebrows, imitating Frances. "Yes, a vodka gimlet. Of course." She turned onto the road. "I can't believe you've never been there!"

"I don't like restaurants."

"Why?"

"I just don't." She didn't want to tell Julia she never ate in front of strangers, for fear she'd choke on her food.

"You'll like this one, I promise!" Julia smiled.

Martha forced a smile back. Next to Julia, in her simple yellow dress and cotton sweater, she felt overdressed and conspicuous. With every step the buttons on her shoulders rattled and the swishy black and white gores of the skirt tangled around her legs.

In one of the oldest houses in Atkinson, the Ramshead dining rooms were small and pine-paneled, each one catacombing more darkly into the next under smoky low-beamed ceilings. The carpeting was a jarring red-and-green plaid that disoriented her now as she trailed after Julia and the maître d'. Holding her glasses steady, she made her way cautiously past the linen-covered tables that were lit with candles flickering in slender glass chimneys.

"Oh, this is lovely. Just perfect," Julia assured the maître d', a slight, gray-haired man, as he held out her chair and then Martha's.

Martha took a deep wheezy breath and tapped her chest as she slid into her chair. She realized she had sat down too quickly for the maître d' to ease her chair closer to the table the way he had Julia's. With a snap, he shook out their linen napkins. He draped one over Julia's lap, then tried to place the other in Martha's lap, but she had gripped the arms of her chair and was trying to jerk herself closer to the table. With each impact of her knees, the table jumped, the crystal trembled, the flatware rattled, and the candle sputtered, splattering wax on its clear globe. Smiling, the maître d' continued his presentation of napkin and menus.

"Stupid chair," Martha muttered, smoothing out the napkin. "The chair's too big. That's what happened."

MARY McGARRY MORRIS

"Let me get you a smaller one," the maître d' offered, pointing to the opposite corner.

"No!" she insisted, gripping the arms. "I'll keep this one." After he left, she glanced around to see who had been watching. Julia was reading her menu. Heads bent, the couple at the next table held hands, laughing and speaking in low tones.

Julia leaned toward her. "Now, fill me in. Tell me what you've been doing with yourself."

Martha regarded her blankly. "Nothing." She shrugged.

"Nothing! How boring, Martha. Aren't you looking for another job?"

"No." Martha turned the napkin over and smoothed out the other side. Julia's attention was as irritating as this couple staring at her. Every time she turned to catch them, they glanced away.

"Martha?" Julia said sternly. "I was in the Cleaners last week, and Birdy Dusser said she'd seen you."

She looked up, surprised. "Did she say anything else? About me, I mean."

"Well, just that she felt bad you weren't there anymore."

"She said that?" Martha took a deep breath. It was odd how thoughts of Birdy only deepened her longing for Mack. In every one of her letters, she had told Birdy what a fine man he was. Careful not to reveal his name, she only referred to him as HE, capital letters. Though each one began with a salutation to Birdy, it occurred to her now that she had really written them to Mack. A heat stirred low in her belly, and with it a yearning to talk about him, but she didn't know how to begin.

The waiter had brought them wine. Julia lifted her glass. "To cleverness," she said. "To Martha Jane Horgan!"

"Pearl," Martha corrected her. "My middle name is Pearl."

"What a lovely name," Julia said, clinking her glass on Martha's.

"That was my mother's name."

"You know," Julia said, tapping her long pink fingernail on the rim of the butter dish, "the other day I was thinking about you and how last fall you just up and left the only life you'd ever known and how in no time at all you were able to put together a life of your own! That was so exciting!" Julia squeezed her hand. "I was so excited for you, Martha! You did so well!"

She sipped her wine. Grinning, she had this dizzying sensation of watching Julia burrow through a crammed closet, finding each article of clothing she held up, brighter and more colorful than the one before. Now Julia was telling her about the abrupt end of her career after her husband's death. For twelve years she had taught sociology courses at Boston University. And then came a day when she knew it was over. She sold her furniture, gave up her apartment, and loaded her car with the few things she wanted to save from her old life.

"It was so strange. I can still remember it, the very moment. I was walking down the hall, carrying a box of final exams. And all along the way, people said, 'Hello, Mrs. Prine. Hello. Good morning. How are you?' And suddenly everything had changed. Everything looked so different. People I'd known for years suddenly had a . . . a crooked nose I'd never noticed before. Or yellow teeth. Or they had a smell." At this, she looked distressed. "I don't know if I'm putting this very well. But it was as if my time were up. As if something went click and suddenly everything WAS different. Not so much that people had changed, or even that I had changed, but that my time was up in that place, in that order of things. When you don't belong anymore, when there's no place for you, things just don't fit right. They rattle and creak and they sound funny and I guess they even smell! Do you know what I mean?"

Julia poured more wine.

She knew exactly what Julia meant. She meant . . . she meant, she meant something wonderful. It had to do with her heart being filled with Mack and the bite of this pale-yellow wine on her tongue and these words, these words . . . Oh God, it was so wonderful. The dining room had gradually filled, and with it came a conflation of talk, the babies, the scampi, the anniversary, the car he wanted; heads lowered in this intimacy, this communion. Love had assembled them, and she was among them. The woman across the way looked at her. Her fingers grazed a row of buttons. The woman smiled and looked away. Their food was being served.

MARY McGARRY MORRIS

"The same thing happened to you last fall, didn't it?" Julia asked, eating.

"Well, not exactly," Martha said, folding her hands on the edge of the table. "Frances and I had a fight and so I packed a suitcase and I walked all the way into town and in one day I got my room and my job and this dress!" She laughed. "I did more in that one day than I'd ever done! Ever in my whole life!"

Julia's stare made her uneasy. "That . . . that was wonderful! You took charge of your own life, Martha!" she said through clenched teeth. "But why on earth are you back? Why aren't you on your own, doing something?"

The air conditioner vibrated loudly and the room grew damp and chilly as all the voices surged in crosscurrents of dread and accusation, and she had to lean back from her plate, because the odors of garlic and fish and seared red meat suddenly sickened her. She reached for her wine but her hand hit her goblet and water sloshed into her plate.

"Oh, what a shame. We'll get you a new one!" Julia said, lifting her arm for the waiter.

"No!" Martha said, grabbing her wrist and holding it down. "Really. It's fine. I like soup." She laughed nervously, picking up her spoon. "Please don't make a big deal over it. "Please don't." Panic caught in her throat, like a deadly shard of glass any abrupt movement might dislodge, and she sat very still, staring at Julia.

"Of course not," Julia said, staring back. It was in a deft monotone that Julia began to describe her flower garden with its raised and straw-banked beds and her neighbor's fiendish toddler who had beheaded every aster and then she asked about the plans for Steve's birthday party, and by the way who was that man Julia had seen in the driveway when she picked her up tonight?

Martha sighed with relief as Julia pulled her onto this safer shore. She told her about Mack, and his book, which she had seen on the coffee table. She described the worn dust jacket, and its picture of him as a young man with dark curly hair, sideburns, and a thick mustache. "He's very smart. But he does these strange things. At first they scare me and then, then, when I see he's only kidding, then I can laugh. But

A DANGEROUS WOMAN

at first it's hard to know, because of the way he . . . he . . . I don't know what you call it."

"Throws you off balance?"

"Yes! Throws me off balance." Smiling, Martha absently stirred her food. That was exactly what he did.

"Well, I'd be careful of someone like that," Julia said. "Someone like that can be very manipulative."

Martha's head shot up. "Mack's very careful of my feelings! He doesn't want me to be hurt!"

Julia's eyes closed heavily and she took a breath. "That's very kind of him. But I would hope he . . ." She seemed flustered. "It sounds as if you like him. Do you? I mean, in the way a woman likes a man?"

She stared at the mess in her plate, embarrassed by such a personal question.

The busboy poured them both more water. When he left, Julia whispered, "You can tell me. I won't tell anyone. I swear, Martha. I never would."

Eyes lowered, Martha nodded. Suddenly she looked up, grinning so wildly she had to cover her mouth.

"That's nice. That's very nice, Martha," Julia said with wide wet eyes. Her smile twitched and her hard swallow was visible. "This is none of my business. But I'm your friend and I have to ask. Has anything happened?" There was a pause. "I mean, you know, physically."

"No." Unable to look at Julia, she moved the food around in her plate.

Julia sighed. "I'm sorry! I'm so relieved! It's just that, well, you know. Some men, they, they gravitate toward . . . how can I put this . . . toward women with problems. With emotional problems." Her voice had dropped to a whisper. "And you do have those, Martha. Right? You know that? Which is partly why I wanted to have this talk with you tonight. You see, I have this idea. You know about Harmony House, right?"

Yes, she knew about Harmony House.

"Well, that woman who was at the house with me was Tyler Spaulding. She's the new director there, and I've just been appointed to the board," Julia said. "And that night I saw you fixing the toilet I thought, How perfect. And I told Tyler the same thing and she agreed. They could use someone like you, and you'd have a place of your own, right in town, near everything."

"What do you mean? A job? Like what Mrs. Ross does?" Martha asked, naming one of the counselors who used to retrieve Hock when he got too boisterous in the Cleaners.

"All the residents have certain duties. Some, of course, are so simple they're almost token. But someone like you, well, you'd have a great deal of responsibility, Martha. A lot would be expected of you." Julia smiled.

"A resident?" The word repulsed her.

"Yes!" Julia nodded eagerly.

"I'm not retarded!" she exploded. A hush fell over the room. People were looking at her.

"Of course you're not. I know that!" Julia reached for her hand and Martha pulled it off the table.

"I want to go home," she said.

"Martha, listen to me. Harmony House isn't just for the retarded. They deal with many different levels of impairment, intellectual, emotional, psychological, even social. Martha!"

She stood up and pushed her chair in to the table. Julia followed her outside, and no matter how she tried to explain herself, Martha refused to speak to her.

When they pulled into the driveway, Martha opened her purse. "Thank you for dinner," she said, placing a twenty-dollar bill on the dashboard.

"Martha!" Julia sighed, handing the money back. Martha threw it into the back seat and got out. "Listen to me!" Julia cried, following her toward the garage. "I'm sorry! Martha!" She grabbed her purse. "Listen to me!"

"Leave me alone! You just leave me alone!"

"Martha, you don't understand!"

A voice came from inside the garage. "Everything all right out there?" Mack peered around the corner of the building.

Martha ran upstairs. As she unlocked her door, she saw Julia walk back to Mack.

"Nothing better happen to her, do you understand?"

"What the hell're you talking about, lady?"

THIRTEEN

—o—

Mack was gone. For the past twenty-four hours, Martha hadn't seen him. He'd said he'd go and now he had and she was all alone and she knew that for the rest of her life no one would ever love her again. She pulled down all the shades and curled up on the couch in front of the television, not caring if it was morning or afternoon. She watched soap operas and old movies, alert only to the timeless constellation that was love. Everywhere, China, Brooklyn,

Los Angeles, England, men and women kissed with arms around necks, around waists, and then women wept and, from slamming doors, men stalked into the dark streets, the metronome of their footsteps along the pavement the saddest sound she had ever heard. She cried until her eyes were swollen and raw. There were babies born, and rings flung into storm-swirled gutters, and a sweep of brilliant sunsets. Someone was banging on the door. She sat up, rubbing her arms. It was the early morning of another night spent on this hard couch with the television still going. There was a chill in the air, and she clutched her robe at her throat as she opened the door.

Frances pushed it wide and stepped inside. She switched on the overhead light and turned off the television. She talked on and on. Her life, her needs, her problems. Money. Steve. Her responsibility for Martha. The burden it all was. Martha sat on the couch. She said nothing. She felt nothing. Frances declared herself through with any more of these breakdowns. Martha bit her ragged cuticle, chewing as she looked up. There was nothing left to care about, not even Birdy. She was dead inside. She chewed off the rest of her cuticle, then swallowed it.

"I gave you the chance to stay here. But look, look what it's come to." She waved her arm at the sour rooms. "You've got one day to pack your things and move them into the house." She turned to go.

"No!"

Frances spun around. "Or maybe you like Julia's plan! Is that what you want? To live in a home with retarded people? Isn't that nice? People thinking you belong in a place like that. What did you tell her? All of a sudden she's speaking in riddles. For Godssake, Martha, all I'm asking, all I've ever asked, is that you keep things in check, that you stay in control. And if you can't, then I have to."

Martha held her breath, waiting. Julia must have told her about Mack. She recognized the disgust in Frances's eyes, and now all the shame would be dredged up again—that night with the boys, and Frances's horror of people, especially men, getting the wrong idea about her.

"Please don't rock!" Frances said. "Just get up and pack your . . ."

"I'm staying here!" she interrupted. "I don't want to live over there."

"Martha," she began, then sighed. "There's more to this than what

YOU might want. You've seen what I've gone through in the last few years, trying to keep things up. And now, without your father, this place is just about unmanageable. I can't do it alone anymore." Here, now, a point in her eyes sharpened. "I need full-time help and I need it cheap and I think Mack would do it if he had a place to stay."

Martha grinned.

"Oh, you're amused, are you? You seem to be forgetting a very major point here. This is my apartment! My garage! My house! My property!" Frances said, banging her fist on the table. "And I will decide who lives where!"

"All right," she said, trying to bite away her smile. He was still here. And he would stay.

Frances looked at her. "Well, that's good," she said, touching her throat uncertainly.

<hr />

Now that Mack had moved into the apartment, Martha was settled in a large sunny room down the hall from Frances's. She was careful to stay out of his way, and if they found themselves in the same room, she made sure she left first. He was outside now, scraping and repainting the shutters and all the exterior doors, according to Frances's list. At night, when he was through working, he went straight up to his apartment and typed steadily until the early hours of the morning. Now she knew where he was every minute of the day.

Frances's good mood seemed unshakable. Steve had come twice in the last two days. The pressure was off. Anita's therapy seemed to be taking hold. She had even gained a little weight, and today her daughters were taking her shopping in Albany. Steve and Frances were on the deck, finishing their drinks before they went out to dinner. Martha sat at the kitchen table, eating spaghetti she had made. She had offered Mack some earlier, when he came inside looking for Frances, but he said he wasn't hungry, adding, "Thanks anyway."

Thanks anyway, she kept thinking. Thanks anyway, as if she were nobody, as if nothing had happened.

She set down her fork and looked toward the open window, where

A DANGEROUS WOMAN

173

their voices carried in from the deck. It amazed her that Frances could be discussing interest rates now with someone whose sticky pelvis had risen from hers less than an hour before. No sooner had Steve arrived than, arms entwined and hips touching, they had gone quickly up to Frances's room.

Afterward Steve had showered and changed into the new clothes Frances had gotten for him. When he came downstairs, his cheeks buffed pink and his sparse hair wet in long strands across his head, he had greeted Martha with his old exuberance. He had missed her, he said, trying to hug her. Blushing with the thought of where those arms had been, she had stiffened and pulled away.

"They have such hopes for their mother," Steve was telling Frances as they came inside. "They've just given it their all these past two weeks. I don't know what they'll do if she doesn't make it."

"You're not serious!" Frances scoffed. She mixed him another drink. "Good Lord, if they're not used to the merry-go-round by now . . ."

"No! No, this time it's different. She's different," he said.

"It sounds like you're the one with false hope, Steve," Frances said.

"Did I say false hope?" He sounded surprised.

"Yes, you did. You certainly did," Frances said. But Martha knew he hadn't.

"She's here. Finally," Frances said as a car turned into the driveway.

Julia came into the kitchen with Tyler Spaulding, whose eyes went right to Martha.

"Julia!" Frances said sharply. "I only made reservations for three."

"Steve, this is Tyler Spaulding," Julia said, then, with a quick glance, returned Frances's wide-eyed grimace.

"Good to meet you," Steve said, easing the young woman onto the deck, away from Frances's obvious fury.

"Hello, Martha," Julia said as Martha got up to rinse off her plate. She wouldn't even look at Julia.

"What is she doing here?" Frances demanded.

"She just popped in on me." Julia sighed. "You don't mind, do you?"

"You could have told her you had other plans!" Frances said.

"I could have, but I didn't," Julia said with a forced smile. "So let's just go on and make the best of it."

"No!" Frances insisted. "Not this time. I'm sorry!"

"Frannie!" Julia said, looking uneasily toward the deck.

"I don't think you understand. This is the first time in weeks that I've gone out with Steve, and I have no intention of having it ruined by Tyler Spaulding," Frances hissed.

"Frannie! Come on!" Julia coaxed, reaching for her friend's hand. "This isn't like you."

"No!" Frances pulled back. "I'm tired of the way you set me up with these PEOPLE, these bizarre friends of yours."

With the two women by the door, Martha was trapped at the sink. She kept washing the same saucepan.

"Frannie, you are classically overwrought. You're being . . ."

"Oh! Go ahead. Analyze me. Which is exactly what this evening is all about, isn't it? You love putting me under the microscope and watching me squirm!"

"Frannie, I can't believe you're saying these things!"

"No, Julia. What you can't believe is that I'm on to you. From now on, run your own life and stay the hell out of mine!"

Martha turned the water on full-force. Julia picked up her purse from the counter and tried to set the strap on her shoulder, but it kept slipping off.

"I'll tell her I don't feel well," she said.

"You do that," Frances said, going into the living room.

Julia stood behind Martha and sighed. "I didn't mean to insult you the other night," she said in a thin voice. "Or Frances either. I really didn't."

Martha squirted detergent into the saucepan.

———□———

As soon as they were gone, she climbed the stairs to the garage apartment.

"What is it?" he called irritably at the door. Clean-shaven, he wore only striped undershorts. She glanced past him, pleased that he hadn't changed anything in the apartment. He smelled of soap and there was a razor nick on his chin.

"I'm right in the middle of something," he said when she told him she had to talk to him. "Couldn't it wait?" he asked, his expression cold and distant.

"No, it can't wait."

"What is it, then?" he asked, drumming his fingertips on the door frame.

"It's about that woman the other night. Julia Prine, the one that brought me home? I'm sorry about what she said to you and I hope you're not mad."

"I'm not mad," he sighed.

"I didn't want you to think I said anything to her."

"I didn't think you did."

"I didn't. I swear!"

He winced. "Good. That's good, Martha. Well, I better get back to work."

"Are you writing a book?"

"Well, trying to."

"What's it about?"

"I'm not sure yet." He stepped back. "I better get to work and find out."

"Did you eat yet? There's still some sauce left."

"I'm all set. Thanks," he said, starting to close the door.

She pushed it open. "I really came over for something else!"

"What's that?" he sighed, his eyes sinking heavily.

"Why can't we be friends?" She stared fiercely and would not blink.

"We can be," he said warily. He shrugged. "We can be friends."

"Then you have to look at me and you have to talk to me!"

"I can do that." His smile seemed detached from all the rest of his somber features.

———□———

The day began with warm, blinding rain that streamed down the window glass. After breakfast, Martha overheard Frances talking on the phone with Julia.

"Steve says I'm an explosion waiting to happen. . . . Oh, he's fine. We're both fine now. This whole thing with Anita's just so bizarre. I can't deal with it. I guess I'm getting like Martha; you know, just blow up and say whatever's on my mind. . . . When you said that, just the thought of her in a place like that threw me. . . . She's fine. . . . I thought the move would really upset her. And that's had me all geared up too, expecting her to flip out on me. But she never even argued with me when I told her. And then it hit me—I think she's got a thing for Colin Mackey . . . the handyman. I swear to God! You should see the look on her face when she sees him. . . . For Godssake, Julia, don't be ridiculous. . . . She's . . . Julia, of course he knows she's not a normal young woman. . . . What do you mean, leading her on? All you have to do is look at her and she'll either hate you or love you, you know what that's like. . . ."

The rain ended with the sun's abrupt glare down through all the trees, smearing every window with a blinding sheen. A silvery steam rose from the mountainside and distant hills. The phone rang throughout the morning. Outside, Mack was hammering. Cars ran. A whole world moved.

"She's not a normal young woman. We all know that. . . . She is not a normal young woman. We all know that," Martha chanted, her chest heaving. Eyes closed, she lay on the bed with her arms crossed under her head. "Oh, didn't you know? Martha is not a normal young woman. Oh no! Not at all! Everyone else is, though!"

She sat up suddenly and looked around at the mess of clothes and towels and shoes strewn everywhere. It seemed that it had happened days ago, the frenzy of tearing clothes from drawers, from the two closets and all the shelves. Her arms ached. The back of her wrist was swollen and bruised, and she was exhausted.

Slowly, piece by piece, she forced her sore, angry hands to pick up everything, to match socks and refold underwear and hang up shirts, until the room was in order again.

A DANGEROUS WOMAN

She heard Mack's voice in the hallway and she opened the door a crack. Frances was coming this way with a purple garment bag over her arm. Mack followed, carrying two large boxes, which he deposited in the room across the hall while Frances watched from the doorway.

"Whose room's that?" he asked, coming out.

"It's a spare room now," Frances answered, closing the door. She had been storing supplies for the party in there so that Steve wouldn't see them. "But when I first moved over here from my brother's apartment, that was the room I stayed in."

"Right next to the master bedroom," Mack said. "I see."

"Oh no," she said with a laugh. "Believe me, Horace Beecham was a gentleman.

Mack turned, grinning. "I don't believe you."

"Just a minute! I think you've got the wrong idea here."

"I was just kidding!"

"I don't like your kind of kidding."

"I'm sorry. Really."

"Just be careful how you speak to me. Be very, very careful!"

He looked at her. "Are you serious?"

"Extremely. And there's something else you better keep in mind. My niece," she said, lowering her voice. "Please don't encourage her in any way. She gets these . . . these violent crushes on people. And they're very hard to get out of."

"What do you mean?" He sounded stunned.

Martha tried to close the door, and Frances turned suddenly. "Oh! Oh, Martha!" she said, looking flustered. She opened the door and held out the garment bag. "Here. I got these at Wickley's. Try them on so I can see which one I like best on you."

"What is it?" Martha didn't understand. Her eyes went to Mack, but he looked away.

"Dresses. For Steve's party," Frances explained. "And also, I've got an appointment for you with Helmut to see if he can do something with your hair. He . . ."

"No!" She swatted the bag away. "I have my own clothes! I don't need you picking things out for me!" She kept glancing at Mack.

MARY MCGARRY MORRIS

178

"Oh yes, you do, if that . . . that costume you had on the other night is any . . ."

"Don't you humiliate me like that!" Martha exploded. "Don't you talk to me like that in front of . . . in front of people!"

Now Frances turned and looked at Mack. She smiled. "What do I mean? THAT is precisely what I mean."

Martha slammed her door.

"Bitch," Mack muttered as Frances went down the hallway. "What a bitch!"

FOURTEEN

———◇———

Mack stood in the kitchen doorway, drinking orange juice. He had spent the morning scraping and priming the window shutters that were lined up on newspapers around the garage.

Martha was scrubbing the slimy grout in the tiled backsplash over the sink with an old toothbrush she kept dipping in bleach water. After this last chore on the list Frances had left for her, she was going into town to buy a dress for Steve's party and get her hair cut. Mack would see that she could be just as normal as anyone else. She was paying more attention to her appearance, and it was already starting to work. More than once in the last few days, she had glanced up to find him looking at her. She was trying not to hound him, to stay out of his way, forcing herself to ignore him when they were in the same room, even though her heart would pound and her hair would stand on end, the way it was right now.

"I wonder how come nobody ever made a fuss like this over my birthday?" he said.

"When's your birthday?"

"It was. Last week, as a matter of fact!" He reached past her to put his glass in the sink.

"Really? I wish I'd known!" Seeing him wince, she quickly asked, "So, anyway, how old are you?"

"Too old!" He pushed open the door.

"No, you're not! You look young."

He turned from the door. "You know, speaking of old, it fascinates me, Horace Beecham and all his money, and your aunt ending up with everything. What did your father think of Beecham?" he asked. "What did he say about him?"

"Not much, really. My father was awful quiet." Her eyes hungrily scanned his face, then held on his soft thin mouth.

"What about Beecham marrying his sister, just a young girl—didn't that bother him?"

She tried to remember if her father had ever said a word about it in her presence. He hadn't. The most she had ever heard had come from the old women at the boardinghouse, and the way they told it, Frances Horgan had been a teenage tramp who had seduced a lonely old man, knowing he would do the honorable thing and marry her. There were even rumors that her affair with Steve had begun right under the old man's nose. Martha didn't believe any of it.

"I keep thinking about it," Mack said. "A wealthy old man like that, marrying such a young girl. And such a poor girl. Do you know any of your relatives?"

She told him that the only ones she had ever met had been the young couple who had been looking for work the same day Mack had come. He asked her if she had ever been to the Flatts. She hadn't.

"Would you like to? Wouldn't you like to meet your relatives and hear all those old stories?"

She shook her head. "I don't like meeting new people. Are you writing about this?" she asked, suddenly wondering. "Is that what your book's about?"

"They're still crooked, aren't they?" he said, adjusting her glasses as he might a crooked picture, and as soon as he removed his hand, they shifted again, one lens higher than the other.

———□———

The bus let her off in front of Cushing's, where she went straight to the Ladies' Department and picked three dresses off the rack. Trapped in this stuffy little stall, she still hadn't undressed, because the limp curtain over the doorway kept gaping open, which gave her no privacy, with the young women on both sides of her parading back and forth between stalls to show each other their outfits.

"God, I feel like such a horse," one woman said from outside Martha's stall.

"God, I feel like such a horse," Martha repeated under her breath, holding the curtain shut.

"What?" the woman called.

"Just go," she muttered. "Will you just go."

"I didn't say anything," called the other woman.

"Someone did!" the woman said, swatting Martha's curtain on her way to her own stall.

"I guess some people have nothing better to do," said the other woman, her arms rising over the top of the stall as she tugged off a black shirt.

"I guess some people have nothing better to do," Martha whispered. Glancing down, she noticed the glint of straight pins in the dust. She picked them up and quickly pinned the curtains together, from top to bottom.

"Kath? I'm outta here!"

"Me too, but wait'll I dress!"

She tensed on the edge of the narrow bench, waiting until she was sure they were gone, before she took off her clothes.

She was about to try on the third dress when the salesgirl's spiked heels clicked into the dressing area. "How ya doing, hon? Need any help?" called Leona Huessel, younger sister of an old schoolyard tormentor. "Oh," she said, trying to part the curtain. "Somebody pinned it." She yanked the curtain open from the side and stuck her head in.

Embarrassed by her dingy underwear, Martha ducked against the wall, huddling close to the curtain.

"Oh! There you are!" Leona Huessel said, looking to the side.

Martha crumpled the dress to her chest.

"How're you doing?" Leona Huessel smiled. "Need any help?"

"I'm done," she said, not moving.

Leona Huessel stepped right into the dressing room with her. With a disapproving frown, she scooped up the two dresses Martha had dropped on the floor. "Did you like any of them?"

"I'm going to buy those," she said. She still hadn't decided, but seeing them over Leona's arm alarmed her.

"Great! I'll just take this one too," Leona said, reaching for the dress she still clutched. "And I'll get you rung up and . . ."

"No!" Martha said, pulling back on the dress.

Leona's hand fell from the dress. "Sure. Take your time," she said before she hurried out onto the floor.

With her dresses in a shopping bag, Martha climbed the stairs to the second floor. In the shoe salon she bought a pair of black canvas flats with long skinny straps that the salesman demonstrated three times how to wind and tie around her ankles. The salesman took the new shoes to the register. While Martha was putting her old ones back on, a woman came in and sat in the opposite chair. She could feel the woman staring at her.

"Hello, Martha. How have you been?" the woman asked, and now Martha looked at her. "I'm Patsy Bell," the woman said. "Steve's . . ." There was an imperceptible blink. "Steve and Anita's daughter."

"Oh!" Martha sighed with a smile, remembering the day they had spent together years ago. That euphoric fall afternoon of hot dogs and cold prickly sodas at the fairgrounds, with pale cotton candy, had sparked Martha's near-hysterical certainty, amid the bright throngs of people and gaudy, spinning rides, that somehow everything had changed, so that the polite, freckled child who held fast to her adored father's hand and with prodding said little more to Martha than "Hello, thank you, would you care for some of my popcorn," would be, by virtue of all the cruelties she did not commit that day, Martha's best friend forever. Afterward, for months and months, her yearning for Patsy Bell careened through her consciousness like a wobbly wheel even she found disconcerting.

Though they never again went anywhere together, Patsy's life provided the vicarious data necessary for imagining what normal life was like. In a sense Patsy became that childhood friend who had moved far away, to another state or country, but still kept in touch. As Steve would describe Patsy's birthday or appendectomy or new kitten, Martha would memorize every word. And then, in those painful conversations with new people, or with other children, she could mention that Samantha was the name of Patsy's favorite doll. No, thank you, she didn't eat peanuts; her friend Patsy hated peanuts. Patsy's favorite color was green. Patsy won a ribbon for archery her first summer at camp. That was a blue ribbon. Now she had a bow and arrow on her charm bracelet. Patsy's charm bracelet was silver. Patsy-cake, Patsy-cake, Martha's friend. Bakes her a cake as fast as she can. Until, finally, Frances had forbidden any mention of Patsy's name.

"I was sorry to hear about your father," Patsy said. Her tanned arms were covered with freckles. Short and kittenish, with feathery red hair and green eyes, she smelled of lavender. Did she still remember that day at the fair, Martha wondered. Probably not. She had been married and divorced; she was a high-school French teacher; she had been to Paris six times; Steve said she even dreamed in French.

She nodded, realizing Patsy was waiting for her reply. "Yes. He died."

"I remember what a strong, quiet man he was. Such bearing about him."

Again she nodded. "And your father's a very nice man too!" Oh, that was stupid. That was so stupid. "It's almost his birthday, isn't it? His sixtieth! Are you coming to the party?"

"Apparently not." Patsy looked at her.

"It's a surprise party. Over a hundred people." She took a deep breath and thumped her chest. "Oh, I shouldn't have said anything. I'm sorry. I'm awful sorry," she said, getting up. "I shouldn't have said anything!"

Patsy smiled wearily. "Don't worry about it," she sighed.

"I don't know what I was thinking of. I guess that's what happened, I just wasn't thinking." She laughed nervously. "I haven't seen you in so long I got nervous. Actually, I was thinking of that day, and you probably don't even remember—I mean, you've been to Paris six times—but I thought that was a wonderful day. I always remembered that day."

Patsy looked at her. "What day is that?"

"The day we went to the fair with Steve and . . . my aunt."

"Oh yes," Patsy said, nodding with a weak smile. "We were just little girls, weren't we?"

"Do you remember all the rides we went on?" she asked, grinning. "And the elephants Steve won for us? Mine was pink and yours was blue! They had little black hats, do you remember?"

"No, not really. I don't remember the details."

"I do. I remember EVERYTHING about that day."

"Well, that's nice it's been such a pleasant memory for you," Patsy said. She glanced toward the salesman who waited at the register for Martha.

"I could call you sometime and we could talk about that day," Martha offered, and she did not need such a stricken look to know, as the words hung in the air, that the last thing in the world Patsy Bell wanted was a call from Martha Horgan. She picked up her bag. "I better go. I have an awful lot to do and so I better go." She started toward the register.

"Martha!" Patsy said, following her. "It's just very awkward," she whispered. "I mean, under the circumstances." She looked right at Martha. "It's always been very hard. I hope you know what I mean."

———◇———

She never took elevators. She paused on the stairs for breath. One more flight and she would be on the fifth floor. She kept thinking about what Patsy had said, what she had meant. If things had been different, they might have been friends; the only barrier all these years had been Steve's and Frances's affair.

On the fifth floor, she pretended to look at cosmetic bags while she tried to work up the courage to go into the beauty salon. She kept glancing at the pink doors. She didn't know what to do once she got inside, go sit in a chair or wait for someone to help her. She didn't even know what to tell them about her hair. Her father had always cut it. In the last few months, she had tried to trim it herself, but it always came out uneven.

Behind the glass case a young woman with blonde hair and bright-red lipstick and long red fingernails stared at her.

Martha's face reddened and she dropped the cosmetic bag. "I'm just looking!" she insisted, folding her arms to show she wasn't a shoplifter. "That's all I'm doing, just looking," she muttered, chin at her chest.

"I'm tryna get your flair," the woman said, looking her up and down. "I'd say you're . . ." She bit her lip. "Intro!" she announced, pointing, pleased with her choice. Picking up a long white tab, she read, "The Intro woman is serious and quiet-minded, but her heart's all razzama-tazz." The young woman held out the tab. "See. It tells your colors and your scents."

The Intro woman is introspective and creative, Martha read. At home in cool greens and vibrant blues. Her scents are woodsy and clean, like rain in a pine forest. . . .

"These are the ones that, like, go with your flair, with Intro," the young woman said, setting a round gold box on the counter. Its lid said INTRO in raised black letters. "It's like a whole beauty supply for your life-flair. See. It's got all your colors, your Cool Greens, your Electric

Blues," she said, reading the various tubes and bottles and pencils and cylinders, her slick red lips catching the glint of the cut-glass chandeliers. She glanced at her watch. "I'll tell you what. If you got time, I could do like a make-over for you. That way, you get the kit at regular price and the Intro cologne by Dorene for like half." Each sentence ended like a question. "Sit here," she said, patting the tall stool. "It's a one-week promo. Today's the last day." She shook out a black-and-gold plastic bib and tied it around Martha's neck. "I love doing Intros," the young woman said. Pencil in hand, she leaned close to Martha. Her breath smelled of coffee and the peppermint gum she nibbled. "You're all so sexy," she murmured, tracing a line of deep blue around Martha's unblinking eye.

She tried to keep a straight face while the young woman brushed and stroked her face, but her smile kept breaking through. Her eyes closed now with the gentle whisk of the brush and the young woman's breath on her cheeks.

"Wow!" the young woman said, and she held up a mirror. "You look beautiful!"

Without her glasses, all she could make out was the red shimmer of her mouth. When she put on her glasses, the mirror was gone and the young woman was wrapping the makeup and cologne in gold tissue paper. "You look great," she said with a bright smile as she handed Martha her change and her glossy black-and-gold bag. "But you really oughta have your hair done. Some new way. Layered and off your face."

Martha asked if that was what she should tell them in the beauty parlor. Shrugging, the young woman said it was up to her; that was just her suggestion. "What do you usually have done?" the young woman asked.

"Well, this is my first time," Martha said.

"Oh, so you must be new here, like me," the young woman said. "I thought you acted a little strange, like you didn't, you know, know the routine." She locked her register and told Martha to follow her. She'd take care of everything. "And I'll get you Carmela. She's like excellent."

The waiting room was crowded. While Martha looked at a magazine, the young woman talked to the receptionist. "You're all set with Carmela," the young woman came back to tell her. Martha stood up and took her hand. "Thank you," she said, with a hearty shake. "I just want to tell you you're a good worker. And that's very important. Thank you. Thank you very much."

"Yah, well." Blinking, the young woman pulled back her hand. "Have a good haircut, now."

---□---

Carmela's stony breasts jabbed Martha whenever she leaned close. Her unfiltered cigarette burned to a long acrid ash in the tin ashtray on the counter while she told Martha all about her ex-husband, who raced cars in Burlington, and the doughnut maker he had impregnated while they were married, and her sister, who had a tumor in a place Martha did not care to know about; and her three Siamese cats, and her son's wrestling team—she thought his coach was getting ready to ask her out. " 'Course, I happen to know he's still married. But I figure I'll deal with that river when we cross it. God, your hair's thick." She lifted a strand of hair and looked in the mirror at her. "There's like a whole section missing. What'd you do, get gum in it or something?"

"It got caught," Martha said. "I was late. It was a PlastiqueWare party and my friend invited me. Her name's Birdy. The thing got stuck." She gestured at the curling iron on the counter.

"Oh yah," Carmela said, lighting another cigarette. She took a long drag, then blew the smoke over her shoulder. "You used to be at the Cleaners, right? Yah. Sure, I know Birdy. God, we go way back, me and Birdy."

The scissors snipped so near her temple she squeezed her eyes shut.

"So, all right. Martha Horgan. Sure. Now I know who you are." Carmela kept cutting near the top of her ear. "How 'bout her and Getso? Now, there's a twosome I never would've even dreamed of. Really. I mean Getso! Ugh." She shuddered. "He's like such a loser; can't keep a wife or a job. At least my . . . ."

Her eyes shot open. "He got fired!"

"Wouldn't surprise me. I hope you know we're getting shorter and shorter here," Carmela murmured, tilting her head.

She couldn't believe it, Getso fired. That meant her job back and her room in the boardinghouse back and then Mack could come and see her there.

"It's awful short," Carmela said, puffing hairs off the back of her neck. "But I think you're gonna be real happy with it."

She put on her glasses and looked in the mirror. With her head a cap of fuzz and her thick glasses banding her face like goggles, what she saw was the startled, gasping expression of a swimmer who had just popped up out of the water.

On her way out of Cushing's, she bought a scarf and tied it under her chin. As she hurried down the street, she shielded her face from her own reflection in the passing storefronts.

At the door to the bookstore, she paused to catch her breath. If she were going to get to the Cleaners before they closed, she had to find a book right away. She paced through the cluttered little shop, but only a few titles were familiar to her. The salesclerk perched on a stool, his large hands folded on his knees.

"Anything special you're looking for?" he asked as she turned the corner again.

She told him no and took a deep breath. She was so intimidated by all these books she could barely look at them, much less take one off the shelf and open it. She hadn't thought picking out a book for Mack's birthday would be this hard. What if she chose a stupid book, one he considered a terrible book, a book only a fool would buy? She turned to go.

"Is it for you?" the clerk asked.

"For my friend," she said, wincing.

"What kinds of books does your friend read?"

"I don't know." She had to get out of here. "He writes them. He's writing a book."

"Oh! Well, now," the clerk said, slipping one off the shelf and handing it to her, "then I'd say this is a must, Miss Horgan."

A DANGEROUS WOMAN

He rang up the sale. Miss Horgan. She had never seen him before in her life. It was depressing. Miss Horgan, her own name, a lamentation tolling on the tongues of strangers.

By the time she got to the Cleaners, the red-and-white "Closed" sign had already been pulled over the glass door. She peered inside past the curled edge of the shade. She thought she heard voices, so she banged on the door, then listened, but no one came. They must be going out the back way. She hurried down the side alley and gave a little whoop at the sight of Birdy's old pea-green Buick at the entrance to the lot. Laughing to herself, she opened the front door and slid inside. She swung her bags into the back seat, but kept the book in her lap to show Birdy.

She knew by the sun's glare on the dirty windshield that Birdy wouldn't be able to see her right away. When the back door to the Cleaners finally opened, she sat forward eagerly, but it was Mercy who stepped onto the loading platform. She wore black shorts and a black halter top. She must have changed after work to go somewhere, Martha thought. John would never allow an employee to dress like that.

Maybe Mercy and Birdy were on their way to another PlastiqueWare party, she thought as the door opened. She closed her eyes, praying that Birdy wouldn't still be mad. She covered her mouth and squealed into the muzzle of her palm, "Don't be mad. Don't be mad. Please, Birdy, don't be mad."

She opened her eyes. Getso and Mercy were up on the platform, kissing. He pressed against her, grinding his pelvis into hers.

Her hand inched up to the hot door handle, but it was too late. With Mercy in the lead, they raced down the stairs, Getso's bootsteps on the metal treads echoing like gunshots through the narrow lot. Getso grabbed Mercy's wrist and, with a squeal, she broke free and ran toward the car. He snagged her by the waistband of her shorts and dragged her, laughing, back into his arms. Inches from Martha's face by the open window, they squirmed together, the car sagging and creaking. She closed her eyes, sickened by the smell of Mercy's sweet perfume.

"Oh . . . oh, Gets," Mercy sighed.

MARY MCGARRY MORRIS

"Let's go back in," he moaned.

"Oh God. I'm so wicked sore."

He laughed.

The door on her right opened. Mercy started to climb in, then jerked back, screaming, when she saw Martha. Getso hollered and banged his fist on the hood. Martha scrambled out of the car and ran, emerging from the alley just as the northbound bus turned the corner. Panting, she ran alongside and kept hitting the door until the bus squealed to a stop.

"For Chrissakes," the red-faced driver groaned, pleating open the door. "Don't you ever do that again, Martha Horgan!" he gasped as she lurched past him to a seat. She was the only one on the bus.

"You scared the hell outta me!" he called, glaring at her through the mirror.

She buried her face in her hands. Poor Birdy. Poor dear Birdy. Now this betrayal. She had to tell her. She had no choice. She looked up. Her bags! She'd left everything, her dresses, shoes, and makeup, in Birdy's car. All she had was Mack's book.

---□---

The joke was that, of the 123 people Frances had invited to the birthday party, only 158 had accepted. Some of Steve's Dartmouth buddies were coming, one all the way from Texas and one from Utah. Everyone they knew would be there, and yet Steve still hadn't caught on; but now that Frances thought of it, that would be typical of his maddeningly selective myopia. Steve only saw what he chose to see. To look the other way had become such a personal beatitude for him that sometimes she just felt like shaking him, slapping some sense into him, screaming, anything to force him to face the folly of what his daughters were putting him through. Her pen rolled onto the floor. Her hands were trembling.

Needing calm, she took up her list. She still had to deal with a dress and shoes for Martha and an appointment for her with Frances's beautician. She crossed off ice sculpture; the caterer had finally located an ice sculptor in Burlington to do the scales of justice with Steve's age in the higher scale. Check on linen rental. . . . There was a thud against the house and she looked up, startled. It was only Mack taking down the ladder. He had rehung the shutters. She got up and stood by the door, watching him carry the ladder back to the garage. Instead of a belt, a length of rope held up his shorts. The untied laces in his sneakers whipped the ground as he walked. For such a disorderly man he was certainly getting things into shape around here.

It irritated her, though, the way he watched her. Accustomed to men's stares, she usually enjoyed them, but somehow it was different with Colin Mackey. It was almost as if he were studying her, looking for something. Well, whatever it was, it seemed a small price to pay as long as she didn't have to worry about loose boards and balky engines and strange sounds in the night.

She could see someone coming up the road. It was Martha, with a green-and-pink scarf tied around her head. Once in the driveway, she hurried after Mack to the garage, and when he turned around she handed him something.

"Here. I got this for you," she called, panting.

"Martha! It's not my birthday," he said. "I was kidding!"

"Well, I'm not going to bring it back, so if you don't want it just throw it away!" Martha sounded upset. Frances tensed. That's all she needed was for Martha to fly off the handle and have Mack quit the way Billy Chelsea had.

"Of course I want it. I just feel guilty." He reached out and put his hands on Martha's shoulders.

Frances couldn't believe her eyes. What in God's name was he thinking of? She threw open the kitchen door and stormed onto the deck. Martha turned and Frances was stunned to see her cheeks glazed in plum colored circles, her eyes circled with garish liner, and her hair . . . "What did you do to your hair?" she cried, rushing at Martha. She tore off the scarf. "My Lord! What did you ever do?"

"I got it cut," Martha said, chewing on her lip. She touched the side of her head.

"Cut! Martha! You got shaved! Like a dog in the heat!" she cried.

MARY McGARRY MORRIS

"How could you let someone do that to you? Do you have any idea what you look like?" She threw up her hands. "You couldn't!"

Martha turned stiffly and went into the house.

Mack stared at her. "Why did you say that to her?" he asked.

"She looks bizarre! She looks like something out of a cartoon!" Her voice quavered.

"That was lousy!" He looked back at the house.

"Whatever it was, it's none of your business," she snapped.

He looked at her. "I don't understand the way you treat her. It's strange. . . . It's cruel."

Her head came up, and for a moment she was too shocked to speak.

"Did it ever occur to you that maybe what she needs is a little kindness?" he said.

"Did it ever occur to you that you don't know what the hell you're talking about?"

"Oooo!" He smiled. "That occurs to me just about all the time."

Look at him laughing, she thought. Judging her the way Julia did, thinking, if she had only done more, kept at it long enough, dragging Martha from doctor to doctor, then surely by now she would have found the right medicine or therapy, the magic cure. It was not for lack of kindness or love but, rather, that immutability people call bad luck or fate. Some cats were black and some were gray. Some men were short, some women tall, as Martha would always be Martha, immured in her own oddness and pain; and she knew enough by now, was absolutely convinced that the most, the best she could do was to keep Martha from harm.

"Don't encourage her," she said. "Do you understand? Can't you see what's happening?"

His face drained. "No. I guess not."

"She watches you. She can't keep her eyes off you. She hangs on your every word with that foolish grin, and the pathetic thing is, she doesn't even know how obvious it is, how . . . how sickening. I told you, she gets these crushes, these . . . these terrible attachments to people. Don't you understand? That's why she let someone butcher her hair like that. And that makeup! She did it for you."

A DANGEROUS WOMAN

"Then I'm flattered," he said, staring at her.

In his eyes there glimmered something, a hunger that was the next moment so quickly, so coldly hooded that she thought, Yes. Yes, he would be flattered. "If I were you, I'd be scared," she said.

"That too." He smiled.

And it came to her that, in his battered way, he was an appealing man, which made him all the more treacherous.

He picked up the ladder and started toward the garage with it.

"Wait, I need you to roll up three rugs and leave them in the hall. They're being picked up early in the morning for cleaning," she called.

He kept walking, and she followed him into the garage. "Did you hear what I said?" she demanded.

"I heard you." Grunting, he hoisted the long wooden ladder onto the hooks Floyd had installed on the side wall.

It pleased her that everything had its place. Here there was order and containment. "The waxer's in the car," she said. "I'd rather you did the floors tonight. I've got a girl coming to clean tomorrow, and I'd like the floors out of the way."

Squatting down, he emptied one paint can into another. His shorts pulled halfway down his backside, and she looked away from the hairy cleavage, offended that he made no effort to hitch them up.

"I'll wax your floors tomorrow," he said, his hammer tapping the lid tight on the can. "They'll get done."

"No! I need them done tonight!" she said, her voice rising. "I have it all worked out."

He stood up and squirted paint thinner into a rag and scrubbed his fingers, working the rag under each nail. "I told you. At night I write."

"I don't think one night is too much to expect under the circumstances!"

He threw down the rag. "Look, why don't I do us both a favor and just get the hell out of here?"

She smiled. "Fine, but the only problem is you owe me a week's work!" She had advanced him a week's pay.

"No problem at all. You'll get your week." Now he was smiling.

MARY MCGARRY MORRIS

FIFTEEN

—————◻—————

The next morning, Martha was polishing all the silver in the house, urns and flatware, nut dishes, candy dishes, the tea-and-coffee service, so many pieces that the kitchen counters and table were covered. Dawn was on her hands and knees, washing woodwork. She was a tall slim high-school girl one of Frances's friends had recommended.

Mack opened the refrigerator. He had finally made it over to the house after another insistent call from Frances. He looked exhausted. Martha knew his light had stayed on most of the night, because she had been up herself, writing Birdy a ten-page letter about what she had seen in town yesterday.

"Do you realize I've been waiting forty-five minutes for you?" Frances said.

Mack's eyes flicked coldly and, whatever he had been about to say, he swallowed in a smile. "Forty-five minutes, that's nothing," he scoffed. "Hell, some women have been waiting a lifetime," he said, winking at Martha as he sat at the table with a glass of juice. He looked down at Dawn. "Now, this is what I call a work crew." He leaned over and asked the girl her name.

"Dawn," came her soft voice.

"Dawn, that burst of light that spawns this mighty thirst," he said, holding up his glass.

Dawn wrung out her rag in the bucket, and a wedge of her fine straight hair slipped over her red cheeks. Smiling, Mack sipped his juice while he watched her crouch down to scrub the black rubber baseboard under the cabinets.

"If you don't mind," Frances said, glaring at him from the doorway.

He jumped up and Dawn giggled nervously.

In the hallway, Frances showed him how to run the floor polisher. She stepped aside now and gestured for him to turn it on. He did, and it skittered out of his hand.

"Bear down!" she called, stalking him as he got hold of it again, letting it take him where it would, along the hallway, bumping off table legs and the brass umbrella stand. "Steer it!" she called, charging back up the hallway after him. "In a straight line!" She was still shouting when the machine died.

"If you want this done, then leave me alone!" he said through clenched teeth.

"I don't just want it done. I want it done right," Frances spat back.

"Then I guess you better do it yourself!" He threw down the cord.

"I don't think so, Mr. Mackey!" she said, kicking the cord back at him.

They glared at one another.

Dawn watched from the dining room. Martha held her breath until she saw Mack smile and pick up the cord. Without a word he plugged it in and steered the polisher so expertly down the hallway that she knew it must have been an act.

By mid-afternoon all the hardwood floors were glassy with wax. In the kitchen Martha and Dawn were cleaning the pictures and mirrors Frances had taken down before she left for Hanover with Steve. Martha turned her rag in the grimy whorls of this gold-leafed frame. No matter how hard she tried to put her mind on other things, images of Getso and Mercy kept seeping in, poisoning her thoughts. "Nothing but cheating liars. What do they care? They don't care who they hurt. What do they care?"

She realized Dawn was staring at her. The girl looked away.

"I'm hot," Martha tried to explain. "But I don't care."

"You're lucky your hair's so short. Mine feels like there's this hot towel on my head," the girl said, her slender arm drawing the hair from her neck in the most fluid gesture Martha had ever seen.

"Want some juice?" she asked, and Dawn eagerly said yes. When she had been this age, girls as pretty as Dawn had fascinated her. She still remembered the little wrinkles that formed at the corners of Katie Holt's eyes when she smiled or the pink dabs of Sylvia Bredder's tongue as she wet her lips. Once a group of girls complained to the principal that they could not concentrate in class with Martha Horgan always staring at them. She never looked at one of those girls again, and if they came anywhere near her, she turned her back on them.

"Is that Mrs. Beecham's husband?" Dawn asked as Mack passed the doorway with a roll of musty jute padding slung over his shoulder.

"No!" Martha said, so emphatically that Dawn glanced at her. "He just works here."

"He's kinda cute," Dawn said, licking pulp off the glass rim. "You know, for an old guy."

On this trip down the hall, Mack stopped. "When's Mrs. Bitchum coming back?" he asked.

Ignoring Dawn's giggle, Martha told him not until later tonight. She sniffed, certain she smelled liquor on him.

"When she does, tell her I did everything on her list. Tell her I'm done for the day and if she doesn't like it . . ." He winked at Dawn who blushed. ". . . please tell her I love her," he sang, "please tell her I care," he crooned with his arms up, swaying in a little dance around Dawn, who couldn't stop giggling. "Hey!" he said, peering at her shiny red face. "You find this amusing? You think a man's humiliation and servitude are funny? Do you?" he demanded, scowling.

Martha was shocked that he would speak to Dawn like this. She hadn't done anything. Sometimes she felt as if she were watching two different personalities fighting to be one man.

"Well . . . no, I . . ." Dawn stammered.

"You do! Of course you do!" Head down, he paced around her. "Everyone needs a victim. But some of us need to BE victims. Case in point, myself. Now, if you don't believe me, ask Martha. She has witnessed the depths of my suffering and degradation."

Martha stared at him, her glasses askew, mouth slack.

"She knows what I am, don't you, Martha?" he said, turning with a smile so lethal she felt the nick of its blade at her heart.

After Dawn went home, Mack dove into the pool and swam for a long time. Martha watched from her window. She had heard him tell Dawn he was going into town, and she wanted to catch him before he left. As soon as she saw him climb out of the pool, she hurried outside with the envelope. He sat on the edge of the pool with his legs dangling in the water. The warm wet patio smelled of sweet alyssum and chlorine.

"The floors look nice," she said, coming up behind him.

"You think so, huh," he said, then squinted up at her. "That Dawn was something," he said, laughing, shading his eyes. "Wonder how old she is."

"Sixteen!" he groaned when she told him. "See, that's my problem. I forget how old I am. It's a real shock some days to look in the mirror and see this mug staring back. It's depressing." He swung a leg out of the water and stood up. "What's that?" he asked, pointing. "Not another letter!" He looked at her. "Why do you keep doing this? Don't you think it's kind of weird?"

"No, you don't understand!" She told him about seeing Getso with Mercy, and how much Birdy trusted them. "I have to make her see the truth . . ."

"Martha!"

". . . to see what a liar he is . . ."

"Martha!"

". . . how evil. . . ."

"The truth is," he roared, "SHE DOESN'T CARE!"

"Well, I care!" she said, hitting her chest. "I care!"

"Why?"

"Because I'm sick of people's lies about me!" She looked away. "You don't understand."

"No, I guess not. Here, give me the letter," he said, taking it from her. "I'll take care of it."

"You'll mail it in town?"

"I'll mail it in town."

"It's already stamped."

"Already stamped."

"I put two on. It's so thick, and I wasn't sure."

"Two! Great! Now, starting right now, let's get into a new program here." He popped open a beer, took a long guzzle, then wiped his mouth. "First of all, I want to tell you how nice you look."

Her mouth careened into a crooked smile and she shrugged self-consciously.

"You do. You look real nice. And I like your hair. I do. I like it like that. It's different, which is okay. It's okay to be different." Water dripped down his legs and puddled at his feet. "You got it done for the party, right?"

"Not really. I don't like parties."

"What don't you like about them?" he asked, toweling himself off.

"The whole thing. Just parties."

He finished his beer and opened another can, offering her one. She shook her head no. "What if you went with someone? You might like it better if you had someone to be with. Someone to talk to?"

"I don't know," she said, grinning in disbelief. "Maybe."

"Do you like to dance? That's another thing. If you go with someone, then you've got your own dance partner all night long."

She shrugged and he kept looking at her. "Do you know how to dance?"

"No."

He laughed and held out his arms. "Okay, here we go. Colin Mackey's one easy lesson in fake dancing." He set her left hand on his wet shoulder, and he held her right hand as well as his beer. "Look at me, look me right in the eyes, and when I take a step back you take a step forward. That's right. Now, two back, and two the other way. That's right. Follow your feet, but don't look down. Just look at me."

Staring at him, she tried to follow, but she got confused every time he brought her hand to his mouth so he could sip his beer. She grew stiffer with each step, until her knees had almost locked. She kept stepping on his toes, so he stopped and told her to take off her shoes. He opened another beer.

"That's it. You're getting it," he said, when he had set her hands in place and started to move again. "Here, let's loosen up a little. Don't be afraid of touching." He pulled her closer. "Perfect strangers touch when they dance, and nobody gets the wrong idea. That's right. That's it. One, two, three, one, two, three," he hummed. "One, two, three."

Her eyes blurred with his closeness.

He was smiling. "I see you're ready for the hard part. Now close your eyes and keep moving. That's it. Just go where I take you. Trust your partner," he murmured, turning in tight circles. Each time he took a drink, her hand brushed his mouth. Her pants grew damp against his wet bathing suit. "You never danced with anyone before?"

"No."

"Well, I'm honored to be your first partner."

Was he feeling this same way, thinking the same thing? Was that his heart pounding against hers?

"I was thinking, you should call that fellow who was here, that big guy, Mount, and invite him to the party."

"No!" She started to pull away.

"Martha!" he said, not letting her go. "I just meant he'd be somebody to . . . to be with. And besides, he likes you. Can't you tell?"

"I want to be with you. I love you!"

"Don't say that!" His hands tightened on her arms, his face darkening. "Don't even think it. Do you understand?"

Understand? What was there to understand, with strange children chasing her, and her own father so seldom acknowledging her that, when they did speak, she would dig her nails into her palms, then race to a light to study the pattern of blue runes in her flesh before they were gone. "I can't help it. That's all I want," she gasped, holding on to him.

His face drew close, his breath ravenous, as if for some vital element she exhaled. "I know what you want," he said hoarsely. "Same thing I want. Same fuckin' thing we all want."

His room was hot and dark. They sat fully clothed, legs outstretched on the bed. The bottle clinked against the glass, and she heard his long swallow. She felt feverish. Without her glasses, her eyes burned, and for a moment she couldn't tell if they were open or closed. The ceiling fan turned with a slow rubbing sound, and somewhere by the bed a cricket chirped weakly. He put his arm around her with a dismal laugh, then sat there a moment, the two of them staring across the room. He turned and kissed her temple, her ear. "Does that feel good?" he whispered.

"Yes," she whispered back.

"Do I make you feel good?"

"Yes," she whispered.

"Well, if Dr. Feelgood can bring a little happiness into this world, what the hell's wrong with that?" He touched her face, one cheek, then the other.

A DANGEROUS WOMAN

"Nothing," she whispered back, reaching for his hand.

"It's a tough job, but somebody's gotta do it. Okay," he said, standing up suddenly. "Time for therapy. Take off your clothes." He went into the kitchen and took a can of beer from the refrigerator. She pulled her shirt over her head, and the hair on her arms bristled in the fan's breeze. She wiggled out of her pants. When he returned, he stood with his back to her, staring out the window while he drank his beer. Waiting in her underwear, she fiddled with the bedspread fringe, finding it peculiar that love could feel this lonely.

"I'll be ready in a minute," he said, lingering by the window, as if he were watching for someone, someone to save him. When he had finished the beer, he turned, crunching the can in one hand, then dropping it. It bounced on the floor. "You ready?" he asked, stepping out of his bathing suit.

"Yes," she said faintly, rolling her bra and panties into a ball. He lay on top of her, at first unmoving, his mouth at her ear. She could feel his chest pumping in and out against hers.

"Is this what you want?"

"Yes."

"You think this is it, don't you?" he whispered. "You think of me and you burn inside. I remember feeling the same way after my first time. Christ, I followed her around for weeks. I couldn't sleep. I couldn't eat. I couldn't talk straight. It's all I wanted to do. The minute she came near me, the minute I heard her or smelled her, it's all I could think of. You know what I mean?" he asked, and she tried to tell him yes, she knew exactly what he meant, but it came out sounding like a long wet moan.

He rose up on his elbows, all the while talking, crooning, to the rhythm of his hips against hers. She was acutely conscious of the heat in the room and the dwindling light and the anger in his voice, the mounting disgust, and yet she didn't care. It felt too good. She felt too good.

"It's like being on fire, isn't it? Burning. Burning inside. Gets up in your eyes and you're blind. Just like booze. You think, Well, just one more time. . . . But each fire's worse and worse. . . . Isn't it, baby? No way to put it out. Jesus, I remember. . . ."

Her head tossed and turned. Sweat ran down her throat, between her breasts, and made sucking sounds against his heaving chest.

"I was only fourteen," he grunted with a movement so wrenching that her eyes opened wide on the fan, its wreath of blades turning around his head. "But this . . . this is pathetic. You don't want me. This is what you want. It's all you need . . . all anyone needs! Just this . . . Here! Here! Oh my God! Here!" he moaned, then collapsed, his hairy legs sprawled over hers, his arms pinning her shoulders.

She gazed at the whirring blades with an amniotic half-blindness. Her chest ached as she held her breath under his dead weight. After a while, he rolled off and lay with his back to her, facing the wall. She waited for him to say something. Finally she sat up and gathered her clothes from the floor.

"Mack?" she called softly when she came out of the bathroom.

"Don't say anything," he warned from the dark bed. "Just go."

———□———

Steve seemed to be driving slower and slower. Frances laid her head back and closed her eyes. The play had been so bad that she had fallen asleep during the first act. Embarrassed, Steve kept nudging her awake. "You're snoring," he whispered. "People keep looking back."

Later, when he thought he had caught her dozing again, he squeezed her wrist. Irritated, she almost said something; instead, to make light of it, she pinched his leg, and his look of disgust shocked her.

He had been fidgety and distracted all through dinner, barely touching his food, then finally admitting he had already eaten. Patsy had barbecued lamb chops for the three of them. She had listened with a fixed smile while he described the skewered vegetables Patsy had grilled with a lemon-and-mint marinade.

"I had no idea she could cook like that," he said with a ridiculous note of wonder in his voice.

She had poured more wine, buttered a roll, and with deliberation cut off another piece of swordfish, pleased, as she chewed, that not one negative word had passed her lips.

Now, as they came down Route 4 past Killington, he hunched forward, as vigilant over the wheel as if he were navigating through a blizzard. She laid her hand on his thigh, patting it. Poor Steve, being put through this charade now, after all those loveless, painful years. She squeezed the back of his neck, saddened by the hair bristling from his neck. She would remind him to get a haircut Friday. He reached back for her hand and held it while he drove, squeezing it until it hurt.

"Frannie, I don't know how to tell you this. Remember how I said the girls were planning a trip for me and . . . their mother. It's the sixteenth through the twenty-third. It'll do her . . ."

"But that's your birthday. You can't go then. Not on your birthday, Steve. You can't, damn it!"

There was nothing he could do, he insisted. In a way, it was out of his hands.

"The girls wanted to surprise us," he said. "Their mother and me," he added quickly, she knew, to blunt his use of the word "us."

She let him talk. Anita was doing so well. The girls were happier than he had ever seen them. Patsy had moved into the house, and she and her mother were redoing her old room. Anita had gained nine pounds. "She sleeps through the night now. . . ."

"Tell me one thing, Steve," she interrupted, unable to stand this ridiculous account that sounded more like a baby's birth than a grown woman's recovery from alcoholism. "Are you going or not?"

He started to say something, but she stopped him. "Just answer that one question. Because, if you go . . . if you dare go, then we're through. Do you understand? Do you?"

He nodded.

"Well?"

"I won't go," he said.

"What will you tell Patsy and Jan?" she asked.

"That it's not a good time," he said. "I don't know . . . Something. I'll tell them there's a big case I'm working on. . . ."

"Why don't you just tell them the truth?" she said.

The tires squealed as he pulled off the road. In the moonlight, he looked old and pale and defeated; like Anita, she thought with alarm.

He smiled wanly. "I find myself in the impossible position of having two families, neither of which I can please."

"I'm not your family."

"You are. You've always been. You know that!" he said, so fiercely she fell silent; and in the silence heard something rattle inside him. Sighing, he rested his forehead on the steering wheel. "They talk and they talk and they talk and it's always about guilt and responsibility and honesty." He looked up, and his voice broke. "And it tears me apart."

"Steve," she sighed. "Oh, Steve."

"It's getting worse. I can't sleep nights. I have this dream. I'm locked in this closet, this dark, narrow closet, and little by little water seeps in under the door and it gets higher and higher, up to my chin and then my mouth and then my nose. And I'm holding my breath and my eyes are wide open. And I can't even scream. I . . ."

"Damn it, Steve, why are you letting them do this to you?"

"I'm not just talking about them. But us too. And all this pain . . . all this . . . this agitation," he said, watching her.

Her mouth fell open, her insides seized now with a danger she only faintly remembered. He had always been weak. How had she ignored it all these years? How had she loved him?

"I owe her something," he said.

"What about me? Damn it, Steve, what do you owe me?"

———□———

"Gone? What do you mean, he's gone?" Frances asked.

Martha sat up in bed, her eyes swollen as if she had been crying all night. This morning Frances had realized that Mack's car wasn't in the driveway or the garage. The apartment was empty, save for a balled-up dirty sock in the bathroom and, on the kitchen table, a book, *The Art of Fiction*.

The Art of Fiction, she kept thinking. Damn him for walking out on her like this at the worst possible time. *The Art of Fiction*. All his talk about finally being able to write. Everything the man said was fiction. That was his only art. And she had fallen for it! When she knew better! When she knew exactly the type he was, exactly what he had in mind, her—that's what he'd had in mind, and in her desperation she had been willing to overlook that.

"Why are you crying?" she asked, coming closer to the bed.

"I'm not crying," Martha answered dully, sinking into the blanket.

"What happened? Something happened! I can tell by your face. You did something, didn't you?" She yanked away the blanket. "Oh God, what did you do?" she groaned. "What in God's name did you say to him?"

"Nothing!" Martha screamed, springing up from the bed.

"Stop it," she panted, trying to block Martha's flailing hands.

Grunting, Martha grabbed her hair and yanked her head back with such force that she staggered and fell against the side of the bed. Stunned, she sat there, staring up at Martha, who stood by the door, pounding her chest and pleading in a thick voice, "I'm sorry. I'm sorry. I'm sorry. I'm sorry. . . ."

In the bathroom, Frances leaned close to the mirror and examined the scratch at the corner of her eye. Thank God, it wasn't turning black and blue.

"I'm sorry!" Martha kept calling from the hallway. She banged on the door. "I didn't mean to do that. I'm sorry!"

She splashed her face with cold water, dried it, then dabbed the cut with makeup. So it had come to this, she thought, and for the rest of the night and the next day it began to seem as natural there as a birthmark.

———□———

The blue-and-tan cruiser was parked in the driveway. Sheriff Sonny Stoner stood in the kitchen in his frayed blue uniform, describing the accident to Frances. Mack had fallen asleep at the wheel of his car and careened through the Gere family's back yard, uprooting their maple saplings. She had no idea who the Geres were, but Sonny's tone suggested that months of this admirable family's labor had just been obliterated. She was immediately defensive. Sonny had better not be looking to her for any kind of charitable indemnity here.

"I picked him up after his stitches and I figured I'd just stop by and double-check," Sonny said, his weary solicitude as grating as ever. She had read an article once that quoted Sonny as saying that he believed in justice and the law, but that one did not always guarantee the other. It certainly didn't in his personal life. No matter whom he had slept with or how many times he had looked the other way, everyone's opinion of Sonny Stoner was unwavering: he was a good man. As far as she was concerned, the real bottom line with Sonny, as with Julia Prine, was self-enhancement. How much more pleasing their own images probably seemed to them in a mirror of fools.

"He's telling the truth. It's done," she said, gesturing back at the deck.

"The more he didn't want me to bring him here, the more I figured he owed you something," Sonny said.

"I'd advanced him a hundred dollars," she said.

"That's what I figured," Sonny mused, looking toward the door. "Asked me to let him get his stuff out of his car, then leave him up on the highway. You know, those poor Geres, they don't have any insurance either."

"What are you getting at, Sonny? This has nothing to do with me. This isn't the same as the windshield."

"Hell, I know that. It's a shame, that's all. Guy like that you keep throwing the rope to, and he can't ever seem to hold on."

"All I ever expected was a day's work," she said, so there would be no mistake about her motives. Sonny better not think she was running some halfway house here.

"I don't know how you're doing it without Floyd." He stood in the doorway and looked out. If an annual deer-hunting trip together constituted a friendship, then Sonny and her brother had been friends. She wondered if Sonny knew that those three days in the woods were the only times Floyd ever went anywhere. Of course he knew, she thought, looking at the back of his snow-white crew cut, and probably only went because he knew nobody else would go with Floyd Horgan. She thought of that night, years ago, when Martha had burst into the house half dressed and reeking of beer she claimed the boys had sprayed on her. Sonny had taken care of everything. She shouldn't be too hard on Sonny.

She followed him outside. He tapped on the cruiser window before opening the door on Mack, who had been dozing. His right cheek was bandaged with gauze, and over his right ear a matchbook-sized patch of scalp had been shaved and stitched.

"Would you mind telling me what happened?" she asked, instinctively touching the scab by her eye.

"I fell asleep."

"I mean why you left."

"Impulse . . . It was time."

"Time? You couldn't have picked a worse time!"

"I'm sorry. I really am." His head hung, and she thought she heard him laugh. "You still owe me work!" she said angrily.

"Don't worry. You'll get your hundred bucks."

"Well, it comes to a lot more than that now," Sonny interrupted. "There's the stockade fence and two brand-new bicycles, plus your hospital charges and the towing and repair on your own car. And don't forget those maples," he added.

"God no," Mack said through a rueful grin. "How could I forget those maples."

Rubbing his chin, Sonny looked down at him. "You know what I think?" he said, leaning his forearms in the window. "Frances needs work done here and you need money. The way I see it, you got two choices. Here or my place. Here, you come and go. My place, I gotta use these." He reached back and jiggled the keys hanging from the same brass ring as his handcuffs.

Sonny wasn't tossing any ropes now. With just a few words, he had tied Mack up in knots. It startled her to realize how much she enjoyed watching him squirm.

MARY McGARRY MORRIS

Mack looked stunned, almost frightened. "But I told you, as soon as I get to Boston I can send money back. I thought we agreed," he said, peering up desperately at Sonny.

"Well, the thing here is that poor Gere family." Sonny hissed in his breath. "It just doesn't seem right, the way they work night and day, the two of them, just to have somebody come plow it all down and then take off leaving nothing behind but a promise."

"I told you. My word is good!"

"And I believe you. That's why I'm giving you this choice."

"Choice?" Mack said with a high, bitter laugh. "What choice?" He looked in disbelief between Sonny and Frances. "My choice of jailers?"

"Well," Sonny said thoughtfully. "You see, I'm trying to be fair as I can." He leaned in closer. "To Mrs. Beecham here. And to the Geres."

Sixteen

From her bedroom window, Martha watched him spray glistening white paint onto the wicker chairs and tables and the sagging settee, which were spread all over the side lawn on spattered drop cloths. When he was done, he headed toward the house, wiping his hands on a rag. She ran down the back stairs, slid into a chair at the kitchen table, and smiled as he came through the door. "Hot enough for you?" She bit her lip; such a lame thing to say.

"Mmmm, hot," he muttered, opening and closing drawers until he came to the junk drawer, where he fumbled through tangled skeins of string, small tools, and odd utensils, which he kept putting on the counter.

"Watch out for knives," she warned just as a melon baller hit the floor. It rolled by her feet, and she grabbed it. "Here!" she said, grinning. His hand shook, and in the moment's hesitation he seemed about to say something. He turned quickly back to the drawer.

"Your bandage is off! Does it hurt?" She held her glasses and walked around him, straining to see the thin purple line that creased his cheek.

His reply was lost in the clatter of everything being swept back into the drawer.

"What?" she asked, stepping closer. "I didn't hear you," she called at his shoulder. "What?" The room was quiet. She didn't have to yell. Now she felt even more stupid.

"The cut's fine," he said, glancing uneasily at the door, then back to her. "Martha, I know we have to talk. But not right now."

"When?"

"Maybe later."

"I just remembered!" Frances called as she strode across the deck. She came into the kitchen to tell Mack the razor blades he needed were in the cigar box at the top of the cellar stairs.

With an ache in the pit of her stomach, Martha watched him look through the cigar box and, after finding the red box of blades, slide one into his paint scraper. Tonight. He wanted to see her tonight.

"Martha!" Frances said, so sharply that she jumped. "Go up and count the packages of paper plates."

She had no sooner entered the cool spare room that was filled with cartons of paper goods and bags of linen than Frances stepped in and closed the door behind her. Her lips were thin and gray.

"For Godssakes, don't ever stare at the front of a man's pants like that!"

"What are you talking about? Don't you talk to me like that," she warned, her face red. But it was true. She couldn't help it. Loving him was all she ever thought of now. In the middle of the night, she would wake up sweating and writhing with desire.

"Martha, you are so obvious. It's written all over your face." She looked at her. "Oh, would I love to know what happened here the night he left."

"I told you, nothing!"

"Did something get you mad? Did he say something?" Her voice fell. "Did he do anything, Martha?" Her eyes narrowed and she whispered, "Did he do anything to you? I won't be mad, I promise, but I should know."

"No!" she insisted, noting Frances's obvious sigh of relief.

———□———

It was early evening when Frances burst into her room with two shopping bags, which she flung to the floor. "What are these?"

"They're mine! Where'd you get them?" She searched through the bags for a note. Birdy must have found them in her car. "Is she here?" She ran to the window, then started for the door. "She didn't leave, did she?"

"That man," Frances said with a contemptuous gesture toward the driveway. "Getso. He said they're yours."

"He's here?" She was stunned.

"No. He was leaving them down by the mailbox and I came along." Frances looked down at her. "He was a nervous wreck. He said you'd left them in his car. Martha, what in God's name were you doing in his car? I mean, someone like that!" Frances shuddered.

"It's Birdy's car!" she said indignantly.

"But you were in it with him!"

"No! I was waiting for Birdy, and then he came out."

"You were waiting for Birdy, and then he came out," Frances repeated, starting to nod. "Oh! Now this is all making sense." She sagged against the door. "It was another one of your crushes, wasn't it? And then, when everything went haywire, you accused him of stealing. Just like that night with the boys." Frances looked as if she were going to throw up.

MARY MCGARRY MORRIS

"Don't say that! You don't know what you're talking about!"

"Oh God! And that's just what happened the other night with Mack, isn't it? Of course!" Frances threw up her hands. "It's so obvious!"

"Get out! Just get out! You don't know what you're talking about! You think you know everything about me! You don't know anything!" she said, trembling with the need to tell Frances that she had been loved, that it was so much more than Frances even imagined.

"I know one thing! You pester people and you pursue them and you haunt them and you've got to stop it before something terrible happens like that night in the woods."

"I told you, don't talk about that!" she warned, rushing at her. But Frances ran out, slamming the door behind her. She could hear Frances down in the back hallway, talking to Mack. "I'll kill her," Martha muttered against the door. "If she tells him, I'll kill her."

At eleven o'clock she woke up, moaning. She had been dreaming of Getso kissing her, his tongue slimy with phlegm. She jumped out of bed and scrubbed her teeth until her gums bled. She rinsed out her mouth with so much peroxide it continued to foam between her teeth as she stood at her window. The lights were still on in the apartment, and the steady click of Mack's typing carried through the still, warm night. Outside her door, the floorboards creaked, and Frances's bedroom door opened and closed. Martha washed her face and underarms, changed into a skirt and blouse, then doused herself with perfume. She waited ten more minutes, before she ran around the back of the house, staying on the grass to avoid the crunching stones of the driveway gravel.

"Mack!" she called, tapping lightly on the door. He was typing at the kitchen table.

"You said you wanted to talk to me," she said when he came to the door. She bit her lip to keep from grinning. He glanced toward the house, and she assured him Frances was asleep. "We can talk!"

"This isn't a good time," he said, gesturing back at the table. "I'm right in the middle of something."

"I'll wait, or I can come back. I'll go set my alarm."

"No!" He stepped closer to the screen. "I'll tell you now. I'm sorry. I am so sorry. For the things I said and what I did. And now I'm sitting on a time bomb here. She keeps asking me about that night. What did you tell her?"

"Nothing!" She smiled proudly.

"Don't." He stared at her. "Please don't."

"I wouldn't do that, Mack." She laughed and pressed her hands to the screen, against his chest. "Honest! I love you so much. I love you more . . ."

"No! Don't say that!" he hissed against the screen. "Don't talk like that! Don't think like that!"

"I can't help it! I think about you all the time. I ache inside for you. When you left, I thought I was going to die. I wanted to die! I need you so much, Mack!"

He opened the door and pulled her in, out of the light. He put his hands on her shoulders. "You need a friend and I'm your friend. That's all I am. Your friend. That's all I can be. I'll be your friend. I promise I won't hurt you ever again. I'll be your friend. I'm your friend and I'll be a good friend. I promise. Do you understand? Do you?" he demanded.

Dazed, she nodded. Yes, she understood. Understood that she had never felt this way for another human being.

———□———

It was the day before the party. A heat wave was predicted, so Frances and Dawn were testing small oscillating fans in strategic positions on mantels and tabletops. They had been delivered this morning by Frances's friend Bert, who owned the appliance store.

"Looks like an old-fashioned summer hotel out there," Mack said, coming into the living room. He had just finished staking the yellow canopy that would extend over the serving tables. He had been up since early morning assembling the umbrella tables Frances had rented. "Hey, kitten, c'mere," he called up to Dawn, who was perched on top of the stepladder. "I need a hand out there."

"I'm so tired," Dawn sighed.

The piano keys plinked as Martha wiped them with a damp cloth.

MARY MCGARRY MORRIS

"I'll help you," she said. His declaration of friendship had only made him more distant.

"That's okay," Mack said, grabbing one of the fan cartons and flattening it. "I need a break from the sun a while anyway." He reached for another carton.

"Don't!" Frances said.

"Just take me a minute," he said.

"No! Bert can't sell them without the boxes."

"He's going to sell them?" Martha asked.

"Yes," Frances said, with a look. "He's going to sell them." She set a fan on top of the piano.

"That's not right, unless he marks them down. They'll be used." She kept looking at Mack.

"Well, that's Bert's problem, not mine," Frances sighed, rolling her eyes.

"Yes, it is your problem," Martha snapped, determined not to be humiliated in front of Mack and this high-school girl, especially by Frances. She could feel their eyes on her. "It's a question of right and wrong! It's not right to use an appliance and then go sell it like it's brand new!" She hit her open hand with her fist. The world was filling up with people like Bert. Bend the rules, turn things just the slightest bit this way or that, until nothing anyone said or did could set things straight. Liars and thieves, like Getso. But not her. She was an honorable woman, someone Mack could trust and depend on. Someone he could love.

"Dawn, that one's not doing anything," Frances called in a strained voice, trying to ignore her.

"Which one?" Mack asked, looking around.

"Just like that time at the Cleaners. Same thing," Martha continued, determined to make her point.

"The one on the top shelf," Frances said.

"Oh, I did that," Dawn said. "Here, I'll move it."

"This man came in for his blazer and it wasn't even cleaned yet. So John told Mercy, 'Just pre-spot it and give it to him. He won't know.'

But I told him! I marched right out there and I said, 'Excuse me, sir, this isn't right. They're lying to you. This blazer has only been pre-spotted. This blazer has not been dry-cleaned and I do not think it's fair. Not at all. Not fair at all!' "

They stared at her—Dawn from atop the ladder; Mack with the reshaped carton against his chest; and Frances with her mouth agape.

"You didn't really?" Frances asked.

"Yes, I did! And I'm glad I did! And if Bert tries to sell these like new fans, I'll stand right there, right next to them, and I'll tell people." She looked at Mack with a surge of triumph. "I will!"

He looked away.

"Oh, Martha," Frances sighed. "What do you care?"

"I care! I care about a lot of things!"

The door closed, and she realized that Mack had slipped outside.

———□———

She felt better down here in the cool dark cellar. She was exhausted and jittery. Every time she blinked, she heard pinging sounds inside her head. Every noise made her jump, and her hands tingled with numbness as she wiped out the freezer chest and plugged it in. Unused for years, it had mildewed and still gave off a dank, brackish odor, even though she had already washed it three times with soapy bleach water. Now she began to clean the old refrigerator, with its small round motor set on top like a robotic head. Mack's legs kept passing the narrow mud-spattered cellar window as he carried out stacks of plastic chairs to the tables. She could hear Julia's voice upstairs. She and Frances were hanging new dotted-swiss curtains in the kitchen.

A truck swung into the driveway, then pulled close by the open cellar door. Mack told the driver the ice went down to the freezer.

"I deliver," the driver said. "I don't set up."

"There's someone down there," Mack said.

"Who?"

"Who? What do you mean, who? Just bring it down."

The dolly's thick wheels banged down onto each stone step. The truck driver peered through the glare of the doorway into the dim cellar. "Anybody down here?" he called. "I got five more of these."

"Five more what?" she asked, turning. He stared at her. She felt flushed and short of breath. This stocky balding man in white coveralls was Harold DeLong, whom she hadn't seen since high school.

"Pallets," he said, then nodded at the freezer when she did not respond. DeLong waited by the door while she shoved the bags into the freezer.

"Here," she said, thumping her chest and walking away from the dolly, which he dragged back up the stairs. She wheeled around. She had to get out of here before he came back. From overhead, through the black floorboards, there was a crash, then running footsteps. She cringed as Frances chided Dawn. "No! I never told you to put them there. Now look what you've done!" A broom whisked across the floor, sweeping up the clinking glass pieces.

At the sound of DeLong's voice, she backed away from the door and wedged herself into the narrow cobwebbed space between the refrigerator and the flaking chimney. She blinked as the loaded dolly banged heavily down the steps.

"Here we . . ." DeLong said, then called out nervously: "Hey! Where'd she go? What the hell . . . Jesus Christ, I was afraid of this," he muttered, bounding back up the stairs. He came back with Mack, who squinted in the shadows. "Martha? Martha!" he called. He walked past her twice, returning each time to the freezer, where DeLong waited with his arms folded. Mack began to unload the ice himself.

Cobwebs stuck to her hair and her back.

"You a relative or something?" DeLong asked.

"I just work here."

"Where do you think she went?" DeLong asked, looking around.

"I don't know," Mack grunted as he swung the bags into the freezer.

"I know her. We went to the same high school."

"Yah?"

"She's still pretty good-looking, you know, considering."

"Yah."

"She seem . . . weird? You know, a little strange?"

"What do you mean?"

"Strange! You know, like mental." DeLong said, stepping closer. "I used to feel bad, the way she got treated, but then, after what happened to my buddies, I mean, Christ, try and be nice and, the next thing you know, rape charges."

She bit her lip and sucked in the blood.

"What do you mean, rape charges?" Mack asked.

"Well, that's how it started. But then, you know, the truth always submerges, so everybody backed way off, because she . . ." DeLong made a lewd jabbing motion with his fist. "Hey, she knew. She was always begging for it. And then, what the hell, alone in the woods, partying with twelve guys. I mean, you know."

"What happened?" Mack asked, staring at him.

"Basically, she took 'em all on and then, after, she freaked out."

Mack kept staring. "That's impossible. No. That couldn't be true."

"Hey," DeLong said, his fingertips at his chest. "Why would I lie? It's commonly knowledge. Not only that, I know this guy Getso, he goes with Birdy Dusser. Gets is one hell of a tough guy, and he's scared shitless of her, him and Birdy both. Look, take my advice and just watch your step. Seriously, for what it's worth."

"It ain't worth shit now, buddy," Mack said under his breath, watching DeLong pull the dolly back up the stairs. As the ice truck started out of the driveway, Mack paced back and forth, then came to a sudden stop and yanked aside a large cardboard box, scraping it over the gritty floor. "Martha?" he called softly, then, taking the steps two at a time, bounded up the stairs into the kitchen. He opened the door and asked if she had come up there.

"No. Not up here," both Julia and Frances answered.

"You sure? She didn't come outside," he said.

"Oh for Godssake," Frances groaned, coming to the top step. "She's not going to start this again. Not now! Martha!" she ordered shrilly. "Damn it, Martha! If you do this to me now . . ."

"Damn it, Martha. Damn it, Martha. Damn it, Martha," she whispered, her head rigid against the flaking whitewash of the fieldstones. Their footsteps moved closer. Just go away. Just go away. Just go away. Go away. Go away. Go away.

"Martha!" Frances gasped and grabbed her wrist, wrenching her from the tight space. Cobwebs spun out dryly from her hair, and little stones and chips of paint fell onto the floor. Frances's nails dug into her flesh. "What happened?" she demanded, shaking Martha. "Tell me what happened!" She turned to Mack, whose face was gaunt. "Did something happen?"

"I don't think so. I don't know," he said, staring at Martha.

Julia came down and walked her up to her room. "You're shaking. You're afraid, aren't you?" Her eyes flickered toward the stairs. "It's him, isn't it?"

"Oh no," she said, meeting Julia's troubled gaze. "I could never be afraid of Mack."

———□———

Frances waited for Mack to put his dishes in the dishwasher, so she could lock up. It was only ten-thirty, but she had to go to bed. Everything was ready for the party. Tomorrow would be devoted to getting herself ready; she had a noon hair appointment, and then she would get her nails done.

He closed the dishwasher and she followed him to the door. He opened it, then shut it and turned back to her. "I keep thinking what a nightmare that must have been for Martha that night in the woods. I keep picturing it, how horrible it must have been." He shook his head. "And then for them all to get off scot-free like that!"

"I don't think you understand the position we were in. And how much more of a nightmare a rape trial would have been for her," she said, annoyed that he was bringing it up again.

"But she hadn't been raped."

"No, but everyone thought she had been. I told you, that was the rumor."

"It doesn't make sense."

"She said they touched her and poured beer on her, and that's what they said too. But they said she let them, that she wanted them to."

"Wanted them to poke her with sticks and spray beer on her? That's bizarre!"

"The point is, people believed it, which is understandable. Don't forget, Martha can be rather bizarre."

He had been staring at her. "Do you believe it?"

"No." She looked away. "Part of it. I don't know." She waved her hand. "I couldn't deal with it. Floyd and I, we just wanted it over. There wasn't a thing to be gained by pressing charges, except more humiliation for her."

"You're probably right," he sighed.

Probably right, she thought. Why was she even discussing this with him, of all people? She reached past him and opened the door.

"Still, it's a shame she's had to endure the rumors all these years."

"If they are rumors," she snapped.

"If?" he said.

"If!"

"Of course they're rumors. I mean, you should know better than anybody."

"Maybe that's the problem. That I do know better than anyone." She smiled wearily. "Good night," she said, closing the door.

Every time Martha got nervous, she closed her eyes and held her breath and counted to twenty-five. She wore one of her new dresses and her new canvas shoes, but the laces wouldn't stay up, so she had to keep untying them and crisscrossing them around her ankles. She had put on her new makeup, but then she felt so self-conscious that she had washed it off before coming down to the party. Traces of blue still smudged her eyelids, making her look heavy-eyed and tired.

Frances's insistence that she didn't have to come tonight only made her more determined to show Mack that she could talk to people and act as normal as everyone else here. It was only nine o'clock, but the starry night seemed ready to burst with heat and the band's frantic rendition of "Cherry Pink and Apple Blossom White" as the trumpets squealed over the din of expectant voices. The guest of honor was fifteen minutes late.

Inside the softly lit house, the fans turned in lazy crosscurrents of sultry air. From the doorway, she scanned the crowd for Mack. The band played a slow song now, and the few couples dancing appeared to be gliding over ice as the pale-gray decking shimmered under the glowing torchlights. She moved her feet, trying to recall the steps Mack had shown her. "One, two, three, one, two, three," she counted under her breath, turning slightly, then more, until her back was to the deck. "One, two, three." That was it!

"Excuse me."

She turned, embarrassed to find a young man with slicked-back blonde hair waiting to get by. She moved aside, and he opened the door.

"May I?" He grinned, lifting his hands.

"No!" She stepped back and folded her arms tightly. "I don't want to dance with you!"

He blinked. "Hey, no problem! Noooo problem at all." He hurried past her.

She came outside and sat alone at a table below the deck. She watched the women, in their pale dresses or long skirts with loose slouchy blouses, sipping their drinks and laughing brightly while their quick eyes alighted on everyone.

From down the road, a horn sounded three long toots, the signal for Steve's arrival with the Pierces, who had told him Frances was having a small dinner party for him. The long white convertible rolled into the driveway and the band began to play "Happy Birthday" with all the guests on their feet, singing. Steve just sat in the front seat, stunned and shaking his head. And now, to applause and raucous whistling, he got out and embraced Frances in a long tender kiss. A few women dabbed at their eyes as the couple climbed arm in arm onto the deck, smiling at each other.

"Speech! Speech!" called various voices. Steve held his hand over his eyes and peered out at everyone. "Bob!" he called, laughing. "Sandy," he laughed, pointing, and turned to say something to Frances. "I don't believe this!" he said, scratching the back of his head. "Golly!" He stood in silence for a moment on the edge of the deck, clutching Frances's hand. When he began to speak, his hoarse voice trembled. "I'm the luckiest guy I know and the happiest, to have all this. All my friends, all my good, good friends . . ." His voice broke and it took him a moment to begin again.

Frances smiled, her long black hair and tanned strong body vivid against her white linen dress. Just an hour ago, she had been in tears because the ice sculpture had started to melt and the caterer was short two waitresses (she had called Dawn and her girlfriend to fill in).

At the bar Mack was ordering a Scotch. Next to him was a muscular woman in a pale-blue sundress, her frosted blonde hair cut as short as a boy's. Steve was thanking them all for their "loyalty and kindness all these years and above all . . ." Again his voice faltered, and he hung his head. "For your . . . your understanding," he said, dislodging the words with a vigorous nod before turning away. Frances's face locked in a dark smile as everyone cheered and clapped and called up to him. Martha knew Frances had been offended by his appreciation of everyone's "understanding," clearly a reference to their relationship.

Mack laughed while the woman in blue dug through her purse. She took out a pen and paper and wrote something down, which she read back to him. Grinning, he nodded. His yellow shirt was buttoned at the collar, and one leg of his wrinkled chinos was spattered with stiff coins of white paint.

His wet hair was fastened in a stub at the nape of his neck. One, two, three. Her feet practiced the steps while she sat watching him. Maybe, when the music started, they would dance together.

"Hello, Martha!" a woman said. She looked up to see Lisa Brown, an old friend of Frances's. Lisa was originally from Mississippi. She and Frances had been inseparable for a few years, until some displeasure of Frances's, some imagined or exaggerated slight, had caused a breach. Lisa's first husband had been a close friend of Steve Bell's, and the two couples had often traveled together. Lisa's second husband was from Burlington, she was explaining now to Martha, who was staring at the blonde woman in blue silk. Every time Mack laughed the woman did too, with an almost imperceptible shimmy of her shoulders. Mack gestured and the woman lifted a locket from her neck and opened it. He bent close to see it, his face inches from hers. He said something and she smiled.

"Are you still living here? I heard about your father. . . . I'm so sorry. I felt terrible. When I heard, I kept remembering all those times here when Frannie and I'd make such messes in his . . . Martha?" She put her hand on Martha's arm and gave it a quick squeeze. "Honey, you're rocking," she drawled softly at Martha's ear.

She caught herself and sat perfectly still. Mack had wandered away from the bar and stood by himself at the edge of the patio, looking at the gleaming black Cadillac that was pulling into the driveway. The back door opened and out slid a small woman in a bright-green dress and white shoes that seemed too wide, too substantial at the ends of her birdlike legs.

"Oh my God," Lisa Brown crooned. "It's Anita Bell."

Steve's wife leaned down into the car to speak to the driver, then stood a moment, facing the pageant of stunned faces. She took a deep breath, folded her arms, and stepped off to the side, blinking nervously.

"I don't believe she is doing this," Lisa hissed through a smile, the same fixed smile of the other incredulous women. "I haven't seen her in years. My God, how she has aged. Poor thing just shriveled all up into an old lady. She looks like the oldest woman here, and I know for a fact she is not." Lisa shook her head. "She must be awful drunk to do this."

Anita Bell was sober, but shaky, weak-looking, ravaged by a lifetime's illness that had not only damaged cells and organs, but had invaded her spirit, leaving her tentative and pathologically shy. She lifted her head with a deep breath before approaching the nearest group of women. Startled, they seemed, without ever moving, to have reassembled themselves, their positions, their attitudes, and they quickly smiled, raised a hand, bent to brush the little woman's rouged cheek with theirs. Still, though, she held herself back just enough to signal some difference between her presence here and theirs.

"Poor Steve," Lisa Brown murmured, leaning forward as he came out of the house. With the long dragging step of a man wading through water, he made his way to his wife's side. People reached out and patted his arm as he passed. His hand at Anita's elbow, he steered her away from the astonished women. At the edge of the driveway, he stood talking to her, his head bent low and his shoulders hunched, for she was a diminutive woman. With Anita, he looked tall, while next to Frances, who was his height, he had always seemed short and slight, almost insignificant. Steve's face was close to Anita's, obviously to smell her breath and determine either her sobriety or the degree of her drunkenness. She spoke for what seemed like a long time. Head bent, he listened, nodding.

Frances had finally emerged from the house. Flanked by a cadre of friends, she stood on the deck, her shoulders so squared that all the bones in her long slender back strained against the taut skin. Bill Pierce held out a drink, which she took with an exaggerated sweep of her head and a bright, blurred smile.

Martha stared, remembering her conversation with Patsy Bell. Was this her fault? She could tell that Frances was struggling to appear unfazed. Anita shook her head, her gaze up at Steve steady and resolute.

He obviously wanted her to leave, and she was just as obviously refusing.

Up on the deck, the band played a slow, raspy jazz piece that Martha vaguely recognized. With his saxophone resting on his belly, the bandleader, a heavyset white-haired man, glanced down at the crumpled note he had just taken from his breast pocket. "Ladies and gentlemen," he began.

Stricken-faced, Frances took a step, but it was too late.

"The first song of the night is for," he read, "my darling, for my best friend, Steve, from Frances. 'Melancholy Baby'." He brought the saxophone to his mouth and began to play the first sad, sweet notes.

MARY MCGARRY MORRIS

Steve nodded cordially at the bandleader. Beside him, Anita blinked nervously, staring off into the floodlit trees. And on the deck, Frances's hand was pressed to her mouth.

"Come on, now," the bandleader said, gesturing down at Steve. "Let's you and the little lady take the first dance of the evening together now. Come on, now," he coaxed with a wave of the saxophone, "do us the honor." He began to play, and when Steve still had not moved, he stepped up to the colored spotlights and focused the smoky blue glow onto them. Anita mechanically lifted her arms to her husband, and there, on the edge of the driveway, they danced in the tight, measured steps of a couple on a crowded dance floor, each staring dismally into the distance. The spotlight caught the pinkness of Anita's scalp through her sparse dyed hair.

"That's just so sad," whispered a young woman who had just knelt down by Lisa.

"Isn't it, though?" Lisa whispered, staring at the stiffly moving couple.

"Frances Beecham ought to be so ashamed," the young woman said. "Look at that poor thing, her whole life's gone by and what's she got to . . ."

"Shut up," Martha growled, turning to glare at the young woman, who shrank back. "What're . . . who . . ." the young woman sputtered.

"Martha, honey, you just calm down," Lisa hissed. "You hear me, just . . ."

"Martha!" Mack said, bending in front of her so that he was all she could see. His breath cooled her face. "Let's take a walk."

They walked around the pool, across the gently sloping lawn, all the way up to the stone wall that divided the house grounds from the dark overgrown orchards beyond.

When she told him what had happened, he laughed. "I'm sure Frances is used to that kind of talk," he said, starting to lean back against the wall.

"Don't!" She grabbed his arm and he froze, his eyes widening on her. "That's all poison ivy," she said of the dark shiny leaves cascading over the stones. She took her hand away.

"Danger, everywhere I turn," he laughed uneasily, looking around. He was snapping a twig into small pieces. Below them the band was playing "Pretty Woman," with Bill Pierce at the microphone singing in a wobbly, self-conscious baritone as he looked between Steve's two women, Frances and Anita, fixed at polar ends of the party.

Mack cleared his throat. "You look very nice." He shook his head. "I feel guilty about your glasses, though."

"Here," she said, slipping them off and handing them to him. She waited while he twisted and bent them. Without her glasses, not only was the distant party a blur of lights, but all the voices and music were so muted, they seemed to be coming from far away. She moved her feet in those three little steps. One two three. One two three. It occurred to her that this might be the only thing she did not need glasses for. "We can dance if you want," she said, stepping back, one, two, three.

"Here you go," he said, returning the glasses. He watched her put them on. "Still the same, though."

"Oh no," she told him, insisting they were straighter. "I can tell." He stood so close that she ached to touch him. "I've been practicing, so, if you want to dance . . ."

"I hate to dance." He picked up another twig.

"Then why did you teach me?"

He laughed. "Must have been some other tall dark handsome stranger."

"It was you," she said coldly, not finding him the least bit funny.

He looked at her for a moment, and the neat scar shone in all the night lights, the stars and moon and blazing torches and floodlights, like another mouth, like a thin smile on his face.

They both watched a woman in a short twirly white dress and a man in bermuda shorts and a red sport jacket strolling arm in arm toward them. They smiled and nodded, both the man and the woman, regarding her with curious eyes. Finally the woman greeted Martha by name. Looking down at the ground, she pretended not to have heard.

MARY McGARRY MORRIS

Mack asked who they were. Friends of Frances's, she told him. "They used to come in the Cleaners," she added, lifting her head now that they were walking toward the party.

"And did you use to ignore them at the Cleaners too?"

"No. We used to talk about their dog, Brunilda. Every time they came in, that's what we talked about."

"So why didn't you just say hi now and something like, 'How's Brunilda doing?' "

"I don't know," she said, watching them stop at the bar. "It's different here."

"How's it different? You know them. They're the same people here as they are in the Cleaners."

"It's different." She shrugged. "I don't know. It just is."

"You just think it's different, that's all."

"It is different. At the Cleaners I learned all the rules, what day in meant what day out, and blue-bags–laundry, red-bags–cleaning." She laughed a little. "When I was there, I could make everything be right. I can't do that here."

He looked at her, his mouth so pinched she thought he was angry with her. "It's tough without the rules," he said, tossing the broken twigs over the wall.

An hour had passed. The bandleader, to compensate for his gaffe, had not once stopped playing. The night had become a frenzy of music. One song led wildly into the next. The waitresses were still passing hors d'oeuvres on round silver trays. The covered chafing dishes were being set up on the buffet table. Anita Bell was ensconced in a small circle of women, all her contemporaries. She said little, but gave her complete attention to whoever spoke. Steve stood near Frances, but they had barely spoken to one another.

Mack had been drinking steadily all night. Martha watched him turn from the bar with another drink just as Dawn came by with a newly filled tray. He put his arm around her and accompanied her from guest to guest. Blushing, she giggled so helplessly that Mack had to speak for her.

"Excuse me," he said loudly to the two couples who were talking to Mr. Weilman, "would anyone care for some pâté?"

Julia was sitting with Martha now. Mack had promised to dance one dance with her, and she was still waiting.

"It would seem that Mr. Mackey has had the course," Julia said.

"He's just fooling around," Martha said, annoyed with Julia's tone.

"He's also manic," Julia said, her sharp eyes trailing his continuing skit with Dawn, who doubled over in laughter. Mack had taken her tray and held it overhead on three fingers now as he minced through the crowd. He kept licking his lips and winking at people, especially men.

"He's very nice," Martha said, and Julia managed a weak smile.

"I'm sure he is," she said, and patted Martha's knee.

Mack had struck up a conversation with Anita Bell. They had already walked twice around the pool, and now they stood near Martha and Julia and Mr. Weilman, who had turned Julia's remark about loving orchids into a passionate dissertation on self-propagation.

"There are even some that nature has construed to look so much like female insects that male insects continually and, of course, quite futilely attempt to copulate with them." Mr. Weilman's cheeks burned a feverish red.

Julia leaned against Martha's shoulder and said behind her hand, "I'll hold the ladder while you jump."

Martha looked at her blankly. Ladder? She had no idea . . .

Julia nodded at Mr. Weilman, and then Martha got it.

He paused, trying to remember the name of one that resembled an insect, then, unable to recall it, went quickly on to describe the various ways some insects communicate with one another. With butterflies it was sight; with cicadas it was sound. Gypsy moths emitted pheromones. "And ants and bees as well!" he said, narrowing his watery, bright eyes.

Martha had no idea what he was talking about. Julia turned, her leg outstretched as if for flight. In the yellow glow of the evening, his shoulders sparkled with dandruff flakes, and the white tufts of hair in his ears seemed to shine.

MARY MCGARRY MORRIS

"There is this mighty force," he was saying, "this life-urging impetus. Like a throb in the dark of things . . ."

She listened. It had become a lovely evening. Mr. Weilman was the only person she had ever known to care so much about such strange things. Bits of conversations carried up to her, and she stared in the direction of the brightly lit pool water, and now, quite clearly over all the other voices, for the band had suddenly stopped playing, she heard Mack say to Anita Bell, "You ever hear an old song and think, Gee, I wonder what ever happened to so-and-so? You think, Maybe he died. Must've, he was so good, and now you never hear anything about him. Well, I know where they all are. Every single one of them—movie stars, TV stars, poets, singers, writers, old game-show hosts." His voice rose bitterly. People glanced his way. Anita Bell nodded intently.

"It's the most incredible underground of geniuses out there."

Nearby, people turned, briefly curious, amused.

"All gray-haired and paunchy, hanging out in bars, thumbing rides, passing each other back and forth on the highways, always leeching off a sister or a mother, because after a while, you know, they're the only ones left. The only ones who care. The movement's just too big to support all of us. There's just too many of us." He laughed. "Soon there'll be more of us than them!"

Seeing the long line forming at the buffet table, Mr. Weilman rose with tremulous alarm, anxious to take his place. Mack led Anita Bell toward Martha and Julia. He walked with great care, and when he leaned onto the table one hand shifted, causing him to stagger sideways. He caught himself, but had obviously twisted his hand. Wincing, he rubbed his blunted wrist.

Julia stared up at Anita until Mack finally reached the end of his elaborate introduction of the three women. "We've all met," Julia said. "Naturally."

His face tightened. " 'Naturally'?" What do you mean, 'naturally'?" he said, bending close. "What the hell's that mean, 'naturally'!"

"Well, we've known each other for years." She looked up and smiled.

"You have?" He looked back at Anita, whose pinched expression had not changed all evening. "You mean, you're all close personal friends and I'm an asshole for not knowing that."

"She didn't mean that," Martha said quickly.

"What'd she mean, then?" Mack asked.

Nervously she tried to swallow, instead began to choke.

Julia grabbed her hand. "Why don't you just stop it right now," she said, glaring up at him.

"Please," Anita Bell said in a small voice.

Mack smiled. "Martha thinks I'm an asshole." He looked back at Julia and winked. "She's very perceptive."

"It's getting late," Anita said, turning from the table. "I'd only planned to drop in."

"Don't you be silly!" Mack insisted as he gestured to the bartender with his empty tumbler.

"He makes my skin crawl," Julia muttered, watching him go.

The woman in blue stopped him. Martha stared in disbelief as he took the woman's hand and led her onto the deck, where they danced together. Mr. Weilman had returned, his plate mounded with food, but after eating a little potato salad, he said he was full.

The band began to play a limbo, and the dance floor cleared, except for Mack. Two women held the pool-net pole, lowering it each time Mack passed under. A crowd formed, clapping the beat. Now, with the pole at its lowest point and his back almost horizontal with the deck, he balanced his drink on his forehead, and had just inched his knees under the pole when he collapsed. Everyone gasped with laughter as he crawled away on his hands and knees.

After the party, Dawn moved along the deserted patio, emptying ashtrays into a tin bucket. In the kitchen, Frances was arguing loudly with the caterer. She complained that the potatoes in the salad had been partially raw and the salmon pâté had a sweet mealy taste.

"A sweet mealy taste!" the caterer cried.

"As if there was relish in it," she said.

"Relish!"

Mack dozed in a chaise longue by the pool, his chin on his chest, strands of hair over his eyes. From time to time, his head bobbed with a crooked smile.

All night long, the ice sculpture had dripped over the raw bar, until the arms of the scales of justice had melted to dull stems. Martha watched the caterer fly from the house, slam the door, and speed down the road in his jeep.

Steve had returned from driving Anita home. Before he went into the house, he paused on the deck steps, looking down at the pool, where Japanese beetles and parrot-green cocktail napkins and a clear plastic tumbler floated on the floodlit surface.

"It's late," he said to Martha. "Why don't you come in now and go to bed?"

"I will," she said. She was hoping Mack would wake up soon.

Inside the house, a door slammed. Then came a thud. Something had fallen.

"Damn it!" Frances cried. "Goddamn it!"

———◻———

In the rainy week that followed, a gray coldness clutched the house, and there seemed to be no way to get warm. The phone rang often, each caller anxious to assure Frances that it had been a spectacular party.

"Thank you," she would reply. "That's so kind of you . . . so good of you. . . . It was fun . . . He was surprised, wasn't he? . . . He was so pleased . . . so happy. . . ."

Actually, they wanted to hear firsthand Frances's opinion of Anita Bell's startling appearance, but she would discuss it only with Mack. Martha was loading the breakfast dishes in the dishwasher. At the table, Mack and Frances were on their third cups of coffee. She had angled herself so she could see Mack each time she looked up from the dishwasher. It pleased her that he was wearing an old plaid shirt of her father's.

"Apparently they were in on it. The two girls. They put her up to it. No!" Frances suddenly corrected herself. "Not put her up to it!

They . . . they managed it. They staged it—that's the word I want. 'Staged'!" She shook her head. "To hurt me. To humiliate me, that's why! You have no idea how good I've been to those girls over the years, how kind. On their birthdays it would be me who'd remind their father. Me who'd spend days shopping for just the right gift, the perfect card. She'd be off on one of her binges somewhere, and it would be time for back-to-school clothes or Christmas presents, and who do you think always took right over? Never say a word, just do what had to be done. And I never expected a thank you back. Never! But this! I mean, this just tears me apart." She shook her head, then looked away as if to hide tears.

Mack set down his coffee cup. "What did you expect? You must have expected something," he said.

"Well, I didn't. I cared about Steve, and so I cared about his daughters, and it was that simple," she said, her voice cracking. "I never wanted anything back."

"No, I don't mean that," Mack said. "I mean, you must have known they resented you."

"Me!" She touched the napkin to her eyes. "What did I ever do? It was never my fault!"

"They've probably blamed you all these years for their mother's misery, for her drinking."

Frances stared at him, her mouth caught in a stunned smile. "You don't understand. That woman was a hopeless drunk before I even knew Steve. I'm more a wife to him than she's ever been." Mack leaned forward as if he were going to say something, but all he did was nod.

SEVENTEEN

——o——

In the weeks since the party, Frances
had only seen Steve once. Tonight he hadn't gotten here until eleven—
too late to go anywhere, so they had ended up in the study. With the
only light the candles flickering on the paneled walls and ceiling and
the dark leather furniture, the room closed over them. She was determined not to say a word about the party. Before long it would be just
another joke they would vie to tell year after year. Actually, it was

funny. It really was. She couldn't wait for Steve to see Mack's imitation of the bandleader, his rolling eyes and syrupy voice crooning into the microphone. She and Steve had been through too much together to let Anita's inappropriate behavior come between them.

Sipping her vodka and tonic, she felt uneasy being the only one drinking. Steve had just wanted seltzer water. She could tell he had lost weight. Well, that was one benefit of not having been out to dinner in weeks. She, on the other hand, had gained weight, now that she was cooking dinner every night for Mack and herself. Martha would sit down and eat with them, but she always made a point of preparing her own food. Sometimes it almost seemed as if there were some competition going on, as if Martha were trying to show she was the better cook. Her moods were becoming more erratic. She hung on Mack's every word, one minute laughing too hard, the next relentlessly pressing some abysmal point. And then there were nights, when hunched over her plate, she would eat in bitter silence, refusing to say what had offended her. She made Mack nervous, but his patience with her and his kindness surprised Frances. He was a man of greater depth than she would have ever guessed.

"It just doesn't seem fair," Steve mused, squeezing the wedge of lime into the fizzing water. He licked his fingers.

"What's that?" she asked, laying her head back on his shoulder. God, she had missed him. She laid her hand on his thigh and felt such a sudden surge of desire that her face burned. She was having a stroke, and only love could save her. Only Steve. She began to unbutton his shirt.

As if it were the paw of some annoying pet, he removed her hand from his chest and set it on the sofa. "I don't know. . . . Seeing the girls so happy, it . . . it tears me apart. I think of how much they've missed. . . ."

She forced her eyes onto the shelf of books, all red leather, gold lettering, hand-tooled. Horace's Kipling. Mack had wondered if Horace had ever read them. She doubted it. Maybe that's what she should do. One by one, she would read them. The gaps on the shelves marked what Mack had borrowed. She would ask him where to start. Reading bored her, even the best-sellers her friends raved about. She needed action, throwing herself so completely, so fully into the task at hand that nothing else mattered.

". . . yesterday they went to a movie together." He shook his head and sighed. "A matinee. And then they came by the office. I watched them get out of the car, and they were laughing so hard, the three of them, they could hardly stand up. It just . . . it just tore me apart."

"Why?" she said, sitting up. She looked at him.

"All those years. They could have had all that with their mother. SHE could have had all that." He shook his head and sighed. "All that time . . ." He turned, and she was startled by the rawness of his eyes and the bitter set of his jaw. "Time! It's like a chunk of me is gone. I can't even stand to see them so happy. I keep thinking of all that TIME, all those years. They laugh and they talk and I can't even join in. There's no place for me. That part of me's dead. I keep wondering why she waited so long. And it tears me apart. It really does, Frannie." He put his hands over his face. "I'm afraid I have no feelings left," he gasped.

"Why should you?"

"She's my wife. They're my children."

She looked at him, containing herself so that she would not blink or flinch. Calmly, softly, she said, "Steve, why are you doing this to yourself?" She bit her lip to keep from adding "to us."

"It's the strangest thing. I've had this horrible emptiness, this sadness. I go to bed with it and I wake up with it. Some mornings I can barely lift my head off the pillow. . . ."

She held his hand. She had felt the same way these last weeks. Without him, she had felt so incomplete. Even as a young woman, she had been his strength, and he, hers. "Poor Steve, you're depressed, that's all."

"She says it's"—and here he gave a wry, bitter smile—"bereavement. Like grief, as if someone had actually died. She said she's seen it before, that I've lost the old Anita and I don't know how to deal with Anita the way she is now, so I'm filled with mourning."

"She? Who said that? Anita?"

A DANGEROUS WOMAN

235

"The therapist."

"That's bullshit!" She jerked her hand away.

"I don't know." He looked at her. "But that's just what it feels like."

She pointed, and his sudden cringing sickened her. She could just see them all cowing him, his daughters, Anita, the therapist. "You'd better not be discussing me in your . . . your sessions!" Her finger stabbed the air with each word. Of course he did. They all did. His bleak silence confirmed it.

How could he? Especially after what they had done to her. Maybe he didn't know that party had cost as much as a wedding and taken almost a year to plan. Maybe he didn't realize what a laughingstock she had become, what a fool she felt like with all their friends, the entire town. And now he dared discuss her with THEM.

No, no, he tried to tell her. She didn't understand. She didn't know what had happened.

"I know what happened! And so does every single person who was here that night!" she said. She started to reach for her drink, then drew stiffly back for fear she might throw it in his face or dump it in his lap.

"But you don't know why," he said, whining the way he used to on the phone with his daughters when they wanted him home; when there had been another crisis; when Anita had passed out on the toilet or she had brought some blithering bar pal home to drink with her.

"I know why! Because those two horses of yours wanted to rub my nose in it for everyone to see, that's why!"

"Frannie!"

"After all I've done for them, after all I've been through! After all I've given up!"

"It was Anita! The therapist, she made her. She said she had to face the thing head on. That she had to deal with the situation. She had to do something."

"So she told her to come here? To barge into my home? Into OUR party? That was her advice? Who is this idiot? What's her name? I'm going to call her. I can't imagine that kind of therapy. I mean it, Steve,

I'm going to do something!" She could just see her, some dippy little know-it-all like Julia's psychobabbling friends. These people were everywhere, on the radio and TV talk shows. Magazines, newspapers. Imagine going to some stranger with your problems. It was sickening. She had learned long ago with Martha what frauds they were. All their pills and talk, when nothing ever changed but the dates on the bills. Some things, some situations just had to be accepted. That was good mental health, to be able to recognize and come to grips with reality. That was strength.

"No. No. She didn't tell her to actually come here. What she told her, what she said, was that she had two choices, to either end the marriage or . . . or to confront the thing head on."

"Thing? What thing? Her drinking?"

There was a silence. "Us, I guess. Our relationship."

"What?" she was incredulous. Anita's problem was Anita. Everyone knew that. She listened in amazement as Steve explained that the therapist had told Anita that for years she had been the victim of their relationship. The therapist said it was an insidious situation because, while Anita had been victimized, she had also been the one who had allowed her husband's affair all these years as a precondition, a rationalization, an excuse for her alcoholism.

"What?" Frances kept saying. "What? This is bizarre! What are you saying?"

He tried again to explain.

"Wait! Wait!" she interrupted. "In other words, all these years, when everyone whispered how cruel this was to Anita, how unfair, we were the sad sacks, you and me—the two of us. WE were the victims . . . of her, of her weakness." She laughed bitterly. "What you're saying is, her drinking's what's kept us together all these years. That's what you're really saying."

"Of course not," he said. "You're twisting things."

"No," she said thoughtfully. "Maybe the therapist is right when you think of it, when you follow the logic of it. But, really, you were the one calling the shots all these years. You had it both ways, didn't you?" She smiled and leaned close, whispering behind her fingertips, "Poor innocent Steve. His wife's drunk and Frances Beecham's had him in her clutches all these years. Poor trapped Steve . . ."

His face reddened, and she could just picture all the groveling in the therapist's office: Steve with his head bowed, awaiting their absolution. What would he do to earn it? How far would he go? What would he tell them? She had been a fool. She had wasted her youth. Her life was two-thirds over and she would die alone.

From the hallway came the creak of the stairway. Martha. Of course, Martha. Always and forever and ever, Martha. Horace used to tell people there were ghosts in his huge house. Whose ghosts, a friend had once scoffed. The house wasn't old enough for ghosts; having built it, Horace was its first and only occupant. To this, Horace had replied, "My ghosts, the ones I bought." The truth in this suddenly sickened her.

"You know something, Steve?" she said, her flesh cold in this heat. "It just occurred to me. Because of you, I have nothing. Nothing."

His head shot up, but whatever he had been going to say he sighed away. "This hardly looks like nothing, dear," he said with a sweep of his arm.

"You know what I mean. You know exactly what I mean."

Again his head cocked. His bitterness stunned her. His eyes narrowed, and sweat beaded on his upper lip. He clasped her hand in his. "If you have nothing, Frances, it's because of who you've wanted to be all these years. You've always preferred the sanctuary of being Mrs. Horace Beecham." As he leaned closer, his thin, almost leering smile frightened her. "Don't you see, you've been married to a dead man all these years. A dead man!"

She pulled her hand away and slapped him. Shocked, she remembered his saying once how Anita thought nothing of hitting him with her fists or brooms or vases.

Eyes wide, he touched his cheek. "Poor old Horace," he said, chuckling. "Everyone warned him. They told him it wouldn't last the year. Little did they know just how faithful you'd be."

"Get out!" she screamed in a lunge that half-toppled him from the couch and left her trembling on its edge.

She locked the door and turned off all the lights. She sat back down

MARY McGARRY MORRIS

and finished her drink, holding the glass to her mouth a long time. It seemed vital that she consume every drop, every sound, every smell. She was exhausted, but every nerve tensed with the fear of sleep. This was the last of caution, she thought, her eyes scanning the shadows with mounting dread. Now there was only this room and that wild place she had come from. She had gotten so far on the shortest of tethers. She would die alone, in the dark of this room, alone, if she didn't get out of here, if she didn't do something. She ran along the dark hallway to the intercom at the bottom of the back staircase. On the seventh buzz, his staticky voice answered, "What? What is it?"

"Mack? Mack, are you up? It's Frances."

—□—

Every day at noon, they met at the pool, by degrees turning the chaise longues, angling them throughout the afternoon, their long oil-slicked bodies gleaming in line with the sun. The cocktail hour began at five, and then they would sit out there until the sun set. For the last two nights, they had eaten at the club, not getting home until midnight.

Martha watched them cross the moonlit driveway, their arms around each other's waists until they came to the narrow stairway up to the garage apartment. Laughing, they stumbled in to one another and then Mack stepped back to let Frances enter first. The lights never came on. For the next few hours, she watched the windows leak a deeper darkness into the night.

It was finally morning now, and she was listening for the squeak of a door or the sag of a floorboard that would signal Frances's return. To make sure Frances hadn't slipped in unheard, she peeked into her room and saw the bed still littered with Frances's clothes. In the cold morning light, the tangles of bright skirts and shorts and cotton dresses, so heedlessly tossed, were as shocking as if she had come upon her aunt's naked body.

"Bitch!" she muttered, grabbing a dress and throwing it across the room. "Bitch . . . the bitch . . ." She was flinging the clothes onto the floor.

"Stop that!" Frances ordered from behind. She reached for Martha's upraised arm. "Put that down!" She yanked Martha's hand to her side.

Frances's eyes were puffy, the wrinkles around her mouth and nose darkly embedded. "What are you doing?" she demanded, staring at the mess of clothes on the floor.

"Nothing," Martha muttered. She began picking up the clothes and putting them back on the bed. Head down, she hurried past Frances into the hallway.

Throughout the day, she was conscious of their watchfulness. Even now, from her room, she could see them by the pool, looking uneasily toward the house every now and again, their heads turning suddenly, squinting, startled as if the distant boom, the flash of wings, the child's cry on some errant wind might be her.

Behind them, the pool shimmered. Frances rolled from her back onto her stomach, then reached across and laid her hand in the small of Mack's back, her fingertips tucked under the elastic of his swim trunks. Quickly his hand swung back to remove hers. Laughing, Frances slapped his backside. He turned over and sat up, his eyes scanning the house, the way one would a darkening sky.

She stepped back, suddenly remembering a time when the school nurse had called her father to come and take her home. She had fallen in the schoolyard and skinned both palms and then wouldn't let the nurse even look at them. Her father's tall stiff presence coming down the hallway had struck her as that of a stranger. He had seemed totally alien to her. When he stepped into the office, he spoke to the nurse, who kept her back to Martha (. . . there were things Mr. Horgan should know . . . not like other children . . .). She had been afraid of her father that day. His voice was different, his shoulders set too straight, his head caught as if in mid-blow. He was defenseless. In town, as long as he came on Beecham business, he was respected and catered to. But on his own, he was a fragile man, and she was his greatest flaw. Just as she had now become Mack's.

She remembered the sudden terror that had risen in her skull, and the cold air meeting the gravel-studded flesh of her palms as her father offered them up to the nurse, and the look that had passed between them, father and daughter, the cold unyielding acknowledgment that there, out there, the world was dangerous, and that survival depended upon acquiescence. There, her father would not tolerate strangeness. It was only at home that he left her alone to flourish in her abundance of quirks and terrors.

She watched from the side of the shade. Frances was reading beneath the brim of a floppy straw hat. Mack sat on the side of the chaise, facing her. He leaned forward expectantly. When Frances finished reading, she looked up and said something. He smiled, nodding as she spoke, and then she handed back the sheaf of papers. Martha realized that it must have been something Mack had written. Her hand hit the window shade and it snapped up. Every time she pulled down the shade, it snapped back up against the roller. Finally, with the two of them staring up at her, she got the shade down.

Eighteen

Mack sliced a cucumber and shredded half a head of lettuce. Next he sliced a carrot, dropping it unpeeled into the bowl.

"Reminds me of my old short-order days," he said.

Martha kept stirring the onions and peppers round and round in the sizzling butter. She made a hamburg patty, and the slap of her hands on the cold raw meat came like a throb, a painful nakedness, an intimacy so acute it disoriented her that he stood so far apart. She turned dizzily toward the stove.

"I'm on a new regimen," he was saying. "Good food, fresh mountain air, and no booze!" He sat at the glass table, facing her. "I feel great," he said, starting to eat. "I can think straight, which for most people isn't any big deal, being able to think straight—but for me, it's a tremendous shock. I've been so used to this mush brain, I forgot what it's like to go from point A to point D or G or whatever, in a straight line."

She didn't say anything.

"Well, anyway." He sighed. "It feels good."

She stood with her back to him while her hamburg fried. The grease splatters rained onto the stove top. She flipped the hamburg and it sizzled in the grease. She turned, oblivious to the spatula dripping grease down the front of her shirt. "Did you tell her?" she asked.

"Tell? Did I tell . . ." His face paled. "No! Of course I didn't! I wouldn't. No!" he said, coming closer. "And you mustn't either!"

"I know what's going on, you know. Don't think I don't!"

"Nothing's going on. Frances and I have become good friends. Martha, she says I can stay here as long as I want. You don't know what that means to me, what that's worth. This is the end of the line for me, the last stop. You know when I knocked on your door that first night?"

She nodded.

"I had no place to go and not a friend left on the face of the earth, but the worst of it was, I didn't even care. I haven't cared for a long time about anything. And now there's so much to care about. I care about you and I care about this place and I care about Frances; I like her. But I'll be honest. What I care about more than anything else is my writing. It's going almost too well. I wake up every morning now panicky. I keep thinking it's no good, that it must be lousy if it's so easy. And then I read it and I swear to God it seems like somebody else wrote it. There'll be certain phrases or even whole sentences I won't remember writing. And you see . . . what I'm trying to say . . . in a way, it's . . . it's like what happened . . ." he said, his face moving closer in his hungry, draining way. "The things I did . . . Jesus, they were brutal. It's like the same thing—the dark side of it—only it's disgusting. It's so disgusting. It's like . . . like fouling yourself in your sleep!" His eyes were bright and his face strained with the force of some vile expulsion.

The back door creaked open onto Julia Prine, and Mack hurried out of the room.

"Martha," she said calmly, though her cheeks flushed with alarm. "You've gotten grease all over yourself." She wet a dish towel and from under the sink took a bottle of pine-scented cleanser and began to scrub at the spots on Martha's shirt front. "Are you all right?" she asked.

Martha nodded, her eyes thick with tears.

"What did he say to you?" Julia demanded. "What did he do?"

"Nothing," Martha insisted.

———□———

That night Steve called. His voice was low and indistinct, as if he had to muffle it at his end. Martha carried the phone into the study, where Frances sat reading a book Mack had chosen for her.

"I'm busy tonight," Frances said to him. "There's nothing to discuss. . . . You already did. . . . You made yourself perfectly clear the last time you were here." She hung up and sat for a few minutes before she crossed the driveway and went up to see Mack. His typewriter had been going all night. It stopped, but then, a few minutes later, Martha was relieved to hear the typing start, and then she saw Frances come down the stairs and return to the house.

It was long past midnight when Martha raised herself on one elbow, her hand at her mouth, her eyes wide. She crept out of bed and listened at her closed door. When the footsteps passed, she turned her knob, and held it from clicking, while she opened the door a crack. At the end of the dark hallway, Mack was closing Frances's door softly behind him. She tiptoed down the hallway to the linen closet, where she huddled in the deep alcove, and listened to them groaning, each panting the other's name. She covered her ears, imploring them to stop . . . stop . . . stop. . . . "Stop it!"

"Stop that!" Frances cried, pulling her from the dark doorway. "What's wrong? What're you doing in here?" Her free hand clutched the front of her robe closed.

"It must have been a nightmare," Mack said, trying to catch his breath. Wrapped in a sheet, he stood behind Frances with sweat dripping from his nose and chin. "Martha, you were having a nightmare, weren't you?"

"You're all right. Everything's all right. Just go back to bed now and everything will be all right," they coaxed her back down the hall, their raw voices writhing together, each reeking of the other.

——□——

All week long, she had stayed out of their way. If they came into the kitchen, she fled into the study. Since the last few days had been overcast, neither one of them had gone out to the pool. So she did, in pants and an old shirt of her father's. She brought out a magazine, which she glanced at from time to time to keep from staring at the house. She saw the light in Frances's bathroom go on, then a few minutes later watched Mack come out and hurry over to the apartment, his eyes downcast as if he had no idea she was there. Closing the magazine, she curled up on her side against the bite of the wind through the trees.

On Wednesday, Julia drove up and found her like this. "Martha? Martha?" She kept prodding her shoulder. "Are you all right? Martha!"

She feigned a deep sleep until Julia finally went inside, and then she ran around the back of the house and tiptoed up the dim rear staircase to her room. She could hear the two women's voices down in the kitchen; at times Frances's voice rose shrilly. After Julia left, Frances banged on her door. "Why are you doing this?" Frances demanded, rattling the knob. And when she didn't respond, there was a moment of quiet, and then Frances said, so close against the door that there seemed to be a stir of air in the stale gray room, "Go, then! Why don't you just go and let me be!"

At night, she was awakened by the briefest sounds, an owl's sudden hoot, a tree branch lashing the brick, the curtains gasping in and out over the sill. Fists clenched, she trembled with every murmur, every creak of the sagging springs, until finally, inevitably, it began again, the dull rhythmic rub of the bed frame under their pummeling wet bellies. Turning, she spread herself hungrily to the black damp chill and started the cold snap of her flanks up and down, up and down, all the while thinking of him. The next morning, she dragged out of bed, as weakened by their lovemaking as they were, the three of them limp and disheveled.

The calls had come to seem like rituals in a ceremony that had to be performed a certain number of times before Birdy would come to her. First she would call her at home and listen to the recording, which she now found strangely soothing. Next she would call the Cleaners. As soon as one of the women answered, she would hang up, wait a while, then try again. The space between calls was growing shorter and shorter. One of these times Birdy was bound to answer. She longed for someone to talk to, so she could understand what was happening here. On her last call to the Cleaners this morning, John had screamed her name into the phone, so she had forced herself to wait two hours before making this one. She had just picked up the phone when she heard a woman's voice on the line, answering, "Sheffield Publishing."

"Mr. Burke, please," Mack said. She could tell by the static that he was using the phone in the apartment.

"May I ask who's calling, please?"

There was a pause. "Uh, Colin Mackey. I'm one of his authors!" he added in a rush, as if to get that in before she could hang up. "He's my editor!"

"I'm sorry, Mr. Mackey, but Mr. Burke isn't in right now. Could I take your number and have him call you back?"

"That's what they said yesterday, and the day before, and he still hasn't called me," Mack said.

"I'll give him your number, sir, if . . ."

"He's already got the goddamn number. Go look on his desk. There must be thirty little pink slips there that say Colin Mackey! Colin Mackey! Colin Mackey! Goddamn it, I have to talk to him! Do you understand?"

"Yes, Mr. Mackey, I'll tell him you've called and that you're very anxious to speak to him."

Mack groaned. "Oh God. I'm sorry. I apologize for that."

"That's quite all right, sir. I'll give him . . ."

"Miss! You see, I'm starting to feel a little desperate here." His voice cracked. "Look, between you and me, I know what the problem is. I know why he won't call me. But would you tell him—would you write this down, please?—that I'm going to pay back every cent, every penny I owe him. All I ask is that he just listen to what I'm doing. That's all I ask."

"I have that, sir. And I have a lot of calls coming in right now. So I'll give him that message. Thank you." The woman hung up.

His bitter laugh sent a chill through Martha. "Yah, okay. Thank you. And thank him, the son of a bitch, the fucking no good faggot." He banged down the phone.

Later that afternoon, Mack told Frances that Leland Burke had finally called him back. Martha's head shot up at the obvious lie. The phone had rung only once all day, and that had been a wrong number. She tiptoed out of the study and stood near the living-room door. He lay on the sofa with his head in Frances's lap. She was running her fingers through his hair.

"It's the dialogue he wants me to be tough on. He reminded me how much I do of it. Too much." He raised his head. "He's right. I just go on and on with it."

"Does he want to see it? Have you sent him any of it yet?" Frances asked, her voice catching with this girlish apprehension it took on lately whenever they discussed his book.

"He's good. He'll listen. He'll give his writers all the time they need, but he wants the whole thing."

"But what if you finish it and he hates it?"

"He won't hate it! How can he hate it? He knows how it's going. This morning he made me read him half a chapter."

"What did he say?"

A DANGEROUS WOMAN

"After I finished, there was this quiet, you know. This silence. And I thought I was going to be sick, and then he said that's what he's been waiting for all these years. My big book, he said. He blew my mind."

"Oh my God, Mack, I'm so happy for you!"

Martha tiptoed down the hallway, and suddenly Frances was behind her.

"You're doing it again! You've got to stop this lurking!" she called as Martha ran up to her room. "It's driving me crazy! Or is that what you want? I think it is!"

As soon as Frances left for the club, Martha hurried across the driveway and up the stairs to the garage apartment. She had to knock for quite a few minutes before Mack finally opened the door.

"Everything okay?" he asked, looking past her to the house. "Something wrong?"

She held the heavy flannel shirt closed at her throat. All the day's rawness had lodged in her bones. "I want to talk with you."

"You caught me at a bad time."

"I always catch you at a bad time."

"I'm working, that's all I meant, Martha."

"I can wait. I'll be quiet. I won't say a word." She'd love to sit in here and watch him write.

He had been shaking his head. "Besides," he said, "Frances will be back any time."

"So?" she said, her gaze so unwavering that he looked away. "What's wrong with me being here? This is where I lived my whole life."

"You know what I mean, Martha. You know what she thinks." He looked at her fearfully.

"She thinks I stare at you and I follow you and I eavesdrop on all your conversations."

He winced with each declaration, and when she stopped he looked surprised.

"But I don't do it on purpose. Sometimes I look up and I see you looking at me. Why do you do that?" She tried to make it sound like a reasonable enough question. She forced a weak smile.

MARY MCGARRY MORRIS

He shrugged. "I'm just looking. It's a normal reaction. Two or three people in a room, you look at them."

"That's right. And it doesn't mean you're staring, right?"

"Right."

"And when I say something and you hear me, it doesn't mean you're eavesdropping. You couldn't help it. You just heard it, right?"

"I guess so," he said, still unable to meet her gaze.

"And I wasn't eavesdropping either. I couldn't help it. I just heard you."

Now he looked at her.

"Nobody's called you on the phone all week. In fact, the only calls you ever get are from Frances. Nobody named Leland Burke called here."

"I called HIM."

"But you didn't talk to him."

"No, I didn't," he admitted.

"You lied to her."

He nodded stiffly. "Are you going to tell her that?"

She shook her head no.

He almost seemed amused. He leaned back against the door frame. "Of course you are!"

"No! I won't. I swear I won't!"

"Oh, I see. I get it. One more dagger over my head," he said, still smiling. "Why don't you just tell her, Martha? Go ahead and do me the favor."

"No."

"No, I mean it. I want you to! Why drag it out!" He waved his arm in disgust. "Just do it. Get it the hell over with."

"I'm sorry, Mack. I won't say anything. I promise I won't."

His eyes glazed with panic and he stared past her. "What the hell am I doing here? Jesus Christ!"

"I'm sorry," she whispered. "I shouldn't have said anything."

He looked down, blinking as if surprised to find her still here. "Martha, do you want me to leave? Wouldn't it be easier if I left? Tell me what to do! Tell me! Tell me what you want and I'll do it."

A DANGEROUS WOMAN

"I want you to love me, but you love her!" she moaned, driving her fist into her palm. "I think about it and think about it and now I don't know what to do anymore."

As he stepped closer, his face darkened and his eyes paled. "Listen to me! That has nothing to do with love. Nothing! Do you understand?" he growled.

"Then what is it? What do you call it?" she cried, swinging at him in the rage she felt night after night.

He grabbed her arms and backed her against the railing, pinning her with his leg. "It's a fuck. I fuck her like I fucked you," he said, then released her so abruptly she staggered sideways. "And the only time it's love is when I fuck myself," he said, laughing.

She felt her way down the steps. She needed help. She needed to talk to someone before something terrible happened. She ran into the house and dialed Birdy's number. "Please, please, please," she whispered as the ringing began. "Help me, Birdy. Please help me."

"I'm sorry, but the number you have just dialed . . ."

"Martha!" Frances called from the kitchen. "Steve's on the phone. He wants to talk to you."

She lay by the pool, her chest rising and falling with the slow steady rhythm of deep sleep. In her early teens, this ability to lie perfectly still for hours had provoked her father into taking her to a doctor in Albany. "What she does," the doctor had said, "is work herself into a temporary state of catatonia." It was a kind of self-hypnosis, a hysterical paralysis, the doctor explained. "Paralysis" was the only word her father would be able to recall of the entire fifty-dollar consultation. After that, if she did not respond when he tried to wake her, he would shake her, calling her name loudly, his breath on her face thin with fear. It came to be her way of gauging his love.

"Martha!" Frances called again now, then slammed the door when she still didn't move.

Steve wanted her to come into his office and sign papers so her father's will could be probated. She couldn't even talk to him on the phone, much less take a trip into town.

The last few days here had been terrible. Frances blamed Martha because Mack seldom came over to the house. She knew something had happened, but neither one of them would discuss it with her. Frances and Mack were barely speaking.

Frances came off the deck and stood over her. "Steve's called three times," she said, even though Martha still hadn't opened her eyes or moved a muscle. "I'm so sick of this. I told him it's your business. Not mine. But, of course, we know that can never be true, can it?"

Silence. Martha took her breath in long measured draughts. An airplane buzzed in the distance. From inside the house came radio music and the drone of the vacuum cleaner. Dawn was cleaning.

"Lay there, then," Frances hissed, bending close to her. "For all I care, you can rot there."

———□———

Martha was tired all the time. She was asleep in her room when the banging started. She opened her eyes, confused.

Dawn was knocking on her door. "Martha!" she called. "It's that friend of Mrs. Beecham's, that guy Steve? I told him she's not here, but he said he wants to see you."

"I'm busy," she said, looking around at the mess. Yesterday, after another blow-up with Frances, she had threatened to move out. Dumping out her drawers and closet was as far as she had gotten.

"He said it's important." Dawn paused. "He said he'll come up if you want."

At that Martha swung open the door. "I'm cleaning," she explained as the wide-eyed girl stared in at the dark piles of clothes.

All the while Steve spoke, she was conscious of how dirty she must look. She hadn't showered in days. Her pants smelled. She crossed her legs and held her arms close to her sides. "Yes," she murmured, nodding in reply to some question she had barely heard and did not understand, but she knew by Steve's gesture toward this typed and seal-embossed document that she was supposed to sign it.

"Take your time. Read it. People should," Steve said, going to the window. His hair bristled over his collar, and his suit pants bagged at the knees, and the toes of his cordovans had been scuffed colorless. She could tell by the way his wrinkled jacket sagged from his shoulders that he had lost weight. Steve had joined the unloved, whose ranks included herself.

She moved her eye up and down the page, then handed it back. He gathered his papers, examining each one with exaggerated attention before returning it to the manila file with her father's name on the blue tab. "So!" he said. "How're you doing?"

"All right," she said, and he nodded, busying himself with the straps on his worn briefcase. He fumbled with the buckle. "And how's Frances doing?"

"Good."

"That's good. So!" he sighed, bending over the windowsill and looking toward the garage. "Where's the handyman? Mackey. He still around?"

"He's over in the apartment. That's where he writes. Well, not right now. Mostly he writes at night. Sometimes he'll type for hours. His light'll be on and all I can hear is his typewriter."

"I wonder what he's writing," Steve mused. He turned from the window, smiling at her. "Who knows, maybe he's writing about you, Martha."

Her hand flew to her mouth. "I don't think so," she said, and she began to cry, all the hurt of these last few weeks finally erupting.

He flinched, his expression roiling with pity and repugnance. "Martha, I didn't mean to upset you," he said. "I didn't mean that he might be writing about you for any particular reason." He looked more closely at her. "Do you see much of him? Does he spend much time over here?"

"No," she sobbed. "Because he hates me. He hates me."

"Martha! I'm sure he doesn't hate you. Why would he hate you?"

Just then a car tore around the driveway, and he hurried to look out the window. He wet his fingertips and smoothed down his hair.

Frances was angry to find Steve with Martha, who was red-eyed and blowing her nose. "I told you to forget it," she said to him. "This is what's wrong. Everyone treating her like a child. Julia's right! I should let her fend for herself. Why should I be the one . . ."

"Frannie, what's going on?" he blurted. "You won't talk to me on the phone. You're avoiding me, aren't you? I love you, Frannie," he whispered hoarsely. "I need you. You're my whole life!"

Frances's mouth fell open. "Your whole life! How do you figure that?" she said with a laugh.

He said he missed her so badly he was barely eating or sleeping anymore. He couldn't concentrate at work. It felt as if a part of him had died. She laughed again, and now he paused, looking at her as if he had just come to an enormous decision. He slid the case folder into his briefcase, then stood with his hand on the doorknob. "I'm done here. But you mean too much to me to just walk away without telling you something about your friend Mackey. I made a few phone calls, and, Frannie, there's a publishing company in New York he owes over thirty thousand dollars to for a manuscript he got an advance on and never finished."

"I'm aware of that."

"He still sends them outlines of books that never get written. Now they just ignore him."

"I know all that. Mack already told me."

"And it doesn't bother you?"

"No, why should it?"

He swallowed sourly. "Because now he's telling them he's found a patron who's willing to pay that all back for him."

"And he has!" She laughed. "Steve, I'm just taking your advice. You're the one who's been telling me all these years it's my own money, that I should say the hell with Horace's accountants and just do what I want with it." She smiled sweetly. "And so I am!"

Poor Mack, Martha thought. He needed Frances's help more than he had been able to tell her. Now she understood both his bitterness and his desperate fear of Frances's finding out about them. Frances had bought him.

"Don't be ridiculous," Steve said. "He's a bum. A down-and-out bum."

"No, he's an investment, Steve. As you well know, time's been the only thing I've ever dared invest." She smiled. "Now I think I'll try money."

Steve closed his eyes and sighed. "This is my punishment, isn't it?"

"Oh no, Steve. I'm just following your good example. Rehabilitation is so gratifying."

N I N E T E E N

―――――――□―――――――

"Slow down!" Martha kept calling. Mack was driving too fast for these narrow back roads.

"I'm only going thirty-five," he called back, grinning.

"Where are we going?" she asked again.

"I told you, it's a surprise!"

"Please tell me. I hate surprises."

"You'll see. We're almost there."

Here the road tunneled into the leaning shade of wild ash in which the white birches flashed past with a reach of ghostly limbs, and now this stand of tall spindly pine so dense the lightless lower branches, rubbed bare of needles and even of twigs, had fused to a black impenetrable fence. The car slowed with the road's steep dark climb. At the top he pulled off to the side, gesturing to the three houses below, the two on the left, small weathered boxes onto which square rooms had been appended, both flat corrugated roofs pierced by identical silver stovepipes. Long-legged chickens strutted past the wheelless, windowless, rust-eaten vehicles tossed up in their common front yard like recent glacial rubble. Behind the second house there was an ancient snub-bodied mustard-yellow milk truck with ball-fringe curtains sagging on string across the windshield. At the driver's door a lush white clematis climbed a strand of wire. Nearby were the sprocketed skeletons of old bikes and a baby carriage with its brittle canvas faded an inky blue, its rusted handle severed.

"That's the main house," Mack said, pointing to the larger, two-story house across the road. Its only adornment was a narrow porch from which the roof had been recently removed. Pink tufts of insulation protruded like raw flesh from gaps where clapboards had been crow-barred away with the roof. On the porch, to the left of the front door, was a bronze-toned refrigerator. Atop that was a silver ice bucket filled with orange plastic flowers.

"You ever been here before?" Mack asked.

"I don't know. I don't think so." Its unyielding tenacity was familiar; reminding her of thrift and the bare, hard using of things. "It's . . . it's . . ." The words eluded her.

"The Horgans," Mack said. "Your father and Frances grew up in that house. His cousin's there now, and across the way there's his cousin's two sons, and down back, you can't see from here," he said, gesturing, "in the trailers, are the two daughters and, I think, another son, and all their families."

Nearby, through the rock-ribbed hidden ravine, ran the Cold River. That was the sound she could hear, the rush of the unseen river like dry leaves rustling beyond the still trees.

MARY MCGARRY MORRIS

"Maybe I came here when I was little. I don't remember," she said, the dampness so pervasive she could taste its piney greenness.

"Fascinating, isn't it? This is where Frances Beecham grew up. She lived right down there. In that very house. Probably looked out that very window down on this same road."

"Is this the surprise?" she asked uneasily.

He turned abruptly, his arm over the back of her seat. "You're going to meet your family! Come on!"

When they got out of the car, a shaggy black-and-white dog shot around the side of the house, barking and digging its paws into the dirt in its half-friendly challenge. The door was opened by a slight gray-haired woman in red pants and a flowered sleeveless smock. She came off the porch, her head at an angle, squinting, her nose twitching as if to determine their scent.

"Anardelia? It's me, Mack. And this is Martha."

"Oh my God," she cried, coming closer. "Now, look what's here! Can you just stand it." Smiling, she examined Martha from every angle. "Sorry I didn't make the funeral," she said with a righteous jerk of her head. "But when a man turns his back on family . . . Well, like Earl always said, there's no sense arguing with the dead, and besides, Floyd had his reasons." Again she smiled at Martha. "But look at you!"

They sat in the bright room that was the parlor end of the kitchen. A partition of unpainted sheetrock filled the wide oak doorway that had once led to other rooms. Anardelia explained that her granddaughter and her husband were converting the house into a two-family. They had started work on it last week.

"That's Velma," the woman explained with a gesture back at the patched opening, "married to Binky, one of the Herebondes. Distant something or other, way on back. I can't keep track. Earl did. He had all the connections right up t'here." She tapped the top of her head. "He's the one I told you Miss Francie-pants cut cold."

"Miss Francie-pants!" Mack laughed. He sat back on the afghan-covered sofa, legs sprawled, arms stretched along the high roll of the sofa back.

"That's what we called her when she was just that high." The woman held out her hand. "Little bit of a thing, and just as different as the day was long. That came from being spoiled so. The mother died having her, and then, some years after, the father died too, and, Lord, what use was Floyd, living on the Beecham place? So me and Earl raised her a few years, but of course, with seven of our own, we were busting at the seams, so when Floyd married Pearl we went and said, 'Now, Floyd, you got to take some responsibility here. By then she was twelve or thirteen maybe, and raising hell like you never seen before. I can't tell you the nights I sat out on that porch watching the moon rise and the moon set, and then I'd go wake Earl up, and off he'd go till he found her."

She patted Martha's knee. "But look at you. Earl'd feel good to see you here. He always said, 'They can say what they want, but they won't ever know until they walk a mile in her shoes.' "

The windowsill was jammed with pots of spindly geraniums, their limp hairy leaves drooping in the dusty sun. The woman had twice offered them coffee, which they had twice refused. Something cold, then. Heat poured into the room. Did they want ginger ale or beer, she asked, half out of her seat. Mack said beer was fine and looked at Martha, but she shook her head and went on chewing the soft side of her thumbnail. She was disappointed. The little she had been interested in was already past, her father and her mother, so now she only half listened. The woman returned from the porch, where she had gotten a beer from the refrigerator. Martha's stomach felt queasy at the pop of the tab and the foam on the rim. She watched the fervid set of Mack's jaw, his teeth bared to the can, his eyes closing as he sighed with his first long swallow. He and the woman continued talking. He seemed familiar with most of her stories. Anardelia was telling him how, on the pig man's wedding day, his house had been burned to the ground by his bride's addled brother; how, when Doe Friester won the Tri-State lottery, she gave up drinking and joined the convent—a belated vacation, they called it—and now old HotTop, whom she'd divorced years before, was suing both her and the Sisters of Sweet Pity for all his back alimony. Mack roared with each story. From the other side of the partition came the piercing scream of a startled baby.

MARY MCGARRY MORRIS

In a moment more, Velma came down the stairs with a squalling red-faced baby over her shoulder, bringing with her the sweet close smell of talcum powder. She regarded them with the same blank docility Martha remembered from their first meeting.

"He's the one I told you wanted to know the family history," Anardelia told her granddaughter. "The same one you and Binky saw. That time up to Beecham's!" Anardelia was clearly exasperated with the girl.

"Oh yah," Velma said.

"She's got blank spots. Drugs," Anardelia confided, taking the infant into her arms. She licked her pinky finger and kept dipping it into the sugar bowl before she put it into the baby's mouth. Velma moved between the refrigerator on the porch and the pan of boiling water on the stove, where she was heating a baby bottle.

When the bottle was warm, the girl took the baby from her grandmother and sat on the couch next to Mack while she fed it. The girl stared over the narrow coffee table at Martha. "You ever find a handyman?" she asked when her grandmother went to the porch for another beer for Mack.

"Him," Martha said with a nod.

"Need any help?" Velma asked with a quick look at Mack as she fitted the baby to the sweaty curve of her neck and patted its square little back. "Binky said it's too big a place for one man."

Mack said she had a point and he'd certainly mention it to Frances. To this, the girl gave a bitter snort. Mack touched the baby's flat nose with his finger, his face close to the bobbing pink head as he cooed to it.

When his second beer was gone, Anardelia gave him another. Velma had gone upstairs to change the baby's diaper. Mack looked tired, his eyes slipping into an unfocusing brightness. Anardelia rambled on with a story of her sister's breast surgery in Pensacola, Florida. Now she was telling a story about her brother Lyle, who delivered spring water. Velma returned without the baby and sat down. When Anardelia paused for breath, Martha told Mack she wanted to go.

"Just a few more minutes," he said, setting his empty beer can on the coffee table.

A DANGEROUS WOMAN

"Stay. You gotta meet Lyle," Anardelia said. Her brother Lyle stopped in every afternoon. "For a crap and a nap, he says." Anardelia laughed.

"I want to go," Martha said, standing up. Anardelia was disgusting. No wonder Frances and her father had never come back here.

"Now, we gotta meet Lyle," Mack said, grinning.

"Sit down, honey," the woman said. "You gotta meet Lyle."

"I'm going," she told Mack, who kept grinning.

Velma giggled.

Martha sidestepped past the coffee table to get outside. Not only were they making her nervous, but she was afraid the beer would turn Mack's meanness on her.

"I heard all the stories, but now I seen for myself," Anardelia sighed.

"What do they call it, what she's got?" Velma asked. "Binky said mental."

"Shh," the grandmother said. "She's family."

--------□--------

The sky darkened, and suddenly it was raining. Even with the wipers sweeping back and forth, the windshield blurred with the downpour. She couldn't stop smiling at him. Being alone together was wonderful. Mack glanced at her and said there was more to the surprise. She said that, after meeting Anardelia, she wasn't sure if she wanted any more surprises.

"She's a very nice woman," Mack called as he drove.

"That Velma kept staring at me. I hate that. I hate being stared at."

"Velma's a burn-out. It was Anardelia I wanted you to talk to. I wanted you to see you've got family, that there's more to life than just Frances and that house. You should be living your own life, with your own job, and your own apartment. You've got a whole history you don't know anything about."

She kept looking at him, so anxious in his speech that his hands flew over the wheel. She couldn't imagine belonging to that family.

"It's becoming more and more apparent to me how important that is." He glanced at her. "It's this stream of time, this constant pull towards something, into something. It's what you don't have."

MARY MCGARRY MORRIS

260

She turned. Was this her blankness? Had he identified it?

"It can't ever be a Birdy or a Billy Chelsea or a bum like me. It's a whole world you don't know about. It's all the big things. It's God. It's a whole history Frances and your father thought they could just turn their backs on and wipe out. But where does that leave you? What does it leave you? With all their fears that they never took the time to explain to you, because they had to be somebody else. Your father didn't dare step out of Horace Beecham's world, and neither did Frances. And in the process, you got lost, Martha."

He turned onto Merchants Row. The rain stopped as abruptly as it had come, and in the sunshine a bright vapor rose from the streets, where rivers of rainwater coursed alongside the curbs.

"So what's the rest of the surprise?" she asked, her heart pounding. She hadn't been here in weeks. She kept looking for Birdy coming along the sidewalk.

He smiled. "I'm going to help you find a job. And we don't leave here until you've got one. We'll start at the first place we come to." He slowed the car.

"No! I don't want a job."

"Of course you do! You have to be independent. A paycheck! A place of your own!" He grinned, and his teeth flashed in the sunlight. "Isn't that what we've been talking about? About putting a life together?" he said, his voice rising.

"You've been doing all the talking. Not me."

"What's wrong, Martha?"

"I don't want to leave you!"

For a moment his eyes ranged from side to side. "I'd come and see you. I would! I'd pick you up and we'd go for rides."

"You would?" Could that be what he meant? Putting a life together. His life with hers.

"Yes!" He laughed. "In fact, we'd probably see more of each other here in town than we do now."

She held her glasses in place and she didn't know what to say.

He peered over the wheel, then pointed. "Let's start up there! The drugstore, Miller's!"

A DANGEROUS WOMAN

She glanced back at him. "They hate me in there."

"They don't hate you! Why would they hate you?" he laughed, shaking his head.

"They do. They just do. I know they do."

"Martha, people just don't go around hating other people for no reason. It's not in the nature of things. Believe me!"

She looked at him. "You ever see a three-legged cow?" she asked.

"No. But I've seen a three-legged dog before."

"The other dogs treat it bad?" she asked, and he said he didn't think so. "Well, then, it probably wasn't born that way. But that three-legged cow was. My father was talking about it one day to Frances, and I could tell the conversation was really about me, so I went down the mountain and I saw the cows coming back to the barn. They were kind of coming along, swishing their tails, you know, like cows do, and then I saw this cow, the three-legged one, kind of limping along off to the side, and when she came to the barn door, one by one all the other cows would bump her. And she just stood there while they did it. Finally they were all in and she just stood there until Mr. Patterson came and swatted her in."

"So what're you saying?"

She shrugged. "There's something about me people hate."

"What?" He looked at her. "Your three legs? Your four arms? Your two heads?"

"I don't know what."

He squinted, as if appraising her through a lens. "I'll tell you what it is. But it's not hate. They're afraid. They're afraid of what they don't understand. What they don't know how to deal with. It's a power you possess, and people fear it." His voice rose excitedly. "You don't even understand it, because, when you look at people, you SEE them. Something in your eyes goes right through people, and it's unnerving, and so they react negatively."

"Like Getso. When I look at him, I feel sick inside." She hit her palm with her fist, and he winced.

"No!" he groaned. "No, forget about him."

MARY MCGARRY MORRIS

262

"I can't! I'll never get a job, and he's the reason why! I can't even say I worked at the Cleaners because of him and his lies."

"Will you try? Will you just try?" Mack coaxed. Suddenly he looked tired.

"Well, not Miller's. It's all teenagers that work in there. They're the worst. I hate teenagers."

He drove farther down the street, passing the yard-goods store, the card store, the candy store. "There." Mack pulled in front of the shoe-repair shop, a narrow storefront with a high-heeled black boot painted on the window. She told Mack what a cranky old man Rufus Hannaby was, but he pointed out how similar the cleaning business was to shoe repairs. No selling. It was service. "And that's exactly what you're good at. Service!" He had almost convinced her. It probably never got very busy in there, and right around the corner, three minutes away, was the Cleaners, and Birdy, dear, dearest Birdy.

When she opened the door, Mr. Hannaby looked up from his grimy bench in a U-shaped island of shoe forms, a heavy-duty sewing machine, and shoe boxes filled with heels, soles, tools, and large spools of greasy-looking black thread. The one light in the store shone on his work.

"What's the last name?" he called, bending close to the oxblood strip of leather he was stitching to the flap of a handbag.

"Horgan. I'm Martha Horgan."

"Check the shelves. See if your name's on a bag. Don't remember Horgan, though."

The wall on the left was covered ceiling to floor with gray metal shelves, lined with brown grocery bags. Each bag bore a crayoned name.

"I'd like a job, Mr. Hannaby. I'm a good worker and . . ."

"A job? A job doing what?"

"The counter," she said, gesturing with the dismal realization that there was no counter. "When people bring things in and pick them up. I used to . . ."

"Do all that myself, girlie. Sorry."

She left the store, smiling, pleased that her name had been meaningless to Mr. Hannaby. Mack's car was gone. She looked up and down the street, but couldn't see it.

"Hey! Hey, Martha!" someone called.

Ahead, sitting against the low brick windowsill of Heartsound Records, were four skinny boys in dark T-shirts and a girl with thick frizzy hair, all about fifteen, all watchful with her approach.

She could just tell. Oh, she could tell from the angle of their heads who they had been waiting for. They had probably been out there for days, weeks, just waiting for this moment. She stared straight ahead, up the bright wet street.

"Martha! How're you doin', Martha?"

"Wise brats. Bunch of hoods, hanging out on the streets all day, oughta get a job and do something useful."

"What'd ya say, Martha?"

"Can't hear ya!"

"C'mere, Martha!"

From behind came the whir of spinning tires along the wet pavement. She jerked around to see a bike at her side, braking to a tight turn in the puddle, its wheels flaring up a wave of rainwater that splashed her.

Dirty water dripped down her arms and legs. "Get out of here!" she yelled.

The boy pedaled away furiously. Holding their sides, the boys and the girl bent forward laughing. "Hey, Martha," the girl warned, pointing. "Watch it! Here he comes!"

Looking up, she half-turned and tried to shield her face just as the bike hit the puddle again and sprayed her with another sheet of water. This time, the boy drove off only a few feet before he stopped. Smiling at her with the bike's front wheel in the air, he reared back like a warrior on his stallion.

She charged after him and he drove off, then turned quickly and came flying toward her again. This time, she lunged forward through the wet shimmer of her dripping glasses, trying to grab him, only to misjudge his distance as he again braked his bike and splashed her. Turning blindly, she took off her glasses and rubbed them on her shirt.

MARY McGARRY MORRIS

"Bastard! You little bastard!" Mack yelled.

Still cringing with the fear of another drenching wave, she put on her glasses and saw Mack walking toward her.

"Son of a bitch. It's a good thing I didn't catch him. I would've killed the little son of a bitch." His voice broke.

She couldn't go anywhere now, looking like this. Not only were her clothes wet and plastered to her body, but her arms and legs were streaked with dirt.

"I was in traffic," Mack said as he drove. He kept looking at her. "I saw it coming. I saw that kid and I knew exactly what was going to happen. It was like watching two magnets being drawn together, and I couldn't do anything. I had to keep going. I couldn't stop it. You shouldn't have gone after him. You should've kept going. You should've ignored him, damn it!"

"He splashed me! How could I ignore him?" She couldn't believe he was blaming her.

"You did just what he wanted. You went after him."

"I tried to stop him!"

"I could tell by watching. They know just how to get you started."

"Started? Started! He started it. What did I do? I didn't do anything!" she cried, slapping her thigh.

"Don't you see? It's a game with them! And you just go right along with it! You encourage it! Jesus!" he cried, hitting the wheel.

She looked at him. His face twisted with the same frustration she had seen in her father, in teachers who had all thought she should have some control over the fiasco that was her life. Of course she should. She wanted to, but did not, never had, and probably never would. And because there seemed to be no reasons for this, no mark they could see, no disfigurement or missing limb, one by one they would abandon her. That was the reason she always reacted so suddenly, loving so fiercely those who would be kind, so that in order to part they would have to tear themselves away from the ancient battlefield that was her heart, gouged and still, and survivorless.

"I'm sorry." She wept, wiping her runny nose on the back of her hand. Sorry for everything, for the brilliant sun in the unblinking sky, for loving him.

"It's not your fault," he said.

They drove in silence down Main Street, past the boarded-up buildings of the fairgrounds, when a truck started to pass, then cut so sharply in front of them that Mack jerked the wheel with a startled cry. The car swerved and he swore. It was the laundry truck, with Getso at the wheel. Martha stiffened, not saying a word, relieved now to see him barrel on ahead of them. "Yah? Oh yah?" Mack said, stepping on the gas, racing after the truck. Ahead, both lanes of traffic were stopping at the red light. Mack pulled alongside the truck. "Hey, asshole," he called. Getso glanced down, and then a wet clot of chewed tobacco hit Mack's windshield with a sickening brown splatter. In a roar of acceleration the truck sped forward, and Mack cursed and jammed his foot down on the gas pedal and pulled behind, staying with it.

"Son of a bitch," Mack bellowed, easing close enough to tap the back of the truck.

"Mack!" Martha cried, horrified. "That's John's new truck!"

Getso swerved into the next lane and took the right turn onto the Creek Road. Now Mack was hemmed in by traffic. Sweat poured down his face. He swore as the truck disappeared from view.

"We should call the police and have him arrested. That's what we should do. Stop up there at the gas station so I can call. I'll call! I'll tell Sheriff Stoner I saw the whole thing!" she kept insisting.

Mack drove past the gas station and turned onto Post Road, then, with screeching tires, took a sharp right onto a shade-dappled road, and then a quick left. After a few minutes, they came to a narrow intersection, its four corners fenced by spring wire. Tiger lilies filled the low culverts along the road. Mack hunched over the wheel, watching the road from the north. The laundry truck raced toward them, and he nodded with a mirthless laugh.

"What are you going to do?" she asked, tensing back.

"Teach that bastard a lesson," he said, pulling forward, angling his car across the intersection. The laundry truck kept coming and coming, then screeched to a stop. Mack sat in the idling car and watched Getso staring down at them.

She looked away. "Please let's just call the sheriff," she begged as Getso blew the horn.

He leaned forward and smiled up at Getso, whose bony face darkened with the steadily blaring horn.

She felt panicky. Mack ground his teeth and stared up at Getso. Getso gestured at them, and again came Mack's strange laugh. What was he doing? The best revenge, the most apt justice, would be Getso's arrest, but now, as the truck door opened, she saw the futility of it all. It would still be her word against his, and what had changed that would make anyone believe her? Nothing. Nothing had changed. He still had them all in his spell. As she watched him jump out of the truck and approach the car slowly, warily, she realized just how badly everyone must have wanted to get rid of her to have taken his word over hers.

"Move the fuckin' car!"

Mack laughed. "Wipe that shit off and then I'll move." He pointed to the clotted brown strings leaking down the glass.

"Hey! You wanna clean off shit, go to a fuckin' car wash, you and your . . . your girlfriend here."

Girlfriend. She grinned at Mack.

"You son of a bitch," Mack growled, starting to open the door, pushing against it with both hands. Just as he got one foot out of the car, Getso banged the door shut on Mack's ankle. Groaning, Mack leaned against the wheel while Getso swaggered back to his truck.

"No, don't!" she cried as Mack got out of the car in such pain he almost fell. He hobbled after Getso and grabbed his shoulder just as he was about to climb up into the truck. Getso turned and Mack crouched, swinging futilely two or three times at Getso, whose lean body and long neck swayed away from each punch. "Don't. C'mon, don't," Getso grunted, his open hands deflecting blows. "Don't be a shithead, now, don't! Just don't!" Almost dancing, he weaved back and forth on the balls of his feet, crouching again as Mack's limping attack dissipated into a frenzy of punches too erratic to merit deflection.

A DANGEROUS WOMAN

Suddenly Mack lunged forward and, with a groan of pain, harnessed his right arm around the startled younger man's neck. In a smear of blunt jabs, he drove his fist repeatedly into Getso's face. Blood spurted from Getso's nose, and with a powerful spring of his body he threw back both arms, catapulting himself free. He hit Mack in the chin, and his head snapped back. His second blow met Mack's cheek. Mack's eyes rolled, and he sank to his knees, then doubled over, leaning on his forearms.

Stunned, she ran to Mack and squatted next to him.

"He shouldn't've done that!" Getso cried, his voice cracking. "That was stupid. That was really stupid." Getso got into the truck and seesawed it until he was headed back the way he had come.

She had to help Mack into the car. His lip was split, and his cheek and right eye had started to swell. By the time they reached the house, the eye was almost closed. He refused her help getting out of the car. He had just limped to the garage stairs when Frances ran across the driveway.

"What happened? Was there an accident?" Frances demanded.

Mack turned, and Frances gasped at his misshapen face and bloody teeth. When he tried to talk, it sounded as if there were stones on his tongue.

"Look at you! Look at you!" she cried.

He spoke again.

"The Flatts," Frances exploded. "Why? Why in God's name would you go there?" She looked at Martha by the car, its hot dusty hood making pinging noises. "Was it your idea? Was that it? I won't have them crawling through my life again, do you understand? Do you?" she cried. "See what happens," she panted, gesturing back at Mack, who sagged against the railing. "See what they do! That's what I grew up with! That's what your father and I had to get away from—but not you! Not you!" Suddenly she sprang at Martha. "Get out! Get out of my house! Get out of my life, you stupid, stupid fool. I'm through with you! I won't be embarrassed by you anymore. I won't be hurt by you anymore! I'm through with you! Go back to the Horgans!"

MARY MCGARRY MORRIS

Martha's mouth hung open as Frances shook her. Go back to the Horgans? They were nothing to her. Frances was her only family.

"It's beyond me. It's too much for me! You're too much for me, and I refuse to be responsible anymore."

Again Mack tried to speak.

"You don't understand," Frances told him. "It's like a curse."

"Don't blame her," Mack said, forming the words with excruciating effort.

"I want her to go. I just want her to go!"

"But it wasn't even them," Martha said. "It was Getso."

Frances looked at her. "Getso? Him again? Oh, Martha, just go!" she groaned. "Go and leave me alone!"

TWENTY

———□———

Steve Bell was in his office, writing on a yellow legal pad, when Miss Eldredge buzzed him. He buzzed back twice, his signal that he could not be disturbed right now. This brief had to be ready by morning. One of the younger attorneys had left it until the last minute. Steve's desk was stacked with case folders. Beside him on the floor was another stack, finished and ready to be filed. He had gotten more work done in the last month than in the previous eleven. He arrived by seven most mornings, usually ending his days at seven or eight at night.

His practice had become his whole life. It was the one area in which he was confident and resolute. The work made him feel like a young lawyer again, fastidious in detail and hungry for the flaw, the tear in the opponent's argument. The practice of law was once more an invigorating experience. In many ways he felt like a man who attends church all his life, then one day, for no apparent reason, discovers the meaning of his religion and, in it, himself. Thus far, this rejuvenation had not spread into his private life. Evenings with Anita passed minute by weighted minute. As soon as he stepped inside his house, he grew old and tired, stooped by an unassuageable weariness. An old man read in his chair and slept in his bed and made tedious love to the shell of the fragile woman who claimed to be his wife. The constant pretense was draining him. He had lost a great deal more than he was allowed to mourn; Anita's youth had been numbed and shriveled by alcohol, and she had returned this pathetic creature with haunted eyes and thin, almost transparent flesh. It was the right thing to do. It was right and just, or so they said. But he knew it was not. No, he had wasted himself on a sour-breathed broken woman he should have left years before, when he still had his youth, when he still had an excuse, and courage.

And so he came here, seized with his clients' quest, exacting in the name of justice and truth all that was their due, even if it resulted in another man's penury. Somehow, he thought, it might be contained here; somewhere in all these documents and books might be the only courage necessary now, the courage to see him through the dark, block-shaped hours that piled one upon another to form a night.

There was a tap on his door, and then Miss Eldredge stepped quickly inside.

"It's Martha Horgan. I don't think she should wait much longer."

There were three people in the waiting room, two middle-aged men and Martha. She perched on the edge of the green wing chair. Her lap was covered with pieces of the tissue she was twisting. Set around her were two bulging shopping bags, a brown grocery bag, and a small frayed suitcase. The men watched her over their magazines.

A DANGEROUS WOMAN

". . . have to go," she muttered, sliding her feet back and forth.

"Martha," he said quietly. "What a pleasant surprise." He started to pick up her bags, but she quickly grabbed them.

"I need my father's money," she said the minute they were inside his office. He closed the door and asked her to sit down, but as if she hadn't heard him, she stood by the desk, still holding the bags.

"What's wrong?" he asked. She looked terrible. Her dress was wrinkled and her arms were streaked with dirt.

"I have to get a place to stay and I don't have any money."

"Did you have a fight with Frances?"

"No. She had one with me. And so now I need money. I don't have any money! I want my money!" She set down her bags, then dug in one and pulled out a large red wallet. "Can I have my money?" she asked, gesturing expectantly with the wallet. Her mouth trembled. It was all he could do not to laugh. Martha's directness had always amused him.

"The will's being probated," he said, and then, seeing her mounting impatience, explained what that meant.

"How long will that take?" she asked.

"Probably just another week or two," he said. Enough time for this latest crisis to have passed, he thought, noting how deftly his mind shifted into the crisis gear he knew so well from his years with Anita: say this, when you mean that.

She sank into the chair. "What am I going to do?" she asked, her panicky eyes so watery and distorted behind her thick lenses that he winced and had to look away.

He capped his pen and closed the folder. He stood up and told her he would give her a ride home and help her resolve this thing with Frances. He smoothed back his hair, wishing he'd gotten it cut today. The thought of seeing her sent a flush through his entire body.

He regretted that he had never given Frances much help with Martha. Their individual sorrows had served as ballast, a balancing between them. And, to be honest, just as he had always seen Anita's drinking as a selfish indulgence she preferred to continue, so had he regarded Martha's eccentricities as a way of forcing attention from her cold rigid father and allowing her great control over Frances.

"No!" she said. "I'm not going back there."

He bristled. This blank defiance rattled him, and it occurred to him that, for a man who had never wanted trouble, who couldn't bear discord, he had certainly taken all the wrong paths in his choice of profession, wife, mistress.

"Then I'll call," he said, and dialed Frances's number. She answered immediately. Nodding, he listened, murmuring, "I see. Of course. Yes. I understand," at key moments, expecting, hoping she would ask how he was doing. But all she said was that Martha had brought this on herself; that she was through with everyone's burdens. From now on, she was going to lead a real life, before it was too late.

"Of course. I understand," he said, and hung up with a tightness in his chest. A real life. Colin Mackey.

"Well," he sighed. "I guess you do need some money." He unlocked the bottom drawer of his desk and removed his personal checkbook, which for years had borne only his name. He would have to change that, add Anita's name. No, give her another month. If she stayed sober, then he would order new checks. "A thousand," he said, ripping out the check.

"But I thought my father had ten thousand in the bank," Martha said, peering at it suspiciously.

"That's what's being probated. In the meantime, this is an advance."

"Thank you!" she said, slipping the check into her billfold. "Now, what do you want me to sign?" She folded her hands on the edge of the desk and looked around.

"You don't have to sign anything. I trust you." He smiled. "You're probably the most honest person I know."

She smiled. "I am!" She bit her lip and thumped her chest. "I'm very honest! Thank you." She stood up and shook his hand, and her fingers felt small and cold in his.

———□———

A DANGEROUS WOMAN

273

The only sound in the Cleaners was the shimmy of the plastic-sheeted clothes hanging on racks under the huge exhaust fan. It was three-twenty and Birdy Dusser was alone at the counter, reading the newspaper. She reached into her basket and broke off another piece of peanut brittle, which she put into her mouth. The phone rang and she took the candy out of her mouth before she answered.

"Cleaners!"

Her head jerked up. "Hello? This is the Cleaners!" Her toes curled against the pull of silence at her ear. She hung up quickly, waited a moment, then took the phone off the hook. She hurried to the glass door and peered up and down the sunny streets. A dog, two young boys, and that was all. She put the phone back in its cradle.

This morning's incident with Getso was starting to get to her. Just lay low, she had told him. She had him switch routes with Charlie for the next few days. Better to have him out of town and out of trouble. He said he had warned Mackey, had begged him not to fight, and she believed him. He said one look at Mackey, bleary-eyed and old enough to be his father, and he knew if he hit him he might kill him. Getso was all for calling the cops before Mackey did, but she knew what John's reaction would be. This time he would fire Getso.

She put the peanut brittle back in her mouth and returned to the paper. The candy clunked against her teeth. It was too quiet in here. Barb was on vacation and Mercy had gone home sick right after Getso left.

She looked up. It sounded as if someone were coming up the back stairs. But after a few seconds of straining to hear, she felt silly. If there were any drivers out back, she would have heard a truck down in the lot.

John was right. This entire mess was her fault. She never should have hired Martha in the first place, but she had looked so pathetic that day, dragging through the door, head down, muttering her lines by dismal rote, fully expecting to be rejected again. She turned out to be the most eager and the most conscientious worker Birdy had ever trained. But then that became part of the problem too. Even the slightest variation in routine upset her. And, if such a thing were possible, she became too efficient, working like a machine at top speed, gears spinning, sparks flying, edging closer and closer to a breakdown.

Birdy sighed. She had allowed Martha to become too emotionally dependent on her, and then, when she started seeing Getso, the poor thing had been devastated. Well, if anything, she had learned a good lesson. And so had Getso. She chuckled softly. If Martha Horgan's fury wasn't the surest cure for light fingers, she didn't know what was. Since that day, Getso didn't dare pick up a penny from the sidewalk. Martha had made him an honest man.

Maybe it had all worked out for the best. Martha was better off at home instead of being harassed every day on the streets. The shortages had ended. Of course, now that Getso was living with her, what bills did he have? Poor guy, most of his check went to support three kids, two of which he swore weren't even his.

"Hi, Birdy."

"Martha!" Her hand flew to her heart.

"I didn't mean to scare you. I came up the back." She kept gesturing behind her. "I wanted to make sure Getso wasn't here."

"He's out on delivery. He should be back soon," she added quickly, feeling a little safer seeing Martha's shudder. Martha looked as if she hadn't bathed in days. There were dark circles under her eyes, and her skin had a yellow tinge to it. One of her bulging shopping bags had split along the seam, and an olive-green sock hung out of it. Maybe she was just bringing in her laundry, Birdy tried to tell herself.

"I've decided to live in town again. My aunt and I aren't on the best of terms right now." She rolled her eyes and laughed nervously. "And now it's so late and I've got so much to do. I've got to get my old room back and I've got to cash a check and . . . and . . ."

Was that all she wanted? "How much is it for?" Relieved, Birdy rang open the cash drawer.

"Oh! A thousand. Oh no!" Martha shook her head and waved her hand.

"Dollars?" Birdy gulped.

"I didn't mean for you to cash it. I was just saying all I have to do." Her voice broke. "Birdy, I need my job back."

"There's no way, Martha. You know John!" It was maddening how she could be so thick, so insensitive, so blind to the truth. Once, in frustration, she had taken Martha's glasses and looked through them, thinking they might reveal Martha's perception of reality.

"But if you tell him I didn't steal anything, he'll believe you! He'll listen to you! You know he will! And you know I didn't take any money. Steve Bell just said the same thing. That I'm the most honest person he knows. I am! You know I am!"

And she was, Birdy thought. Too much so. Was that what Martha saw through those thick dirty glasses, the world in black and white, no gray, no shadings, just the cold sharp edges of starkness, of good and evil, love and hate?

"How can you keep believing him? Do you know what he did today? He beat up a friend of mine! And now I can't even live at home. He took away my job and my home and my best friend. Every time he sees me, he yells things, and today he spit tobacco on my friend's car." She dropped her bags and ran toward Birdy. "How can you let someone like him even touch you? He's disgusting. He . . . ."

"Stop it!" Birdy insisted, her hand out, pointing to keep her at bay. "Do you hear me? Just stop it!"

Tears streamed down Martha's face. "How can you choose him over me?"

"Martha! This is bizarre!"

"But how can you, when you know he's a thief? When you know he's taking Mercy out, the two of them out there, kissing and rubbing against one another. They're not your friends. I am. I am! I am!" Martha tried to smile. "I mean, you don't even have to answer my letters and I still keep writing. Now, that's a friend, a real friend!" She was grinning, grinning through tears.

For a minute, she couldn't catch her breath. She didn't know what to say. Mercy and Getso. All their kidding and pushing and tugging on one another. All his trips over there to fix her temperamental water

MARY MCGARRY MORRIS

heater that always seemed to go on the fritz after her husband left for second shift. Today Mercy had left right after he did. No. They wouldn't do that to her. She had been too good to them.

"Help me, Birdy. Please help me. I never had anything. And then I came here and I had everything."

Birdy shook her head and laughed bitterly. "Then you didn't have much, Mart. Take my word for it."

"I know sometimes I tried too hard. But this time it'll be different. I've changed. You know my friend, he . . . I'm in love with him and I know he wants to love me back. Oh, Birdy, please help me. All I want is a normal life. I did it before and I can do it again. I know I can!"

"You're asking the wrong person for help, then. It's your aunt you should be talking to. She's the one that kept you here before. Have her talk to John."

"Frances?"

Numbly Birdy explained how Frances Beecham had subsidized Martha's salary, even providing Martha's Christmas bonus, with a little something to John for all his trouble. "So don't be asking me anymore. Okay?"

"But no one else will help me! You're the only one. Please, Birdy," Martha begged. "Please help me!" She threw her arms around Birdy, sobbing and kissing her face.

"No, Martha!" she cried, shoving her away. "I can't take this anymore. Just leave me alone! Don't call me! Don't come here! I don't want anything to do with you anymore, do you understand? Will you please leave me alone?"

With Martha staring at her, Birdy turned away, her chest heavy with all this sadness, this treachery in the world.

She watched Martha struggle down the street with her bags. Her dress hung on her skinny frame. Just trying to be human was hard enough, but imagine, on top of that, having to be Martha Horgan, she thought, staring, as if her eyes could pave a safe path for Martha until she was out of sight. It was the least she could do.

Miss McDonald, the teller, was a tall overweight young woman with short dull baby-fine hair that she had finally gotten permed and frosted after months of cutting curly hairdos out of magazines and laying them over a photograph of herself. Her new look made her feel cute, bouncy, almost petite. Even her walk had changed, and there was no question but what people were reacting differently to her now. Roger, whom she had been dating for almost a year now, was calling twice a day from the garage where he worked. Last night he had given her a silver ankle-bracelet strung with a pearl.

"For no reason at all," she was telling Jimmy, the next teller, as she initialed her customer's paycheck. Her customer was a short older man with four long green cigars sticking out of the breast pocket of his tweed suit coat.

"Oh jeez, what'd your mother say?" Jimmy asked. He knew how much her mother disliked Roger.

"I didn't tell her." She wet her thumb and counted five brand-new twenties out to her customer. She stretched her leg back to show Jimmy the ankle bracelet. "And it's not like I hid it on her or anything," she said, sliding the man's pass book and deposit slip under the Plexiglas divider. "Have a good day," she said. The man remained at the window, counting his money, double-checking all the transactions.

"So what do you think did it?" Jimmy asked, his long fingers flying over the keys as he tallied up. His cage was still closed.

"The perm. The whole change thing, you know," she answered. She wished he would open up. Martha Horgan was in line. Oh God, look at her trying to pick up all the clothes that had spilled onto the floor when the little boy behind her bumped into her bag and tipped it over. All down the line, people were picking up shoes and shirts and photographs and giving them to her. The little boy's mother handed Martha a plastic food-container with a blue lid. "I'm so sorry," she said again.

Still kneeling, Martha peered up at her. "You should keep a better eye on him."

"I know. But he's just so tired of waiting."

"Poor service. That's why. It's the manner of the modern marketplace. That's what my boss always said." She got up and thumped her chest and took a deep breath.

Biting their lips and staring at the floor, people tried hard not to laugh.

"Yes, well . . . here we go," the woman said, wide-eyed, as the line moved up one.

"Next'll be the diamond," Jimmy said, turning his CLOSED sign around so that his name showed. "And then what will Mother do?" he asked. He looked at her, pursing his lips and batting his lashes.

With her son clinging fearfully to her pants, the mother moved stiff-leggedly up to Jimmy's window.

The man with the cigars took a lollipop from the Styrofoam cup and stepped away. Martha Horgan moved her bags up to the teller line and set her check on the counter, keeping her hand on it as if she feared someone might race by and grab it. "Cash, please. Eight one hundreds, five twenties, ten tens," she rattled.

"You didn't sign it," Miss McDonald said, pushing back the check and a pen.

Muttering, Martha signed the check.

"Well?" Jimmy persisted as he waited for the woman's account to come up on the screen. "Or will you just not mention that too?"

"That would be different. I mean, God, that would be SO different." Imagine a fifty-dollar perm-and-frosting special changing your whole life like that, she thought, smiling at Martha, who glanced up at her. God, her eyes were intense. She had never realized what a pretty face Martha Horgan had behind those thick glasses. Scary, though. She had waited on the aunt before. Gorgeous lady; affected and cold as ice, but if she thought anything was wrong with her accounts, she'd start to shake.

"What are you waiting for?"

"Oh . . . your check . . . I didn't realize you were done."

Martha Horgan peered at her. "You don't give very good service!"

At the end of the line, Wesley Mount scraped his feet and cleared his throat uneasily. Miss McDonald was so embarrassed. He was creepy, but, still, it flattered her the way he always stood off to the side and waited for her window to be free. Two years ago, he had sent her a poinsettia at Christmas, candy on Valentine's Day, and then, on Saint Patrick's Day, he brought her a pot of shamrocks and asked her to dinner. When she told him she couldn't, his eyes brimmed with tears and he could barely speak.

"I'm sorry, Miss Horgan," she said softly now, the color rising in her cheeks.

"She's in love," Jimmy told Martha with a toothy grin.

"Oh, don't," Miss McDonald said, head bowed, covering her eyes.

"See?" Jimmy laughed. "She's enraptured."

"Then she shouldn't work here. Good service is prompt and attentive, and she's not!" The counter trembled as she banged her fist on it.

"Oh," Miss McDonald sighed miserably, unable to raise her eyes to the stricken gaze of the customers.

"Martha? What's wrong?" Wesley Mount asked, bending to Martha Horgan.

"I lost my temper," Martha said in a small voice. She hung her head and closed her eyes.

"Here," Mount said, quickly stuffing her check into her open purse, then snapping it shut. "Let me just give you a hand here." He picked up her bags while she looked on meekly.

He steered Martha down the street and through the door of the luncheonette, settling her in the first booth (better air, give her more of a sense of openness by the window, the feeling that, if she had to, she could get right outside), and now, at the counter—quickly, so as not to leave her alone too long—he asked the waitress for a glass of ice water—no, make that two. Empathy. Communion. You are not alone. Your suffering, my pain. His favorite was, My cheeks are wet with your tears. Wesley Mount was conversant with pain. Hysteria, Anger, Grief, Despair, these were the threads in the unique fabric of his calling; a hand on the shoulder, the ability to show people that, in their time of loss, they were not alone. It was happiness, the plodding sameness of normalcy, that left him tongue-tied and fearful.

MARY MCGARRY MORRIS

280

The funeral parlor had always been his home, and so death had been natural and unmysterious to him. The body was a wondrous machine, but a machine all the same, and when it broke down, it was not so much that life seeped away as that death took over. Death was not a void, but a force, and, like his father and grandfather before him, Wesley Mount had mastered the ritual and protocol its presence required.

Martha drank the entire glass of water, then sat back, panting a little, her firm breasts rising and falling. He forced his eyes onto her lovely face. She burped softly into her hand.

"You were thirsty," he said, noting with pleasure her perfect skin with its gentle glow, the narrow bridge of her nose, and her finely freckled prominent cheekbones. There seemed to be dust on her arms. There was a streak of dirt down the front of her dress. Where had she come from? What had she been doing? Just being near her excited him. Like his sister, she was a high-strung, unpredictable woman. Her mouth trembled, and it fascinated him that he couldn't tell if she were about to smile or frown.

"I like water," she said.

"Here, have mine."

She drank half of that, and hiccupped.

"Are you hungry?" he asked, glancing at his watch. It was four-thirty. Tonight was old Will Delaney's first viewing, at seven. The Delaneys were a family of talkers who would come early and leave late. There would be no chance of seeing Martha tonight.

"No, thank you," she said, her chest heaving with silent hiccups.

"Would you like a cup of coffee? Or maybe you're a tea drinker?" he asked hopefully, being one himself.

"No, thank you." She covered her mouth.

The waitress came to the table, and Martha stared at her empty glass, her shoulders jerking up and down.

He had to order something if they were going to sit here. "Two turkey sandwiches, and two more waters, please."

"I told you I don't want anything!" Martha said.

The waitress looked at him.

"They're both for me, thank you." He smiled.

A DANGEROUS WOMAN

"I'm just not hungry," she said when the waitress left.

"Of course. If you're not hungry, you shouldn't eat. That's the trouble with a lot of people today. They eat just because it's breakfast time or lunchtime or dinnertime. They eat and they're not even hungry."

She nodded. "Habit. I guess it's habit. I do that." She looked up with such a troubled expression that he had all he could do not to blanket her thin hands with his own. "I have a lot of bad habits."

"I doubt that," he said. When she didn't reply, he asked if the bags meant she'd be moving back to town.

Yes. In fact, she was on her way to Mayo's, she told him with a long gasping hiccup.

"That's wonderful!" he said. "Well, certainly more convenient for you," he added in a more somber tone. He ran his hand down his tie, surprised it lay so still over his clamorous heart.

The door opened on two young men, who sat down at the counter. They both ordered french fries and large root beers. They kept glancing back at Martha, whose loud hiccups racked her chest. At the counter, the waitress turned to see what was going on. The young men huddled over their drinks.

"Take a long deep breath," Wesley advised, and, closing her eyes, Martha tried, but just keeping her head erect appeared to be an effort.

"Do you have a paper bag?" he called, and the waitress looked up quizzically. "To put over her face," he explained, gesturing.

"She's not that bad-looking," one of the young men squealed, and the other buried his face in his arms, helpless with laughter.

Wesley barely heard them. After a lifetime of grim jokes at his own expense, such cruelties seemed as intrinsic to existence as seeds in watermelon.

"Shut up," said the waitress as she rummaged under the counter for a bag, which she brought over quickly.

He told Martha to breathe deeply into it.

She opened the bag. "It smells like fish," she gasped into it.

"You're hyperventilating. Now, breathe deeply. That's it. There . . .

MARY MCGARRY MORRIS

there now. Get a hold of it, now. Control your breathing, in and out, in and out. Everything will start slowing down, your heart and your lungs. Everything's getting right back in rhythm. There, there now," he kept saying.

Suddenly there was a wrenching hiccup, and she threw the bag onto the table. "My check," she gasped, opening her pocketbook. She tore through it, removing a book, a scarf, a balled pair of stockings, pens, a bag of seeds, gum, slamming them onto the table until she found her wallet.

Everything there charmed him, especially the seeds. She must have been gardening; that explained the dust on her arms and her sweaty, frazzled state.

"My check is gone!" she said, her stare so fierce that he wondered if she thought he had taken it.

"In that middle section," he said, pointing.

"Oh," she said, finding it. "I thought I left it at the bank," she said, slapping her chest with relief.

He could tell by the watchful way she placed it in the billfold that she did, she probably thought he had had her cover her face so he could steal her check. As he watched her putting everything back into her bag, he began to feel sad and alone, as if she had already left him. She looked up and blinked, her mouth twitching so self-consciously that he longed to reach across the table and draw his fingertips over her soft lips and soothe those tremulous eyes. But this time he would be cautious. There would be none of the smothering attention, the nervous phone calls, the barrage of flowers and candy, the searches for greeting cards listing the qualities of friendship, his heart aching as he licked the envelope because what he really meant was love; every day of his life, thought of little else, as he dressed and manicured and perfumed himself in his quest. He had prepared the corpses of the poor, the sick, young and old. Beyond the effects of disease and injury, there was little the bodies ever revealed. He could not gauge greed, charity, patience, cruelty, kindness. But he could always tell a lifetime without love. There was a tearless distance to the eyes, and at the mouth an unripe tautness, the flesh so toneless its touch repelled him. It was, if such a thing were possible, a deathless death.

—□—

From the kitchen, Claire Mayo could hear the ladies setting the table in the dining room. They liked an early dinner on summer Wednesdays, because the band concert started at seven. Tonight Claire was running late. Sweat beaded the old woman's upper lip as she kept trying to thicken the lamb stew. She could barely see into the tall pot. Lately it seemed that she was shrinking and the house was getting bigger, the steps steeper, the nights darker, the days longer, the gravy thinner.

The door swung open. "We're short one salad bowl," Mrs. Hess called in.

"There isn't any salad," Claire said with some pleasure.

Mrs. Hess looked at her. The door swung shut, and she knew by the buzz of their voices that they were complaining about starches again. They blamed their constipation on the rice. They could complain all they wanted, but she wasn't about to stop serving rice, which came free from the old-age food surplus, along with long yellow bricks of American cheese, butter, and flour.

Next into the kitchen was Ann McNulty. She stood at the sink, sneezing, while she filled the pepper shakers through stiff paper funnels she had cut from notepaper. Cute, always so cute and so clever it made Claire sick to her stomach, seeing crocheted covers on every tissue box and wastebasket in the house. All the picture frames were covered with quilted tubes. Now she was knitting a banister cover for the front staircase, which Claire had already said she didn't want, wouldn't use, couldn't stand the sight of, but didn't she sit there night after night, working on the ugly thing that snaked down her lap and around her feet. Little by little she was taking over. They all were.

Ann McNulty came toward her now with the pepper can and said something.

"No," Claire said. "The spices don't need covers."

"It's empty," Ann McNulty said, dropping the can into the trash.

"Smells good," she said, lifting the lid on the pot. "And no rice, I see."

"There's some in the stew," Claire said, staring at her. "For filler."

"And what's in the oven?"

"Macaroni and cheese," Claire said, just as insolently as she could.

Ann McNulty hurried out of the kitchen, obviously dying to report that Claire had done it again; even after their meeting last night, she had gone ahead and cooked what she pleased, when she knew how miserable they were all feeling.

"I don't believe it!" Suzanne Griggs gasped from the other side of the door.

Claire opened the cupboard over the sink and took down the bottle of Metamucil, which she emptied into the stew, muttering as she stirred, "They want fiber, I'll give them fiber. Sitting around here all day like princesses, complaining how bound up they are."

It started after the first polite minutes of passing plates back from the tureen and "Bread, please," "Butter, please," "Salt, please."

"Did you get the prunes stewed, Claire?" asked Ann McNulty, meaning the five boxes her niece had brought by this morning.

"Not yet."

"I thought we'd agreed on prunes. More fruit and fiber, isn't that what we said last night?"

"All those poisons just backing up and not being passed," Suzanne Griggs said with her hand pressed to her stomach. She shuddered. "Every time I think of it, I feel sick."

"Two and a half days." Mrs. Hess rolled her eyes at Loiselle Evans. "This is the longest I've ever gone."

"No, last Christmas," Loiselle said. "I remember you weren't going to eat the stuffing, but Martha had raisins and apples in it, so then you did, and I remember you said it worked."

"She did make a wonderful stuffing, I'll say that for Martha," Suzanne Griggs said.

"And salads. Remember? Martha made salad every night," Mrs. Hess said. She looked down the table at Claire. "I'm not getting enough roughage!" Her lip quivered and her eyes paled with tears. "Look," she said, probing the stew with her fork. "Just rice, meat, and gravy . . . and these . . . What are these disgusting lumps?"

"Powder balls," Ann McNulty said, examining a dripping forkful of the gravy-coated clots of laxative powder.

"Powder balls!" Claire scoffed. "Those are bran seeds, bran pods, they're called."

"Really?" Loiselle Evans asked, bringing a forkful to her mouth. "Does have kind of a nutty flavor," she said with a discerning nibble. "Ummmh!"

"How'd you find out about bran pods?" Suzanne Griggs asked, tasting hers. "I never heard of bran pods."

"The health-food store," Claire lied, pleased to see them so eagerly cleaning their plates. Faster than stewed prunes, and a lot less work, she thought, already looking forward to tomorrow night's rice pudding.

They were still eating when the doorbell rang. In the center of the table was the stewpot Claire had carried out so they could skim the Metamucil balls directly into their plates. The doorbell rang again, and Claire got up to answer it. It took her a minute to recognize the blurred face at the dusty screen. Seeing Martha's hair so short, Claire's first thought was that as either an inmate or patient, her head had been shaved.

"I need my room back," Martha said. "I don't have any place to stay."

"But your room's rented," Claire said quickly. She had heard about Martha's thievery at the Cleaners and how the women there lived in constant fear of her, especially poor Birdy Dusser, who had to get an unlisted number as well as all her door locks changed.

"I'll sleep on the couch," Martha said. "I don't care."

"Now, you know I'd never allow that, Martha!"

"What about the sewing room, then? Nobody uses it, and I'll pay the same rent as before."

"It's not even big enough for a bed, and there's no window!"

"But I need a place to stay!"

Martha tried to open the door, but, thank goodness, it was already

MARY McGARRY MORRIS

latched. Across the street, cars were starting to pull in around the park. Claire could hear the rustle of the women settling into the shadows behind her.

"Then go try Wilmer's on Pond Street. They'll take you, especially if your aunt's still willing to pay the extra fifty a month." Rudy Wilmer would rent to a dog if it paid.

"What extra fifty?" Martha asked.

"Never mind," Claire said. Let her ask her aunt. She was tired. Like a giant lung in the shadows, the ladies breathed in and out, and she could feel them wanting Martha back.

"Tell me!" Martha insisted. "What do you mean, an extra fifty?" She hit the door, and Claire was afraid she'd push her fist right through the brittle screen.

She explained that, soon after Martha had moved in, her aunt had called to see how things were going. Frances Beecham had offered Claire the extra fifty herself, out of the blue, with no particular reason given.

"This time I'll pay the extra fifty." Martha snapped open a billfold. She pressed a check to the screen. "See! I have the money."

"It's not the money. I told you, the room's rented."

"But I don't have any place to stay!" Martha cried. "I don't know what to do! Please, Claire, please help me!" She hit the rickety door, and its warped bottom half banged in and out of the frame.

"My Lord!" gasped Mrs. Hess.

"The poor soul," sighed Loiselle Evans.

"Call the police," Ann McNulty said.

Claire closed the heavy inside door and made her way to the phone. So the stories were true. Martha had become a dangerous woman.

———□———

Dazed, Martha sat in one of the rocking chairs. She had to do something, but she didn't know what. Birdy's words kept zapping through her brain like an electrical charge. I DON'T WANT ANYTHING TO DO WITH YOU ANYMORE. Every emotion had been scoured out of her. Maybe she would just spend the night out here on the porch. She could put her head on

A DANGEROUS WOMAN

one of her bags, and if it got cold, she could cover up with her clothes.

Across the street, all the parking spaces around the park had filled up with cars, and families were shaking open blankets to sit on. The hot-dog and popcorn vendors were setting up their carts.

From inside the house, the water pipes groaned and clanged, as all the toilets seemed to be flushing at once. She looked up curiously as a police cruiser cut through the traffic with its lights flashing. It pulled right up onto the sidewalk in front of the boardinghouse, and a young policeman jumped out and whipped his hat onto his close-cropped head. He adjusted his holster as he bounded up the steps. He stood over her, and now she watched him remove the hat and tuck it under his arm. "Excuse me, ma'am. We've received a complaint about you disturbing the peace and trespassing here at one ninety-nine North Main Street, the premises owned by Miss Claire Mayo."

Not knowing what to say or do, she stared down at her folded hands.

The front door creaked open. "Sonny?" Claire Mayo called.

"No, ma'am. Officer Eddie Firth. Sheriff Stoner's off tonight."

"I don't want a big commotion with everyone looking, but I want her off my porch and off my property."

"Yes, ma'am. I was just telling her that." He stepped closer. "Excuse me, ma'am, um, Martha? You have to get off Miss Mayo's porch. You have to. Right now."

Martha? Who was he? Not Martha, but Miss Horgan. From now on, she was Miss Horgan. She stood up and picked up her things, and he came down the steps with her.

"I'll be glad to give you a ride home," he said, opening the cruiser's passenger door.

Ignoring him, she carried her bags across the street, into the crowded park. She was conscious of people watching her as she searched for a place to sit. She came off the path, stepping between the blankets. The only empty spot was next to a gang of boys in denim vests.

"Excuse me. Excuse me," she said, stepping over a man's leg, hoping to get away before they saw her, but it was too late.

"Over here!" they called. "Hey, Martha! Sit with us! Come on!"

Her ankle turned and she tripped forward but didn't fall. Ahead now, in the farthest corner, was an empty bench. She got back on the path and raced to get to it before anyone else could. People were laughing. She collapsed onto the bench, weak with the realization of Frances's most dire warning. Here she was alone, with nowhere to go and all her possessions in bags at her feet. Her only solace was Mack and her hope that he would miss her enough to realize that he had been wrong, it had been love after all.

The dark grass was dotted with sprawling families and elderly men and women in aluminum lawn chairs, and in the farther troughs of darkness, under trees and huddled by shrubs, the younger people, smoking, passing out bottles and cans from their coolers. To her right, a blonde couple lay on their sides, facing each other. The girl's hand was in the boy's back pocket, and his hand was open on the seat of her jeans. Directly behind them was a large group of teenagers that kept calling out to newly arriving friends. Occasionally they called to the couple, who ignored them.

Young children wandered from family to family. Their tired-looking mothers were so careless, she thought, noticing one little boy stray onto the path, his sneaker laces untied, his hips under his thin pajamas padded with diapers. She tensed forward as he waddled closer and closer to the upper sidewalk, to the traffic passing in a long stream of headlights.

"No!" she suddenly cried, her hand jerking as instinctively toward him as he seemed drawn to the streaking lights. A woman ran up behind him and scooped him onto her hip.

She could feel everyone staring at her, so she narrowed her eyes and focused on the bandstand. A galloping march pounded from the loudspeakers. People began to clap along, and children raced down the paths to march around the bandstand in a blur of heads. At the clash of cymbals, the trumpeters rose in resolute fanfare to the drummer's dark trembling beat. And there, in the midst of the cheering and whistling crowd, she closed her eyes and thumped her chest and kept trying to clear her throat. Silence came, and now, as the band began to play "Beautiful Dreamer," the first clear strains of the violin sent a chill through her.

"So good to see you," Mr. Weilman said, sitting beside her. "I come

A DANGEROUS WOMAN

to every concert, but I barely know anyone anymore. Where did they all go?" he asked, looking around. He shook his head. "To Arizona, that's where. You know, I think there's a whole contingent of Atkinsonians there, and all these funerals I keep going to are just farewell parties. They just pack themselves up in their beautiful caskets and get shipped down there." He laughed.

Mr. Weilman talked throughout the concert. He remembered when this bandstand had been built, to replace the original one of wood, which had finally collapsed in a violent summer storm. The money and materials had all been donated by local merchants. Horace Beecham had been one of the project's prime movers. Horace had had a great sense of civic responsibility, Mr. Weilman said, adding with a chuckle, "Which is probably the only sense the old goat ever had."

He became more animated as the concert went on. A most embarrassing incident had just taken place, he confided, telling her how one day, in the supermarket checkout line, he had bagged his own groceries, then stayed on talking to the cashier while he continued bagging other customers' groceries. Next thing he knew, he had been hired. And now, four weeks later, this very morning, he had been fired for the very disorder that had gotten him hired in the first place, logorrhea.

She glanced across the street. When the concert ended, she would sit here until all the lights went out in the boardinghouse, and then she would go back and sleep on the porch.

"Do you know what an affliction logorrhea is, Martha?" He regarded her pensively. "Do you even know what logorrhea is?"

She shook her head. "No."

"Well, one thing's for sure. It's certainly not contagious, since that's the first word you've spoken to me tonight."

MARY MCGARRY MORRIS

290

TWENTY-ONE

———o———

Mr. Weilman lived on a narrow tree-lined street of closely set houses, their dark yards walled by ancient tangles of spirea, forsythia, lilac, and honeysuckle. "Careful," he warned, stepping around the two tricycles and a go-cart on his front walk. "Left where they fell at the bedtime knell," he said with a chuckle, setting down her suitcase while he unlocked the front door.

As he showed her through the house, he explained that he had been giving away all but his most necessary furnishings. Now each bedroom contained only a bed and a chest of drawers. In the dining room, the mahogany chairs sat seat-down on top of the table for easy cleaning. He had already given the buffet, the tea cart, and the silver chest to a young couple down the street. "I don't need them, and I'd rather see them go to people I like than have it all end up someday with strangers," he explained. Their footsteps echoed down the bare hallway.

The living room ran the length of the house, with an acrid-smelling fireplace set between two bays of uncurtained windows. In this long high-ceilinged room there were only two worn green chairs on a thin red-and-blue Oriental carpet that had most of its fringe chewed away. Against the wall, on a square table with cut-glass drawer pulls, was a tall brass lamp with a dented shade. The teetering piles of books under both windows made her think he had given away his bookcases, and probably just recently.

In the fall there were mice in the walls, he said, and in the attic, an occasional bat. There were some nights when he would wake from a sound sleep convinced the old place had sprung to life with all its creaking and groaning and, from the dark side of the attic door, hissing if he came too near. He said he had begun to think of the old house as an enormous conveyance, straining at its moorings, wanting to lift off as soon as enough ballast had been discharged.

Everything was clean, he assured her, turning on the light in the kitchen. He scrubbed the bathrooms, floor and fixtures, himself once a week, the tub walls every other month. The rest was done monthly by a cleaning service. "When was the last time you ate?" he asked, pulling out a chair for her at the drop-leaf table.

She said she wasn't sure. But she wasn't hungry, so it didn't matter. If anything, she felt sick to her stomach. She sat down and braced her chin on her hands, watching dazedly as Mr. Weilman slapped ground meat into a patty, which he fried and served to her on a paper plate along with a Styrofoam cup of coffee. This way he had no dishes to wash. "I travel light," he said and she wondered if he had also given away his dishes. Chewing dryly, she got the meat caught in her throat, but because he was so anxious to please her, she kept at it. He sat down and watched her eat, his gaunt old face glowing with pleasure.

"You know," he said, "there's no sense looking all over town for a room when I have all these empty."

Exhausted, she sipped her coffee.

He smiled hopefully. "What do you think?"

"Would you mind?"

"Mind! I'll mind if you don't! In fact, you can move in for good, if you'd like. Might as well! Two lonely souls, seems like the logical thing to do."

That would be perfect. Mack could visit her here with much less attention than at the boardinghouse. She covered her mouth to hide her nervous smile. "I don't go out at night. You could lock all the doors by seven." She tried to remember what other rules Claire Mayo had posted on the foyer pillar. "I never shower longer than five minutes and I never leave a room with the light on."

He considered this. "Interesting." He rubbed his chin. "So, if there's a light on, you must remain in the room."

"Yes," she said, then shook her head. "No!" He'd been catching her in these word traps since childhood. These were precisely the convoluted conversations Frances and her friends had so little patience with.

"Then who turns it off?"

"I do."

"But I thought you said you never leave a room with the light on."

"I never leave a room with . . ." She pointed up as his eyes flickered eagerly. "UNTIL I turn off the light. First," she added, happier than she had been in weeks.

———□———

It was noontime, and now the phone just rang and rang. Every time she called, it was always Frances who answered, never Mack. After four days of this, she was beginning to wonder if he had left. She hung up and dialed again; this time she counted the rings. She hung up on fifty. Next time she would wait till sixty. He might be out in the orchard or swimming in the pool. She dialed and began to count. Downstairs, Mr. Weilman's back-porch door slammed again, and she lost track. Was she on thirty-seven or forty-seven? Her hand shook as she pressed the buttons, then began to count each ring. "One, two, three, four . . ."

BANG! Bang! Bang! It was the door again. She hurried out of the bedroom. Someone was down there banging it on purpose. All morning long, there had been a constant stream of neighborhood children in and out of the house for water, crackers, chalk, to use the bathroom. Right before Mr. Weilman left to take her check and her deposit forms down to the bank, one thin little girl in a rumpled sundress had limped in, sobbing, with blood from her scraped knee trickling down her shinbone. She had fallen off her tricycle in Mr. Weilman's driveway. He knelt in front of her, his quivering hands attempting to pull the little red string through the bandage paper, as he asked in an endlessly patient voice how many times had he warned her that his driveway was different from hers. His had two pebble-studded concrete ramps just wide enough for automobile tires, with a broader strip of grass growing in between. The little girl shrugged and her chest heaved with the aftershock of a tearless sob. She kept looking at Martha, hunched over the table, filling out the new account forms Mr. Weilman had gotten for her yesterday.

"Maybe a hundred," Mr. Weilman said, stretching the bandage over the cut. "Or maybe a thousand," he sighed, getting up.

"But I was careful," the girl said.

Martha's head shot up. Oh, and didn't she remember that tone from her own childhood, that pathetic little whine that could turn so venomous so fast. I WAS CAREFUL. BUT SHE PUSHED ME. IT'S NOT MY FAULT. SHE DID IT.

"Careful isn't careful enough, or else you wouldn't've fallen off and you wouldn't have that cut!" she blurted, instantly regretting the childishly gloating tone and cadence of her voice.

Both the girl and Mr. Weilman looked at her, then glanced at one another.

MARY MCGARRY MORRIS

"So there you go, Hilary," he said, lifting the child off the chair and setting her down on the floor. "Almost as good as new," he called as she limped outside. The door slammed and Martha winced.

Mr. Weilman looked at her. "She's only four," he said.

Well, she hadn't said anything then. But now she would. The brats. Listen to them down there. He wasn't even home, and they thought they could just run in and out of here whenever they felt like it. Poor old man, she thought, racing down the stairs, he let everyone run all over him. In the few days she had been here, she had seen more traffic in and out of this house than in all her years at home; at Frances's, she corrected herself, wheeling around the corner. In the kitchen, two children were trying to pour lemonade from a heavy glass pitcher into a trayful of small paper cups. With each pour, lemonade sloshed into the tray.

"What are you doing?" she gasped, bearing down on them so quickly that the child with the pitcher jumped back and knocked over two of the cups. Martha yanked the dripping pitcher away from the girl and set it in the sink.

"We're making freezer cups," the boy said behind her.

"Oh no, you're not!" she said. "No, sir! Not in here you're not!"

"Mr. Weilman said we could," protested the boy. His hands were dirty and his arms were streaked with the drying sticky lemonade. Small dark splatters of it were on the floor. "He always lets us," he said, licking between his fingers.

Fat little face and those hard little eyes . . . Ooh, she didn't like him . . . not at all. . . . No respect . . . Listen to him sputtering on and on about lemonade and freezer cups, fresh thing. As if it were his right.

"It's his turn," the girl offered timidly. She had retreated to the door, where she waited with her hand on the latch.

The boy kept explaining the same thing, that it was his turn. He said it again now as he started to open the refrigerator to retrieve the pitcher she had just put there.

"No!" she cried, slamming the refrigerator door so hard he jerked along with it. "Now get out of here! Go!" she ordered, then steered him by the shoulders onto the narrow side porch. His thick-lidded eyes regarded her sullenly through the screen.

"C'mon, Josh! That's Marthorgan!" the girl said, the very word embodying the nightmarish creature that had been breathed suddenly into flesh-and-blood life before their eyes.

"That's Marthorgan. That's Marthorgan," Martha said in a singsong. She watched them dart across the shady street into a sunlit strip of side lawn, then around the back of a gray house that, like all these houses, was filled with children like them, messy, cruel children. Marthorgan. That's who they saw. Marthorgan. And there wasn't a way she knew how to change it. She had always hoped that contained somewhere in all this turbulence there was a quiet normalcy that would one day emerge to deliver her into the world, confident, calm, and likable. As a teenager, she had lain awake countless nights trying to figure out what made her different, trying to determine what was good about herself. In an effort to find her best feature and capitalize on it, she would study her slender feet and hands, her long neck, her thick hair, her wide mouth, bright eyes, her full breasts; but no matter what the fashion magazines advised or the mirror reflected, she knew the flaw was too deep.

Lately she had begun to wonder if her vision, her perception might not be too keen. Most people invented their own truth as both armament and balm, like Mr. Weilman thinking he was being good to the children by giving them the run of his house when it was as plain as the nose on her face what was going on here. They thought he was a fool and probably had some name for him too. "Marthorgan, Marthorgan," she chanted as she began to scrub the sticky mess from the counter. The wet paper cups sat swelling in the tray of lemonade. All at once she threw down her rag. She would leave the mess here and let him see what a disaster his carelessness had caused.

The phone rang. A woman asked to speak to Mr. Weilman, and Martha told her he wasn't back yet.

"Who is this?" the woman snapped.

"I'm a friend of Mr. Weilman's." She wasn't about to give her name to some stranger.

MARY MCGARRY MORRIS

"Is this Martha Horgan?"

"Who are you?"

"My name is Laura Barrett. I'm Joshua's mother. I live across the street in the gray house. Joshua tells me that you shook him and pushed him and . . ."

"I didn't shake him and push him!"

"Well, that's not what Joshua says, and that's not what Jennifer Hoffler says!"

"He wouldn't leave, so I put my hand on his shoulder and I opened the door and . . . and that's what happened." She covered her eyes. Her heart was racing. The brats. See what happened when they didn't get their own way.

"Don't you ever touch my son again! Do you hear me?"

"He was very fresh to me!"

"Then you should have called me! If this ever, ever happens again, I'll have you arrested for assault and battery, and don't think I won't!" The phone crashed in her ear.

She closed her eyes and took a deep breath. Mack. She had to talk to him. She missed him, missed being near him, hearing his voice, or washing the dishes he would leave in the sink, or just smelling his citrusy cologne. She dialed, and he answered on the first ring.

"Mack! It's me, Martha!" she cried, grinning and slapping her forehead with relief.

"How're you doing?" He hesitated. "Is everything all right?" he asked in a low voice.

"Everything's all right! How are you? Did those cuts heal? How's your ankle? It's not broken, is it? I've been so afraid you broke it. And then, every time I called, Frances answered, so I started to think maybe you left or you were in the hospital or something. And then nobody answered."

"Hey, slow down." He laughed, and it made her laugh. "I'm fine. My ankle's fine. It was just one mean bruise, that's all. I haven't answered because when I'm writing I always disconnect the phone, and then these last few days nobody's been here because we drove up to Quebec City. So what've you been doing? Isn't this weather beautiful?"

"Mack!" she interrupted. "I've got a place to live now. I'm at Mr. Weilman's."

"Yes, I know that."

"You do?" she said, laughing, pleased that he had tracked her down.

"Frances told me," he said.

"Oh. How'd she find out?" she asked.

"I don't know. I didn't ask."

"Well, when are you coming to see me? You said you would!"

"I know," he said, so tersely she realized Frances must be nearby.

She closed her eyes. "Will you come here? Please? I miss you," she said in a small pinched voice.

He didn't say anything for a moment. "Is everything all right? Are you okay?" His voice had fallen to a whisper.

"I need to see you," she gasped. "You said you would."

"Don't. Martha, please don't."

"I mean as friends. I mean we can just talk. That's all I want. I just want to talk to you."

"No, I can't. It's better this way. Believe me. You know why. I've told you why."

"Because of her! Because you love her!" She was crying.

"Martha, listen to me. The night you left here, she asked me again if anything had ever happened. And if it had, she said she wanted me out, right then and there."

"What did you say?"

"What do you think I said? If I tell her the truth, then I'm gone. You don't want that to happen, do you?"

"Well, what good does it do if I can't even see you? You might as well be gone." She looked up. "So go ahead and tell her! I don't care, I'll even tell her myself!"

"Look, stop it! Just calm down. I'll come see you tonight, and we'll talk. Be on the corner, and I'll pick you up at eight."

———□———

An hour later, when Mr. Weilman came home, she found him in the kitchen, pouring the sodden paper cups of lemonade into new cups. He put them in the freezer, and then he began to wipe off the countertop and cupboard doors. He worked in silence, and then he sighed. Laura Barrett had been waiting for him outside. She had told him what had happened. Martha tried to explain why she had made the children leave. Her voice grew thinner and thinner. "They could've turned on the stove and started a fire." She leaned wearily against the table and closed her eyes. She knew she was right. Of course she was right. But, as always, she had turned it into something wrong.

"You don't like children, do you, Martha?" he asked quietly.

"I like children!"

"No, you don't. Admit it. You don't." He put the dishrag in the sink and turned around. "But I do. I like them very much," he said, fixing her with a stern eye. "Do you understand?"

— □ —

First she put on the dress she had worn to the PlastiqueWare party, then she took that off and put on a brown plaid skirt, but the wool felt too picky, so she took that off and threw it onto the heap of rejected clothes. She was getting that panicky feeling again. She had to stay calm. Nothing could go wrong. She wanted Mack to see her calm. Finally she changed into black pants and a pink shirt. She even put on lipstick and eye liner.

Mr. Weilman had continued to be not only quiet for the rest of the day, but sad. It occurred to her now that there hadn't been another child in the house all afternoon. He ought to be grateful for the peace and quiet, she thought, coming down the stairs. He was in his den, asleep in his recliner, his chin on his chest, with the newspaper blanketing his lap. This was the only room that still had all its furniture, and it seemed cluttered and dark compared with the rest of the house.

She touched the old man's arm lightly and called his name, but he didn't respond. The corners of his sagging mouth were white with spittle. "Mr. Weilman," she said, lifting his cold hand. "Mr. Weilman!" she called in alarm. Was he in a coma? Had he had a stroke? A heart attack? "Mr. Weilman, please wake up!" Was he dead? She patted his cheeks and his eyes shot open.

A DANGEROUS WOMAN

"Wha . . . wha . . . don't hit me!" he cried, cringing from her.

His fearful look saddened her. "I was just trying to wake you up," she said. He stared up dully as she explained that she was meeting a friend and probably wouldn't be back until late. "I've got the key, so you can lock up and go to bed," she said.

She hurried along the dusk-stilled street, past the plain wood houses and the tired voices of children whose mothers were washing away the day's grime before putting them to bed.

She turned the corner, then slowed down, disappointed not to see Mack's old car. A low white sports car inched toward her, its hubcaps flashing like spinning blades under the streetlight. She darted behind a tree, and the sports car pulled up to it.

"Martha!" Mack called, leaning to open the door for her.

Tanned and with his hair cut short, he looked wonderful; handsome, she thought; the scab on his chin the last trace of his fight with Getso. His navy-blue blazer, white polo shirt, chinos, and loafers made her wonder if he was wearing Steve's clothes. But he was much taller and broader than Steve. Seeing how dressed up he was, she regretted changing into pants. She hoped they weren't going anywhere too fancy.

"You got a new car?" she said, settling into the soft black leather seat, which molded itself to her body. She folded her arms to hide the stain she had just noticed on her shirt.

"It's Frances's new car," he said, turning the corner. "As a matter of fact, I'm on my way to pick her up at the club."

"But I thought we'd . . . I thought we were going to talk." He was dressed this way for Frances.

"We are," he said, pulling into the high-school parking lot. The tall arc lights flooded the empty lot and surrounding grass and buildings with a luminous pink cast. She looked up at the dark granite blocks, hating the school as much now as she had when she had gone there. The tennis courts were on the other side of the high hedges, and she could hear the rhythmic whack whack of a match being played.

"Okay, let's talk. What would you like to talk about?"

"I don't know." She shrugged. "Anything."

He drummed his fingers on the steering wheel. "Have you been looking for a job?"

"No. Not yet."

He nodded, staring out the window and not saying anything. "Now, see, if you had a job, we'd have that to talk about."

"We can talk about your book," she said. "How's your book coming?"

"Pretty good," he sighed, then hit the wheel. "Actually, I'm a little bogged down right now. This last week's been rough. Between going away and all Frannie's company, it's been hard getting much work done."

"That's all she really cares about, you know, her friends and her parties. You should write somewhere else." She leaned toward him. "I just thought, Mr. Weilman has three empty bedrooms. You could take one."

"I'm very happy with my . . . with this arrangement. It's me. I just have to discipline myself more."

"I hope you know she's not really going to pay all that money to your editor, don't you?" she said bitterly.

"She says she is. . . ."

"Well, that's a lot easier said than done!" she interrupted. "You don't know how cheap she is!" she said with a nervous laugh.

"But I believe her. She really wants this for me. She says she wants me to have a fair shot." He put his arm over the back of her seat. "I don't say this to upset you, Martha, but your aunt is a very kind and a very generous woman."

"When she wants something!"

"I guess we're all a little bit like that."

"I'm not!" She looked at him. "I'd do anything for you. Anything."

"Martha."

She stared at him. "I will. Anything you want. Anything you ask me, I'll do it for you, Mack. Anything."

He looked away, then took a deep breath and turned to her. "Martha, listen to me." His face under the lights was washed with sweat, and his eyes glistened. "I did a terrible thing to you. . . ."

"No, don't say that!" She covered her ears.

He grabbed her wrist. "I said listen! I want this straight! I want you to understand. I took advantage of you, and I hate myself for it. I despise what I did and I despise what I am. But there's nothing I can do about what happened. Nothing! I was drunk! I was sick and twisted and foul and disgusting." He brought his face close to hers. "But I'm not now. THAT I can change. I can be good. I can finally do something! Martha, I can write. It's all I care about. It's the one thing that matters. It's the only time I ever feel anything. It's the only time I feel human. It's the only thing in my life that's real. It's all that I want. Do you understand?"

"But don't you want to be happy? Don't you want a happy life?"

"There's no such thing!" He shook his head. "Not for me. That's what I'm trying to tell you." He held up his finger. "The one thing I want is to write. Frances is making that possible. And nothing and no one can get in the way of that."

"You mean me. That's what you mean, isn't it?"

He nodded, and she didn't know what to say.

"Are you still going to come and see me?" she asked hopefully.

"No. There's no point to it. It's not fair to you."

"But I love you!" she blurted, unable to contain it any longer.

He started the car, and her head jerked back as he tore out of the parking lot.

TWENTY-TWO

———o———

Two more weeks had passed, and she was still staying with Mr. Weilman. She missed Mack, and yet every time he answered the phone she would hang up without saying anything. At night she would close her eyes while she lay in the tub, picturing him at Mr. Weilman's front door, begging her to let him in. And oh how she let him dangle night after night in that doorway while she pretended to make up her mind.

Though Mr. Weilman denied it, she was certain Frances called every few days to check on her. One way or another she would manage to stay in charge, even if she had to send spies to do it. At this very moment, Julia Prine was in the den with Mr. Weilman, supposedly to drop off flyers from Harmony House. There was an art auction next month, and Mr. Weilman was one of the chairmen.

Martha was in the kitchen, washing the sinkful of peanut-butter and jam knives and all the spoons the children had used this morning to make lemonade. When Julia came, Martha had locked the door and told the children they couldn't come in because Mr. Weilman had company. She was enjoying the quiet. For a few days after that incident with Joshua Barrett, the mothers on the street had declared Mr. Weilman's house off limits as long as Martha Horgan was there. But it didn't take them long to get sick of having their own kitchens torn apart and their toilets plugged up with huge wads of toilet paper. One by one the children had straggled back. The house had become the neighborhood way station, and Mr. Weilman was happy again.

Most of the mothers were her age, and some of them had even gone to high school with her. She hadn't realized who Laura Barrett was until she saw her watering her front lawn with her son, Joshua, the brat. Laura Barrett's maiden name, Hopewood, had been paired in alphabetical sequence with Horgan all through school. Laura had made it clear at an early age that they might have to sit together or work on the same science project but no one could make her like Martha Horgan.

The thought of these women having lives that were so ordinary and so remote from hers was fascinating. When she was growing up, the second she climbed off the school bus and entered the isolation of her home, the pain of her school hours seemed light-years removed. Now being so near these women was as exciting as it was bewildering. From the second floor, she could see just about every house on the street. During the day she slipped from window to window, watching them unload bags of groceries from their station wagons and tear down their front walks to pry apart scuffling children. At night, she saw them greet their returning husbands, who for the most part were slimmer and younger-looking than their wives. The man diagonally across the street, in the pale-green house, didn't usually get home until after midnight. At first she thought he worked long hours, until she began to notice how his car was parked in the morning. Sometimes the front wheel was up on the curb. Sometimes half of the car would be sticking out of the driveway into the street. Last night he had left it in the middle of the road. His wife had run out this morning at five and backed it into the driveway, and then she ran inside, looking up and down the street before she closed the door. So this was it, she thought, watching Sandy Lark from the yellow house tiptoe through her side yard barefoot in her bikini to get the mail; this was how everyone lived, everyone but her.

She dried the last of the silverware. She could hear the children. During the day, even though she usually avoided the kitchen, their presence still permeated the house, with the terror of their screams and shrill laughter and constant tears at every window.

Hearing footsteps, she spun around and checked to make sure the door was still locked. She closed her eyes and took a deep breath, feeling dizzy and lightheaded, the way she had all week. The house's airiness seemed to be turning on her. She wasn't sure what it was; there wasn't enough confinement here, or maybe there just weren't enough rules.

"Martha!" Julia said from the doorway. "How are you doing? I was just telling Ben I haven't seen you in ages."

What else had she told him? That if she gave him any trouble one call to Harmony House would get her out of his hair? "I'm fine, thank you."

"Are you working?"

"No!" And she didn't want any make-believe job at Harmony House either, thank you.

Julia looked at her watch. "How about lunch? Do you feel like getting out? We could drive up by Killington. I don't have any appointments un . . ."

"No. I have to get Mr. Weilman's lunch."

"Then let's take him with us." She started for the door.

"I don't want to go! I'm not even hungry. Take him. I don't want to go."

"Well, we'll do it another time, then." Julia looked at her. "Martha, are you all right? I mean, are you happy here?"

"I told you, I'm fine."

"Frances tells me she's worried about you."

"That's her problem."

"To tell the truth, I've never seen her so happy." Julia looked at her. "I think she's really serious about this Colin Mackey."

Her tears rose with such blind suddenness that she bumped into Julia on her way out of the kitchen.

———□———

Later that afternoon, Wesley Mount called to ask if she might like to go on a picnic with him. A picnic! No. Absolutely not. She couldn't, she told him, and after she hung up she realized she hadn't even said goodbye.

After dinner, Mr. Weilman talked her into accompanying him on his nightly walk downtown. He had asked her every night this week and she had refused. But now that she was down here she didn't mind at all. They walked slowly, because he had been feeling weak all day. The stores were closed, and there were only a few cars passing by. She was amused by his running commentary as they paused at each window. "Now, there's a handsome suit, reminds me of a suit I had. . . . Look at that camera; you know, there's a tribe in South America . . . Doilies, lace doilies, it all comes back, doesn't it? See the bank, the Granite Trust over there? They had the first elevator in town. People came for miles around. They'd stand in line for a chance to go up and down. Come on. Let's see if the lobby's open," he said, taking her arm.

"I hate elevators," she said.

"Really?" Mr. Weilman said, cocking his head the way he did with the children, as if they required a level of hearing far more profound than anyone else. "Why would you hate elevators?"

"They give me a funny feeling. I'm always afraid I'll get trapped inside."

"Well, what would you do if you were in a skyscraper and you had to get to the fiftieth floor?"

"I'd go up the stairs."

"You'd climb fifty flights of stairs rather than use an elevator?" He laughed when she insisted she would. "Have you ever done that? Climbed that many stairs?"

"I've never been in a skyscraper before."

"Never? How about in New York City?"

"I've never been there."

"What big cities have you been to?"

"Burlington. And once I went to Albany." Both trips had been in her early teens, to doctors, who wanted to continue seeing her. Her father had viewed their proposed treatment as gimmicks to keep wringing money out of him. Sitting and talking never cured anything, as far as he was concerned. Wasn't there some pill or an operation or something that would set her straight, he would ask, absolutely disgusted to be told no. After all, if something was broke he fixed it. There was always a way to make things right. We're not talking about a balky engine here, Mr. Horgan. We're talking about a psychological condition that's only going to get worse. We're talking about your daughter. Marthorgan.

Mr. Weilman had stopped in the middle of the sidewalk with his hands clasped to his chest. "Would you like to go to New York City with me? I love the city. My wife and I used to go all the time. I'd love to show it to you. Would you come with me? We could take the bus and we could see a show and . . ."

"No! I can't, Mr. Weilman."

"Of course you can. We'd have a wonderful time."

"I can't."

"But why?"

"I don't know. I just can't."

He looked at her. "Please tell me why."

"I don't go to new places. I just can't. I can't."

A DANGEROUS WOMAN

"But why can't you? What happens? What are you afraid of?"

She stared at him while she tried to put it into words. "It feels like pieces of me are falling off. Like I'm losing myself. These parts of me," she gestured, "I can feel them dropping off."

"You poor dear," he said, taking her arm with such an anxious grip that she was alarmed. As they hurried back, she kept glancing over her shoulder to see what he was afraid of, but there was only the quiet darkness at their heels.

———□———

The next morning, as soon as Mr. Weilman left for the supermarket, the front-door chimes rang, but when she went to answer it, no one was there. She closed the door, and then the kitchen buzzer sounded. Thinking someone had gone impatiently around back, she hurried into the kitchen. The minute she opened that door, the front chimes rang. It went on like that, with her running back and forth between the two doors. She knew it was the children, but if she wanted to catch them in the act she'd have to get ahead of them.

This time, instead of running through the house, she left the front door slightly ajar and waited with her hand on the knob. Her eyes flickered toward the green tremble of the hydrangea bush in the dining-room window. Twigs snapped and leaves rasped against the screen. So that's how they got back and forth unseen: they had been tunneling through the thicket of shrubs and cedar trees against the house. Now, sure enough, the kitchen buzzer rang. They held in the button until the electric buzzing had intensified to waves of jagged light in her eyes. All at once, the buzzing stopped.

"Marthorgan!" a child called.

She kept her eyes on the dining-room window. There . . . Now the shrub quaked, its branches dragging across the hazy screen. They were on their way, the brats. Oh, she could just picture them, dirt-smudged and giddy with sweat and terror, creeping up the steps, then, on their hands and knees, passing under the bay window. Footsteps; oh, the bold brats, listen to the thundering herd of them, not even caring. . . .

MARY MCGARRY MORRIS

She tensed as a shadow darkened the slit of the open doorway. The chimes played, and she both threw open the oak door and pushed out on the sagging screen door, banging it into him.

"Get out of here, you brats . . . you . . ." she screamed, pushing him away from the door, hitting his chest with both hands, with the helpless realization that, like some careening driverless vehicle, she was out of control.

"It's me . . . Martha . . . it's me," said Wesley Mount as if it were dark and she couldn't see him.

"Those brats! It was those brats," she panted, running to look over the railing at a thin gray squirrel that shook its frayed, dusty tail at her.

———□———

He returned later that night, after calling hours ended at the funeral home. The three of them sat on the porch while Mr. Weilman told Wesley Mount about his peace of mind and his better health since he had stopped his chemotherapy.

"It's not for everyone," Wesley agreed.

"If I were a younger man like yourself, there'd be no question. But at my age the cure's worse than the disease."

"It's a quality-of-life issue, no doubt about it," Wesley said, marching his feet from heel to toe while he sat there.

Mosquitoes bit Martha's ankles and arms, and now they were buzzing at her ears. She scratched her head and stamped her feet. She wanted to go inside. "Bite me," she muttered, waving her hands at her ears, "but they never bite anybody else."

Mr. Weilman looked at her and chuckled. "Do you know, I just found out that Martha's never been to New York City. What do you think of that?"

"I don't know," Wesley said. "I've never been there either. But I've been to Albany," he added quickly.

"Then we should go. The three of us," Mr. Weilman said, his pale eyes glittering under the dim porch light. "What a trip that'd be. I know that city like the back of my hand. The places I'd show you!"

"I've got an assistant coming on after Labor Day," Wesley said, glancing at her. "It shouldn't take him too long to get the lay of the land."

"Then we're going!" Mr. Weilman leaned over and took her hand. "Now, don't say no, Martha. Give it a chance. Say you'll think about it. Say maybe. Come on!" He squeezed her hand. "Please say it."

"Well. Well, maybe."

Mr. Weilman smiled, then yawned and slapped his knees. "I guess it's that time. Lately the night never seems long enough."

———□———

He went inside, and they sat so still they could hear the stairs creaking on his way up to bed.

"A trip to New York with Ben would be quite an experience, wouldn't it?" Wesley finally said.

"I'm not really going. I just said that. I didn't want to make him feel bad," she said. She was beginning to feel protective of Mr. Weilman. When lawn-care people or siding salesmen called, she told them he wasn't home. Yesterday a magazine salesman and a woman selling window cleaner had come to the door, and she had turned them both away. The trouble with Mr. Weilman was, with no intention of buying anything, he would invite every single one of these people in and listen to their pitch, and then he would start talking, and the next thing you knew an hour had passed and they would be making up excuses why they had to go.

"Oh, of course not," Wesley said.

They sat in silence for a few moments.

"What a night," Wesley said, leaning forward to see the stars. "Makes you never want winter back. It's so long and cold," he sighed, looking at her.

"I know," she said. "It is long."

"Too long."

"Umm, too long," she said, wincing. Now what?

They stared at his limousine, parked just past the maple tree so it wouldn't end the night filmed with sap or pollen dust. Wesley began to rock, and the porch floor creaked.

"Think it'll hold me?" he asked, stopping the rocking chair.

"Oh yes. This is a good porch. Good and strong. Very good wood." She swallowed hard and closed her eyes. Go home, she thought. Just go and leave her alone. What did he want? Why did he pester her?

"They don't build porches like this anymore," Wesley said.

"Why did you come here?" The question burst out of her.

His head jerked back. "Well . . . I . . . I thought . . . I . . . I . . ." He swallowed with a thin strangling sound. "I just . . . just wanted to see how you were doing and . . . talk to you." Suddenly seized by three violent sneezes, he shook out a large white handkerchief and blew his nose. "Allergies," he gasped, and sneezed again. When he looked up, his eyes were red-rimmed and teary. "I enjoy your company," he said in a congested voice. "I like to talk to you."

"Well, I'm not a very good talker—I mean, conversationalist."

"Oh, but you are. Really!"

His earnest expression made her laugh. "No, I think you just like to talk, that's what I think!"

"Actually, I don't. And you may find that hard to believe, since that's such a part of what I do for a living. I have to meet people. I have to talk to people. I have to talk them through things. I usually say the same things over and over. But then with other things it's hard." He was folding his handkerchief smaller and smaller, into a tight perfect square. "I might give the impression of glibness or maybe a certain ease of expression, but socially I'm really quite . . ." He looked at her. ". . . miserable at times."

"Birdy said you were shy in school." She bit her lip to contain all the other things Birdy had said, how in high school he had been picked on so much his father finally had to send him away to private school.

"I still am." He held out his hands and raised his eyes in an almost prayerful attitude. "Here. Out in the world. But if you and I were in the funeral home right now and you were . . . Well, when you WERE there and your father was there, for instance, I knew what I was supposed to do and what you'd need and what I had to say to everyone. I could do that." He nodded emphatically. "I did that."

"And you did a good job. A very good job," she said, nodding, grateful that he said nothing about her breakdown over her father's coffin.

He smiled shyly. "Why, thank you. That's very kind of you."

"Oh, I wasn't trying to be kind. I'm just a very honest person."

"And I like that about you," he said, so softly she could barely hear him.

———□———

She could not believe she had agreed to go to the movies with him. She had been a nervous wreck over this for the last two days. She would call him and tell him she was sick, which wouldn't be a total lie. She had almost fainted getting out of bed this morning. As the day went on, she had felt better, but what if it happened as they were going down the aisle of the dark theater and she just sank into a silent heap and he kept on going looking for seats and nobody knew she had even fainted until someone else came along trying to find seats and they tripped over her.

Mr. Weilman came into the living room while she was looking up the number of the funeral home.

"You're not ready," he said, obviously disappointed to find her in the same old skirt and baggy shirt she had worn for the past few days. "He'll be here in fifteen minutes."

"I'm not going," she said, dialing. "I don't feel well."

"Getting out will make you feel good," Mr. Weilman said.

"Mount's Funeral Home," answered the recording. "We are not able to come to the phone right now. At the sound of the tone, if you would leave your . . ."

She'd tell him when he came.

Wesley arrived at exactly six-thirty, the grandfather clock on the landing and the door chimes both ringing at once. She had the feeling he had gotten ready hours ago and ever since had been driving around looking at his watch. He wore a double-breasted blazer with monogrammed brass buttons and a wide red tie. Before she could say anything to him, Mr. Weilman had insisted on taking their picture. He posed them in the front hall, where they stood with frozen, strained smiles while he fiddled with his camera. He was always taking pictures of the children, and yet he never seemed sure how to work his camera. Martha wondered if he ever bothered putting film in it or, like the freezer cups, whether it was just another way of catering to the children.

Wesley said he was afraid the tickets would be sold out. He patted his face with his folded handkerchief.

"Smile," said Mr. Weilman, ignoring him.

"That's okay. I don't think I can go," Martha said.

"Be just a minute now," Mr. Weilman said. "I'm waiting for the red light."

"Well, I suppose we could always make the second show," Wesley said.

"Here we go!" said Mr. Weilman.

"I look awful," Martha said.

"You always look so comfortable," Wesley said, turning to her. "I admire that in a person."

"Smile, Wesley," Mr. Weilman called. "You look about as happy as an undertaker!"

"I never take good pictures," Wesley said, turning back. He folded his arms.

"I don't either," she said, folding her arms.

"Oh, I'm sure you do, you're so pretty," Wesley said.

"Say 'cheese'!" The camera flashed, and it seemed to suck Mr. Weilman toward them in its beam. Wesley caught the stumbling old man and held him upright, while Mr. Weilman insisted he was fine; looking through the aperture for so long had disoriented him.

After Wesley remarked what a hot, muggy night it was, they drove downtown in silence. She kept searching out her window for something to talk about.

"I like that statue," she said of the sculpture ahead on the corner.

It was a sleek bronze dog straining back on its invisible leash from a parking meter.

"Really? I never quite got the point," he said, stopping at the light. His face was beaded with perspiration.

"Birdy said it's how people are in this town. They don't want to be forced into things," she said, pleased at how well that had come out.

The light changed, and he pulled into the parking lot. "I don't go to the movies much," Wesley said quickly, as if he thought she should know. He patted his temples and upper lip with his handkerchief.

The TriStar Cinema was in the middle of the shopping center that had been built on the site of the old railway station.

"Me neither," she said, trying to unbuckle her seat belt. She twisted it into her lap to get a better look at it. She tried to shake it open.

"There," Wesley said, reaching and pushing in the tab. "That one doesn't get much use."

They walked toward the theater entrance, where two girls were smoking cigarettes in long white holders. They had the same dry frizzy hair, black-lined slits for eyes, and white faces pinched up like mean little lap dogs. Martha tensed, expecting them to say something. She hurried by, surprised at the silence.

After Wesley bought the tickets, she followed him to the refreshment stand. Seeing such a variety of candy gave her a panicky feeling. She didn't know what she wanted. Nothing, that's what she'd say, and avoid saying anything stupid. She was relieved to see that he had already ordered two large popcorns and sodas.

The minute they sat down, the lights dimmed and the previews began. They were in the fifth row from the front. Martha smiled up at the screen. Everyone was beautiful. Even homely people managed to look beautiful up there. As soon as her eyes adjusted to the darkness, she looked around. There were only about fifteen or twenty people in the theater. She kept trying to see if she knew any of them.

"What's wrong?" Wesley whispered.

"Nothing."

"Aren't you going to eat your popcorn?"

"Yes." She had forgotten about it. "What movie is this?"

He looked at her. "Oh, I'm sorry. It's *Blue Lie*. It's a French movie. I was going to ask you which one you wanted to see, and then I got so bollixed up at the ticket counter, I forgot. It's a mystery. It got excellent reviews. But if you don't like it, we can get tickets for another one."

She assured him this was fine. Just being here was good enough. The movie was starting. The music was so loud the walls and floor vibrated.

"You don't mind subtitles, do you?" he whispered.

"No," she said, eyes wide on the screen, where a beautiful woman with long dark hair threw back a satin sheet and stepped out of bed completely nude. She walked across the room and opened the closet door, but hanging inside there were only men's suits and shirts. She picked her own clothes up from the floor, then sat on the side of the bed and began to dress. The camera followed the slow caressing rise of her stockings up her leg to her glistening thigh.

"I'm sorry," Wesley whispered. "They said it was a mystery. I'm really sorry."

"That's okay," she whispered, holding her glasses steady. The room flooded with light as a door opened beyond the bed. From the doorway a muscular young man in jeans gestured for the woman to hurry. As she rose from the bed to embrace him, the camera focused on the blur of sheets, then zoomed in on a man's head on the pillow, his eyes frozen in horror. There was a bloody flap at his throat where it had been slit. Martha screamed and covered her eyes, and behind her someone laughed nervously.

Wesley grabbed her hand. "It's just a dead man," he whispered.

"I know!" She pulled her hand away, angry with her childish outburst. No one else had screamed.

During the most explicit sex scene, she and Wesley stared up at the screen. Though not a limb or thread touched, she was so acutely aware of his nearness that her face flushed and her eyes burned. Desire seeped into every corpuscle, and now everything reminded her of Mack. At the end, she tried not to let Wesley see her cry, but the tears streamed down her cheeks. He passed her his scented handkerchief and took her half-eaten popcorn tub onto his lap while she blew her nose. The lights came on, and people were leaving the theater.

"Are you okay?" he whispered, leaning in to her.

"It's just that it was so sad," she gasped, grateful that he sat waiting until she was ready to go.

They drove slowly along Main Street to Sewards Dairy Bar, where Wesley ordered two chocolate ice-cream cones. He took a handful of extra napkins, which he tucked under his arm. He passed her cone through the window and then, when he got in the car, he laughed because she was still eating the popcorn.

"I always try and make things last," she explained, wrapping a napkin around the stem of her cone. "Except ice cream," she said. "That's one good thing you can't make last. There's no dilly-dallying with ice cream." She licked wide brown swirls as she turned the cone faster and faster.

She stopped. His mouth quivered as he watched her. She felt stupid. She wished she hadn't come. She had been acting like a goof, and now he was looking at her the way Birdy used to when she had gone too far, when she was out of control and didn't know a way on earth to get back.

"Would you like to eat your cone here?" His eyes widened. "Or I could bring you back to Mr. Weilman's, of course. Or we could just ride around and eat our cones." Again his mouth trembled. He wet his lips.

"I don't care," she said, her voice thickening with the ice cream. She kept clearing her throat and swallowing.

"It's up to you. I really have no preference." He pulled onto the road, licking his cone as he drove.

Stung by his clipped tone, she didn't say anything. He was annoyed that she couldn't make up her mind. Well, then, he could just drop her off right here, for all she cared. Who did he think he was?

Suddenly the dusty windshield was mottled with enormous raindrops. Even at high speed, the wipers couldn't keep up with the downpour. Wesley put on his emergency flashers and coursed slowly through the glare of rainwater flowing along the road.

MARY McGARRY MORRIS

"Don't worry," he shouted over the hollow rain beat on the roof. "I'm an excellent driver. I'm very experienced." He glanced over frowning. "Is your seat belt buckled?"

A few moments later, he pulled into the driveway of the funeral home. Here, he explained, he could drive right under the portico and keep her dry. Or they could just sit in the car, she thought, looking up at the dripping-wet bricks, and for a second she was afraid she had said it out loud when he said the same thing, only adding, "But this might be a long storm."

Seeing her hesitation, Wesley reminded her that there hadn't been a wake tonight. She scowled. That hadn't even occurred to her. She had been wondering what they would do in there, what there was to talk about. She wished he'd stop staring at her the way he did when he thought she wasn't looking; and those sighing sounds he kept making. Like panicky little cries. What? Was he offended? Disappointed? Bored? Oh, this was such a mistake, the whole evening, a terrible mistake she would never ever make again.

"Shall we?" he asked, opening his door.

"Shall we? Shall we . . ." she snapped, about to say, Shall we what, keep getting on each other's nerves like this? But he was already out and hurrying around the front of the car. He held the door open, waiting for her and smiling.

The foyer reeked of chemicals so strong they seemed to seep right into her pores. Her eyes watered and she had to keep fanning her hand under her nose.

"It's the polish," Wesley explained. "Linseed oil and turpentine. I did all the woodwork today. This, believe it or not, is the original finish. Hand-rubbed," he said, stroking the oak wainscoting, which gleamed under the cut-glass chandelier. "I do it every six months. It's amazing how thirsty this wood gets." He looked back at her. "How dry the air is," he added, and there it was again, that sigh, like a faint whimper, and suddenly she was aware of the enormous silence here. "I'll make some tea," he said.

Wesley led the way up the burgundy-carpeted stairs, through a torrent of nervous facts. He said the rooms here on the second floor had been home for his parents, a brother and sister, and his grandfather Henry, who had started the funeral service in 1891. His parents were both "deceased," and his brother was an engineer in Toledo. He passed the first door on his right, then opened the next one, into his living room. The only rooms he used up here were the kitchen, one of the bedrooms, and this square high-ceilinged parlor with its green velvet sofa and matching chairs. She was amused by the sway of the thick gold fringe on the base of the sofa and chairs every time Wesley walked by. The lamps were shaded in pearly-gray leaded glass with ornate metal bases. All the mahogany tables and radiators were topped with white marble slabs. The fireplace opening and mantel were black marble.

Martha went into the bathroom and stayed there a long time while she tried to think of something they could talk about. When she came out, Wesley was in the kitchen, filling the kettle with water for tea. She sat at the table, which was covered not only with a white linen cloth but with a cushioned table-pad as well.

He set down two vinyl placemats and the cups, creamer, and sugar bowl, arranging them so that their handles pointed in the same direction.

She cleared her throat and thumped her chest. "Where's your sister live?" she asked. That was the question she had finally come up with in the bathroom.

"Hawaii."

"What's her name?"

"Ginger."

She smiled. "That's a good name. Ginger." She should have had a name like that. Ginger Horgan. She pictured herself tap dancing on a stage with a top hat and a black baton. She felt lightheaded and oddly buoyant, as if she were playing a part up on a movie screen.

Wesley didn't sit down until the water had boiled and he had filled both cups. He was perspiring. It was too warm up here for hot tea, but she dunked her tea bag up and down and didn't say anything. He said the only air conditioning was downstairs. He hated opening the windows while it was still raining, because then he'd have to go around with a towel and dry all the sills. He loosened his tie and asked if she minded if he took off his jacket. When he did, she could see through his thin nylon shirt how his undershirt strap hung over one shoulder.

"What does your sister do in Hawaii?" She wanted to hear more about Ginger.

"She eats too much and talks too much and her latest husband is a very disreputable sort," he said testily.

"I still like her name." She was disappointed.

"Well, you wouldn't like her. She's not like any of the Mounts. She got in more trouble growing up. My father always used to say he didn't know where she came from. He said it so much that I actually used to think she just showed up at the door one day and moved in." He kept checking his watch before he finally fished out his tea bag and squeezed it. He dribbled milk from the creamer onto a teaspoon, measuring four spoonsful into his tea. "I haven't heard from my sister in over fifteen years. Isn't that strange?"

"No. My father didn't speak to his relatives for thirty years. And my aunt still doesn't."

Suddenly there was a boom of thunder, and she grabbed the table.

"You jumped," Wesley said, laughing. "You're very high-strung. You must be creative. Do you paint or do anything artistic?"

She liked to cook, but that wasn't what he meant.

"My sister was an artist. Would you like to see her old paintings?"

She followed him into the living room, where the paintings were either still lifes or landscapes. Each landscape seemed to depict the same red barn or covered bridge. She was disappointed that they were so flat and childish. She wanted Ginger to be a brilliant artist. "They're very nice," she said. "And the frames are really beautiful." The heavy frames were far more impressive than the paintings.

Wesley thanked her. He had found his sister's canvases in the attic and had them framed. "They give me a sense of family," he said.

He took her down the hall to show her how he had renovated part of this second floor for business use. "People can't understand living with your business the way I do, but, then, I can't imagine coming home every night to an empty house."

She wondered if a corpse in the house kept it from being empty.

He opened a door and turned on a light so she could see inside. Soft music began to play. "It used to be the master bedroom," he said. Now it was the casket-display room. The satin-lined caskets seemed suspended in midair on their Plexiglas stands. Overhead, the recessed fixtures flared a soft ray of light down into each casket. Propped on every pleated or smocked pastel head-pillow was a plastic card embossed with the model name of that particular casket. Nearest the door was the "Homeward," a coffin of polished dark mahogany. Beside it, in rock maple, was the "Godspeed." She pictured it with retractable wings and exhaust pipes jetting from the end.

Wesley opened the doors of an enormous walk-in closet. He pressed a button, and tinted lights glowed over a rack of men's dark suits and women's pastel chiffon dresses in clear plastic bags that swayed in ghostly undulation as they passed. Price tags hung from the sleeves.

"It saves the bereaved having to go shopping in a regular store," he explained. "And it keeps some of them, the deceased, from looking, well . . ." He looked around, grimacing. "Tacky," he whispered. "You know, if you ever need a dress for something, don't buy one. Just come by and pick one out." He glanced at her. "And I've got a lot of size eights in there. In fact, I just got a new one that would look beautiful on you," he said, searching through them until he found a pale-blue cocktail dress with seed pearls edging the neckline. "Do you like it?" He held it under his chin.

"It's nice," she said, uneasy with the intensity in his eyes above the shimmering dress.

"You know, you've got classic features," he said, then turned abruptly and hung up the dress.

"No, I don't," she scoffed.

"You do! And, believe me, I've done enough reconstruction to recognize good bone structure," he said, coming close, squinting and angling his head in professional appraisal. "I'd say you have just about perfect symmetry."

"I do?"

"Oh yes. Your cheekbones are exquisite." His voice was steady and calming. "You're beautiful."

She grinned, and his whole expression seemed to rush toward her, his warm breath melting over her like wax. He cleared his throat. "Would you mind if I hugged you?" he asked, so softly she could barely hear him.

She shrugged. "I guess not."

He put his arms around her, and at first they stood politely together, with only their shoulders touching. And then his arms tightened and hers lifted and they held each other with an urgency, not of passion, but of great relief.

TWENTY-THREE

Mr. Weilman tapped on the bedroom door, then backed in with a spoon and a jar of applesauce on a silver tray. "Guaranteed to stay down," he said, unscrewing the lid.

Martha's dizziness had become so constant that she had to will herself up and out of a chair, slowly, ever so firmly, and the same thing coming down the stairs, her eyes guiding her feet to every step. The worst of it was her shaky stomach. For the past week, she had been living on saltines and ginger ale. Mr. Weilman said it was the same flu that had gone through the neighborhood.

"Baby food?" she asked, shuddering. Just the thought of it sickened her.

"Reba Lewis sent it over," he said.

"Reba Lewis?"

"In the green house," he said. "Katie's mother."

Reba Lewis was at least the fourth neighbor Mr. Weilman had consulted about her nausea. Laura Barrett had even sent over her own chicken broth.

Mr. Weilman sat on the edge of the bed and offered her a spoonful of applesauce. As soon as she swallowed, her stomach heaved. She gagged, and Mr. Weilman held the tray to her chin. She had never felt this sick.

Wesley Mount had called or come by almost every day, but she still couldn't talk to him. It was more than this illness; she was mortified every time she thought of her hungry embrace in his apartment. He probably thought she had been aroused by that dirty movie. On her dresser were the five get-well cards he had sent in the last five days. He had also sent a fuzzy yellow wind-up duck that waddled noisily around with a sign that said "Get Well Soon!" Yesterday he had brought her a can of English peppermints and a vase of red gladioli. She could hear him downstairs now, urging Mr. Weilman to call a doctor. There was dehydration to consider here, as well as her electrolyte levels. What seemed a minor imbalance could quickly flare into a critical condition. Mr. Weilman assured Wesley he was monitoring the situation, and he reminded him of his own medical experience these last two years. Wesley countered with his far vaster experience, and what he often saw, the end result of negligence.

"Negligence!" Mr. Weilman's indignation resounded up the stairs.

"I don't mean you, Ben," Wesley assured him. "I mean anyone who ignores the signs of a potentially grave condition."

She pulled the sheet over her head, and the tented heat swelled with her own staleness. She curled smaller and tighter, drifting in and out of sleep while, from the street and yards below, the children's voices caught in the flow of her dreams, a cry, a word, a twig, a red feather, a whiffle ball, a frayed paper cup bobbing and glimmering, then sinking out of reach. She ran after them, but they fled, and finally, when she understood that they would never stop as long as she chased them, she stopped and watched them go, watched them grow smaller and smaller, and then they disappeared.

"Martha. Martha? Can you hear me in there? Martha, it's me. It's Julia."

As she struggled to wake up, Julia explained that she had just dropped off tickets for the art auction. "You were in bad shape last week, but now you look even worse," Julia said, brushing cracker crumbs off the sheet.

She couldn't even remember Julia being here last week. Without food, she was growing weaker. Her appetite and memory might have dimmed, but it was strange how her senses seemed to have heightened. If Mr. Weilman sighed in the kitchen, she could hear it. Daylight was blinding. The weight of the sheet on her toes was painful. She let herself be propped against the pillows so that Julia could take her temperature. It was normal, Julia told her, staring at her as she shook down the thermometer. She went downstairs, and returned with a glass of ice water, which she told Martha to sip slowly. She backed through the door now with towels and a basin of tepid water. She wrung out a washcloth and rubbed it with soap while she quizzed Martha about her bowels. Had she had any headaches, backaches, chest pain, coughing, sputum, sinus pain, ringing ears, double vision? Julia handed her the washcloth, and Martha took off her glasses. Julia dipped them into the basin and dried them on the towel, reeling out her string of questions while Martha washed her face and neck. She could feel the skin tightening on her bones. The air was sharp with Julia's spicy perfume.

"Any bladder infections? Any burning? Any discharge?"

As she shook her head, it occurred to her that this illness might be the final, fatal stage of what had been consuming her all these years.

"When was your last period?"

She couldn't remember. They had always been so irregular she had long ago given up keeping track. They came when they came. Every four weeks. Six weeks. Two months. Blinding migraines and twisting cramps, wrapping up the pads and hiding them in her pockets until she could tuck them deep down in the trash so she wouldn't have to listen to Frances's smug sigh, "Oh, so that's why." Sometimes she would forget, and by the end of the day her pockets would be stuffed with the foulness. When her periods didn't come, she was always grateful.

"You must have some idea. Think, now," Julia said. "Did you have one in July?"

"I don't know."

"There was the Fourth. Steve's party?" Julia coaxed.

"No." This was so embarrassing, and it certainly had nothing to do with her periods. She had never been sick like this with them.

"June?" Julia asked, returning her glasses.

She couldn't remember. June. What was June? How could she have forgotten? In June, Mack had come. "May," she said. The end of May. The night of the PlastiqueWare party.

Julia didn't say anything for a moment. Her face reddened. "Could you be pregnant?"

"What?" She stared at Julia, stunned by the question.

"Could you be pregnant?" Julia repeated in a choked voice.

"No!" Her hand flew to her mouth. "I don't know. No! I couldn't be."

———□———

Julia's twenty-minute trip to the drugstore and back seemed to take hours. Martha lay on the bed now, with the sheet drawn to her chin. To this point, the procedure had been painless, but so awkward that they had barely spoken. Julia sat on the bed reading the instructions, and then she told Martha to go into the bathroom and urinate into a paper cup and leave it in the sink. When Martha came out of the bathroom, Julia went in with the pink-and-blue box, the pregnancy-testing kit.

Things were clinking in there; water was running; and now the toilet flushed. All she wore under the sheet was her pajama top. She lay with her eyes closed and her ankles locked. The noon heat was heavy, and yet she was covered with goosebumps. The sheet felt cold everywhere it touched her.

She remembered her only other internal examination, her feet in cold metal stirrups, her rump dragged by the tiny pug-nosed nurse to the end of the sweat-damp paper-covered table, the humiliating position an almost unendurable misery, with the doctor's voice beyond her sheeted legs warning her against the coldness of the speculum widening inside her flesh.

"Please hurry, please hurry," she whispered, starting to shiver. The possibility of pregnancy brought not a single image to mind. All that was real was this taste of sourness and this fatigue like a vast inertia, a deadness from which she could not rise.

The bathroom door opened, and Julia came out holding up a paper stick. Wincing, Martha hiked the sheet up to her knees. At least the stick was tiny compared with the doctor's instruments.

"Martha?"

"Go ahead. I'm ready," she said, uncrossing her legs and pulling the sheet up to her waist. She spread her legs and held her breath, dreading the insertion.

"Oh, I'm not . . . You thought . . . No. Oh, Martha!" Julia yanked down the sheet, covering her. "It's done," she said, leaning close and explaining the procedure: she had dipped the stick into the urine. "See. It's pink." Sighing, she sat on the edge of the bed. "I did it twice to be sure. It turned pink both times."

Neither one spoke. Martha looked away. What did that mean?

"Pink means you're pregnant."

"Pregnant"—what on earth could that possibly mean?

"Do you want to tell me who the father is?" Julia asked.

She closed her eyes, aware that something, a form, a great wonder was beginning to coalesce. Love, she thought. Was that what it meant?

"It's him, isn't it? Colin Mackey."

Martha bit her lip.

"What will you do?" Julia asked.

She turned her head and tried to cover her smile. Julia looked so troubled. She knew she should be upset too, but all she felt was relief.

"You can't go through with this, Martha. There's no way. And you don't have to do it alone. There's a clinic in Burlington and no one will . . ."

"I'll be all right." She wanted Julia to leave. She had no interest in anything right now other than talking to Mack.

"If you don't let me help you, then you're going to have to tell Frances."

She couldn't believe Julia was threatening her. "Please go. Please!"

"Martha, you can't have this baby!"

"Leave me alone. I'll do what I want."

"No, Martha. Oh God, no, you can't."

"Why? Tell me why," she demanded, sitting up and wringing her hands to keep them from slapping that smug, perfect face.

"Oh God, Martha, think of it. Think what its . . . Think what your life would be like," she said with a look of horror.

"Get out!" Martha said, springing at Julia. "Get out of here!"

After Julia left, she dressed quickly. She felt so lightheaded that she seemed to float down the stairs, then from room to room, with Mr. Weilman dogging her steps, asking her how she felt and what could he get her to eat, what could he do.

"Nothing. I don't want anything." She wanted to be alone so she could call Mack.

He followed her into the front hall. "At least you've got some color. How about some toast?"

"I have to go somewhere," she said, pushing open the door to get away from him.

"Where? Martha! When are you coming back?" Mr. Weilman called as she came squinting down the porch steps into the dizzying heat. "I'll get some fish," he called. "Some scrod, nice and light."

All along the street, the children paused on their vehicles, in their digging and games, to watch her. They knew she had been sick, because

Mr. Weilman had made them whisper and close the door quietly. They darted out from under their sprinklers and stood dripping on the hot dusty sidewalks, but she would not look at them. Shielding her eyes, she concentrated on walking very slowly; the humidity and the heat were sapping what little strength she had.

She was almost downtown before she came to a public telephone. The traffic was so noisy that she had to lean in close to the phone. Mack answered on the first ring, and he actually sounded pleased to hear from her. "I've been wondering how you're doing," he said in a tired, lazy voice. She heard his chair creak, and she pictured him leaning back, stretching his long hairy legs across the desk.

"I've been sick," she said, grinning. Her heart might burst at any moment. She was shaky, excited, happy, terrified. "But I'm better now." She stuck her finger in her ear as a cement truck rumbled by. "I have something to tell you," she shouted.

"What is it? Martha, I can't hear you very well."

"I'm pregnant! I'm going to have a baby!" She waited. "Mack? Did you hear what I said?"

"Umm. Yes."

"Aren't you going to say anything? I'm pregnant."

"Who's with you? Where are you?"

"I'm at a pay phone. I'm by myself."

"Why do you think you're . . ." He lowered his voice. ". . . pregnant?"

"Because the test says I am."

"Test? What test? Who gave you a test? I'm not following this."

"Julia did. She gave me a pregnancy test."

"Julia Prine?" Silence. "Why would she give you a test? What're you talking about? I don't know what you're talking about." Silence. "Martha, are you all right? You're not making sense."

"I'm pregnant. Did you hear what I said? I'm pregnant."

"Yes, I heard you."

"What're we going to do, Mack?"

"I don't know what you mean."

"I mean . . . I mean . . . Well, something." He wasn't being any help at all. He knew what she was trying to say.

MARY MCGARRY MORRIS

"What?"

She shrugged. "I don't know. Be together?" she said in a small voice. "Get married? Something."

"You need an abortion as soon as possible," Mack said. "You can't have your whole life ruined by . . ."

"No! No, you don't understand. My whole life WAS ruined. Now it's changed."

"My God, you can't be serious! Think what you're saying!"

Listening, she closed her eyes. He was making her feel so helpless and stupid. Of course she knew all that this meant. He was right—she hadn't had time to sort out her thoughts—but that was why she was calling him. What? She jerked around, and the short metal cord snapped her back. He kept talking about the father: what if the father denied it; what if he wouldn't support it. "Especially when the father's someone you can't stand," he said.

"You're the father!" She laughed. "What do you mean?"

"I know how you feel about him, and you don't need to be tied up to that all your life."

"What're you talking about?"

"You and Getso. I didn't want to tell you that night and upset you, but your friend Birdy called Frances and told her everything that had happened; how you were always following him, and brushing up against him, and how when he turned you down you accused him of stealing. She said you'd started waiting out in his car for him, and when he told you to leave him alone, you accused him of dating her best friend."

Her head was reeling. Whose best friend? Birdy's best friend? She had been Birdy's best friend. Nothing was making sense. Mack was too far away. If he were here, she could make him understand.

"And when I heard that, everything made sense. Getso grabbing you that day by the store, and then the time he brought the bag of clothes to the house. I haven't said this to Frances, but I think I know what happened, Martha. It was the other way around, wasn't it? He used you, and then he got scared Birdy would find out, so he accused you of stealing to get rid of you."

"Please deposit four more quarters," a voice intruded on the line.

She searched frantically through her pockets and her purse. All she had were bills. Just as the line disconnected, she spotted the Dairy Queen across the street. She darted between the oncoming cars and cut in front of the people waiting in line at the window.

"Hey! What the . . ."

"I just want change," she said, waving a five-dollar bill.

"And we just want ice cream," a young woman said.

She got in line. Tears welled in her eyes. How had everything gotten so twisted? How had the truth spawned such lies? An uneasy silence fell over the line, and people glanced back at her. She stared down at the ground and tried to dab away the tears. Behind her, a woman burst out laughing, and Martha ignored her. As soon as she got her change, she hurried back to the pay phone.

This time the number was busy, so she called the Cleaners and asked for Birdy. Now more than ever, she had to make Birdy see how Getso's poison had tainted everything.

"Just a minute," answered a young voice she didn't recognize. "Birdy! Hey, Bird!" the voice called away from the phone, then returned quickly to ask, "Who's this?"

"An old friend of hers."

"Uh, she's not here."

"But I heard you call her."

"Yah, well, she left and nobody told me."

"When did she leave?"

"A while ago."

"When will she be back?"

"Uh, she won't be, I guess."

She was walking toward Birdy's house. Though she had never been inside, she knew exactly where it was. There had been many lonely Sundays last winter when she would walk the two slushy miles from the boardinghouse to Birdy's, making sure she passed the dark-green cottage slowly enough for Birdy to see her and invite her in.

There it was, so deep in the verdant darkness of the tall pines as to be almost invisible. She ached at the thought of all the pain that little

MARY McGARRY MORRIS

house must contain, and how betrayed Birdy must feel to think that Martha had repaid her kindness and attention by chasing after Getso. It wasn't fair that one man could be so evil, so selfish, so coldly calculating, so powerful that he had managed to destroy her only friendship. And now, to protect himself from the truth, he was spreading these lies about her, this filth. He had obviously brainwashed Birdy. She had read about such things in magazines and seen it on talk shows, and here it was happening in real life. By isolating Birdy, he had made her his psychological prisoner, his love slave. It sickened her.

Birdy's car wasn't in the driveway, but that wasn't unusual, since he drove it all the time. Birdy probably had to walk everywhere now. The shades in the second-floor windows were pulled down. Maybe Birdy was up there in bed. Martha's heart swelled as she tapped lightly on the lace-curtained door glass. She put her ear to the glass and listened.

Birdy didn't answer the front door, so she came along the driveway in slow careful steps over the slippery golden pine needles. The back door was open. She pressed her face to the screen and peered inside. The tiny pink-and-white kitchen with its tulip-patterned wallpaper was like a picture in a magazine. She could smell cinnamon and warm herbs.

"Birdy?" she whispered a few times, then listened. She tapped lightly and called again, this time louder. She could hear water running and the sound of muffled music. She stepped inside, closing the door soundlessly. There were unwashed breakfast dishes in the sink, and on the cutting board half of a green apple, its flesh beaded with moisture. The knife Birdy must have just used lay on the counter, its blade still streaked with juice. On the wall by the refrigerator, the telephone bore Birdy's new number, written on a strip of masking tape. Sitting down, she whispered the number over and over to herself. She folded her hands on the edge of the table, careful to contain herself in this one small space so that Birdy would see that she had always known her place and had never overstepped the boundaries. As much as she wanted to, she wouldn't even peek into the other rooms. Absolutely not. There was a banging sound, and her eyes shot to the ceiling, then followed the footsteps that moved back and forth overhead. The milk-glass light fixture trembled over the table, and a door slammed. Birdy was coming downstairs. She stared at the doorway, her smile bursting into a joyous grin.

"Jesus Christ!" Getso said, jerking back, his scarred eye ridging higher into his forehead.

She jumped up from the table and stood frozen, staring.

There was a white towel around his neck, and all he wore was a pair of shiny black bikini underpants. He whipped the towel off his neck and tried to cover himself. "What the hell're you doing in here?"

"Birdy. I have to see Birdy." She could barely expel the words.

"She's not here. She's at work."

"They said she's here."

His stringy wet yellow hair dripped down his neck and slick shoulders.

"Well, she's not. She's at work. So you better go. Go ahead, now." He gestured at her with the towel. "She's not here."

"Don't you lie to me," she said, gripping the back of the chair. "I know she's here. They told me she was here."

"Yah, because that's what they're s'posed to say." He stepped closer. "Don't you get it yet? She wants you to stop bothering her. So go on. Get the hell outta here," he said, his face twisting contemptuously.

"Bothering her!" she cried. He should talk about bothering Birdy. After all his lies and his cheating . . .

"Yah, bothering her, like this," he gestured disdainfully. "Like here you are, you just walk in."

She stared, mesmerized by his vileness, amazed that he could not only face her, but act so offended, so disgusted by her. "No matter what you do, you can't stop the truth from coming out. No one can do that. No one can stop the truth," she said, pleased that she was starting to calm down.

"Jesus Christ, Martha, will you get the hell outta here and stop bothering people," he snarled, grabbing her arm and pushing her toward the door.

She struggled and her glasses fell to the floor and now everything was murky and shapeless. "Bothering people," she groaned, trying to twist away. Oh God, she felt his crotch at her hip. What was next? Of course. That's what had been on his mind all along, with his leering comments and his filthy lies. She yanked her arm free, but he grabbed her again, and she staggered back against the counter. He pulled her toward him, and she writhed in his hold, her face rubbing against his hairy chest. Groping behind her, her hand closed over the cold-handled knife. His arms dropped with the first stab.

"Bothering people! Bothering people! Bothering people!" she grunted with each blow. "People bother me," she cried, her eyes fixed on his, glassy with their stunned horror. "But nobody thinks of that! Nobody cares about that!"

Gasping, he leaned on her, his wet head against hers, his flesh settling over her with the stony, sighing weight of an exhausted lover. And then he sagged down to the floor in sections, folding increments of joints and tissued flaps. Like spent wings, his arms hinged close to his sides, folding as he curled smaller and smaller in the widening bloody shadow that was seeping onto the shiny white tiles.

She found her glasses on the floor and put them on; the right lens was shattered. She put the knife in the sink, and then she turned on the cold water and watched the pink water swirl into the drain as she rinsed her hands. She had to stay calm. But she couldn't think clearly with her heart pounding in her head like this.

It was all she could hear. She was on Prospect Street, and a motorcycle passed, but the only sound was the blood pumping in her brain. Had she turned off the water? She thumped her chest, unable to remember. Oh God, what if the sink plugged up and the water overflowed onto Birdy's new floor. Poor Birdy, what a mess she would have to clean up.

Not knowing any formal prayers, she murmured her own as she hurried along. "Dear God, please don't let the water be on. Dear God, please don't let the water be on. Dear God, help me."

She could call the new number. Maybe Birdy was upstairs and if she got down in time she could turn it off. Where was her purse? She must have forgotten it on Birdy's table, and now she had no money to call.

Cars raced by. People stared at her. The smashed lens in her glasses glared with sunlight. She tried not to run. Teeth bared, a German shepherd bounded to the edge of its yard, barking savagely through the thin dusty boxwood. "I hope that dog is leashed. There's a leash law in this town," she muttered, breaking into another half-trot. She caught herself, walked a few more feet, then ran again, panting, "Have to call Birdy. Have to call Birdy." But her head was starting to ache, and she had forgotten what she had to tell her.

Ahead was the boardinghouse. She would use their phone. The call would be catalyst enough. With the sound of Birdy's voice, she would know what to say. She ran up the porch steps, but the door was latched, so she rang the bell. Three of the ladies appeared at once, Loiselle Evans, Mrs. Hess, and Claire Mayo, who carried a small rechargeable vacuum cleaner.

"Martha!" cried Loiselle Evans, her hands flying to her face.

"What in God's name happened to you?" Claire Mayo gasped.

"I have to use the phone."

"That's blood! Oh my God, that's blood. She's covered with blood," screamed Mrs. Hess, pointing.

"Let me in!" She pushed the door. "I have to call Birdy!"

"Get away from that door," Claire Mayo ordered, pointing the vacuum as if it were a gun.

"Oh, please let her in," Loiselle Evans pleaded. "She's hurt and we have to help her. We have to." She stepped up beside Claire, her pert face at the landlady's ear. "You know we do!" she said fiercely.

Claire Mayo peered at Martha. "Are you hurt?"

"I'm not hurt," she said, and Loiselle Evans sighed.

"Where'd all that blood come from?" Claire's lip trembled.

Blood. The front of her shirt was covered with it. There was blood on her arms and her feet. Again the wave of sickness rose with the realization that he was on her, touching her, sticky and soaking wet against her flesh. "Let me in!" she cried. She banged on the door, and blood spurted from her fist. She looked down at the gash in her palm. Now she kicked the door, and her foot shot through the brittle screen.

"Call the police!" Mrs. Hess shrieked, and Claire Mayo slammed shut the heavy oak door.

MARY McGARRY MORRIS

She was walking so fast that at times she appeared to be skipping. Ahead, on the corner, was the funeral home, its black sign on the front lawn promising in gold script "Mount's Where Caring Counts." She began to run, then, staggering, forced herself to that stiff lurching gait again. She slipped inside, dazed by the sudden shock of air-conditioned air. It took her a moment to adjust to the vestibule's dimness. From nearby came the melodic rise and fall of murmurous voices. Looking through the wide parlor doors, she saw a large candle burning at the head of an open casket. The corpse wore an orange tie, an ugly orange tie. Imagine wearing an orange tie at your own wake. An ugly orange tie. She shook her head to dislodge such an irrelevant, irritating thought. But it was caught, fixed there, that wide ugly orange tie consubstantiating all that was wrong in the world, all the ignorance. "The ignorance," she muttered. "The terrible, terrible ignorance."

The mourners, mostly elderly women, prayed aloud with a priest in a long black cassock. Wesley Mount stood at the back of the room, his arms folded and his head bowed. "Hail Mary, full of grace, the Lord is with thee. Blessed art thou among women and blessed is the fruit of thy womb Jesus. Holy Mary . . ." The priest looked up at her. He took a couple of steps forward, then glanced back at the women, intoning, "Hail Mary, full of grace."

With the priest's approach, Wesley Mount's head rose. "Martha!" he said, reaching her first. "What happened? Are you all right?" He sniffed. "That's blood. Martha, your glasses! What happened?"

"I could tell by the way she was standing there something was wrong," the priest said.

"Were you in an accident?" Wesley asked.

She tried to think. She didn't know what to call it. There was a name for what had happened, but she didn't know what it was. It had to do with honesty. Her eyes darted between the two men. A priest would know the word.

"I think she's in shock," the priest said.

The women's prayers had stalled. They turned and watched from their seats.

"I really think she should lie down," the priest said.

"Come with me," Wesley said, guiding her up the stairs.

Wesley led her to his sofa. He begged her to tell him what had happened. "Are you hurt? Martha, do you have some kind of wound?"

"Yes," she said, showing him her hand. "I do."

"Oh, poor dear," he said, holding her hand in his. He touched the side of her face, and her eyes closed. "This is very deep, so I'll do what I can here and then I'm taking you to the hospital. You've obviously lost a lot of blood." He stood up and kissed the top of her head. "You came to me," he whispered. "Oh, Martha, I can't tell you what this means to me."

It was with great tenderness that he wrapped her hand in a wet towel, then assured her she would only have to be alone for a few minutes. "I'll be right back." His medical supplies were downstairs. When he left, she stood up. She had too much to do to go to the hospital. She went into the hallway, and she could hear the women and the priest talking to Wesley down in the vestibule. Trying to find her way to the back staircase, she stopped in front of a mirror, horrified by the sight of her bloody shirt. Turning, she ran into the casket-display room, opened the closet door, and there it was, the blue chiffon with seed pearls on the neck.

Exhausted now, she trudged along Main Street, her raised hand still wrapped in the towel. She didn't like the way people stared at her. Two women were coming toward her. They were struggling to keep a straight face at the sight of the filmy blue cocktail dress over her pants and her old sneakers. As soon as they passed, one of them burst out laughing. Head down, she kept going.

———□———

Martha stood in the glare of Mr. Weilman's messy kitchen. They had been in here again. The lights were on, the cupboard doors were open, and crumpled paper cups littered the counter and floated in the plugged sink, along with a bloated slice of bread. On the table there was a jar of peanut butter with a greasy knife sticking out of it, and the plastic containers Mack had given her. She picked one up and groaned when she saw the holes that had been punched in the blue lid. It was filled with grass and stones and fuzzy reddish caterpillars. Every single container had been cut. Some contained worms. The biggest held a small green toad. In this one there was a salamander. She couldn't believe it; they had destroyed the only thing Mack had given her. There were in this world a few kind people. She knew she was one, Mr. Weilman was another, but not these children. They were cruel and selfish, and that was the most terrible thing of all.

She dialed Birdy's number. The phone rang twice, and then a man answered. Getso. The minute she slammed down the phone, she realized it hadn't even sounded like him. She dialed again. She tapped her foot. "Oh, Birdy," she sighed. "Oh, Birdy, please answer."

"Hello," the same man answered.

She asked to speak to Birdy Dusser, and the man asked her name.

"I see," he said when she told him. "Just a moment, please . . . It's Martha Horgan," he said and she was sure the high-pitched sound she heard in the background was a cry of joy. She grinned, waiting for Birdy through the scramble of garbled voices, and then she heard a woman's wrenching wail.

"Martha? Ah, Birdy would like to call you right back if she could. Ah, she says she needs your . . ."

". . . he was afraid of something like this . . ." Birdy cried.

The muffled silence came like a struggle of dark wings beating in her ear.

". . . telephone number," the man continued.

She hung up. Now she knew and Birdy knew and soon everyone would know that a terrible thing had happened. A terrible thing. The most terrible thing of all. She dialed Frances's number, and Mack answered on the first ring. "Hello? Hello?" he repeated.

"Hello," she said finally, her forehead pressed to the wall. "It's me. Martha."

"Martha! Where are you? Are you all right? Where are you?"

She could tell by the strain in his voice that Frances was nearby. "Are you at Weilman's? Is that where you are?" he asked.

She bit her lip. "Mack? I'm . . . I don't know what to do, Mack."

"First tell me where you are."

"You know what you said about . . ." She shuddered. "About Getso. Well, those were all lies. He made that all up. I knew the truth about him, so he blamed everything on me."

"Is that why you went there?"

He couldn't possibly know she had gone to Birdy's. That couldn't be what he meant. She was getting confused. She felt so dizzy. He was calling her name. She closed her eyes.

Outside, a woman was calling, "Joshua! Joshua! Joshua!"

A door slammed. She could hear the voices of children, and then the sudden tinny, insistent ring of a bike bell.

"Martha! Frances wants to know where you are. Are you at Mr. Weilman's? Martha, answer me. Are you there?"

"Yes," she whispered.

"All right. She says to tell you she's on her way there. We're calling Steve now, and he'll come too. Frances says to just stay put and don't talk to anyone. Don't answer any questions until Steve gets . . ."

"No, you come! Please, Mack. I need you. I love you. I'm all alone and I'm so sick . . ."

"It's going to be okay." His voice cracked. "Everything's going to be okay. I swear it will. They'll understand. It wasn't your fault. They'll help you."

"And it's not your fault either, Mack. We both . . ."

"Martha!" he said sharply. "Here's Frances. She wants to talk to you."

"Martha, listen!" Frances said, her voice a coil of fear and control. "What happens in the next few hours, everything you say will be of vital . . ."

The back door burst open, and two small boys flew past her, screeching. They dove under the table. Next came a taller boy in a red football shirt. He grabbed one of the other boys by the arm and yanked him out from the sanctuary of the table, dragged him halfway to the door, cursing and yelling that he had done it this time, he had gone too far,

MARY MCGARRY MORRIS

338

and now he'd have to pay. His face twisted hatefully, inches from the younger boy's.

"Coming in here," she muttered, snatching the black iron ladle from its hook over the stove. "Just bursting in on people," she said, her outrage and shock fixed on the boy's blatant cruelty, the loathsome bullying cruelty that had nipped at her heels a lifetime—with every step, walking, running—now finally cornered.

"Josh!" warned the boy who still crouched under the table as the ladle struck the taller boy's back.

"It's Marthorgan!" screamed the little boy who had been grabbed first and now fled onto the side porch. "It's Marthorgan. She's hurting Joshua! Help! Somebody please help!"

So startled was the boy that he never even made it to the door. He was on his knees, his arms huddling his head against the rising and falling ladle. Blood pooled in the indentation at the base of his skull. He sobbed. She looked down at his convulsed shoulders, at his skinny heaving chest. Blood trickled down his neck to a darkening spine under his shirt. Under the table, the third boy pulled a chair close and pleaded through the legs, "Don't hit me. Please, Marthorgan. Please don't hit me."

"Martha! Martha!" demanded a voice from the phone, which turned round and round on its dangling cord.

The boy on the floor moaned.

"I'm sorry," she gasped. She came toward him, then drew back, turning in a small helpless circle, the layers of chiffon swishing and catching on her pants. "Here," she said, offering him a dish towel, which he wouldn't take.

"It's clean," she assured him as the younger boy tried to help him stand up. "Tell him it's clean."

"My head," the boy moaned, sinking to his knees. "My head, oh, my head." His face was dully white, and as he looked up she gasped with alarm at the sorrowful censure of his fading stare.

"Ice!" She thumped her chest. "Ice! You need ice! Just wait! I'll get some ice!" she panted, spiraling out from this numbing core, this inertia, this paralysis where life's rules became all longitude and latitude, the invisible bars that kept her in and kept her out. He shouldn't have barged in here like that. . . . He shouldn't have startled her. . . . Didn't he know there were rules, that when the rules got broken she got jerked off course? That's what rules were for, to keep everyone on the right track. Now look what he'd done. . . . Just look—blood everywhere, and now more people here who didn't belong. It was all his fault. All these women staring at her like this, as if she were some kind of monster, as if she were crazy, and here she was the only one trying to do something for the boy . . . the only one, when she had a million other things on her mind. A million other things, and an aching heart.

The door flew open. "Here," she said. "Put ice on it," she tried to tell the boy's mother. It was Laura Hopewood; Hopewood and Horgan; now Barrett. She was a small curly-haired woman not much bigger than her son, whom she squatted next to, while a large blonde woman in a pink jogging suit peered closely at his scalp.

"Cuts," the blonde woman murmured. "Mostly little cuts."

"Look at her!"

"Look at her hands!"

". . . blood. I know it's blood."

"Ice'll make it stop," she said again, offering the frosted plastic dish. They wouldn't listen. Stupid. Stubborn. Well, if anything happened, they had better remember that she had told them. Ice would do it. Ice would stop all that bleeding.

Laura Barrett begged her son to stand up as she tried to rise with him.

"Laura, don't!" called one of the women in the doorway. Their children peered in between their arms and legs. They looked at Martha. She set the bowl of ice on the counter, picked it right up again, and began to jiggle it, the ice cubes rattling together. She only wanted to help. Couldn't they see that? Hypocrites, staring at her with such dismay when she had seen the way they yelled at their own kids and thought nothing of whacking them over the least little thing.

"Let him lay down," said one of the women.

MARY MCGARRY MORRIS

340

"I'll carry him," the blonde said, bending toward the boy.

"No!" Laura Barrett cried, her hand shooting up to block the blonde. "Joshua! Joshua!" she cried, her face close to her son's. "Oh, Josh! Oh my God!"

"He must've passed out!"

"Probably a concussion . . ."

"Or a fractured skull!"

"The police're . . ."

". . . already called an ambulance," a woman said, hanging up the phone.

"Look at her . . . pathetic. . . ."

"Is he dead?" a child gasped. "Is Josh dead?"

"Marthorgan killed Josh. . . ."

A siren wailed and Laura Barrett looked up. Her cheek was smeared with blood.

She should wipe it, Martha thought, her eyes darting around the kitchen for something to wipe her cheek with. "Here," she said, extending the dish towel.

"Get away from me," Laura snarled. "You get away from me."

"Here," she insisted, touching the towel to the woman's bloody cheek.

"Aaargh!" Laura Barrett groaned in horror, cringing back into the limp fold of the boy's body.

"Martha!" one of the women warned, snatching away the towel. Martha tried to pull it back.

"Get her away from me!"

They kept grabbing at her. She batted them away with her good hand. "He just ran in!"

"Martha, get . . ."

"No! No! You listen! You all listen!" She turned, then turned again. Her fingers dug tracks through her sweaty hair, and she had to keep angling her head to see through her one good lens.

"They're here," a woman called at the door.

Her mouth was so dry she had to keep wetting her lips. "I've been sick and he just ran in! He was hurting that boy," she said, pointing to the stern-eyed child by the door. No one listened. They looked outside. Heavy footsteps mounted the porch steps. A man and a woman in dark-blue jumpsuits and dusty black shoes ran into the kitchen. They gently eased the boy onto the stretcher they had just unrolled. Laura Barrett looked on, her arms clutching her stomach. With her thumb and fore-finger at the boy's thin wrist, the attendant nodded, her lips moving silently. The other attendant flipped open a square silver box and plucked out a white plastic ampule, which he split open at arm's length, then passed back and forth under the boy's nose. Suddenly the boy's head twisted to one side.

"Okay?" the attendant asked, bending close. "Can you hear me?" He looked up at Martha as the boy grunted. "What's his name?" he asked her.

She shook her head. She couldn't remember.

"Joshua! Joshua! Joshua!" responded a chorus of women's and children's voices.

"Joshua? You awake now? Wake up, Joshua. C'mon, kid. C'mon! Open those eyes. That's a fella. . . . There you go. . . . C'mon, now. . . ." The attendants lifted the stretcher between them.

"Mommy," the boy groaned.

"Oh, Josh," sobbed Laura Barrett as she followed him outside.

All the women and children hurried after them.

On the other side of the screen door stood the boy who had been under the table. He had seen everything. He would be able to explain what had happened. To get his attention, Martha snapped her fingers, but his gaze was rapt on the departing ambulance. She pressed so close against the door that the little hairs on her upper lip were drawn like filings to the screen. She could taste the hot dusty metal.

"Little boy! Little boy," she called in a low voice, but he didn't hear her. A long blue sedan slid up to the curb, blocking Mr. Weilman's driveway. From it emerged a short redheaded man and a taller, older man with a cigar stub in his mouth. They were both in shirtsleeves. One of them must be the boy's father coming to get her, she thought. She opened the door an arm's width, enough to grab the back of the younger boy's shirt.

MARY MCGARRY MORRIS

"Help! Marthorgan! Mommy, help!" the boy screamed, and the two men broke into a run.

She yanked the boy inside, slamming the door shut and turning the lock when she saw their grim-faced charge onto the porch. They shook the door and banged on the glass, peering in at her. The little boy gasped as she pulled him into the living room with her. She checked to make sure the front door was still locked, and then she closed the two open windows. Everything she touched was smeared with blood. "You come with me," she ordered the child as she dragged him toward the stairs. "You've got to tell them what happened," she grunted, wrestling him up each step. He struggled, so that his sweaty arms kept slipping out of her grasp. Her cut hand was bleeding onto his arms. He tried to kick her. She stopped on the top step and shook him, demanding that he calm down and listen to her. "You're my witness and I want you to tell them the truth!"

"Don't hurt me. Please don't hurt me," he panted as she dragged him from room to room while she locked the windows.

After she locked the door to her room, she ordered the boy to sit on the straight-backed chair in the corner. His feet dangled over the floor. One sneaker had fallen off, and his sock was black with dirt. He watched her pace back and forth, then sink onto the edge of the bed with a sigh.

"You know I didn't try to hurt Joshua, right?" she asked, and he nodded. "He was hurting that boy, your friend. And it startled me."

He stared at her.

"Answer me!" she said.

"You didn't ask me anything," the boy said.

"I did! I most certainly did! Now, don't get me mad. That's all I ask. Just don't get me mad!"

"I won't." He shook his head.

The commotion from the driveway had spread around the house. Voices came from everywhere. They were even in the back yard. A herd of feet stampeded over the hot dry lawn, then up and down the incline at this side of the house. Women's voices. Children's. Men's. There was a scratch on the drawer of the mahogany night stand. She wet her finger

A DANGEROUS WOMAN

343

and rubbed it. Mr. Weilman had better not blame her for that. He'd better not. Downstairs, the doorbell rang ceaselessly, and there was such banging on the doors that every wall vibrated. The lamp shade trembled. The window shade trembled. And now, from another part of the house, came more banging. "Go away," she whispered, looking toward the window as a man's voice, amplified, drowned out all the other sounds.

"Martha Horgan!" the voice boomed. "This is the police. We just want to talk to you, Martha. Please open the door and let Zachary come out."

There was no sound for a moment other than her own insistent petition, "Leave me alone, just leave me alone, leave me alone, just leave me alone." She did not thump her chest or wring her hands. Never had she sat so motionlessly. She looked closely at the air, at the thin yellow light in the air. "Shh!" she said to the boy, thinking the sound she had just heard had been him.

"I didn't say anything," he whispered. Tears ran down his face.

Next came the loud scrape of metal dragged along metal, then the voices and running footsteps. The footsteps were right under the window, and now they seemed to be ascending the very clapboards.

"Martha! Martha Horgan!"

Reflected in the bureau mirror was a man's large freckled face at the window screen, the red-haired man. With a kind of dreamy astonishment, they stared at each other in the mirror. As long as she didn't turn around, he might not be real.

"Detective John O'Toole, Miz Horgan." He smiled, and just above the sill held up a plasticized card that flashed in the sunlight. "I'd like to talk with you," he said. When she didn't respond, he repeated it, while he jiggled the bottom of the screen and bowed the frame with a springing sound. He lifted the screen a few inches.

He was going to climb in here. No! "No!" she cried, running to the window. "Don't you come in here! You can't come in here! You have no right to come in here!"

"I have to talk to you," he said in that smooth voice, his eyes never blinking from hers.

MARY McGARRY MORRIS

She saw now that he stood at the top of a metal extension ladder.

"Go sit down now," he said, lifting the screen a couple more inches, his eyes fixed, as if his stare alone might immobilize her. "I just want to make sure the boy's all right. I've got a son myself and there's n . . ."

All the color drained from his face as she rushed toward the window and yanked it down. He stared through the glass while she turned the dull brass lock.

"Martha," he started to say, but she pulled down the brittle paper shade.

She could hear the hollow thud of his feet on the rungs as he scurried to the ground. Downstairs, the phone had been ringing and ringing. A policeman's voice boomed up again from the street. "Martha Horgan, come out of the house. Martha Horgan, this is the Atkinson Police Department. We just want to talk to you, Martha."

"I have to go to the bathroom," the boy said.

"No!" she snapped.

More cars and trucks were pulling up outside. She stood by the window and peered down the side of the shade at a white van that said "WHVT" on its side. A dark-haired young woman in a yellow suit spoke into a microphone while a man in baggy jeans and a T-shirt trained his shoulder-mounted camera on her. People bunched in behind her and waved at the camera. The woman gestured toward the window, and everyone looked up.

Martha spun around as the boy slid off the chair. "You sit down! Don't you make me nervous now, do you hear?"

"I have to pee," he whined, jamming his fist into his crotch.

"You wait! You just wait! I don't know what to do here."

The boy's face puckered and he took a deep breath, which he held with widened eyes.

Brat. She looked away. He could hold his breath all he wanted, but she wasn't going to fall for it. "Stop that!" she demanded.

"I didn't do anything." He paused. "I'm a good boy," he said hesitantly, as if it were a theory he was testing on her.

A DANGEROUS WOMAN

"Then act like one! Good boys shut up and they don't make people nervous."

A sob tore through him. "Please don't hurt me. Please don't," he cried.

She looked at him and shrugged with a helpless gesture. Hurt him? How had any of this come to be? All she had ever wanted was to be happy and to be loved, just to be like everyone else. She buried her face in her hands and leaned forward on the sagging old bed. "Now I've done it," she whispered. "Oh brother, now I've done it."

There were footsteps in the hallway, then the click of a key in the lock. The bedroom door opened slowly. Mr. Weilman looked in, his eyes rheumy and tired. "Are you okay, Zack?" he asked the child, who jumped up and ran to him. "C'mon, Martha," the old man said wearily.

"It was an accident," she said. "I was on the phone and I was sick and the boys all ran in. . . ."

"I know. I know."

"It wasn't my fault."

"I know," he said sadly.

She stood up then and set her chin and stared at him. "This is what you get for letting those kids run wild in here!"

"Martha, this is Detective Honing," Mr. Weilman said as the short gray-haired man stepped into the room.

"Come on, Marthor, Martha," he caught himself. "We have to see what happened here." With his hand clamping her elbow in the stern manner of her father, he steered her down the stairs and out onto the front walk, toward the long blue unmarked police cruiser. One of her sneakers had come untied, and the lace flicked up and down along the pavement. People stood on the front lawn and on the sidewalk and in the road. Such silence, they didn't laugh or say a word, but stared, squinting through the glare of the sun at the tall woman in her bloody blue cocktail dress. The bright eye of the television camera moved right along with her. Speaking in a hushed voice, the reporter said, "It appears that this afternoon's sudden and terrifying hostage situation has

MARY McGARRY MORRIS

come to an abrupt and quiet end. Police are taking the bloodstained woman to . . ."

"Move aside!"

A round-faced child in a ruffled sundress gripped her mother's fingers and asked loudly, "Is that her? Is that Marthorgan?"

"Shh," came the reply.

TWENTY-FOUR

The waiting camera crews whipped down their cigarettes the minute the cruiser was spotted coming along the tree-lined street to the courthouse. Down in the parking lot, a cluster of women marched in a silent circle. Each of the long black crosses they held over their heads bore the stenciled date on which a woman had been raped. One woman held up a white poster board on which had been printed in red ink MARTHA WASN'T CRAZY—JUST MAD

AS HELL. Two women carried a black banner stitched with white satin letters that said EXCULPA: AN EYE FOR AN EYE.

Children straddled their bikes, hoping for a last glimpse. It was expected that from here she would be taken straight to the state mental hospital. The cruiser idled for a few moments at the curb, and then the doors opened and Sheriff Stoner guided her out of the back seat, solicitously, as tenderly as if she were his bride or mother. Ducking his head, a weary-eyed man in a rumpled suit climbed out after her. The door slammed and the children stiffened, some even backing up, as they stared at Marthorgan, theirs always to goad and manipulate, now this docile manacled creature, with her smashed, crooked glasses, groping past them, as if they were not even there. The real horror was not in Getso's murder or their friend's injury, for in torture and death they were as well versed as any child. No, it was her submission and that flatness, that emptiness that comes with the sudden end of power, them over her and her over them. They held their breath and did not move. Even after she had climbed the steps and gone inside, they remained very still.

The courtroom was so jammed that folding chairs had been set up along the back and side walls. Despite the crowd and the press and the sensational nature of the arraignment, the room remained strangely quiet. Martha was acutely conscious of every sound, the creaking chairs, the rumbling air conditioning, the humming fluorescent lights, the electric sputter from the judge's microphone, and the squeak of one of Steve Bell's scuffed shoes as he paced back and forth.

With his damp head slightly bowed and his hands clasped behind his back, Steve paused and looked up at the judge. He had been droning on for the last ten minutes. She couldn't keep her thoughts straight, much less concentrate on what he was saying. He had stressed the importance of staying calm and attentive during the arraignment. No outbursts. No thumping. No muttering. Blinking, she held her glasses and tried to refocus her webbed gaze on his back. Frances had a new pair for her, right there in her purse, but Steve insisted she wear these. He had also instructed her to keep her thickly bandaged hand visible on the table.

Her back ached and her legs were starting to feel funny, so she tilted her chair back and rocked a little to get the cramps out. Suddenly conscious of Judge Hennessey's scrutiny, she froze, and the chair dropped with a thud. She propped her chin on her hand and with her one clear eye stared intently at Steve. The arraignment wasn't supposed to last this long. Last night in jail, and then on their way here in the cruiser, Steve had explained each step to her. The recitation of the charges had already taken place, and now they were discussing bail, which, Steve had warned, the judge might refuse, pending a psychiatric evaluation. Actually, she didn't care what that fat man up there with his wild black eyebrows decided. Steve's precise explanation of the court's procedures and requirements had been like listening to the customs of a foreign country being described. Curiously interesting, but she couldn't see what any of it had to do with her. They could do what they wanted, but she wasn't going to have an abortion and she would never betray Mack. Never! And that's what this was all boiling down to. She wanted Mack to know that it would be their secret for as long as necessary. She kept glancing back, hoping for some sign from him, some acknowledgment. He sat directly behind her with Frances. Deeply tanned, he wore a linen jacket of the same pale blue as his eyes. She turned again, and the muscle in his cheek clenched. She gave a little wave now, and Frances nodded, her sharp little smile intended, like jagged glass, to keep her in her place.

Across the aisle, Birdy was flanked by her plump sisters and the two former Mrs. Getsobiskis, a bitter wall of puffy-faced women. Birdy's head trembled. It had taken all three sisters to maneuver her down the aisle and into her chair. No matter how hard Martha tried to make eye contact, Birdy stared past her. She hoped Birdy knew how sorry she was for all this pain and commotion, not to mention this entire morning she'd be losing from work. She wasn't like Mercy and the rest of them, insensitive and inconsiderate.

She tapped the dark-suited arm of Steve's law associate and gestured toward his pen. The young man looked confused. "The pen," she said. "I have to write something."

A hand closed over her shoulder. "Shh," Frances reminded her with a deep squeeze. Steve was still talking.

With her face close to the paper, she wrote, DEAR BIRDY, I AM SORRY FOR EVERYTHING AND I WANT YOU TO KNOW IF THE FLOOR GOT RUINED, I WILL PAY FOR REGROUTING OR A WHOLE NEW FLOOR, LOVE MARTHA. She tore the sheet off the long yellow pad and folded it and folded it to the size of a matchbook cover, then printed Birdy's name, drawing a tiny smiley face in the belly of the "D." She turned and handed it to Frances. "Pass it over," she hissed.

Frances glanced at it, then shook her head with wide, glistening eyes.

Steve's voice filled the room. Everyone sat with heads hung. A few people nodded.

"Then give it back!" Martha demanded. She held out her hand until Frances returned the note. Turning the other way now, she reached out with it as far as she could. "Here," she hissed, looking down the row of shocked faces. "Pass it!" But no one would take the note or even look at her.

Feet scraped. Heat and dust filmed the long narrow windows, casting the distant mountaintops with a somber purple haze. Steve looked up at the judge, then took a step closer, as if to share a confidence. "There have always been those among us for whom the wind's a little too strong," he was saying, "the sun just a little too bright. And in a community like ours, they are as much entitled to their place here as they are to our acceptance and our good will. And we expect their families to provide for them and to be as vigilant as possible for their safety and ours."

People were glancing at her. She held her breath, and her lips quivered in a dry, fixed smile.

"This is not a family matter any longer. No, this is a matter that concerns us all. Each and every one of us." He peered over his glasses at her. "Because this is more than a violated woman who in her outrage and confusion struck down her assailant. This is vastly different, and you know why this is vastly different. Because fifteen years ago, when we should have acted in Martha's behalf, we not only looked the other way, but we made a choice. We chose the assailants over the victim. Because she was an emotionally unstable young woman, we declared her honor and her future to be of less value than her tormentors'. And our message was loud and clear: Martha Horgan didn't count. She doesn't matter. You can taunt her and chase her and you can poke her with sticks and you can use her and you can finish what you started to do to her fifteen years ago, because this court of law and this community don't care about Martha Horgan."

"If it please the court," the young prosecutor protested. He stood up, shaking his head and sighing. "Your honor, we've all been very, very patient—under the circumstances," he added, and at that Steve Bell's head went back. "But Attorney Bell's arguments, to be charitable, are grossly premature. He is attempting to try his case right now, right here, and that is wrong!"

Both the prosecutor and Steve Bell moved closer to Judge Hennessey, who covered the sputtering microphone with his hand while he whispered something.

Steve shook his head angrily. "No!" he said loudly. "Absolutely not. Your honor, Martha Horgan should be released on bail into the custody of her aunt, Frances Beecham, who this court surely knows will guarantee . . ."

Martha turned with a hopeful smile at Mack, who slumped in the chair, staring down at his folded arms. Behind him, Julia Prine nodded at Martha. At the end of the row sat Wesley Mount, erect and still in his crisp white collar, his eyes never wavering from the judge.

"Martha needs immediate medical attention, your honor, the very best her family can provide, because she is at risk, your honor, with a pregnancy. A pregnancy that must be terminated, because she has been raped. Raped by Jimmy Getsobiski, who tormented and abused her and . . ."

"No!" Martha cried, shaking her head, stunned that Steve would say such a thing, tell such a disgusting lie in front of all these people. "He never did that. He never . . ." She shuddered, repulsed by the words.

". . . raped me. That never happened!" She looked right at Birdy now, who was crying. "Never! I swear!"

———o———

They sat in the conference room adjacent to the judge's chambers. The pictures on the dove-gray walls were the judge's own pen-and-ink drawings of his favorite places in town, the bandstand in the park as well as the statue of the dog straining back from its invisible leash.

Bail had been denied, and the judge had ordered a ninety-day psychiatric evaluation. When Steve had continued to insist she needed the abortion, the judge reminded him sternly that no person, and certainly no court of law, could force Martha or any woman to terminate her pregnancy, no matter how troubling the circumstances.

They were awaiting the arrival of the psychiatric nurse Frances had hired to accompany Martha to the state hospital in Waterbury. The prosecutor had halfheartedly objected, calling a private nurse "preferential treatment," but, his decision made, the judge seemed anxious to placate not only Steve but Frances, his two old friends.

Martha's hand pressed against her stomach, too flat for anything to be growing in there. She tried to picture cells clustering, a fetal mass, a miniature child, anything, but nothing of clarity, no image came to mind. There was only the sensation of fullness, of a swelling tenderness that made her smile.

Frances fidgeted with the jet clasp on her purse. She seemed dazed. She looked at Martha and shook her head. "There's no way she can have this," she said. "There's no way! What is Tom Hennessey thinking of? This is like a nightmare!" She turned to Mack, who hadn't yet said a word. "Tell me when this is going to end," she groaned.

"Frances!" Steve said sharply. He had barely acknowledged Mack's presence. He reminded Frances that there were some vital things he wanted to tell Martha before it was time to leave. He pulled up a chair and sat so close their knees touched. "This is the time for absolute honesty," he said. "You mustn't hide anything from the psychiatrists, Martha. Their opinions are going to make or break this case. You've got to level with them. There's no trying to protect my reputation or Frances's or anyone else's. From now on, it's only you that matters here, do you understand?" He leaned in closer.

"Answer him!" Frances said through clenched teeth.

"I understand."

"It may horrify you to tell them about what happened at Birdy Dusser's, but you've got to! You've got to do it. If you don't, if you try and pretty the thing up, then it's going to look as if you murdered him in cold blood. Do you understand what I'm saying here, Martha? Do you?"

"Answer him!" Frances hit the table with her fist.

"Yes." She could feel Mack's eyes on her. It would be so much easier if he would only give her a sign, some gesture, acknowledging what they had shared, their secret she now carried.

"Martha, the brutal fact here is that, without an abortion, there's not a judge or jury that will believe he raped you."

"But he didn't," she said flatly. They wanted her to lie. Like everyone else, they didn't care about the truth, only themselves. Their truth was whatever way they twisted and shaped the facts. And that was exactly why Getso was dead: because each lie demanded another lie, and another. She looked away.

"Martha! Listen to me! You can't deny what happened. You have to end this pregnancy!"

She sat back and closed her eyes. The world moved farther and farther away. Muffled voices passed along the corridor. Telephones were ringing, clocks ticking, a heart beating. This, she could suddenly comprehend, a heart in time with hers. She gripped the edge of the table.

". . . can't expect Frances to burden herself raising a child now, at this point in her life," Steve was saying.

"Oh my God," Frances groaned, covering her face with her hands at the prospect.

"Well, let's be realistic," Steve said, shrugging. "That's what'll happen with a murder conviction or any institutionalization."

Frances looked at Mack. "Maybe she'll listen to you," she pleaded.

MARY MCGARRY MORRIS

"Yes," Steve said. "I bet she will." He smiled at Mack. "I bet you're the only one she will listen to right now."

There was a tap on the door, and then it opened. "There's a nurse here," the white-haired court officer said to Steve, who told him they needed a few more minutes.

When the door closed and Mack began to speak, Frances nodded hopefully. "We got to be good friends, didn't we, Martha?" He cleared his throat, then coughed into his hand.

She nodded, her crooked grin making them look uneasily away.

"And I remember you telling me things about Getso. About how he repulsed you so much that if he just came into the same room you'd feel sick to your stomach."

She nodded, pleased that he remembered.

"And about that night in high school. And how you couldn't re-member much of it because you'd blanked it out. You said you could make yourself do that. You said, if something was unpleasant enough, you'd either forget it or change it around in your head to make it seem nicer. Do you remember telling me that?"

"No." Had she? No. No, she knew she hadn't. Why did he say that? What was he trying to tell her?

"Well, this is the same thing, Martha. But now your life's at stake. In a way, everyone's life." He looked at her. "Don't you see what everyone here is telling you? Don't you understand?"

She smiled. "Yes!" she said eagerly. Her breath caught. He wanted her to know he understood the pressure she was enduring for him.

"So don't be afraid or ashamed. And I'll help you. I'll be right there every step of the way—with Frances and with Steve. I'll explain what happened, just the way you tell me. And there's no reason for you to go through with this pregnancy. Listen to me, Martha," he said, staring now into her eyes. "It's wrong. This isn't what you want. Believe me, this is a mistake, a horrible mistake!" His face had twisted into something hateful and ugly. The knuckles on his fists were sharp and white.

"Not for me it isn't!" she cried. "Maybe for . . ."

"It is for all of us," Frances said. "Martha, Mack and I are getting married this winter. You can't do this to me! Not now! Please!" She reached for Steve's hand. All at once, he looked old and haggard. "Steve! This is not the way I planned on telling you," she whispered. Tears filled her eyes.

"I'll back you to the hilt," Mack said, the fierce rush of his words all that held up the ceiling, supported the walls and floor, so that if he stopped talking everything would be sucked into the silence. "Every step of the way. I can verify everything. I mean, there's so much in your favor. Even this," he said, taking a paper out of his pocket and unfolding it. "This letter you wrote Birdy. Even here it tells how he was always after you. Listen: 'Dear Birdy, You have to believe the things I tell you about Getso. Ever since my first day at the Cleaners he has been after me because he knows I know the truth about him." He looked up and held out a stack of envelopes. "And all these other letters. The motive's so . . ."

"You never mailed my letters?" She couldn't believe it. "You lied. You said you mailed them!"

Mack glanced at Steve. "Maybe she wouldn't even have to testify. She gets so damn nervous. I could relate everything she told me about him." He gestured at her. "I mean, look, why reduce her to this?"

"And what would that be? What would you relate?" Steve asked, his gaze keen on Mack, who could not keep it. "Tell us."

"What she told me about herself and . . . and about what happened."

She swayed gently with the rising pitch of his voice. As much as it hurt, she finally understood. The truth did not matter. It never had, never did, never would. The emptiness was at the center and the center would always be empty. Only love could fill it and she would never be loved and all at once this knowledge, this terrible certainty, was unendurable.

"And what did happen?" Steve asked with the lightness of a page being turned. The room was quiet. There was no sound, no sound at all. "Martha, you tell me," Steve whispered. "Tell me what happened."

She stared at Mack, but he closed his eyes.

MARY McGARRY MORRIS

"Martha?" Steve reached across the table for her hand. "What happened? Tell me. Tell me the truth."

She bit her lip and tried not to smile. "We made love," she said softly, and the smile jerked across her face.

"Oh my God," Frances groaned, covering her mouth as if she were going to be sick.

Martha leaned forward, desperate for Mack to say something, but he just kept shaking his head from side to side. "He's ashamed. He's afraid to say it. He won't say the word," she tried to explain to Steve, who stared down at the table. They all did now; they couldn't bear to look at her. "It's because I'm so disgusting! You see, I make him sick. Just like I make everyone sick. Sick, sick, sick. I am a bad person, a very, very, bad, bad person." And now, with this final truth, birds flew from her mouth, ugly black flapping wings that crackled so close they made her cringe and wince. Her hands writhed, the claws twisting and turning. And soon there would be stillness here and peace here in this dark place, the safest place, where there was only room for one. For her, and she understood this now, finally. Someone spoke. She cocked her head to listen. It was a man. A man. He was saying, he said, this was what he said, exactly what he said, and she would never forget it:

"I was drunk. And you see . . ." His voice broke. ". . . she had never been loved."

"In other words, you raped her!" Steve said with loathing.

"No!" Frances gasped. "No!" she said again, looking from one man to the other.

"He raped her! The son of a bitch raped her!" Steve cried, banging the table with both fists.

"I took advantage of her." Mack nodded. "I did."

"You raped her!"

"I was drunk."

"And when you were drunk, you raped her."

"Whatever," Mack sighed, looking up with an almost shy smile. "But Martha won't call it that. She thought it was love. And maybe it was," he said, that is what he said, exactly what he said. And when he was gone, forever and ever gone, and she was alone, forever and ever alone, those were the words she remembered, the most important words, and nothing and no one could ever change them, and she would write those words, exactly those words, in all her letters to all her friends.